BOOK II

HUNTER OF THE CATS

BOOK II

HUNTER OF THE CATS

THE LAST CAT

ROBERT QUADE

Strategic Book Publishing and Rights Co.

Strategic Book Publishing & Rights Co., LLC
USA | Singapore
www.sbpra.net

ISBN: 978-1-68235-257-1

Dedication:

To Sister M. Melfrida who taught me the love of the arts.

REBAH

1868

CHAPTER I

RETURN

The dark figure leaned far over the rough rope railing of the bobbing brigantine and stared at the black sea which reflected a multitude of twinkling stars. Boredom had become Jason's number one enemy since leaving Mobile. He hated spending time by himself. His mind became too active when he remained alone all day. On the port side of the undulating ship patter of bare feet from a nameless sailor on some unknown assignment interrupted the pensive man's reverie. Jason's shoulder muscles contracted. He had seen more than one black person thrown overboard on his trip from Africa to Alabama, and just because this reverse trip didn't contain the below- deck hideousness of the first crossing it didn't guarantee safety to the black passenger. That horrifying experience of the slave ship coupled with the confinement in a dark cellar on Duval Street in Mobile finally came to an end when that damned Masai, Hunter, bought him for Andrew Harrison and the plantation known as Whispering Willows. Jason spread his legs for balance and prepared for an attack by the white man rushing toward him, but the flat-footed sailor ran past Jason, and grabbed one of 200 many rope ladders that spider-webbed the masts of the ship and clambered upward into the darkness. Jason maintained his guard. It was possible the first sailor meant to divert his attention, which would allow a second sailor to perform the cowardly deed of murder. Even though the influence of that devious overseer, Hunter, and the plantation's business no longer had any power or presented any threat, Jason could not alter his color and the white men still could not accept black people as equal human beings. Sheriff Bubba and his Ku Klux Klan had proved that point many times.

"I wish this damned trip was over," Jason muttered to himself. He remained on guard against an attack for an additional five minutes before finally concluding his macabre suspicions as groundless.

Four days had elapsed since the rapidly moving vessel had entered open sea. After a brief stopover in the Port of Miami to load cargo, the Green Mermaid headed toward the welcoming shoreline of the African Continent.

Jason's tiresome horse ride from Unionville to the bustling seaport of Mobile had proved a long and hard trek but well worth the arduous journey. He mentally savored the completion of his long-sought revenge on his old boss, Hunter. By now, Lulu, Hunter's doting whore, surely had taken Shamrock Enterprise's ledger books to Hunter's partner, Sean, a ruthless schemer equal to Hunter's cunning. Sean would now know of Hunter's white alias, "Mr. Wilkerson." The wily Irishman would force Hunter to sign over the bank account in South Carolina which Hunter had Gregory Ellis, a carpetbag lawyer from Ohio, establish so that Hunter's business would flourish without suspicion as to the true color of the owner of the account. The alternate choice of not signing the account over to Sean could amass for Hunter suffering of unspeakable tortures at the hands of Sheriff Bubba, the Grand Wizard of the local chapter of the Klan. Hunter would also have to cede the plantation Whispering Willows to Sean, since it too bore the name of Wilkerson on its deed. Jason rubbed his hands together and produced a throaty chuckle. Yet there was more to come for Hunter's much deserved downfall.

When that infatuated whore of Hunter's, Lulu, discovered the astronomical amount money Hunter had hidden in the South Carolina account and how he had delayed their marriage all those years with his lies, she would unite with Sean to cause Hunter additional misery for the rest of Hunter's life. Jason doubted if the gold stashed at the Underground Railway cabin on a small island in the middle of the swamp at the plantation would come to light. Hunter would probably use some of that stash in an attempt to escape his torment. Jason believed this revenge better than a rapid death of the hated overseer. With death everything ended quickly, but the anguish Jason had plotted would last for years and spawn new problems for Hunter. Jason had triumphed over that Masai bastard, but gratification had not filled his vengeful soul. A frown furrowed Jason's brow. He felt more loss than gain from his first triumph against the entire Masai nation he swore to destroy.

Jason straightened up and relaxed a little. Having to stay in his narrow cabin day after day with nothing to do but think and scheme made him over-anxious and restless. The confinement of his quarters had made his body ache as well. The captain had warned Jason that some members of the crew found it difficult to accept a black man as a paying passenger. They believed Jason had taken advantage of some white plantation owner's misfortune to finance this trip. Ever since the end of the war, many people accepted throughout much of the South that blacks stole anything that came within their grasp and they were a lazy lot. To forestall any problems, the captain counselled Jason to exercise only at night to have meals served in his cabin and leave his cabin, during the day only responding to the call of nature. So far, no trouble had developed, but the damned inconvenience of remaining in a hot cabin all day only exacerbated Jason's natural ill temperament. The cool nautical breeze massaged his face.

To no avail he stared upward at the snow white billowing sails in an attempt to discern the agile figure that had just climbed the rigging. The refreshing nocturnal breeze, so welcome to the African-bound passenger, made the sails resemble a shroud against the black sky.

Shroud? What made Jason think of death at a time of his great victory? Death, Victory's surrogate at times, demanded equal payment to its chest pounding brother. "Stop," he thought. Jason vehemently shook his head to dispel the morbid thoughts and walked at a swift pace toward the bow of the teeter-tottering ship. Why this depression? No matter, Jason thought. He would balance all his emotions once he returned to his native Africa.

Africa. He had a score to settle there, too. Rebah. Yes, Rebah. Already a very special plan, better than his revenge on Hunter, had begun to form. Unlike Hunter, who had always treated him fairly, Rebah had personally injured him. My God, Jason hadn't meant to think of Hunter in those terms. Hunter belonged to the treacherous Masai tribe and deserved the current anguish inflicted upon him. Jason, who descended from the Ibo tribe, hoped Lulu, in conjunction with Sean, would make the conniving son-of-a-bitch's life unbearable. All of his ex-boss' scheming would come to nothing now. At last Hunter would be put in his place. Where had Jason heard that phrase before? Ah, yes, Bubba. He or one of the sheriff's KKK cronies said it every time Jason had entered the small Alabama town of Unionville on Hunter's or plantation business. But thanks to Jason's contrivances, Hunter now worked for Sean, instead of Sean working for Hunter. Jason calculated the greedy Irishman would squander the construction business in about two or three years, sell the plantation, and would return to New York with the rest of his imported Irish trash now residing at Whispering Willows. They would return to work again with the Boss Tweed gang.

The spiteful man had a much to consider, especially where Rebah and his filthy Masai tribal connections entered into his yet unformed plans. His mind rapidly refocused on his past accomplishments. Jason relished the mental image of Hunter in dirty rags clearing the land or picking cotton. Jason's pace slowed as he approached the farthest end of the bow. Just below, the ship's figurehead, a Green Mermaid clutching a conch shell, stared out to sea. Somewhere onboard the ship's bell rang. Jason had never understood the meaning of the number of chimes. The disturbing noise that occurred every hour irritated him. Once the resonance ceased, the restless man concentrated on the ship's heading. The craft's bow plunged up and down at a frightening rate drenching him as he clutched the damp ropes fanning out to the port and starboard side as the vessel raced through the turbulent sea. For some unknown reason, Jason had discarded his sea sickness the second day out during that nightmare trip from Africa to Alabama, and it had not returned on this reverse trip. Jason rested his abdomen on the single metal peg at the bow where the two ropes met and found the rough rocking of the ship a welcome feeling. His thoughts then shot down to the cargo hold and the fifteen bales of cotton for sale when he arrived at Dahomey. The sailors laughed at the dumb nigger who had no better sense then to attempt to sell raw cotton on a continent with no cotton mills. Some white trader would rob the black moron blind and sell the bales in Europe for a nice profit.

Once again Jason chuckled to himself. Sometimes one could use prejudice to one's own advantage. He had learned that much from Hunter. Jason acquired the cotton bales two weeks after purchasing his return fare to Africa on the Green Mermaid. When Hunter questioned him about the cotton purchase, Jason claimed they were for sale on the black market in order to obtain a little extra cash. Hunter seemed pleased at the time. At long last it appeared Jason had taken an interest in making a little private profit. Jason omitted telling Hunter he had removed some of the gold from the horde concealed at the deserted cabin in the swamp. He had hidden two large, heavy ingots of gold near each end and two in the center of the tightly packed fifteen bales. Any more gold and the weight would have made the handlers suspicious. In addition, he hid 200 two-inch ingots in various places in his trunk and in the four pieces of his luggage he had sent ahead to Mobile. As further insurance, he added another fifty in a knapsack and fifty more in a money belt. Who would ever suspect an ignorant black trying to vend raw cotton in Africa would have so much gold? And not one ounce belonged to that greedy walking outhouse of a boss he had left behind. In time, if some mishap on Hunter's part occurred, Sean would question Hunter's spending habits and force Hunter to reveal the location of remainder of the island treasure. That thought made Jason chuckle again.

The bow of the ship sprayed another fine mist over Jason. The thoughtful man looked down and studied the foamy, white froth as the bow parted the jet-black water. It seemed to Jason the smiling mermaid figurehead enjoyed spraying him from the conch shell she caressingly held in her hands. How refreshing it felt to the lone passenger. He turned to face the deserted deck and leaned against the adjoining peg. He could barely discern the helmsman in the stern due to the dipping and swaying of the vessel. This time, from the angle on the where he stood, the billowing sails reminded him of the fresh wash hung by Lulu at Whispering Willows. Once more visualizing the pretty woman at the plantation, Jason thought of how she would have made a nice companion on his return trip, but she had become too involved with that loathsome Masai. Let the bitch stay behind and make Hunter's life miserable. The unsatisfying taste of revenge resurfaced. Again Jason attempted to redirect his thoughts. He had his whole life in front of him now. To hell with her. When Konte reinstated him to Ifa's priesthood of the Golden Stool, all women would accede to the restored priest's slightest wish.

"What in the hell is the matter with me?" he muttered. In the past he fed his animus on hatred and anger, and now his life had turned around, he should feel better than this. He tried to bask in his current vengeful achievements, but somehow he felt hollow. As soon as he reached Dahomey and took control of his life, his mood would improve. Jason turned and grasped the front metal peg on the bow.

But he always had control of his life, at least since Hunter had bought him. Hunter made clear from the beginning; Jason bore the nomenclature of employee, even though he'd had to bear the title of Master Andrew's slave publically. In addition, Hunter paid him well, offering him a partnership, and at times had even sought Jason's advice. Hunter had also shielded him from the owner of Whispering Willows, Mr. Harrison. Only Sean and Bubba treated the plantation's bookkeeper with prejudicial scorn that Jason had no choice but to accept. Hunter had carefully explained to Jason his need for Sean and had spent extra time with Jason explaining that need after a particular nasty three way session with that carpetbagging bully. Bubba had proved a hopeless case. An ignorant person always may learn, but a stupid one, never. My God! Jason realized he always had control over his life, although he had never felt like it. Hunter treated him as an intelligent employee and, if given the chance, Hunter offered to help him succeed in America with any endeavor Jason might have chosen, but only if Jason wanted to remain and ceased demanding his return to Africa.

"What in the hell am I thinking about?" the distraught man thought for the second time. "That damned man wouldn't save a pig from slaughter if there was no profit in it." Hunter and Rebah thought alike. After all they came from the same background.

Suddenly, he became aware of the money belt around his waist. He had worn it since before he came on board but only now did he feel its presence. Rebah made him remember it. Jason would need a lot of gold to get revenge on that two-faced son-of-a-bitch. Holy Ifa! Jason rejoiced in feeling anger again. He left his post and walked toward amidships, only this time on the starboard side. The damned ship's bell rang again. He wished he knew the real time and not just all that clanging. A dark figure emerged from below decks. The helmsman's relief tipped his hat to Jason, drew his pea coat tighter, and headed for the stern. For the first time, Jason noticed the chill in the air that had penetrated his wet clothes. The lone passenger headed for the hatch leading to his cabin. He paused momentarily at the rope railing to stare at the ink black sea matched by its ethereal mantle. Jason liked nights without a bright moon. Without town lights or the moon he could appreciate the true beauty of the heavens. He recalled the night he left that hellhole in Mobile with Hunter to take up residence at Whispering Willows and the first time he had ever ridden a horse. Jason's concentration on the myriad of stars during the trip made the bouncing up and down in the saddle less painful. The liberated man wondered what happened to the rest of those poor souls who had shared that rat-filled cellar while awaiting their fates as a plantation owner's property. From what Jason had seen of other plantations, he considered himself damned lucky to have met Hunter. Now, what the hell made him think like that? In Africa a perfidious Masai had drugged and sold him into slavery. Another Masai had bought him as a slave in America. The entire Masai nation needed extinction. Jason reached out for his hatred and anger but found only a strange and unusual emptiness. Again, he consoled himself that this nagging depression would certainly pass when he arrived at Dahomey. It must.

Doggedly, the distraught man headed for the open hatch to descend into his cabin before daybreak. He glanced over his shoulder for one last look at the twinkling stars. One particular stellar group caught Jason's attention, but the off duty helmsman blocked a full view. Jason waved the man to one side and pointed.

"You sailors know the name of all of the stars. What do you call those over there?" he asked the man.

The sailor turned and stared to where Jason pointed and smiled. "Oh, those. That is called Orion, the Hunter." The helmsman inched past Jason and descended the narrow stairs for a hot meal from the galley's cook. Afterward to his quarters to sleep before the noisy activity on deck began at sunrise.

The pink sky on the horizon warned the solitary black man of approaching dawn as Jason returned above deck. He leaned once more on the ship's fence-like rope and stared out over the sparkling ebony sea. Soon all the night's lights would fade. Jason never heard any more of the other bells announcing nautical time but spent the remainder of the night staring at Orion.

CHAPTER II

ARRIVAL

Jason delighted in the beehive of activity on the bustling docks at Dahomey. He considered this homecoming an African welcome which he interpreted as the beginning of his new life. He still felt uneasy and nervous but he hoped that would soon pass now that he had arrived home. The ship had docked for over an hour and the huge labyrinth of cargo crates on the muddy quay testified that the scurrying seamen had performed their hard work well since arrival of the Green Mermaid. The longer it took to unload the consignment the less time the crew had to spend in searching for the rewards of the completed trip. Jason leaned on the rope railing and scrutinized with exhilaration as some of the sailors paused in their laborious job to respond to questions from curious onlookers interested in the contents of the crates and the more private questions presented by some overly made-up ladies concerning their heavenly delights available this evening. His goods and luggage remained onboard because the Miami and Mobile cargo had priority for unloading over transferring bales of cotton to the dock, but soon they would take their place beside the other freight already neatly stacked on the crowded pier. Jason gave a sigh of relief. He had arrived safely home to Africa where he belonged and that allowed him enough time to relax just a little and perform his personal business in his own good time. No one would show interest in fifteen bales of cotton when other enticing merchandise from Mobile and Miami already congested the dock. That fact gave him breathing space to settle into his new life. During the rest of his trans-Atlantic voyage, Jason had solidified his plan for obtaining retribution from Rebah. Now he had to make it a reality. He straightened when he heard the familiar, authoritative, heavy footsteps of the Green Mermaid's captain. Jason turned and smiled at the robust seaman.

"Good morning, Mr. Jason. Your cargo and luggage should be coming up soon. Is there anywhere you want it to be delivered?" the smiling captain asked in a jovial voice. The round, ruddy-face sailor could afford to display such a good humor. The profit from this delivery would provide a week, if not more, of whoring and drinking with his crew who currently flirted with some of the attentive working girls on the landing who responded with a wink or a smile at any sailors' interest.

"No, thank you. I'll have somebody pick it up by nightfall. I also wish to thank you for a very pleasant trip." Jason replied, offering his hand as a sign of sincerity.

The captain glanced down at the offered hand. "You're welcome." The captain merely tipped his hat, nodded, and turned away. Jason ignored the obvious snub and began to wonder if the captain or members of his crew forced his isolation during the crossing. Back in Alabama, Sean and Bubba had produced much sharper and certainly much more verbally colorful snubs to any overture or inviting gesture made by a black man. Jason merely smiled, shook his head, and walked toward the bustling quarterdeck of the ship. The scurrying line of stevedores ignored the black man as he inched his way down the gangplank through the maze of cargo and exited onto an equally busy street that ran parallel to the quay. It had a wide horizontal street intersecting it that lead to the center of town.

Jason surveyed the dirty scene around the busy docks and the nearby buildings desperately in need of paint. Nothing much had changed in Dahomey, except for the conspicuous absence of the slave-holding baracoons. Those derelict ships moored on land had no other purpose than rapid destruction by fire if any antislavery ship flying a hostile flag to the slavers approached the port. Except for their gold value, the human cargo kept inside these wooden torture chambers had no meaning to the slavers. In case of emergency, and the necessity of igniting them, replacement of the incinerated goods presented no problem to sellers who labeled the lost souls as sub-human beings. Fire proved a more practical solution than spending years in some British prison or even a hanging for slave trafficing. The technical dissolution of the slave trade to North America and the increase in legal trade fostered a most welcome change to the waterfront. Dahomey no longer needed the baracoons now that Europeans had retranslated the word, slaves, into colonial servants. Jason stifled a laugh. The nightmarish seizure of individuals, the living hell during deportation to unknown places, and the dehumanizing sale of many others and him had ended. The new words had a much nicer ring to the ear and provided a little guilt regarding the jingle of coin in the white mans' pocket. Black-skinned people could now remain in their own country as second-rate citizens and rape its rich resources for white men's profit. Only in the East did slavery prevail as an open and large scale business totally ignored by the pious Westerners. How convenient for all concerned.

Notwithstanding the drug's affect that hampered his observation skills on his initial visit to this hotbed of corruption, the muddy streets of Dahomey seemed a little straighter and wider to Jason. More European-style houses dotted the landscape, but the stagnant harbor still stank of offal. Attempting to outdo the harbor stench, an unknown liquid containing a plethora of flotsam trickled toward the harbor water in two ditches paralleling the broad center street of town and had many side streets contributing to that foul flow which terminated at the quay. Spring-like boards spanning the filth provided the only means to cross from one side of the street to the other if one desired to keep shoes and lower clothing clean of the sewerage and contend solely with street mud. On the quay, a new wooden pier had replaced the space once occupied by the inhumane baracoons, but the ghost of their existence could still haunt those who had experienced them.

Jason grabbed a passing, half-naked boy who gaped at the black man in European clothing restraining him tightly by the arm.

"Do you know the Aqua Brothers' Trading Company?" Jason asked in Swahili, keeping a firm grip on the astonished lad. He had heard Hunter mention the brothers as middle men in the slave trade and other legal or illegal enterprises. He knew the brothers controlled other members of a cartel called Egbo. If cruelty and corruption had other names, Egbo defined both words no matter the language. The drunken ramblings of a slaver called del Coelho first introduced the brothers' names to the observant captive, Hunter. Even though Hunter had not yet completed the rite of manhood and years had passed since he first had encountered their names he remembered them. It always amazed Jason that Hunter never forgot names or events and had the ability to recall information, good or bad, recent or remote at the snap of a finger. Some of this information he relayed to Jason as a grounds for his second-in-charge at Whispering Willows as an incentive not to return to Africa. Jason never shared with Hunter his obsession of obtaining vengeance on Rebah as one reason for the rejection of all Hunter's arguments.

The captive boy's eyes never ceased scanning the opulently dressed black man detaining him. The youngster nodded his head to Jason's inquiry. As Jason released the boy he reached into his frock coat pocket and withdrew two articles: one, a heavy, brown package about the size of a large man's hand; and the other, a silver coin.

"Give this package to either of the Aqua brothers and to no one else. Tell them Jason will bring them another at eight o'clock tonight if they will store fifteen bales of cotton and his luggage just unloaded from the Green Mermaid. Have you got that straight?" Jason added a little shake to the boy's shoulder to emphasize the importance of the message which alerted the lad that the man who had first gripped his arm like a vise and then shook him like a doll would brook no alterations in his specific instructions. The boy ignored the ill treatment by the dapper, very serious black man and riveted his eyes on the shinny silver coin held between the thumb and forefinger of Jason's left hand. With mouth agape the tiny black head nodded again. The boy took the package with both hands as Jason made the lad repeat the message twice to assure there would be no misunderstanding on the Aqua brothers' part. The little urchin seemed surprised at the heavy weight of so small a parcel. Earning the coin became more important than the weight or contents of the package. It could contain stones or iron bars the little scamp thought as long as he received that silver coin.

"Good, now take the package to the Aqua brothers, and I'll wait here until you return. If you bring me a message from them before the sun lights up all of that large street that runs down to the harbor, I'll give you another coin to match this one," Jason said, as he flipped the money in the air. The gods had showered the ambitious rascal with good fortune today. The coin had not rotated three times before a tiny black hand snatched it in mid-air, and the coin disappeared into a fold in his small dirty loincloth that undoubtedly contained a small pocket to hold coins. A magician could not have made the spry scamp disappear any quicker. After about fifteen minutes of waiting, Jason felt a slight tug at his right coat sleeve. He looked down at the small smiling black face offering him a folded piece of paper. Jason took the paper with his left hand and searched for the promised piece of silver with his right. Just in case Jason decided to renege on his promise the coin had barely appeared in sunlight before the lithe little imp snatched it and both the coin and the scalawag disappeared from sight.

Jason slowly unfolded the note written in English. A sarcastic smile dawned on his face as he read: "The contents of your package are certainly intriguing. My brother and I anxiously await the arrival of you and the duplicate package. We shall see to your luggage and cargo immediately. Eight o'clock will be most acceptable to us. Until then I remain---Your servant, John Aqua."

Try as he might, Jason could not control himself and burst out laughing at the line over the scrawled signature, "Your servant." He wondered what the note would have read had John known Jason's skin color. Still, according to Hunter, people of the Aqua brothers' caliber knew no other colors except gold and silver. He refolded the note, placed it in his coat pocket, and went in search of a comfortable hotel. Alabama still maintained strict segregated hotels, but an open city like Dahomey sustained a bit more liberal attitude in providing lodging to black and white under the same roof. Jason could have afforded the very best hotel the city had to offer, but that would only make people suspicious of how a black man could avail himself of such luxury. He did not want to draw too much attention to himself, so he would find something modest but clean. As to supper, Jason knew he would have to adjust to far less palatable fare than that prepared by Whispering Willows' cook, Morning Glory. What he wouldn't give for a piece of her shoofly pie right now. Oh well, that delectable cuisine belonged to another lifetime. With that thought in mind, Jason ambled down the wide, muddy street toward the center of the bustling city in search of cleaner lodgings than the derelict waterfront offered.

CHAPTER III

PROPOSITIONS

By the time Jason arrived at the Aqua brothers' darkened establishment, night lessened the activity on Dahomey's main streets. Movement and laughter in some of the alleyways assured Jason that not all business had ceased with the setting sun. He had found lodgings at a relatively new hotel called The Lazy Monkey. Though nothing exceptional, it catered to a mixed clientele of black and white which allowed Jason the anonymity he desired. The small room contained only a tidy bed, a petite armoire, a wooden stand holding a pitcher filled with water and a clean white towel hanging on an attached rod, and a small wooden night stand with a coal oil lamp with a red glass lamp shade. Still it was sufficient to satisfy Jason's needs, at least for now. The heavily spiced, palatable stew with many vegetables, a little meat, and thick brown gravy, served with fresh baked unleavened bread in the inn's dining room, sated Jason's hunger primarily because he refused to question the nomenclature of the stew's meat. Besides, he had developed a voracious appetite from scouting Dahomey for the remainder of the day when he left the quay to orient himself to his new surroundings. He had arrived home again, and he had to learn to readjust to his previous way of life in Africa and that included old dietary habits. His hearty meal allowed him to relax a bit longer at his supper table with two additional dark ales added to his bill. After drinking the potent corn liquor acquired by Hunter at Whispering Willows, Jason compared this ale to sarsaparilla. Hmmm! Another readjustment he had to make. He had forgotten the taste of cassava, the local liquor, but knew he would soon enjoy its pungent flavor. If memory served, it proved to have a much better taste than the weak ale he now imbibed. The inn did not stock cassava because most of its guests were of foreign extraction and preferred ale or European alcohols. The Westminster chimes of the grandfather clock just inside the open dining room doors struck seven. Jason once again chortled to himself. He had not heard that sound since leaving Whispering Willows. Mr. Andrew had always checked his pocket watch against the dark oak grandfather's clock that stood in the corner of the library. It certainly sounded much better than the clanging of the Green Mermaid's ship's bell, but, much more important, he understood the announced time. Jason finished his second ale and left the hotel a well sated man.

In order to make his arrival more exact, the expected guest at the Aqua brothers' place of business spent time scanning merchandise through broad windows along the main street and watched merchants close their shops for the night in order to hurry home for a bountiful supper and an evening of relaxation with friends and family. Besides, he needed a little exercise after that satisfying meal. When the proper hour arrived, Jason knocked on the weather-beaten door of a well constructed-building that posted a sign "Aqua Brothers' Trading Company" over its front eave. Jason heard the shuffle of shoes behind the sturdy door. An undetermined number of bolts and latches either slid open or became unchained. A deeply-lined black face, with sad eyes that would make rocks cry, capped by snow-white hair appeared in the crack of the door. Jason's heart sank. All of those facial lines and dispirited eyes on the aged greeter displayed a diary of a difficult life.

"Mr. Jason?" inquired the pitiful figure holding a lamp. Only very important business men or members of the Egbo had appointments with the brothers after dark. The doorman gave a little start that the well-dressed business man with black skin had a special appointment with the Aqua Brothers.

"Yes," Jason replied almost apologetically.

"Mr. Tom and Mr. John are expecting you. This way please," invited the pathetic figure. The servant swung the door wide and indicated with his left arm which held a lamp for Jason to enter the large semi-dark room.

Jason stepped through the doorway, past the old man who kept his eyes lowered as if Jason had seen too much of his personal life. The doorman proceeded by well-learned rote to rapidly re-latch every lock and bolt on the thick entry door. The visitor stood observing the near empty room with no windows, but not without noticing in the flickering lamp light fifteen bales of cotton and his luggage neatly stacked in the far left corner. A few sundry barrels and evenly piled boxes occupied the opposite side of the chamber. He felt that all contents of the room didn't escape the watchful eye of the porter. Jason congratulated himself on his storage selection. At the far end of the room, a dim light outlined an entryway. The porter, his lockup complete, walked past Jason, went to the haloed door, and knocked.

"Mr. Jason is here," the porter announced.

"Show him in," a baritone voice responded.

The servant opened the door and ushered Jason into an equally large room identical to the one he left, except it sported two large windows facing west and had a mixture of fine artwork and furniture. African/European artifacts scattered throughout the room spoke to the discerning eye of the obvious regal cost of many of the pieces, including the two divans and four large overstuffed chairs placed in a circle. Jason assumed that particular area was off limits to all except members of the Egbo when business was conducted. The eclectic choices of the brothers forced any visitor with artistic taste from labeling the hodgepodge as amusing, or cheap, just in great need of an interior decorator. A man of medium height with thinning brown hair sat behind a clean, well polished black teak desk. Beside him to his right a man of similar features stood. For a split second the seated man raised his right eyebrow at the neatly dressed black man who approached with his right hand extended. The trader rose, leaned over the desk, and extended his hand.

"Greetings, I'm Tom Aqua, and this is my brother, John," he smiled, jerking his head toward the man standing next to him.

Jason had accompanied Hunter on many of his nefarious business dealings throughout the South and had observed how Hunter had dealt with many of the less than honest and, at times, hostile people. He considered the application of some of Hunter's techniques most appropriate in this situation. Jason took the offered hand and lazily shook it. He looked deeply into the slightly lined, brown eyes of Tom Aqua and saw a cobra staring back. Despite their congeniality, in an instant these two could strike a deadly blow to either a man's person or his reputation without any consideration or remorse. With a sweep of his hand, Tom indicated for Jason to occupy one of the two straight-back chairs in front of the desk. Jason sat, crossed his legs, and gave the brothers an equally large grin which put them on notice he could prove equally as lethal.

"You mentioned something about a package similar to the one you sent earlier?" commented John, getting right to the point.

Jason allowed the comment to linger in the air for a brief moment before replying. "Oh, I have that, but first, I want to discuss a little business I have in mind, and then I'll pay my bill in full." The brothers glanced at one another. Tom gave his brother a shrug and turned his attention back to Jason.

"There is a matter of housing. I wish to purchase a place with complete privacy. For personal reasons, I wish to keep my presence in Dahomey anonymous at least for now. Next, I would like to employ four or five good men to protect it from prying eyes. Lastly, I want to find the whereabouts of five men. One of them is Mbuti."

"Do you have the names of the men you want to find?" Tom asked, finding his visitor's requests contained fewer details than the crafty black man cared to reveal.

"No, but they worked for a man called del Cohelo and, more recent then that, a Masai from Ilorin called Rebah," Jason replied.

John's brow furrowed as shook his head and pursed his lips. "We seem to have a little problem here. del Cohelo met with an unfortunate drowning accident last year. Rebah is easily found without our help; he is second in power only to Long Ju Ju of the Asanti tribe at Ilorin. We really believe that we can be of no further service to you in that area. We still may fill your order for property and staff."

"I'm sorry to hear about Mr. del Cohelo. I am quite familiar with Long Ju Ju and the Golden Stool, and I would prefer that Rebah knows nothing about this search. That is why I was recommended to seek you out," Jason said cryptically. This time, John raised both eyebrows.

"Is there any specific time limit in which you wish this accomplished? You know that such a search, especially with secrecy involved, could be long and very expensive?" John's tone would close the conversation for any native-African black within a hundred miles.

"Would five ingots of gold be enough?" Jason replied, uncrossing his legs and leaning forward. He still maintained his smile at the obvious ploy.

Surprised, the brothers looked at each other in disbelief. Where would a black man get a gold nugget let alone five ingots of gold? Still ---

Jason reached inside his money belt and began to extract ten more of the two-inch gold bars to equal the package he had sent earlier. The brothers stared in amazement as each gold bar clanked on the teak desk.

"Here is the package I promised to deliver. I'm sorry you find the task too difficult. Since I have kept my end of the bargain and have paid my debt, I hope you will be discrete until I can find someone else for the search. I shall return tomorrow to discuss the property and staff employment. If there is anyone you know who would be willing to do the search, you may have them contact me at The Lazy Monkey." Jason rose to leave.

John rushed to block the door and prevent Jason from leaving. From behind the desk, Tom joined his brother. "No! No! No! No! We didn't say we wouldn't do it. We just said it would be expensive."

"Good. Then I hope we have an agreement for the five ingots of gold," Jason said as he resettled in his seat. "When you find me a place and the men to guard it, transfer my luggage but not the cotton bales to my new residence. When I come to pick up the keys to the house, I will make sure you receive two of the promised ingots. After all, you will need some cash to initiate the search. Oh, and I would appreciate a receipt for the money spent. I know that it is not necessary, but it is an old custom I have had in practice for years, and I would hate to change it now." Jason relied heavily on his past experience as bookkeeper at Whispering Willows. Hunter had always provided him with receipts even for the smallest purchases.

"When the remainder of the contract is fulfilled, you will receive the other three ingots. Any transition from gold to local currency I trust you will do at a fair market price, including a fair broker's fee. Of course I shall keep a close eye on the exchange rate," Jason grinned. "It's just another old habit of mine and you know just how difficult old habits are to break." The brothers recognized they dealt with a person versed in business affairs, and Jason warranted close scrutiny. Hunter had taught Jason well.

Jason shifted his weight in the chair, widened his smile, and crossed his legs while the stunned brothers remained standing before him. Jason realized he had the advantage of this meeting and decided to profit from it. "Oh, yes, there are gold ingots hidden in the bales, but I knew that I could trust the Aqua brothers. You come highly recommended by my former employer and now partner who also is adept at remaining anonymous." Jason kept his smile, closed his eyes, and gently nodded his head toward the pair. The brothers responded by doing the same, acknowledging that this mysterious venture contained a silent partner.

Jason continued. "There are other ingots I can lay my hands on just in case, shall I say, these grow legs and walk away. I would have to send for their replacement though. That would mean additional expense to me in recovering the ones that disappeared, but my partner would make sure, restitution with a reasonable amount of interest was paid. Certainly I would not require that all of the interest would be monetary." Hunter had freely used Sean's name in many business dealings without the Irishman having any awareness of his doing so. Jason wondered if the same intimidation would work using an unnamed person residing at an unknown place.

Without alarm, the brothers again nodded to acknowledge the veiled threat. "Besides, if all goes as I have planned, we shall have a good, profitable, long-term relationship. Now do we have a contract, or not?" Jason uncrossed his legs and waved an open palm toward the brothers then placed his chin on the fist of his arm resting on the chair arm to give the appearance of relaxation which he did not feel. Jason gave a silent sigh of relief when the brothers replied in unison, "Indeed we do." Hunter's devious methods worked.

John offered Jason an extended hand and pumped it vigorously. Unlike the captain of the Green Mermaid, John's colorblindness became apparent if any transaction involved a large amount of money. Jason had just proved another of Hunter's adages; enough gold can remove any obstacle. "I think that you can move into your new home tomorrow. I have the prefect place in mind that my brother and I recently acquired. As to the five--er--gardeners, they will be there tomorrow afternoon." Almost as an afterthought, Tom cordially added, "Oh! And you'll need a housekeeper and cook. Jason cocked his head to the side and raised both palms outward as if he had received a generous gift. Jason then covered his mouth and gave a slight cough and said, "Of course, they will be as discrete as the gardeners."

Tom rubbed the palms of his hands together rapidly and with a slight nod of his head added, "Definitely. We shall include all of them in your monthly personnel payroll."

Not duped by the brothers' plan to plant spies, Jason congenially countered, "That's very considerate of you, but as I am purchasing the house, I would prefer to pay the personnel myself. Of course you will receive a finder's fee, but I shall be their employer with the right to screen, set their salaries, hire, and fire any or all of them at any time. The rest of the personnel needed to search for the whereabouts of the individuals I wish to locate I leave in your more than capable hands. Aside from what you will pay the searchers, the one who finds the desired people within a month will receive an additional bonus of twenty gold bars. Every month after this and the next the bonus will be halved. The same twenty gold bars will be given to each of you if the project is completed in the two months. Please purchase the best iron safe money can buy and have it delivered to my house. Until the safe arrives, I can think of no better place for the bales than here under the watchful eyes of the Aqua brothers. Again, I must stress that during all of these transactions discretion is a key factor," Jason emphasized as he rose, walked between the condescending brothers, and strolled toward the door with a huge African mask hanging on it. If he paid a high enough salary to his staff, it would seriously curtail spying. Any breach would mean immediate dismissal and loss of a salary higher than any person or business in Dahomey had to offer. He could also use the interview to discover others who would consider working for him and not just those recommended by the brothers.

"Meet us here tomorrow at three," Tom said. "We'll have someone escort you to your new lodgings where your personnel will be waiting to be interviewed, and we shall be most careful of your belongings so as not to lose one bole of cotton until the safe arrives."

Jason's sardonic grin widened even more so. "I have no doubt about it. Good evening gentlemen." And with that, Jason exited the museum-like room, closed the door with a sigh of relief, and walked toward the door leading from the building. He hoped the brothers had not noticed the beads of sweat on his forehead. The porter appeared from nowhere and without a break in his stride undid the locks in record time. Jason smiled, paused in the doorway, and asked the porter, "What is your name, sir?"

The doorman visibly startled. Never had anyone ever called him "sir." "Joseph, sir," he answered as he meekly stared at the floor.

"Have you worked for the brothers a long time?" Jason asked with interest.

In a soft voice, Joseph replied, "They bought me when they first arrived in Dahomey to open their business over twenty years ago."

Jason's voice hardened. "Are you still their slave?"

Joseph became alarmed by Jason's tone, lest he had done something wrong to one of the brothers' special clients. "Oh no, sir! When the British made Dahomey a regular stop, they freed me. Now I do a little cleaning, shopping, and take care of the door. The brothers give me food and lodging and a little change for my pocket. That's all I really need."

Jason decided to try to discover in greater detail more information the brothers avoided to relate. "Did you know a Mr. del Cohelo?"

For the first time, Joseph displayed bitterness and hatred in his voice. "He was an evil man."

"What happened to him?" Jason quizzed.

Joseph's tone lightened. "A little over a year ago he came here drunk and demanded to see the brothers. He could barely stand, but he had enough strength to knock me on the floor again. There was a terrible row." Joseph warmed to his story. "Mr. del Cohelo accused the brothers of cheating him. Mr. Tom and Mr. John threw him out. He began yelling in the street something about he was going to the British about Mr. John and Mr. Tom's business, and then he said they were still trading in slaves for the Arabs and refused to employ him in their search for slaves and that they never showed him proper respect for being the best slaver they ever hired. The next day, a sailor going on shore leave found Mr. del Cohelo's body floating next to his anchored ship." Joseph paused and a shadow of a smile crossed his face. "That nasty man must have been so drunk he staggered to the pier, fell off, hit his head, and drowned. The brothers paid to have the body cremated, but there was no religious service." The smile that suddenly appeared on Joseph's face broadened and looked unnatural. "Mr. Tom is such a kidder. I asked him what happened to Mr. del Cohelo's ashes. He told me they were out back, but I know he scattered them in the river. There's nothing out back except the outhouse, and I know Mr. John wouldn't scatter them in there."

The door to the brothers' office suddenly opened, and the brothers' forms outlined the doorway. "I thought I heard voices," Tom said suspiciously. Both brothers had agreed after Jason left that they dealt with no black fool and Jason needed careful observation. "Joseph, you've taken enough of Mr. Jason's time. He has more important things to do than be entertained by you. Lock up for the night," Tom commanded in a gruff voice.

"I apologize for Joseph's ramblings," John said in a much pleasanter tone, "When you are through locking up, kindly step into the office before going to bed, Joseph? Good night, Mr. Jason." John stood back from the opening, allowing his brother to close the door.

Jason knew the brothers had just opened their mental cobra hoods as a warning to him not to pry too deep into their affairs. More prudence became paramount in his dealings with them. At length they would interrogate the porter concerning the conversation for any scrap of useful information concerning this mysterious man who had just employed them. Jason stepped out onto the wide porch as Joseph, indicating by the tone in his voice that he expected a forthcoming inquisition by his employers, courageously whispered, "Good night, sir."

The moist, hot air, after the noxious atmosphere under the guise of diplomacy within the Aqua brothers' establishment, felt refreshing. Jason paused on the porch for a moment. Assessing Joseph's story, Jason acknowledged the fact that he dealt with very dangerous men indeed and had to remain on constant guard in his liaisons with the brothers. Things had gone well for now, but that could rapidly change. Hunter had provided Jason with good lessons in dealing with dangerous people. The shade of Sean McQuinn entered Jason's thoughts, but he dismissed it and focused on his future goals. "Not long now, Rebah. Not long now," he thought. Jason tugged at the lapels of his frock coat, stepped into the street, and headed for The Lazy Monkey.

CHAPTER IV

POWER

Rebah, Ifa's high priest second only to Long Ju Ju, walked to the back of the hut where the dimness created a cooler and more pleasant atmosphere than the rest of the thatch structure he and his family called home. The temple of Ifa, Long Ju Ju's residence and the council hut provided the three main structures of the cul-de-sac of importance in Ilorin. His house had the honor of forming part of those notable configurations at a greater distance from the other structures. He heard his wife and two daughters outside of the entryway pounding rice to make flour for tonight's rice cakes and talking with other women about the quantity and quality of rice recently acquired from the hard bargaining Arab traders who recently paused in Ilorin on their way to Dahomey. Rebah sat down on the straw mat which served as his and his wife's bed and rubbed his eyes with the palms of his hands. He felt extra tired today after his strenuous session with Long Ju Ju concerning the serious decrease of funds to Ifa due to the decline in slave trade. Before the entire lucrative slave trade collapsed, an illness to the previous Long Ju Ju's ensued the old man. The leader of the Asanti nation and guardian of the Golden Stool asked too many questions about his deputy's private dealings with the Arab traders regarding reasons for condemnation of villages for slavery. Long Ju Ju had pointed out that village condemnation increased shortly after the Arabs visited Ilorin and questioned whether Rebah's condemnations dealt with religious or personal reasons. Rebah countered by pointing out that most of the villages condemned did not contain Asanti tribesmen and stressed the difficulty in maintaining proper respect for Ifa outside the Asanti tribe. In reality, Rebah tried to spare selling anyone from Asanti tribe as much as possible, but the hearty people garnered much more gold from their prospective masters in the East than other less robust tribes. Unlike the past when the Civil War raged on the American continent and the need for slaves proved great, Rebah now only infrequently condemned entire villages for some infraction against the Golden Stool and sold their citizens into slavery. To add to Rebah's problems, Europeans had begun to colonize the Dark Continent and needed the black population as servants for their plantation houses and to work in their newly acquired arable fields and rich mines. The pittance paid to the workers by white men enticed the locals to perform even more subservient work than the toiling in the fields or hunting game around their villages for themselves. The income provided better sustenance by its monthly money guarantee for their families rather than the traditional means of obtaining money by crop or animal hide sales affected by floods, draught, or occasional death due to natural hardships.

Rebah stretched out on the straw mat, put his hands behind his head, and stared into the semi-darkness at a rodent crossing a bamboo roof support. He observed how it periodically paused briefly and sniffed to assure itself that the trip harbored no hidden dangers and the possibility of a cache of food at the end of its journey. Things had gone well for Rebah ever since he disposed of annoying Jason and the last avaricious Long Ju Ju who had approved village condemnation but spent most of the profit for excess jewelry, housing, and clothing for his many "wives." Rebah had studied how Mbuti poison, in proper doses, could not only render a man helpless, but kill him. At first Rebah introduced only very small doses of the nerve numbing poison in the old Long Ju Ju's cassava. When the entire population of Ilorin realized the old man's health worsened, it became a simple matter to introduce the lethal dose. Rebah did not miss the old man and his monetary wastefulness.

Rebah could have killed Jason as well, but he would have missed the pleasure of knowing his rival suffered in the chains of slavery, which Jason considered anathema. at council meetings. Jason constantly fought against Rebah concerning village condemnation. The cunning priest had heard from various merchants about the hard life of a Confederate slave in America and since Jason stubbornly impeded Rebah's climb to power through slavery, it seemed poetic that Jason taste what he so vehemently denounced. Rebah laughed softly. He wondered if Jason still lived. His former rival might not even have survived the sea voyage. He really didn't care. Just to have gotten rid of Jason gave him immense satisfaction.

No matter. With Jason out of the way and the election of a new Long Ju Ju, Rebah's rise in the priesthood of Ifa had accelerated. With the demise of the old Long Ju Ju, Rebah and Jason's mentor, Konte, had become the new Long Ju Ju. Konte moved the Golden Stool from its round-robin travels throughout the Asanti nation to a permanent station in the temple at Ilorin. The constant movement of the revered throne may have produced a larger income to the village that had temporary possession of the Golden Stool, but bitter rivalry between villages as to which one would get the holy object next sometimes turned to violence. The single act of a permanent location provided stability to the followers of Ifa and permitted Rebah to centralize his growing power. Instead of attempting to discover slavers in his treks back and forth across the continent for religious reasons, it became easier to deal with potential recruitments to his service when they visited Ilorin after an already devoted employee secretly presented a name and time of the individual's arrival in the city for possible induction into Rebah's plans to increase his power.

Rebah created a far-reaching spy system. Coupled with bribery to other shady individuals from other tribes and the inclusion of a few white men from Dahomey, Rebah's power increased daily. Enough of a bribe made it easy for a renegade on a pilgrimage to Ilorin to denounce his fellow villagers or a white malingerer from Dahomey to point out robust villages for plundering. Rebah gave a promise of immunity to the betrayer who proved his dedication to Ifa by revealing the heresy within a tribe. The betrayer never suffered the same fate as those he betrayed. Of course the addition of monetary rewards to informants prompted an incentive to increase traitors in other villages in order to procure more "heretics" to swell Ifa's coffers. This tactic created a strong power base for Rebah. Long Ju Ju's right hand had cultivated fear throughout Africa with the mere mention of his name. Now, he patiently labored very hard to consolidate his authority before the Europeans made his life totally disagreeable by usurping trade routes and protecting villages from condemnation. The white man, backed by the army of a given country, proved more difficult to handle than terrified villagers, but a few corrupt white individuals always made themselves available to dabble in the slave trade for the right price. Rebah slowly shook his head. Too bad del Coelho had an accident. He certainly had deserved recognition as the best slaver to walk the Dark Continent. When sent on a mission he never failed to deliver some of the best high priced merchandise. The week he died Rebah had just contracted with del Cohelo for another sortie in the Eastern part of the Africa to obtain a minimum of sixty slaves. The slaver stated he had personal business in Dahomey that would recoup a lot of money already due him. His task would only take a couple of days, and then he would leave for the East to begin his hunt for Rebah. del Cohelo's accident forced Rebah to reorganize his plans.

Rebah rolled over on the mat and directed his thoughts toward Konte. Though a kind old man, and, to the Asanti, a well loved Long Ju Ju, he lived too far in the past to see the immense profit in trading with the Arabs for slaves rather than commodity trading with greedy Europeans who took for themselves most of the returns from the sale of the rich natural treasures of the African Continent. This left the native people smidgens of the profit. Besides, the less demanding Arabs accepted slavery as a way of life and usually paid more than the European trade enterprises. If Rebah could obtain a respectable age for acceptance as the next Long Ju Ju, just three or four years more, a mishap could occur to Konte. He could claim Asanti heritage through his marriage, but first Rebah had to build a power base within the Asanti.

Rebah rolled over on his other side and stared at the filtered sunlight illuminating the section of the hut used by the entire family. In order to allow the cooler air inside to circulate, his wife tied back the cloth curtains of their sleeping area which matched the ones separating his daughters' pallets. The rapidly fading sunlight informed Rebah soon his dutiful wife would call him for supper. Already he heard the women gathering various pounding bowls and pestles in order to prepare the evening meal. Bright sunlight flooded the sleeping area as his wife moved aside the vibrant, multicolored, bamboo woven drape that served as a door. Her husband heard her stow the work tools on the shelf, and the rattling of pots alerted him that she had begun the evening meal. Rebah quickly rolled over to face the wall of the hut so she would think he napped. He didn't feel like having a conversation with anyone at the moment.

Rebah's thoughts went back to his rise in the priesthood of Ifa. He had started only with five men -- four Masai and one Mbuti. He now had a cadre of fourteen obedient servants and two more possible inductees scattered throughout different Asanti tribes and belonging the city of Dahomey. He made sure he paid them well and had each of them search other tribes for other possible inductees into his exclusive business in Ilorin. Though it seemed a small amount of personnel at the moment, yearly he added two or three more names to the list. By the time it became necessary to replace Konte, he would have enough men to quell any opposition to those who also aspired to the Golden Stool and prevent his desire to place his backside on the revered object. Contented with the progress of his life, the crafty priest drifted off to a dreamless sleep.

Rebah awoke with a start as the soft hand of his wife touched his shoulder and called his name. He could hear his two daughters giggling in the dining area as they prepared the low table with four bolsters and pillows for the evening meal. The delicious aroma of supper permeated the hut. His wife always provided succulent meals. He hadn't intended to sleep, but it seemed to have refreshed him. His wife returned to the main room to censure one of his daughters for some minor infraction. Rebah sat up and stretched, rose, went into the great room, and gave each of the women a hug. For the first time, he noticed the enlargement of his daughters' breasts. He would have to find them husbands soon. If careful, he could possibly marry them to important village chiefs' sons and further extend his influence. Proper marriages required serious consideration if he wished to elevate his social standing even higher among the neighboring Asanti tribes. Indeed, life had showered many benefices on the possible future Long Ju Ju. Rebah sat down to eat.

CHAPTER V

GOLDEN STOOL

Konte let out a slight groan as one of his attendants placed over his shoulders the heavy tapa ceremonial cape inscribed with protective and enlightening etchings to inspire Long Ju Ju in performance of his assigned duty as Ifa's mediator. Priests designated by tradition to ritualistically paint Long Ju Ju's face for the upcoming ceremony completed that rite over fifteen minutes ago and left the old man alone for prayer and reflection. The shortest day of the year, a day special to Ifa, arrived. Anyone with a grievance could petition Long Ju Ju for justice without having to go through the ecclesiastical bureaucracy, and his ruling became final and permanent. Never before today did Konte dread his role as Long Ju Ju. Something bothered Ifa's high priest and he didn't comprehend the reason. He performed this ceremony many times in the past and had always felt he meted justice wisely. What prevented him from looking forward to today's ceremony? Questions arose but no answers. Like it or not, Long Ju Ju had his duty to perform.

Long Ju Ju exited the preparation area of the temple hut and began his regal walk down the aisle formed by priests and worshippers of Ifa. Though still early morning, the heat produced from the milling crowd and the heaviness of his costume made him sweat. He shifted his shoulders in an attempt to discover a dry area inside the cape, but it seemed the entire garment concealed a hidden river. With his peripheral vision, Ifa's highest priest noticed more than Asanti tribesmen amid the petitioners and witnesses. People from various areas of the African Continent where the religion of Ifa had spread dotted the multitude of petitioners and observers, including some Arabs who inhabited the southern portion of the Sahara. Much time passed since Long Ju Ju or his lieutenant traveled abroad to dispense justice, and only when it became a necessary intervention by Long Ju Ju to decide between foes that may cause a war that made him travel so far from home.

Wisely, these members from the north had the hoods of their jelabas pulled forward to protect them from the hot African sun. Long ago they learned from the Great Desert that exposed skin, especially the head, could easily drive a man insane and kill him in a matter of a couple of hours. They would take no chances even if jungle surrounded them here in Ilorin. The rich costumes and handmade accessories from a melange of tribes from far and near rivaled the splendor of Long Ju Ju's costume. Add the beauty of the Arabs' multicolored robes, and a festive sight greeted any one who had an eye for color and design. The shuffling sound of feet from behind alerted Konte that Rebah and the priestly entourage accompanied him to the throne. He mounted the three stairs of the platform and stared ahead at elaborate throne known as the Golden Stool, representing the very essence, past-present, and future, of the Asanti people and the followers of Ifa. From that humble throne, Long Ju Ju would dispense justice -- a disputed land boundary, a broken marriage contract, ownership of animals, and on and on. The crowd appeared especially large for today's ceremony, and Long Ju Ju sincerely hoped most of them had come to Ilorin not as petitioners but only as spectators or witnesses that wanted to participate in tonight's festivities. Konte observed that if all attendees had petitions, the next feast would arrive and pass before Ifa's agent would complete his business.

As Konte approached the embellished throne. Rebah's tenor voice soon led the chanting which initiated the opening of the Day of Judgment ceremony. Konte's mind left the liturgy and searched for the response as to why a strange feeling of danger haunted him. The priestly chanting came to an abrupt halt forcing the leader of the cult to concentrate on the present situation. Long Ju Ju bowed to all present and sat back on the Golden Stool. One of the officiating priests led forth a young man and woman. A third man stood well back from the approaching couple. The petitioners and witnesses for the first judgment of Long Ju Ju separated into three groups and paused fifteen feet from the platform to give obeisance to the austere figure in his tapa cloak staring down at them. The contingency of each of the pleading members with their witnesses could have made their own tribe. After silencing the cacophony of accusations hurled at the same time by each group, Konte determined the family of the girl who belonged to the largest group on his left negotiated marriage to a young man from a different tribe who belonged to the large group standing in the rear, but she preferred to elope with a young man from her own tribe who formed the group on the right. The political marriage would have ended the enmity between the two tribes. Now new conflict threatened to erupt due to the rash action of the lovers. Konte drew in a deep breath and exhaled very slow. This first case heralded a tedious day for Long Ju Ju.

In early afternoon, Long Ju Ju procured a rest period, but the list of cases diminished by over half. He announced to the multitude of spectators Rebah would make judgments in his absence, and his assistant's decisions carried the same weight as his own. Rebah could not occupy the Golden Stool during

Konte's absence, but as Long Ju Ju's lieutenant he possessed the same power to make decisions. Long Ju Ju walked to the edge of the dais and watched the priests form an aisle for him to re-enter the temple for food, drink, and perhaps a slight nap. Konte watched the excited new petitioners for the next case ignore his decent from the platform and crowd around where Rebah stood.

Konte entered the cooler temple hut and immediately shed the heavy tapa cloak that seemed somehow heavier than this morning. On the low table in the center of the room before the large wooden statue of Ifa, one of the servant priests had prepared his superior's afternoon repast. The tired leader of the Asanti could hear petitioners outside passionately presenting a case to Rebah. Long Ju Ju took a long draught of cassava from the ornately carved wooden cup that had rested on the table and broke open a pomegranate taken from a bowl of fruit beside a pitcher of soothing beverage. A mat spread for an afternoon siesta beckoned the old man invitingly, but Konte's disturbed mind prevented him from enjoying any comforting repose. Something foreboded evil to the Asanti leader, but what? He had not observed anything to confirm his eerie feeling. Had Rebah's well concealed drive for power finally come to fruition? For a moment, Konte pursued that line of thinking. No, his lieutenant's age and lack of a firm power base to enact his plots held that ambitious priest in check for now. Then what? The question hung unresolved. The disturbed leader began to pace the hut with the uneaten fruit in one hand as he sipped the contents of the cup with the other in order to resolve the poignant question.

"Holy Ifa, what is it?" he prayed. Outside, the petitioners' loud pleas overrode the silence in the hut, but no reply to the dilemma came from the god in response to Long Ju Ju's invocation. Konte continued pacing and searching for a response.

"My lord is the food not to your pleasing?" asked the frightened young acolyte assigned to cater to Ifa's high priest. Afraid he had done something to displease Long Ju Ju, the lad dropped to his knees in a supplicant's pose.

Konte started. He had not meant to display any emotion that may reveal his concern about his personal problems. The old man walked to the trembling boy, smiled, and raised the boy to his feet. "No. I believe with all the excitement of the day I'm not as hungry as I thought." Reassured the high priest's anxiety originated from another source, the inexperienced aide nodded and backed out of the doorway. Konte took another sip of inner warming cassava and continued his disturbing deliberations.

After a respectable amount of time that would have served proper for sustenance and rest, Konte slung the heavy tapa cloak over his shoulders again and prepared to resume his Long Ju Ju duties. Ifa's judge remained a little longer in the serenity of the hut to assure his sudden appearance would not demean Rebah's authority in the current judgment he administered or reveal any self-concern about personal problems on Long Ju Ju's part. Konte waited just until Rebah passed judgment on the current case. At last, he stepped from the doorway of the temple. The participating clergy formed an aisle leading once more to the platform. After what seemed to Konte a long walk around Africa, Long Ju Ju once again took his seat on the revered object. Rebah turned and bowed to him and walked to the right of the seated Long Ju Ju and assumed a regal pose.

Two hours of sunlight remained when the last petitioner heard Long Ju Ju's judgment. Konte ignored the exhaustion that encased his body and mind. He refused to display any such weakness before his people. With his duty over for another year and the night-long festivities about to begin, Long Ju Ju would concentrate on other ecclesiastical duties. Any other cases not heard today had to revert to the clerical bureaucracy. All frightful portends began to dissipate. Thank Ifa!

"In the name of Holy Ifa, justice, my lord," a voice from the departing crowd yelled. Konte paused to deal with the latecomer.

The cry came from one of the Arabs. Konte could not see the man's face because of the cowl pulled forward. "Speak, my son."

The petitioning figure stepped forward and pulled the concealing cowl from his head. The holy throne shook as Rebah grasped its back and leaned on it for support as his legs threatened to buckle. "Jason!" he whispered to no one in particular. Konte rose so rapidly that the Golden Throne toppled backward from the weight of Rebah. Other nearby priests ran to upright the revered object. The curious crowd halted their exit and became attentive to this new petitioner that caused panic at the holy shrine.

With measured stride, the vengeful man came to stand within ten feet of the dais of judgment. "I accuse the man called Rebah of dishonoring the name of holy Ifa and committing an abominable act of treachery against Ifa's devout servant by selling me into slavery to further his evil ambition. I accuse him of plotting to seize the Golden Stool in the near future for his own personal use to increase slave trade in the East, and that he did murder the last Long Ju Ju by the use of Mbuti poison to further this ungodly goal, and finally he participated in mass corruption of Ifa's holy ordinances by using village condemnation to supply certain Arab traders with slaves in order to meet his own filthy plans." Jason shouted while pointing a condemnatory finger at the stunned figure standing behind Long Ju Ju. The assembled crowd began to murmur in shock at the allegations.

At the last accusation, Rebah partially recovered himself and regained his balance thanks to the up-righted Golden Stool. "Liar!" Rebah screamed, but his high-pitched soprano voice carried very little weight.

A huge smile broke out on Jason's face. Without breaking eye contact with Rebah, Jason's eyes became hooded for the first time in many months. As if calling lightning from the heavens, the vindictive man pointed a finger skyward. Six Arabs, part of the company who had accompanied the returned native from Dahomey to Ilorin, brought forward in heavy restraints four large, black men and one pygmy. Jason swung his finger toward the new arrivals while he kept his fiery eyes locked on his enemy.

"Do you know these men, Rebah?" Jason paused but received a mute response from the accused man. "They seem to know you," Jason added venomously as he waved for the Arabs to bring the involved men closer to the platform for better viewing by Long Ju Ju and Rebah.

Without waiting longer for a rebuttal, the petitioner approached the dais in front of Long Ju Ju and knelt. "Would you like hear their tale, my lord? You may question them together or individually. They will all say the same thing."

The kneeling ex-priest cocked his head to the side and allowed his incinerating eyes to once more bore into the man desperately attempting to maintain his balance with Long Ju Ju's throne, his only means of support. Rebah avoided eye contact with Konte who stood before it, eyes affixed on the man he thought dead.

"Oh! And Rebah, I have sixteen more men not far from here who can be brought forward to attest to your treachery to Ifa and Long Ju Ju. It took me a while to round them up, but once these four volunteered some names, my task became easier."

Rebah released his hold on the chair and turned hastily to exit into the temple. He must seek solitude and form a rebuttal, but two large scowling priests blocked his egress. The distraught priest looked around like a trapped animal. Finally, he prostrated himself before Konte and in a broken voice exclaimed, "My lord, let me explain."

Konte crossed his arms across his chest and barely audible speech stated, "That is why we have this day."

The quivering man did not look up as he began his diatribe. "This man is lying. He never did like me. He has done this to disgrace me in the eyes of Ifa and yourself. He has paid these men a lot of money to lie about me and has well rehearsed them in the story he wants them to tell. That is all there is to it," Rebah responded desperately.

Konte looked toward his lieutenant's accuser for a response to the charge of perjury. Jason reached inside his robe and drew forth three pieces of paper. "My lord, you are familiar with the Aqua brothers of Dahomey. I have here their sworn statement that they have spoken with the captain of the slave ship that transported me to America. It clearly states that after I was drugged first by this Mbuti and then by these four men, I was taken directly to the slave compound in Dahomey. The captain who had been paid by Rebah expected my arrival in bondage two weeks before he ever laid eyes on me. After a brief stay in a holding pen due to the tide change at Dahomey, I was carried drugged on board his ship to be sold into slavery in America. Arrangements for my abduction and sale into slavery had been made well in advance by the traitor, Rebah, as these men will attest. Here are the papers also signed by the Aqua Brothers confirming the truth of that statement by the ship's captain." Jason approached the stage and offered the papers to Long Ju Ju to examine. With trembling hands Konte accepted the papers. "The second is the captain's statement, and the third is the statement of his first mate to further confirm it. You may also question the other sixteen men I have brought you as to who is telling the truth, but it is especially important that you question the Mbuti. He will tell you about

Rebah requesting instruction in the use of Mbuti poison dosage to make a person ill and how much to administer to kill him. Furthermore Rebah paid this Mbuti for the needed substance to murder the previous Long Ju Ju as well as having him provide the poison dart that immobilized me for my sale into slavery. The Mbuti's other friends will give you details and names of other Arab traders who demanded and received a set number of slaves by request to Rebah." Jason's eyes became mere slits as he approached within arms length to the cowered man after Long Ju Ju received the remainder of evidence.

"My lord, I--" Rebah began.

"Silence!" Konte shouted. The judgmental figure waved for Jason to return to his group. The disturbed high priest knelt, crumpling the papers in his hand, leaned forward, and spoke only to the prostrate Rebah. "For a long time now, I have been aware of your secret plotting, but this act with its irrefutable evidence made public, brought to me on the Day of Judgment from so many people outside of Ilorin, demonstrates your abomination and treachery, not only to me, but against Ifa. Since your actions have been brought to light in a public forum, I can no longer pretend to ignore your scheming. There is nothing more I can do for you."

The man named Konte had knelt, but now the priest and leader, Long Ju Ju, rose to his full height of authority. He passed the evidence to a nearby priest and raised his arms above his head. Rebah's judge pronounced the following: "Hear the judgment of Ifa against this odious pretender to his service. I give the life of this serpent and all his possessions to Ifa's wronged true servant, Jason. Furthermore, I restore my wronged priest to his legitimate place at my right side. Now take this wretched polluter of Ifa's will from my sight. I shall have his head over Ifa's temple before the sun sets." A disgusted high priest started his retreat to the steps leading to the aisle of priests which ended at the temple door while two other priests took Rebah into custody.

"Wait, my lord!" cried Jason. A surprised Konte halted and stared at Jason. Rebah had nothing left to forfeit. Even the wronged Jason dare not overrule the will of Long Ju Ju on reprisal day. "Are you displeased with the sentence, my son?" Konte asked quizzically, ignoring the murmuring from the gathered crowd who could hardly believe the spectacle unfolding before them.

"No, my lord." A humble Jason rested his open palms on his shoulders and bowed to his old mentor. "It is just, but you did give me his life and property."

The odd and uncomfortable feeling that had haunted Konte all day returned. "Speak on!" he ordered, not really wanting to hear what Jason had to say next.

Once more Jason approached the dais and looked up at Ifa's high priest. Konte looked down and could no longer see a trusted friend, a person considered once as a son, but saw a rabid beast of destruction. "According to the decree of Long Ju Ju, I now own this man and all that belongs to him. I reserve the right to dispense my own justice in this case."

Fear lit the old priest's eyes. Something inhuman stood below him. "You have his life forfeited. What more could you want?" Konte asked in a weak voice.

"I don't want his death," Jason growled.

Konte believed lessons given to a waif he had discovered so many years ago wandering the streets of Benin finally reached fruition. He had showed Jason mercy and compassion by taking him under his wing and had nurtured him in the ways of Ifa. Now his moral lessons to Jason came full circle. Konte smiled, descended the dais and said, "I have given his life to you. Do with it as you wish."

Jason stepped toward the two militant priests restraining Rebah. "Here is my sentence." Once more he waved to two of the Arabs accompanying him to come forward and then turned to Konte. "My lord, this is Abram who knows of a deserted oasis in the middle of the great desert that only he uses on his trips to and from Egypt. There's a well and nearby rocks to protect the caravan from the desert sun and provide much-needed water. Hidden in the rocks, he keeps a food supply for his trips. I have paid him to add additional supplies to help feed the keeper of the oasis."

"But you just said that the place was barren. It has no keeper," stated Konte as once again that uneasy feeling began to permeate his person.

"It does now. Rebah will be taken to this place and left. He will receive a regular supply of food. If he strays from the site and is found, Abram's people have instructions to return him. He will remain there the rest of his life contemplating his offenses against Ifa."

Konte frowned but nodded in agreement. Perhaps, his silly fears about today had become meaningless due to the ruthless sentence Jason had just decreed. "It is a much harsher sentence than the one I imposed, but it is just."

With a wave of his hand Long Ju Ju dismissed the case to continue the ritual parade back to the temple.

The two guards started to take Rebah toward Abram when Jason stepped between Rebah and his jailers. "Know the rest of your sentence, Masai," bellowed the angry man.

Konte turned. For some unknown reason, Long Ju Ju's fear just turned to terror. Both he and Rebah gazed upon Jason who displayed an uncontrollable fury which had immobilized the two of them. Both shuddered to think what new condemnation Jason devised worse than the living death sentence just passed.

Jason temporarily turned his back on the curious high priest and the disgraced prelate and waved for a second Arab to come forward. "This, my lord" Jason said staring snidely to the restrained man, "is Ali. It has been brought to my attention that Rebah likes to negotiate in the slave business with the Arabs."

Once again Jason turned to confront his old mentor. By way of introduction, Jason crooned, "Ali is the owner of an establishment in Dahomey that services the poor and visitors to the city who cannot afford the sensual surroundings and pleasures of the more fortunate." Spittle flew from the spiteful man as he turned and screamed at a quaking Rebah and the crowd of onlookers, "His wife and daughters are to be given to Ali to service the poor men and travelers of Dahomey."

Konte stumbled back in shock as Rebah began to scream. "Do anything you want with me, but leave my family out of this. Sell them into slavery, if you must, but not this. I beg you for mercy in the name of Ifa, not for myself, but for them. They are innocent. Mercy, Jason, mercy." Broken and still restrained, Rebah's legs buckled as his equally stunned wardens allowed him to sink to the ground and place his forehead on the ground facing his tormentor.

Jason walked forward and looked down at the sobbing man and whispered, "I, too, was innocent when you sold me into hell, as well as all of those who lived in villages which you condemned in your desire for power. As you forced this innocent, and others like me, to drink the bitter dregs of slavery. Now you must partake of the same cup. Innocent children along with their parents were sold into slavery at your command. Were they less innocent than your wife and daughters?" Jason stepped back and raised his voice for all to hear.

"Finally, all of his livestock is to be slaughtered and a great feast is to be held here in Ilorin to celebrate the justice of Ifa.

All other possessions are to be placed in his house which is to be burnt to the ground and sown with salt. Thus will Ifa be avenged?"

An abashed Konte almost joined Rebah on the ground as he stared at Jason in shock. Never had he heard of such cruelty, even by Rebah or any white man. The priest now regretted he had given the judgment, but Long Ju Ju had spoken from the Golden Stool, and he could not retract. Perhaps reason could prevail. He motioned Jason forward for private conversation.

The old man reached out and placed his quivering hand on Jason's shoulder and sought the young boy he had saved from a life of thievery. "I know you have much bitterness in your heart, my son. Rightly so. But death to him and his family would be welcomed not only by him but by me. If you must send him to his living death, do so, but spare his family who had nothing to do with his wicked deeds. At the very least, demand their deaths, but not this act which is far beyond cruelty. I ask you to reconsider your decision, not for Rebah's sake, but for mine and all I may have meant to you in the past." Konte's hand trembled even more on the implacable man's shoulder as he made his plea.

Cold eyes of a beast stared at the old priest. "A man not too long ago accused me of being panther-like. So be it. It has taken me many years of hunting but, like the panther, I shall now have my prey--all of them." Suddenly, the young lost boy flickered in Jason's eyes. "My lord, I give you my word that, in the future, I shall always be guided by your gentle hand." Instantly, the cat reappeared, "But in this matter I cannot be swayed." Jason's eyes became unfocused for a moment as he stared toward the western sun. "The same man told me long ago that there are many forms of death. This is only one form." Jason stiffened under Long Ju Ju's grip and with no emotion said, "If you command me, I shall reverse my sentence. Otherwise, my judgment remains."

A defeated Konte withdrew his hand and rose to full height. "You know that I want to command you to do it but cannot. If I did that, all past judgments by Long Ju Ju could be questioned. Once Long Ju Ju has rendered a decision from the Golden Stool, it cannot be reversed. I have learned a bitter lesson today." Tears welled in the old man's eyes. "One must not only watch for the dangers that may arise from within a known circle of enemies but from the savage cruelty of ones we considered friends, even one we loved as a son." Konte drew the sweat-drenched cloak around his tired body. "May Ifa guard your conscience and the ability to sleep in peace for the inhumane acts you have done this day. All maliciousness Rebah has done can in no way reach comparison of your action today. It will be a long time before my sleep will be peaceful for the part I have played in this despicable deed."

Konte paused and placed his hands on both sides of the kneeling man's head and made Jason look into his eyes. After careful examination, the wise priest said, "I still see the beautiful frightened soul of a scared, abused little boy I loved. I also see the Black Panther you mentioned devouring it. Kill the beast, Jason; kill it before it kills you."

Konte withdrew his hands, turned and entered the temple hut, leaving Jason kneeling before an empty throne.

SARAH

1869

CHAPTER VI

PRICES

A year elapsed since Rebah's humiliation and downfall. Still, Jason did not enjoy his reinstatement as Long Ju Ju's second in command. Konte did nothing to undermine Jason's position, but the close friendship that had taken so many years to forge no longer existed. At conferences Long Ju Ju listened to his former pupil's advice and sometimes acted on it, but Jason recognized, and grievously felt, an expanding gulf in their personal relationship. Konte refused to allow the returned native to bridge the huge personal chasm created by Rebah's exile. Since that fateful day Jason had not received a social invitation from Long Ju Ju, other laity, or ecclesiastical members of the compound. Long Ju Ju treated him respectfully in deference to Jason's office. Jason received only a regretful smile and a polite refusal in response to his friendly invitations to socialize from everybody. If Jason attempted to join groups congregated in the compound, a thousand excuses occurred to each member to depart and leave Jason standing alone.

To prove himself on the counsel, Jason became a good administrator. He retained a firm restraint on his underlings without the cruelty he had shown Rebah. Although he had a tendency to lose his temper from time to time, no one at Ilorin could accuse him of unfairness. He received respect and obedience without question, but attempts to win friendship proved in vain. The women of Ilorin would have nothing to do with him. They verbalized no scorn in their voices, nor could he find fault with their excuses to absent themselves from his company, but subconsciously he could feel their invisible wall. It seemed the entire city chose to follow Long Ju Ju's example and avoid him as much as possible. Jason seethed. His life had come full circle. He now lived with his own people and should receive better treatment. Despite his grumpy disposition, the staff at Whispering Willows had treated him better than anyone in Ilorin. At Whispering Willows, he easily determined who did or did not like him or at least tolerated his sullen company but not here. Damn them all. Jason must prove to himself that as a man in control of his own life and the lives of others, he needed no one socially.

"Where in the hell did you put the jar of cassava?" he barked at his young servant.

Just inside the entrance of Jason's hut, an acolyte designated as the volatile priest's personal servant leapt to his feet. "On the table in the back, my lord," an astonished voice squeaked.

Jason realized he verbally abused his helper due to his foul mood. If this incident reached the ears of others it would only increase more isolation, if possible. "I'm sorry I yelled. I have a throbbing headache, and the heat is getting to me," Jason responded in milder tones.

The acolyte doubted his hearing. Had the high priest actually apologized? Jason never gave apologies or offer explanations to anyone. The youth became alarmed. "Would you like for me to fetch the shaman, my lord?"

"No, it's nothing. Leave me alone for a while. I may rest."

"Yes, my lord. You didn't sleep well last night. You..." The boy withered in mid-sentence by the ominous look Jason gave him.

“Leave me,” Jason said through clenched teeth with a bit more supremacy than he intended.

“Yes, my lord,” the contrite servant answered, feeling quite relieved in leaving Jason’s presence, especially with the current nasty mood the high priest displayed. Constantly bowing toward Jason, the frightened boy backed out of the hut and sat by the doorway overlooking the compound, in case Jason had further need of him. The entry to Jason’s hut faced other high clergy’s residences, including the largest, belonging to Long Ju Ju. Jason hoped that no passerby heard him yelling at the lad. In the future he must apply more caution when his disgruntled mood presented itself.

Jason walked to the back of the hut, picked up the half filled jar of cassava, and poured another cup. He sipped the relaxing liquid and sat lotus fashion on his sleeping mat. The acolyte correctly observed Jason’s sleeping habits. The depressed man avoided sleep until complete exhaustion overtook him. During sleep, his dreams invited demons from his past to invade his already troubled mind causing him to yell out during the night. This nightmare invasion produced much anxiety from his nearby neighbors and increase of scowls the next day from members of the compound awakened by Jason’s diabolic dreams. Rumors of Jason’s mental condition began to diffuse throughout Ilorin. Jason believed before the Arabs transported Rebah to his new home, the bastard placed a curse on him. He jumped up from the mat and poured more cassava into his cup, hoping it would dispel some of the emotional hurt he felt. Perhaps it would help him to become more relaxed and relieve some of his muscular tenseness. Whether asleep or awake, echoes of Rebah’s screams for mercy still permeated Jason’s thoughts. The insomniac slammed the well used wooden cup filled with cassava on the small table spilling some of the contents on the sleeve of his white robe. It became more and more difficult to avoid thoughts of his nefarious actions both here in Ilorin and in Alabama. He tried desperately to convince himself this haunting had nothing to do with anything he had done. He wanted to even the score for himself and others that had suffered the same fate he had endured. He merely instituted justice, not for himself alone, but for those still toiling under the yoke of slavery due to Rebah's greedy grasp for money and power. All things considered, who ever bestowed mercy on the village members Rebah sold? Who ever bestowed mercy on him as a slave? Who ever cared for his well being?

In asking the last question, Jason's mounting anger vanished into thin air as surprise answers filtered into his disquieted thoughts: Konte and Hunter. Konte always treated him as a son from the first meeting in Benin when Jason attempted to steal Konte's purse. From that day on Konte showed Jason tenderness and compassion. His surrogate parent only nurtured that relationship throughout the years--until now. He rued the alienation of the old man's affection. Jason swore he would never abandon his search to discover a means to mend that breach. He rubbed the back of his neck and refilled his cup. Why did he think of Hunter at this time? The events in America existed in another universe. Jason wanted them to remain there undisturbed. Jason now must concentrate on life with his people in his native land and rid himself of past memories as a slave in America, but how? He took another sip of the cassava and thought of the name Hunter gave him, panther. Jason laughed into the cassava cup almost spilling some of its contents again. His panther nature enjoyed fantasizing about the fall of Hunter as much as it did about the fall of Rebah. For more than a year, Jason prayed to Ifa that Lulu and Sean made Hunter's life insufferable. By now Sean would have confiscated Mr. Wilkerson's bank account in Charleston and returned to New York to live a life of ease. He wondered who owned Whispering Willows now. Before departing for New York, the crafty Irishman would have alerted everyone in Unionville to Hunter's ploys. If Sean had not made Hunter reveal the gold's hiding place, Bubba's scrutiny of that accursed Masai's spending habits would prevent Hunter from using the gold reserve he had hidden in the swamp at Whispering Willows. If Hunter dared touch the gold his skin color would raise questions as to where a black man came by all of that gold. Bubba, the Grand Wizard of the Ku Klux Klan, who officially doubled as sheriff of Unionville, would ensure Hunter would never again take advantage of other people. Jason tried to relish his refractory thoughts of Hunter's downfall, but the tortured man's desire for acceptance of his righteous deeds lacked conviction and caused more turmoil than soothing satisfaction.

Hunter's hypothetical distress could not sate Jason's hunger for retribution any more than the successful ruin of Rebah did. He compared the results of actions to drinking mental salt water. His best laid plans to have Rebah suffer the rest of his life with the knowledge of his family living in forced prostitution failed. Only a day's journey from Ilorin, Rebah seized a knife from one of the Arabs and committed suicide. Damned coward. Jason looked into the empty cup and could not recall when he finished its contents. It didn't matter. Once more he approached the table with its medicinal liquid and continued with the soul searching scene. Only the most destitute of Ilorin attended the feast prepared from Rebah's livestock. Even they took the food and drink out of sight of the temple area to consume it. Neither Long Ju Ju nor any priest partook of the food or drink which they considered tainted. The musicians and dancers hired by Jason for the so called Exposition of Rebah celebration performed to an empty compound. The day after the scheduled banquet, scavengers from land and air, and not the majority of Ilorin's citizens, feasted. Not even the celebration of the Day of Judgment could maintain a gay atmosphere after witnessing the horror imposed by Jason. The celebratory atmosphere that supposed to have consumed the city dissipated at early evening and Ilorin quieted by one o'clock. Jason paused in his reflection and had to admit life had not improved since that fateful day but seemed to decline. He took another sip of the cassava and came to the conclusion that the more he succeeded in his quest for justice, the more he failed.

Even now, when passing to the right of the temple entrance, citizens of Ilorin tried to avoid gazing in the direction of the still-visible blackened area where Rebah's house once stood. None of Jason's vengeance had the end results he planned. Directly after Jason rendered his judgment and to maintain their busy schedule the Arab caravan departed Ilorin with Rebah in tow. At sunrise the next day when Jason exited his hut to enjoy the final phase of his sentence, he took a small step backward when he noticed Konte already stood in front of the temple to helplessly observe the final implementation of Jason's sadistic ruling. Jason began pacing the hut as he pictured Long Ju Ju supporting himself on his ceremonial spear and wore his official robes and facial markings of deep mourning. An army of acolytes waited with pails of water to douse any ember that might threaten the already- dampened neighboring structures. Jason allowed the previous night for the three women to arrange for their journey to Dahomey. Though shocked at first when they heard of their part in Jason's retribution, they reluctantly resigned themselves to their fate as they became aware they had no one to defend them, especially after Jason's rejection of Konte's pleas for mercy. If Long Ju Ju could not dissuade Jason to relent or alter the unfair decision, then certainly no one else could. The women realized they had become blameless casualties of a spiteful individual who at the moment could not distinguish between justice, which he deserved, and unbridled retribution which no human warranted. Their new master made it clear to Rebah's family they could carry into exile only their personal articles and nothing belonging to the disgraced man. Konte spent time with the distraught family while they packed the meager belongings allowed to them. Long Ju Ju left the women's company well after midnight and gave instructions to his acolyte to wake him at first sign of dawn. Sympathy for the anxious women played no part in Jason's decision to allow Rebah's wife and daughters to remain the extra night. Jason's hatred required destruction of everything belonging to the traitor, Rebah. A search of the women's personal belongings before they became severed from their old life insured that not a single trace of Rebah would still exist either in Dahomey or Ilorin. Jason's blood boiled when he thought about the immediate departure of the caravan containing Rebah when Rebah's unwanted act robbed Jason of full retaliation against his adversary. Only a day's journey from Ilorin, Rebah seized a knife from one of the Arabs and committed suicide. Damned coward. He wanted to gloat at watching the offender and the bastard's family as they saw their lives disintegrate. Another failure for Jason. His anger increased at that memory. With an additional gulp of the cassava he continued reviewing that day.

Inside the crude deserted hut the mercenaries assigned to perform the immolation stacked Rebah's possessions into chaotic small piles for easy burning. A large crowd gathered around Rebah's family to offer sympathy as the inferno consumed Rebah's hopes and memories. The outcast's survivors seemed oblivious to the crowd surrounding them but the three women hugged each other seeking succor from the horror taking place in front of them. Within a half an hour the flaming structure finally collapsed into a heap of burning rubble. Five mercenaries hired by Jason raked the hot coals to insure that the structure's contents received equal annihilation as the hut. Jason firmly declared that no physical trace of Rebah must survive but he overlooked the survival of the mental impact of his heinous deed. Jason smirked as Ali constrained the women's hands and led them away. When Jason recalled that incident, his hands shook, and he emitted a small groan. No amount of cassava could eliminate that sight. With pity in their eyes the once happy family looked a final time at Jason before they disappeared from view. Nothing of Rebah showed in those eyes, only innocence. Jason groaned again and took a large gulp from the cup. He could still envision the women's eyes boring down on him. Even now that piteous stare which reoccurred time and again in his dreams caused Jason to shiver. The irate priest standing before the holocaust would have to eventually endure similar torture for his ruthless act as did the victims of his volatile rage. They had no choice in their fate but accepted it. All three women affirmed that Jason would have a very dark future created by himself as a result of his own virulent actions. Jason shook his head in an attempt to dispel those inhuman searing stares haunting him whether asleep or awake. How dare the victims of his reprisal feel pity for anyone, let alone him? He felt nothing, or at least thought he didn't. The women also denied Jason the gratification of a hysterical display. Masai culture would not allow it. They accompanied Ali as if invited to repast at his house instead of a life of prostitution. Hot raked embers smoldered in the late afternoon sun when Jason turned to enter his house. A waving, young priest made him stop.

"Long Ju Ju wishes to speak with you," the messenger informed the gloating priest.

Jason walked to the temple entrance and confronted his pensive mentor. When Konte finally spoke to Jason, Long Ju

Ju's focus on the twinkling embers and the light gray ascending smoke never faltered. "The sentence is not yet concluded," the mild-mannered priest murmured in a mournful tone. Long Ju Ju stared straight ahead at the devastation. "There is still hot ash that must be cooled before the salt is sown. Stand beside me and keep vigil to ensure your decree is enforced to the letter." The old man still never removed his eyes from the pyre.

For the remainder of the night and the early part of the next day, Long Ju Ju remained silent while resting on his spear and would not respond to any conversation with Jason as the mercenaries continued their raking. Offered food and drink, Konte waved sustenance away with the back of his hand. Some citizens of Ilorin passed back and forth in front of the temple unable to gain entrance due to the two figures blocking it. Konte's eyes never wavered from the cooling ashes during the entire night and early morning nor did he acknowledge the facial expressions of understanding and empathy from all who passed. Those who came to view the carnage realized that even a god's ruling may become corrupted by a cold-hearted man. As for Jason, he ignored the scowls of contempt from the same individuals. He had done a righteous thing. An hour-and-a-half before the noontime meal, workers arrived and sowed salt on the now cooled ash. Only after the completion of the macabre assignment of sowing the salt did Konte acknowledge Jason.

"Your act of vengeance is now complete," Long Ju Ju said in a cracked voice. He finally looked at Jason with pity. "Do not even attempt to include benevolent Ifa in this affair. Any of Rebah's actions could not have been worse than yours. These facial markings of grief are more for you than Rebah," Konte's tone altered to great bitterness. "In their greatest wrath, the gods' worst cruelty could never rival yours. Now go. Feed upon your hate and malice. You will find it an empty meal." Konte stared at the wrathful priest a moment longer, slowly shook his head, and commented to no one in particular, "Where did I fail?" He then turned and entered the temple leaving a troubled Jason standing alone in wake of his departure.

Jason sprang from his sleeping mat. He would have to distance himself from Ilorin soon or he would become mad. Jason stuck his head outside his hut. The boy prepared himself for a tirade of verbal abuse from the fiery ecclesiastic. "When is the next procession to collect tribute leaving?" Jason asked, abruptly.

"In two days, my lord," came a stunned, timorous reply.

"Make provisions for me to join the procession. It's time the people see even those in authority care for them. Pack all my ceremonial robes. I want this to be an unforgettable journey for the worshipers of Ifa. We shall show our people we in Ilorin share our devotion with them." Jason didn't wait for a response but replaced the matted curtain and retrieved the cup of cassava he had left on the table. He ignored the rapidly retreating feet as the acolyte ran to accomplish the high priest's command.

After the noon ceremonies inside the temple, Jason informed Konte of his decision to make a pilgrimage to small villages to Quilimane. The old man just nodded. Jason turned to leave the temple when a soft voice whispered, "If, along the way, you find a lost, frightened little boy, bring him back to me, but you…" Konte's voice resembled the softest breeze, "you will find only yourself waiting for you wherever your destination, and you will like your arrival there less than your life here in Ilorin. You have my permission to remain away as long as you like. May Ifa bless your journey?" Jason, who had paused with his back to Long Ju Ju, rapidly departed the temple without looking back.

CHAPTER VII

CAPTIVE

By slowly hacking through the dense leafage, the religious procession fashioned a verdant highway within the thick, green African foliage. Only a mile or two of hard work per day provided access between one small secluded village and another. Each party traversing the overgrown pathways between hamlets must cut new paths over the old due to the rapid growth caused by the humid climate. Heavy rains eradicated the byways as if they never existed. On the positive side, frequent heavy downpours prevented hungry insects from eating alive people making their way through the jungle. Four months elapsed since Jason departed from Ilorin on his self-proclaimed mission of mercy. Only Stout Heart, Jason's steed, and other animals in the caravan, seemed to enjoy the slow pace. The abundance of available greenery allowed the stallion to add extra body weight. The surroundings did not provide uniform bounty to the rest of the entourage. When the rain ceased, the myriad of insects feasted well. Some days the procession advanced only a quarter of a mile due to the combined density of the growth and odious weather. As it groped its way through the ocean of vegetation, the rhythm of the village drums spread word of the cavalcade's presence. Large and small communities along the way provided guides and cutters in expectation of hosting Ifa's high priest. Without them, the trek would have taken even longer. Any delay pleased Jason who wanted his arrival at Quilimane postponed as long as possible but could offer no excuse for rejection of the offered help. He reposed only three to four days in some of the larger villages. With the additional mouths to feed, a longer stay could seriously deplete the village food supply. If needed, Ifa's representative dispensed justice tempered with mercy to petitioners. However, Jason tried desperately to avoid that service because it constantly reminded him of the benefice denied to Rebah. With each decision, Jason could hear Rebah's voice in his mind, crying for mercy. Jason avoided sleep as much as possible. Sleep made Rebah's voice louder.

Those traveling in his company explained Jason's nightmares as visitations from the gods. Despite his poor nocturnal habits, the troubled priest concentrated repressing his temper. That act alone took superhuman strength of will. The villages seemed delighted with Ifa's second highest priest. True to his word, even the poorest of villages received the best rituals Jason had to offer. He filled each village with the peace and contentment before departing, but could not provide the same for himself.

Eventually the ensemble left the jungle behind and penetrated the Serengeti. Dotted by herds of prey and predators, the grassy plains extended for miles. In two or three weeks, the little caravan would reach Quilimane which housed a large temple dedicated to Ifa. At this eastern city resting on the banks of the Indian Ocean, the group would roundhouse back to Ilorin. Jason anticipated the best luxury the city had to offer, a hot bath. Perhaps, it would assuage some of his restlessness.

While Jason sat proudly on his impressive white Arabian stallion reviewing the success of the pilgrimage, a mercenary, one of twenty delegated to safeguard the assembly, ran toward Jason. "There is a small village ahead made of mud and dung instead of bamboo and thatch," the soldier informed his leader.

Weeks of labor to control his temper dissipated in an instant as unbridled rage boiled inside Jason. He recalled similar descriptions of Masai villages made by his former foreman at Whispering Willows. "God-damned Masai," thought Jason. He shifted uncomfortably in his saddle attempting to conceal his inner emotions from those in the procession awaiting his decision. "Let us enter and see if they show Ifa proper respect and offer them the rite of good fortune," he replied calmly as every muscle in his body tightened. Jason had encountered small groups of Masai in Ilorin. Never since his return had such a large group presented the opportunity to exact wholesale vengeance on the abominable sect. For the first time, Ifa blessed his quest for the destruction of this foul race by placing so many within his grasp. He would not fail his god. The mercenary saluted the mounted priest who hooded his eyes to avoid discernment of his true intent. He acknowledged the ceremonial gesture with a slight nod of his head. The guard headed toward the front of the procession to inform the lead priest to progress toward the nearby village.

Jason conjectured perhaps this village gave birth to Rebah and the four other Masai who aided his sale into slavery in America. If not, it resembled the hamlet that once quartered those similar villains. For now, this fortuitous windfall would satisfy Jason's continuing vendetta on the Masai nation. As the cortege neared the community, Jason saw only women, children, and old men. He studied the position of the sun. Of course. Early afternoon meant most of the men shepherded their herds of cattle or hunted game for the evening meal. In the distance, Jason could see a young boy running to inform the men of the new arrivals. Jason decided to delay any retaliatory retribution until every detestable, tribal member presented himself. Under the guise of offense to Ifa, none would escape his wrath.

"Ah. The same as Rebah," a little voice spoke in the back of his mind. Jason reeled in his saddle. "There is no similarity. I want no profit of money or power, just justice," he replied mentally to the little voice. No response came.

Jason rode into the middle of the village and disdainfully glanced at the humble homes. The crafting the women held in their hands gave way to smiles and greetings. A patriarchal man approached the obvious leader on a white horse and bowed. Jason ignored the chief's courteous reception and glowered at the respectful elder. "Where is the temple of Ifa?"

The old man crossed his wrists over his chest and again bowed to the saddled priest. "We are too small to have one, my lord. Ifa's statue is kept in my modest abode and travels with me when we go south," the elder replied.

"Show me," Jason growled as if he doubted the chieftain's word. Due to the harsh tone, all eyes of the villagers lost their luster of greeting and hardened in bewilderment. An eerie feeling suddenly permeated the village. Why didn't the priest show the same proper respect to their tribal chief as their patriarch had done to him? The white stallion sensed negative feelings from his rider and became skittish as Jason alit. Without taking his hooded stare from the village headman, Jason extended his arm with the horse's reins to a nearby priest and said, "Stout Heart is hungry. Give him feed, water, and a good rub down." The visiting entourage had experienced many strange moods in the high priest on entering any village, but on entering this one, Jason's mood greatly disturbed them. Jason released the reins without looking back and, with a jerk of his head, ordered the village leader to proceed to his hut. The old man turned and headed for a large structure at the end of the small village. As one of the priests led Jason's horse outside the compound, the rest of the train coalesced into an aisle from the village entrance to the chief's hut. Jason glanced beyond the village and perceived shepherds and hunters hastening to greet the newcomers. Jason affected to ignore them and followed the elder.

"Well? Where is Ifa's statue?" Jason demanded angrily quickly glancing around the domicile.

The headman looked at the priest with a slack jaw. What had he done to make the priest so angry? "Here, my lord, in the chest with my most precious belongings." The elder replied pointing to an old intricately carved chest at the back of the hut next to his sleeping mat. "The statue of Ifa is the most cherished among all I own," he added with great humility.

"And how can people worship Ifa with the statue hidden in the dark? Ifa is a god of light," Jason said, trying to taper his temper.

Afraid he had committed an act of irreverence; the elder replied defensively, "We take the statue out every dawn and sunset to pray for divine help and guidance."

"I see no place of worship," Jason snapped.

"There is a niche to the right of my door where the statue is placed every morning and evening for worship. If any tribal member wishes private prayer, I remove it from the box and allow that person to use my hut in solitude," the bewildered man retorted. "Here we hold Ifa in great esteem," he added lamely.

Jason grimaced and walked outside to examine the niche and to survey the milling crowd. "Is this your entire village?" he asked, scanning the scene with the sweep of his hand.

The elder glanced at the assembly gathered behind the aisle of mercenaries and priests and nodded. "Missing are some of the young ones who have not yet had the rite of manhood. They are guarding the herds, but, yes, these are all of my people," he said proudly.

None of the men held weapons. The hunters had discarded their arms. Weapons would appear offense to the priest of Ifa, but the shepherds still carried their staffs. Opportunity presented itself for Jason. Like a cat on an unsuspecting mouse, the crafty priest pounced. Jason rapidly advanced on the captain of the mercenaries and shouted, "Surround them. If any resist, kill them, women and children, too, if necessary."

A tidal waved of shock thundered throughout the village as the mercenaries speedily formed a circle around the stunned villagers, thus preventing the men access to weaponries. Twenty-five unarmed men stood helpless against the armed mercenaries. The soldiers herded the entire village into one of the cattle pens and immediately posted guards.

Feeling his victory incomplete, Jason contemptuously shouted, "Have three of your men round up the brats still herding. Leave one man to guard the herds in case the neighboring vermin opt for a raid."

"My lord, what crime have we committed?" asked the shocked elder from behind the cattle rail.

"As high priest of Ifa, I shall not allow you to desecrate his statue by placing it in camel shit," Jason yelled at the stunned elder, all the while waving a finger at the niche. Again, Jason turned to the captain of the mercenaries. "As we leave, I want this village burnt to the ground. Bind this filth," he hissed as he swung his extended arm from pointing at the niche to the confused people assembled in the corral, "Your soldiers may sell them as slaves in Quilimane and keep the proceeds. Ifa would not want any money from camel shit lovers." Jason sneered at the emotionally overcome elder. Cries and screams chorused to Ifa from the women and children, while the men hurled curses at the unjust priest. Only one individual in the crowd remained silent.

After hearing the sentence of Ifa's priest, due to the hopelessness of their situation and in desperation to reach loved ones, villagers pushed and shoved each other like cattle in a stampede. In the melee, Jason sensed eyes staring at him. He surveyed the hubbub of helpless enemies. There! A third of the way back, left of the corral entrance, stood a young woman. She seemed dislocated to the panic surrounding her. Perpetual jostling didn't disturb her. She merely righted herself and continued to stare at Jason. She had skin the color of the finest chocolate and just as creamy. Her sarong disclosed a body that could provoke envy in other tribal women and arouse crazed sexual fantasies in the men. High cheekbones accented the fullness and sensuality of her lips, but her face remained unreadable. No shock. Just---blank. The most striking feature, her eyes, stared through Jason. The stunned priest tried desperately to discern the emotion behind the stare. No hate. No anger. No surprise. Not even a question. Nothing. Just a microscopic examination of every inch of his being. If others in the pen had not jostled her, Jason would have named her a demon not of this world. The brown orbs held an undefined life behind them, a knowing. Knowing what? Jason shivered. She bypassed Ifa's priest's physical presence. For the first time in his memory, Jason experienced fear. Desperately, he endeavored to break eye contact and tried to re-hood his eyes. Too late. She stared at something he could not comprehend. "She must be a witch. First Rebah's curse, then nightmares, and now this girl," he thought. Frantically he gesticulated to one of the mercenaries. "That girl, there," he pointed to the sculpted woman. "Bring her to the headman's hut. I wish to question her."

The mercenary quickly assessed the beauty of the female captive, flashed a smile, and fashioned his own interpretation for the reason of Jason's mandate. The soldier ran to the guard at the corral gate. He pointed to Jason and then to the prisoner.

The guard grinned, nodded, opened the gate, and bulldozed the frightened people aside until he reached the designated girl. Only when the soldier gripped her arm did she break eye contact with Jason. Offering no resistance, she looked down at the grasping hand then into the eyes of the mercenary whispered something to him. The soldier maintained his grip but loosened it as he gave the girl a look of surprise. Jason's legs shook as the mercenary spoke something to the strange hostage. She never verbally acknowledged whatever order he gave, but both captor and captive immediately headed for the gate. Part of the Masai culture included surrendering to the dominant male without complaint. On leaving the prisoners' compound, the mercenary maintained his hold on her arm but walked a step behind giving the appearance of dependence on his prisoner for guidance. Jason ordered the guard to keep her under surveillance until he sent for her.

Oblivious to the pleas and threats of the other captives, Jason walked through the empty village toward the hut of the chief. He paused momentarily and addressed one of his priests. "See if you can find any cassava in this wretched hellhole. Bring it to me in the leader's hut, and then have the woman brought to me." The priest bowed and obeyed. Jason pushed the matted curtain of the hut aside and entered. Now out of sight of everyone, he noticed his hands trembling. "Get yourself under control. They will be bringing the woman here any minute," he thought as he rubbed his hand across his forehead and down the side of his cheek. He walked to the back of the hut, all the while taking slow, deep breaths.

The sunlight runwayed across the dirt floor when the mercenary pulled open the mat door. The shadow of the girl pointed directly at Jason. Jason turned and studied the figure outlined in the doorway. Specific features of this gorgeous creature became blurred as the light silhouetting her body.

"My lord, here is the cassava," came the voice of the priest standing behind the mercenary. It forced the captivated priest to refocus his attention.

"Bring it in," Jason commanded. "Stand over there," he ordered the girl as he pointed to the right side of the entrance. "You're dismissed. Wait outside," he barked to his subordinates. The soldier smiled, nodded, and allowed the mat door to fall in place behind him as he left. The serving priest placed two cups and a jar on a small table in the rear of the hut and retreated after the soldier.

Jason's eyes adjusted to the semi-darkness. The woman had not spoken or moved. He stared at her face with his hooded eyes. That never-failing intimidation became lost on the unwilling guest. Before she could notice his trembling hands, Jason turned his attention to the cassava. With more outward calmness than he felt, Jason slowly filled both cups. He turned to offer her one and dropped both.

On the floor beside where she stood lay her sarong, and the most radiant woman he had ever seen stood naked before him. Her too-perfect breasts accented the curve of her waist that tapered into legs only the gods could have created. She stood proudly erect before the astonished man with her arms at her side. Jason's assurance dispersed when he looked into her unrevealing eyes. The beautiful face appeared fashioned by Africa's greatest artist displayed eyes that accented only emptiness. Jason could not salvage his composure. "What kind of woman are you?" he croaked, "Are you a witch that captures men's souls?"

The empty eyes locked on his. "I am what you want me to be," she replied. Her voice rang true like cymbals of Ifa's holiest rite, but, like the eyes, had no emotion. "Would you please complete your rape so that I may return to my people?" she added as an afterthought.

"Don't be so damned arrogant! With a snap of my fingers I could have you beaten or even killed," Jason snarled.

"I have never doubted that, my lord," the disinterested reply from the unconcerned woman resounded in the hut.

Jason assumed he had unnerved her. "Besides, I can have you anytime I desire," he said dismissively believing he had made her submissive.

"No my lord, you can have my body, but only I am capable of giving you myself," she retorted in the same flat voice that made Jason wonder who controlled this meeting.

Jason felt the mental slap. He had erred. He didn't have the advantage of this interview. She did. He rapidly advanced and confronted her. "Who are you? Are you a witch?" he repeated.

"My name is Sarah, and, no, I am no witch," she replied with unemotional demeanor.

"Sarah is not a Masai name." Jason countered. Sarah remained silent.

He crossed his arms, hoping it would give him a more authoritative look. "Where did you obtain a European name?"

Sarah's composure did not waver. "It was given to me by a missionary after my first tribe had been raided by Arabs and sold into slavery. I was left behind with the elderly and other children the slavers didn't want. Without younger men and women to take care of us, we sought other tribes that would adopt us. I joined this tribe that worships Ifa. This tribe had a Christian missionary and he taught me to read and write English as well as Swahili. Unlike most of my people who affirmed that school and knowledge outside of tribal lore is a waste of time. He believed that girls could be as intelligent as boys and taught some of us how to read and write. Since I didn't have an official family, it was easy for me to attend his class. He died three years ago. Some of us truly miss him even if we didn't accept his god. Our people still believe in the beauty of Ifa---at least until now."

"Why did he name you 'Sarah'?'" Jason feeling less tense and wanted to learn more of this luscious creature.

"He said I was the first girl he had made literate, and, like my namesake, I could do great things."

"Cover yourself," Jason said quietly as he picked up her sarong and handed it to her. He then picked the two cups from the ground and placed them back on the table. Believing he had regained control of the situation Jason said, "I shall have you at some future date."

Sarah replaced her sarong and again stood rigid in the same place. "You are stronger than I. My body is always here for your raping."

In fear of those piercing eyes, Jason again raced across the hut, grabbed Sarah by the arms, and shook her.

"Woman, don't you feel anything?" he shouted, more as a question to himself than as a rebuke to her. Sarah did not react to his threat but continued to stare at him with searching eyes. Jason could have shaken a child's doll and received the same results.

"Guard! Guard!" Jason shouted in such a high-pitched voice that he scarcely believed his ears. The mat door jerked aside so violently it almost ripped from its frame. A mercenary appeared in the doorway with drawn pistol to behold a heavily-breathing man restraining the arms of an extremely docile woman.

"Take this--this thing back to the corral," Jason spat the words through his clenched teeth. He released Sarah with a shove and walked to the back of the hut to refill one of the cups with the soul-numbing drink.

Sarah walked steadily toward the soldier and paused at the doorway. She turned and faced Jason's back. "We all have experienced pain, my lord. Like Mumia of the old olagan's tale, we also have choices. You don't have to build your life around that pain. I chose to throw mine away in a clod of dirt many years ago and, unlike you, I don't feed my pain with anger and hate." Sarah turned and exited the hut followed by the soldier. The high priest turned from the table and threw the cup at the door. "Get out!" he shouted, but she had already gone.

That night Jason drank himself into a stupor in hopes of some semblance of sleep. Hunter constantly had referred to Mumia. Had the gods introduced this girl into his life as another haunting? The cassava did not act like an anesthetic, and the usual demons arrived into Jason's dreams instead. He dreamed of Rebah, Konte, and Sarah with claw marks on their faces pointing their fingers at him standing in front of a burning building. Out of the building came Hunter inviting him to enter. "Follow him," whispered Konte. "The boy you seek is inside. Kill the panther."

Jason awakened in a sitting position with one of the acolyte's hands on his shoulders vigorously shaking him. "My lord, you were having another nightmare," the boy said.

Jason's clothes and covers were saturated with sweat. He merely nodded and said he would feel better now. He rose from his sleeping mat, dismissed the boy, and went in search of dry clothes. He dared not return to the sleeping mat to sleep for fear of a reoccurrence of another nightmare. He picked up the almost empty pitcher of cassava but placed it back on the table without filling his cup. "Dear Ifa, I cannot continue like this," he murmured. Jason sank down on his sleeping mat and rested his chin on his chest. He stared at the bare ground between his legs for the remainder of the night.

CHAPTER VIII

BALM

Sunrise brought no remission to his spiritual turmoil, only an increase in his unbridled animosity toward everything and everyone. Somehow that witch had captured Rebah's spirit and used it to torture Jason's very essence. On the third day, Jason resolved to once more fracture Rebah's and now the woman's mastery over him. "Guard!" he yelled so loud he almost frightened himself. Taking account of the explosive nature of his leader's voice, the foremost of the mercenaries reluctantly peered around the doorway and prepared to dodge some object the high priest might launch. Instead, the wild-eyed priest walked to within six inches of the summoned man and carefully enunciated each word in his command: "Bring me the witch and wait outside." Jason gave the second part of his order to the running man's back.

Within minutes, Sarah, stoic as ever, entered the hut and locked eyes with Jason. After the guard departed, Jason took a long draught of cassava, placed the empty cup on the table, and approached the formidable woman. When he back-handed her right cheek, Sarah's head jerked to the side, but she did not break eye contact with him, nor did she speak or evidence any reaction whatsoever. Jason ripped the sarong from her body, seized her right arm, and threw her onto his sleeping mat. She remained in the same position in which she fell. Quickly the masterful man disrobed and pounced on her. He secured her head and forced his tongue into her mouth. Sarah lay with both hands at her side but would not respond to his passionate tonguing. He spread her legs, which, to him, felt like moving bales of cotton, and penetrated her. His muscular body quickly pulsated up and down. Beneath him came neither sound nor any movement, except that of normal respiration. Again and again he sexually pounded his victim, but her body did not respond, nor did she move. The rapist could feel no sexual gratification in his deed. Jason then made a fatal error. He looked into her eyes. Nothing! Neither positive nor negative emotions became evident. Perhaps he had detected just a little hint of pity. Jason's penis became flaccid without reaching a climax. He stifled a shout as he rolled off of her. Anger swelled within him. Lying beside her, Jason panted and pounded his fists into the mat and began yelling, liberating a maelstrom of years of pent up emotions.

"My lord, do you need help?" A voice called from the other side of the matted door.

"No," Jason screamed, "Go away until I call you."

Oblivious to the scorching streams cascading down his cheeks, Jason squeezed his eyes shut as his breathing became succinct and more strained. He opened his eyes to inspect the haunch of meat that lay beside him. For the first time in his entire life, Jason despised himself. He pressed the palms of his hands into his eye sockets. A low moan escaped from his soul. How different it sounded from those produced by his nightmares. It lacked the howl of anger, panic, or hate. Where did this cry originate?

Through his blurred sight as he lowered his hands, the flank of flesh beside him coalesced into a gorgeous woman. Jason's lower lip quivered as he stared at -- not Rebah's ghost or a witch -- but a kind, fully human, beautiful woman. This time, instead of vacuity, Jason beheld affection and an obligation by both parties to bond, not just bodies, but in spirit. Before he grasped the portent of the moment, Ifa's lonely priest's labored breathing became gulps. Sarah gathered the tortured man in her soft, tender arms and pressed his head against her soothing breasts. The dam burst. Even in his worst abuse at the missionary school, outcast by those around him, and ill-treatment by Rebah, never had Jason cried. Now, in these secure arms he could not stop. His tear ducts drained, and still he sobbed from deep within himself. Sarah held him tightly against her and stroked his head without comment. Jason heard the rhythm of her breathing through her breast which felt softer than cotton boles. As she fondled his head her soothing heartbeat lulled him to sleep. He coiled into a living bastion of remorse and wonderment as exhaustion and an unexplained feeling he had never felt before Sarah entered into his life helping him to slip into a dreamless slumber. He felt secure locked in those defensive arms which would shield him from all physical harm and mental agony.

Jason awoke with a start, and his left hand immediately shot out to feel the empty space beside him. The gods wanted to torture him more; this time with a dream of promise. His heart sunk until he heard a soft voice of reassurance dispel all doubts about the truth of the current beatific experience that overwhelmed him. "I'm over here," it said. Jason turned his head toward the door and saw Sarah sitting by it stringing beads. "I had one of the priests bring you fruit and fresh water," she added, pointing her threaded needle at the back table.

He stood and began to don a clean, white robe. "How long did I sleep?" Jason asked.

Sarah began gathering the beads and wire. "All morning and most of the afternoon. Now that you're awake, I'll go back to the corral," she replied as if she had this conversation with him every day.

"No!" Jason shouted. Panic once more gripped his soul. He didn't want to return to the nightmares. Thanks to Sarah, he had enjoyed the most peaceful sleep he had in over a year. Only one person gave him that and now she wanted to leave him alone again with the succubus of his soul.

Sarah ceased gathering her equipment and stared hard at Jason. "Is that an order, my lord?" she asked in her now-familiar bland voice.

"I could---" Jason stopped mid-sentence. All of his old emotions prior to Sarah's understanding touch welled in his mind. "You are in charge here, not her. She just wants to leave you alone to be tortured again. Stop her from leaving," a voice whispered in his head. Sarah had mentioned Mumia. Odd. Two of the people who tried to help him knew the same tale and referred to it. Jason failed himself in accepting assistance in the first instance. This time, he determined not to lose the comfort this heavenly creature had to offer, even if it meant allowing her to return to the corral. "Of course not! Go or stay as you wish," he said reluctantly in a tone that contained all of the loss he would experience with Sarah's departure.

He walked to the table and looked at the food and the jar of cassava. He raised his eyes and stared blankly at the wall in front of him. He heard the soft breathing of Sarah directly behind him. Again he stared down at the contents on the table. Before him lay one of Mumia's choices. Jason determined at that moment not to become like Master Andrew. Avoiding the cassava, he picked up a date and began to eat.

Gently Sarah placed her hand on the nape of the high priest's neck and lovingly began to rub it. "Jason I have to go back. My people are in pain the same as we were."

Jason's heart skipped a beat as he absorbed the word, "we." Both of them had sustained inequities. Sarah had come to terms with her pain. Even though he now endeavored to understand his torture, Jason could not make that admission just yet. He knew, not felt, but unreservedly knew, that the lovely creature standing behind him represented all the good that existed behind the blackness of his personal destructive panther that controlled his daily living. Even now the spiritual cat attempted to envelop him by encouraging him to force his will on Sarah. "Command her to stay," it said. He felt her gentle hand slide to his shoulder. In confusion, Jason lowered his left hand to the table for support lest his legs give way to the emotions warring inside him. Jason had prayed many times. But for the first time the befuddled priest prayed with his entire being. "Holy Ifa, please show me the path past this beast so that I may be worthy of all that this woman has given me and has yet to offer. Allow me to discover the lost boy Konte trusted and bring that lad back to him. If I could but find that boy again perhaps Konte will return the closeness and confidence I once knew. It is not too late for me, or Sarah would not be here to help bind my wounds. You have proven your love and mercy an infinite amount of times, and now you have brought Sarah into my life. You have no greater gift or help to give and I thank you for it." Jason felt a gentle shake.

"Jason! Look at me," Sarah said in a melodious voice, as she turned him to face her. "From the moment I saw you from the corral, in that glimpse, the gods revealed to me what a magnificent man you really are. I knew in that instant you are my soul's mate for life. I saw the black thing which had taken control of this battered, lost soul, and I refused then, as I do now, to give it the slightest satisfaction or victory. Today I have fought and won a great battle over it, but the war is not over. No matter how many times I win or lose, it will always be there. I can help you and show you other ways of weakening it, but only you can discover a replacement for the beast. I have now willingly bound my life to yours. When that darkness rips at your soul, it also rips at mine. It will take a long time, but get rid of it, my love, and let me take its place," she said, stroking his cheek.

Jason's eyes welled with tears again. "Everything that has been important to me has always been denied. My mother didn't want me and left me at a Christian orphanage. I learned to hate the other throw aways like me that lived there, and to tolerate the beatings and punishments until I escaped. Konte found me and I experienced the first kindness from another person without that person wanting something in return. He became like a father to me and I betrayed all he taught me. In the past Long Ju Ju offered some guidance, but I still felt lost. Then Rebah sold me into slavery. After Konte a man called Hunter tried to help me but I spurned his help because he belonged to the same tribe as Rebah, the Masai. Only more bitterness increased in my daily life by having to work with Hunter. He tried to make me forget tribes, vengeance and hatred and start a new life in a new land. I hated him even more because I believed he only wanted to block my return to Africa for his own benefit. He didn't understand my need for retribution on all Masai, starting with him and then with Rebah. I guess that's why he gave me the nickname of panther. The worst of all the things I did in Alabama was use a poor innocent girl who loved him dearly to bring about his downfall before I returned to Africa. I tried unsuccessfully to make everything the way it was before Rebah sold me into slavery. So far I have achieved all of the revenge I had planned. Yet the more I succeed in implementing my strategy the less satisfaction I get. Konte told me that I was feasting on an empty meal. I have eaten it for so long I know of no other nourishment. Now I have discovered someone I truly care for but you belong to Hunter and Rebah's accursed race. How can I come to terms with that? Must I suffer loss and mockery for the rest of my life?" he said bitterly.

"No, Jason! No," replied Sarah as she gave him a gentle shake. "That is the---What did you call it---the panther talking? You use the word, hate, before you even get to know a person, forcing a person who has never harmed you to wear an undeserved label of enemy, and they could have possibly have become a friend. What if Konte had been a Masai? Would you automatically hate him too?" Sarah put her arms around him and rested her head on his back. "The beast has been in control of you for so long that it doesn't want you to realize your real potential. Even now it is possible that you can accept the beautiful things life has to offer; instead it wants you to exist totally in hate and anger until it eventually destroys you. I can help. So can others, if you let them. Being a Masai, a European, or any other race isn't important. It is the person that's important. Look around you for those who can direct you away from the path of the destructive beast and help you live a more satisfying life without the panther gnawing at your soul. You may find these helpers in the oddest places. But, it's your beast. Only you can deal with it. Today, you have struck it a crippling blow, and it will do all it can to regain control. Look into your heart and see me there. The anger and hate of the beast doesn't want me there. In the future, it will force you to make choices, and its choice will be quick and easy. My help will take longer, as I want you to stop and think, then choose. I tell you the beast doesn't have to win. It's not going away overnight, but now you know what Long Ju Ju and this man called Hunter knew all along. It's there, and now you are aware there is another type of life within you yet to be discovered. Your nightmares are the beast destroying the person you truly are. Give the real you a chance to breathe--to live." She took his head in her hands.

"This is who you really are, but there is something in your life that is missing and has been for a long time. That thing is what the beast fears. Find that missing piece of your life, and the beast will die." She held him and left the hut, leaving Jason astounded.

Far into the night, the memory of the day enveloped Jason, and for the first time he enjoyed his sleeplessness. Sarah! Sarah! Sarah! How could one person transform his life with just her nearness and in such a brief time span? He chuckled about believing her a witch. Perhaps a good witch? He wished she had cast her spell on him years ago. Jason rolled over for the hundredth time and thought of the wonderful, beautiful witch who loved him.

Love! What a strange word for Jason's mind to assimilate. Hate. Revenge. Anger. These passwords constituted his daily living. His muscles began to tense. He had based his life on everything those pessimistic words entailed and suffered the agonizing results far too long. People had not isolated him; he had pushed them away. He unnecessarily hurt many along the way, but none so much as himself. The panther fumed within him, but this wonderful thing called Sarah had encapsulated the empty mental food that fed the beast and felt the bounty offered by Sarah. No matter how thin the shell surrounding his negativity, with Sarah's help, the shell, would harden and eventually destroy the antagonistic reactions of his soul. He desperately needed to not place the heavy burden of his struggle on Sarah alone. He wanted to open his eyes wide to the wonderful world around him, a world made magnificent by Sarah. Her face permeated the giddy man's thoughts. Something tickled his belly from the inside making him want to leap from the mat shouting and laughing. The pain still existed. The beast would not so easily let that go, but now someone wanted, really wanted, to share the burden and make it tolerable. That would help eradicate it.

In his entire life, Jason never experienced this delightful feeling. Damn! Why did he keep thinking "brilliant feeling?" Had Jason encountered something called happiness? Konte's words rang true. The beast served an empty feast and never made him feel like this. The feast Sarah had given filled him to bursting, and still he hungered for more. Jason added this sleepless night to many others, but this one he welcomed.

Most of the priests and mercenaries went about their early morning assignments giving only side-glances to the headman's hut. Since the last assignation with that woman, only his personal attendants attended the high priest, but they reported a calm demeanor had seized him, and the cassava remained in the pitcher. All accompanying Jason on his journey admitted their perplexity at the momentous alteration in their leader. His barometric personality concerned the entire company. No one knew what to expect next. All thought him bizarre before Sarah entered his life. Now, his close attendants conceded she possessed powerful knowledge of witchcraft in order to alter their priest's personality to that of a tolerable human being. Why had Jason not given the order for the village's destruction? Why had he not allowed the procession to proceed toward Quilimane? The mercenaries and priests not part of Jason's personal servants thought perhaps they should consult the shaman concerning the high priest's strange behavior, but that would have to wait. Jason had requisitioned two ceremonial priests to prepare him for some important rite this morning, the first since the company's arrival. Try as they might, not one of priests could think of a major feast that warranted the formal garb and markings Jason had demanded.

The priests exited from the headman's hut and assembled other sacerdotal personages for a grand procession to the corral. At the breaking of the stalemate, the assemblage showed relief and the captives fear. The priests fashioned two lines, chanted the praises of Ifa, and paraded toward the corral. Jason exited from the hut as the last of the priests formed an aisle. He wore a large feathered headdress and matching ankle-length cape. The facial marking could only compare to those of profound mourning. Underneath the ornate paint somberness stressed the importance of the rite. He kept his head lowered all the way to the corral gate. The off-duty mercenaries stood to the side in astonishment. This ceremony proved different from any they had witnessed in the past. Did it bode well or ill to the nervous captives? Memories of Rebah surfaced among mercenaries and priests alike. At last, the soldiers thought they could destroy the village and continue to Quilimane with their captives and do some serious drinking and whoring after their sale. The priests could requisition some other priests at the Quilimane temple to assist them in tending to the ill-humored high priest before joining the mercenaries in their festivities.

The chanting suddenly concluded, and the priests framed the corral, leaving Jason and two mercenaries standing before the closed gate. Jason raised his head and swept his eyes over the incarcerated Masai to allow tension to build. Men and women began to murmur. In the center of the holding area, a frightened child began to cry. Jason saw a woman bend and pick up a little boy. She pressed his head against her left shoulder saying some unheard words of comfort in his ear. The crying desisted, and silence reigned supreme as Jason broke the suspense.

The high priest elevated his hands in an invocation to Ifa to help him choose his words wisely. The droning voice of the man who held the village's fate in his next pronouncement produced the only sound heard. The hostages speculated on the horrifying result once this vengeful priest concluded his prayer.

Jason lowered his arms and placed his crossed hands on his shoulders. "Ifa has punished his most unworthy servant for the distortion of his divine wishes. Since our arrival, he has tormented me with uneasiness and frightening dreams as retribution for my bad judgment. Last night in a dream, holy Ifa appeared to me leading a camel. After the camel had shit, he made a woman and a man appear. 'Take the soil of the earth and strengthen it with the soil of this animal. Build houses with this to protect your family from the wild beasts and to shelter them from the hot sun and torrential rains.' The man did as Ifa bade. He then turned to the woman and said, 'Whenever the camel soils, gather it in a sack to be dried for fire to cook your food and to heat your body at night as well as to build your home. The camel is my gift to you and your people.' He then turned to me and said, 'Hide your face in the dirt before me, arrogant man. I see no shame in these people honoring me with the gift I gave them. Yet you took it upon yourself to speak for me in this matter. I sent no oracle to bid you act as you did. Today, you will go before my people and undo the wrong of your own doing. As penance for your sin, you will give each soldier the equivalent cost of one slave to compensate for their loss resulting from the foolish promise you made to sell my devout followers into slavery, and it will come from your private funds and not from mine at Ilorin. When you return to Iorin, you will fast on grain for one month, and in the second month you will eat only food cooked over camel dung. Now, go right the wrong you have done me. Be thankful your punishment is no worse, and be wiser in the future.' He then disappeared." Jason gently bowed toward the corral. "I cannot go against the wishes of the one I serve, and I beg his forgiveness as well as yours." Jason then lowered his hands to his side and issued a command to the mercenaries. "Open the gates and set them free. I command a big feast be given in Ifa's honor this evening in gratitude to the merciful god's intervention in preventing me from going against his will and causing much harm to those who serve him. Let no priest or soldier injure any of these people or damage any of their goods. The wrath of Ifa will be upon their heads as it fell upon mine if I am disobeyed."

Amid cheers of the just-freed people, Jason solemnly turned and led the procession back to the headman's hut. Everyone looked forward with great expectation of tonight's celebration. Jason had never received such adulation in the performance of any rite in the past. He did his utmost to look penitent and not join in the joyous rioting taking place around him. Jason kept his eyes focused on the ground before him and thought, "Ah Rebah. I did not show these people the mercy that I denied you. I showed it to myself. Divine Ifa, forgive my past behavior and the lie I just spoke, or did you really make me tell the truth? My action now provided quite a different feeling than that of vengeance. No matter! I shall keep my promise, but not in penitence. It shall be performed in great joy and thanks for the wonderful gift you have bestowed on me. Sarah!"

CHAPTER IX

NEWCOMER

After two days of feasting at the Masai village, Jason resolved to proceed on their pilgrimage. He entreated Sarah to accompany him but offered no covenant of marriage or formal status as a concubine. She returned to her hut in silence to contemplate Jason's proposal and the ramifications her decision would have on their lives.

Jason passed the evening without the comfort of Sarah's presence. What did he say, or, in this case, didn't say? At sunrise, the procession packed and prepared to vacate the village. Jason could delay no longer. He trifled with the idea of forcing Sarah to accompany him, as the beast stirred inside him offering that solution to the problem. He had only to call for the guard and have her bound. Though difficult for him, Jason dismissed the idea of using strength to get his way. If nothing else, he learned that force could not produce the solution he desired, but would only exacerbate the problem. The decision must come from Sarah, and not the beast. Still, the temptation lingered. Jason employed all the will power at his command not to summon Sarah and have her brought along as part of his luggage. He worried his sanguine personality proved him irredeemable, and she had abandoned him. At the thought the gods might want chastise him this way, Jason's insides ached. It pointed to the enormity of the repulsiveness of past actions. Regardless, he must accept it. He thought back on Hunter and the tale of Mumia. He must choose. If he were to lose Sarah, that hole in his soul would remain open forever. He frantically endeavored to stay the bitterness creeping over his psyche. Jason glanced around the hut. The priests had removed all of his possessions. He had no reason to remain any longer, and the shuffling of feet and murmur of voices told him the procession had become impatient to leave. Like Hunter's Mumia, he made the choice to leave the decision to stay or go up to Sarah. Jason fought back tears he never had never known before meeting Sarah and exited the headman's hut.

Sarah stood patiently waiting in front of the hut. Her mundane belongings, wrapped in goat skin, rested at her right foot. She gave Jason a broad smile. "I thought you would never come out," she said.

Jason swallowed hard three or four times to thwart his heart from vaulting from his mouth. "I thought that you had decided to remain." His voiced edged with joy.

Sarah shook her head side to side at his doubting. "I have already told you. We are soul-mates. How could I remain? I spent the night saying good-bye to friends." Sarah balanced her goat skin bundle on her head. "Where do you wish me to walk in the procession?"

Jason's knees buckled. His thigh muscles ached from the strain to prevent him from collapsing. He waved to one of the mercenaries and shouted for all to hear, "Give this woman Stout Heart to ride at the end of the procession as befitting the future wife of Ifa's high priest. As a further act of penance to show Ifa I am truly sorry for what I did, I shall walk by her side." Much mumbling came from the crowd, but that sound eventually became a thumping of staffs against the ground and a cheer from the people of the village. Jason got that tickling feeling inside his stomach again.

The soldier ran whooping to fetch the horse. Another removed her bundle to be stowed with the high priest's belongings. Still smiling, Sarah bowed toward Jason as he led her toward his mount. She rearranged her sarong to resemble a pair of breeches. Embarrassingly, Jason felt himself becoming sexually aroused at the sight of her tapered legs. Sarah sensed his discomfiture and broke into a laugh.

As he helped her into the saddle, she whispered, "I hope walking will rechannel some of that energy." Once settled in the saddle, she added, "But save some of it for this evening." Jason's laughter joined hers as the procession began its departure from the jubilant village.

By choice, Jason and Sarah's sojourn to Quilimane turned into self-imposed social isolation, much to the delight of the rest of the assembly. The expeditious transformation in their high priest shocked and pleased the entourage. Though he performed all duties of his executive office in a strict manner, Sarah's presence decreased his volatile behavior and made him more tolerable to those who had daily official business with Ifa's high priest. Jason's temper could still blaze at any moment, but now only serious incidents triggered the outbursts. Although Sarah had a reassuring effect on Ifa's high priest, even she could not bridle all his negative reactions to daily living. In Quilimane, after a particular nasty interview with the high priest, some individuals, whom Jason interpreted as incurable miscreants, sustained mementos of his fury on flayed parts of their bodies. When Jason realized uncontrollable rage had gained control and clouded his judgment, he became, in the private confines of his assigned residence, a sulking penitent. Sarah assumed the role of sounding board until Jason realized the proper course of action he had overlooked. To his credit, Jason's vehemence lessened. After years of blindly trotting down the path of hate and revenge, this new attitude demanded a hard-won character adjustment. However, he did not always experience success in self-control.

Jason lay awake on their sleeping mat in the quarters adjacent to Ifa's Quilimane temple. Was it possible three weeks had passed since their arrival in the city? He listened to the steady rhythm of Sarah's breathing as she nestled on her husband's shoulder with his right hand caressing her short-cropped black hair.

He thought back on their arrival at Quilimane. Jason redeemed his promise to make Sarah his wife. Though both desired a quiet, private ceremony, it proved impossible due to Jason's status. The celebration for Ifa's high priest's wedding persevered for two weeks, but after three days the bride and groom insisted on proxies to preside at the various goodwill dinners offered by well-wishers throughout the city. The newlyweds believed they would grow old and gray before the feasts terminated and allowed them any privacy.

Another five months had passed, during which time Jason dispensed justice and performed the ceremonies his high station required. At times, Jason enforced great discipline on himself not to leap and shout for joy in the middle of some solemn occasion when his mind wandered from the current business and to the sweet face of his loving wife.

Exceptionally difficult judicial decisions he deliberated with Sarah in private confines of their house. She did not comment or offer advice but indulged him by allowing the venting of various facets of the case and inquired about the outcome if he opted for certain decisions. Jason soon mastered reading her face. If it remained placid, the thought process he pursued proved judicious. If her eyes became hard and her brow slightly wrinkled, Jason clued himself to consider alternate solutions to the problem.

Not all the time did Jason's means of assessment prove infallible? When his solution rendered over-harsh results concerning the type of case involved and he rebuffed other avenues of deliberation, Sarah would invent an important task, give him a kiss and a hug, and leave him. After rendering the verdict to some case in which Jason assumed she had disagreed, she would reappear as if nothing had happened. Her oppositions with his public decisions never affected her demeanor in their private life. Toward the end of the third month both reached a pivotal point of view with Sarah's overwhelming lack of participation in his decisions.

Jason sentenced a man to thirty lashes at the public pillory for stealing another's cow. The defendant claimed he purloined the creature for the milk and had every intention of returning the animal to the owner. The defendant claimed his wife's breasts produced no milk to feed their four-month-old son and he could not afford a wet nurse. According to the defendant, his son's need prompted the theft. His applications for employment as a house-boy to a white man met with no success. His previous employer of five years had returned to Portugal, and he had not yet found a new position.

The plaintiff repudiated the out-of-work man's version and alleged the scoundrel appropriated the animal for profit. Law officers created by the Portuguese overlords had returned the cow unscathed, milk still in the udder, in a matter of minutes after the theft. The plaintiff demanded Jason impose the full extent of the law on the villain. The plaintiff assured the judge that stealing cattle could result in expulsion or even death in his village as the ownership of many cattle signifies wealth and respect. Also a member of the Masai nation, the defendant stated he fully recognized the importance of the animal to the plaintiff which strengthened his claim he only wanted milk as he had no desire for exile or death. The latter statement sent Jason into a rage. The damned Masai toyed with the wrong Ibo high priest again.

Later that evening, after rendering the quick decision, Jason spoke to Sarah about it. He decided that the defendant's thirty lashes at the public pillory and the slaughter and donation of the carcass of the plaintiff's cow to the temple provided justice. That way, neither of the Masai won the case. Sarah's eyes became hard and she rose to leave.

"Sit down!" A frustrated Jason shouted.

Sarah gazed blankly into Jason's eyes. "Is that an order, my lord?"

Jason quickly understood he had gone too far. "Of course not! It's just that when you disagree with me, you up and leave. Why don't you help me? If you disagree with my decisions, tell me, and offer other ones," he pleaded.

Sarah walked in back of him, bent over, wrapped her arms over his chest, and gently rested her cheek on top of his head. "Jason, you, not I, are the high priest. It is not my responsibility, or anyone else's, to overrule Ifa's high priest even if I disagree with your decisions. Sometimes the beast makes you make hasty decisions you come to regret. Don't allow it. Take your time and think things out," she offered as she gently kissed his head.

Sarah's gentleness could not assuage his fury. "What did you want me to do? Let those Masai go free?" Jason felt her arms tighten. Even he appalled himself with that declaration. Too late! It had come out.

Instead of a tirade of rebuke or some demonstration of anger, Sarah unlaced her arms and sat beside him. She reached over and placed her hand gently on his cheek. "Come back to me, my Jason." She began to gently stroke his stubbulled face. "Permit me, my husband, to remind you that your wife is a Masai, and the unborn child I carry is half Masai."

Jason startled as if she had struck a physical blow. Unborn child! Sarah had never alluded to pregnancy. The father-to-be sputtered, but no words would form. By gesture, he signaled to his smiling wife to remain seated on the low bench while he went to the table in the middle of the living room for a cassava and to regain his speech. After a healthy draught, he rushed back to her side. "Sarah! I'm sorry I spoke as I did. I shall guard my tongue in the future. I said something without thinking," he said holding her close. "Now tell me, when did you find out?"

Sarah broke the embrace and took both of his hands in hers. "I have known for a week now."

Jason stared at his wife in amazement. "Why didn't you tell me?"

"You seemed busy with your duties, and I wanted just a little more time to pass to make sure." She gave his hands a rapid shake of assurance and added, "Besides, as much as you have delighted in me since we met, I thought you would have known by now. Unless you slow down, we'll probably birth an entire new nation." Jason gave a hearty laugh at Sarah's joshing. "It will be another seven months before the baby is born. You handle the ceremonies and judgments of Ifa, and let me handle this. You wanted my input. Well, that's it."

"But--" he tried to intercept.

Sarah placed her index finger on his lips on the then gave him a quick kiss. "There are no 'buts'. You didn't marry a foolish woman. If I need anything, I certainly will tell you. I want this baby as much as you."

He nodded.

"Then this is one time I shall give the orders." Once again she chuckled and hugged him close. "We Masai are made of sterner stuff then you Ibo give us credit for." Jason took notice of the amiable rebuke. Neither of them again alluded to Jason's prejudicial statement nor his acrimonious decision of Jason concerning the cow as they rose and went to dinner.

Jason gathered the sleeping woman into his arms and brushed a thankful kiss on her forehead. Sarah released a contented sigh and snuggled closer to her husband.

An hour later she could feel the baby moving in her womb. Beside her, the soft snore of Jason made her smile. To feel the baby move in such early pregnancy made Sarah become aware of the vitality of the fetus.

Suddenly, Sarah felt perplexed. Which individual in her life had the greatest need; the one in her belly or the one lying next to her? Another month elapsed since she had informed him of her pregnancy. Sarah could not decide if Jason spent more time in the temple or the house adjacent to it. The judgment concerning the cow on the day of the announcement of the baby passed into history between the two of them. Sarah received via gossip from some of the temple workers the thief had received a gift of a cow found wandering in the streets, and an anonymous benefactor had bought the plaintiff man's dairy products for one week and had it distributed among the poor of the city. A solitary cow wandering the streets of Quilimane? Unlikely! Sarah held her peace. Let sleeping dogs, or in this case, sleeping cows, lie.

Jason rolled over on the sleeping mat and placed his arm across Sarah's extending abdomen. The little one would soon be keeping them awake in protest to the unwanted weight. Sarah shifted and gathered Jason's arm next to her cheek. Her husband roused enough to sleepily remove his arm, shoot a kiss toward his wife, and roll over on his side, turning his back to Sarah. Which of them had the greatest need? The happy woman resolved that neither had the greatest need, but in any given moment, each had individual needs only she could meet. Jason resumed his soft snoring. The nightmares that had plagued him for so long had almost become a thing of the past. Sarah realized she carried one being in her body and both in her soul. She would have to reconcile both of their needs at any given time. Why? She thought the resolution to that question simple, because she had become a wife and a mother-to-be? No! A more substantial rationale solution presented itself. Her mind stretched back eons for the true explanation which solidified into a single word--woman. That thankless juggling act existed since the dawn of time. A warm glow permeated Sarah as she rubbed her abdomen and rested her cheek against her husband's back. Despite all of the bravado of men, she adored the singular title of woman and all it entailed. Sarah closed her eyes and joined Jason in harmonious sleep.

Jason determined to vacate Quilimane and return to Ilorin after Sarah presented him with the joyful news of the forthcoming birth, but his overwhelming official duties prevented immediate departure. He wanted to get Sarah the security of a well-known midwife at his home city before her time came. He discussed with the priests and soldiers the quickest and safest route for return. Unlike his trip to Quilimane, his return to Ilorin required the avoidance of villages.

Jason became bogged down with his duties and trying to determine which of the priests to delegate what duties. Sarah's pregnancy advanced to six months. The fetus became very active, making Sarah wish the pregnancy would reach term. She continued her daily chores over Jason's protests. Her refusal to accept assistance from other women worried Jason greater than the delay of departure. Jason had no choice but to surrender to her obstinacy and her recently developed insatiable desire to consume the entire melon crop of Africa. In desperation, Ifa's high priest began to delegate certain duties to the local officiate without careful consideration whether or not the individual could perform them or not, and had his retinue prepare for departure. Finally, in the middle of Sarah's seventh month, the caravan departed Quilimane and proceeded toward the Great Desert. Arab merchants assured Jason that in skirting the desert he would encounter less populated villages than back-tracking through the Serengeti and the jungle.

Despite the haste, the caravan had to make stops at villages bordering both the jungle and desert. Jason's position as Ifa's high priest forced him to delay in order to perform certain ceremonies and render judgments. Sarah once more reiterated the precedence his high office held over his private life. An anxious Jason bowed to her wishes, focused on his official duties, and allowed Sarah to determine the functioning of their private lives.

The Sahara contained no moderation of duty. It produced unbearable, incinerating solar heat during the day and nights rivaled only by the Arctic Circle. Only sunrise and sunset offered periods of short normalcy. Sarah bore it all without complaint. She sat the standard of climatic toleration for the priests and soldiers. If the high priest's pregnant wife had no complaints, then why should strong men? Despite discomfiture to the entire troop, Jason appreciated that Sarah set the pace. At the onset of diminutive disagreements among his men, Jason could offer Sarah as an example of strength to shame the men into compliance and prevent petty insurrections. To Jason's dismay, more border villages than he had anticipated presented themselves, which further delayed the caravan. Jason wanted to bypass many, but Sarah refused to sanction such an idea that could compromise his role as Ifa's high priest. Placing her needs over the obligations to Ifa violated her neutrality. The little band became delayed an additional three weeks beyond their carefully planned schedule.

On the evening of the fourth week, the procession camped at a nearby oasis. The village they left the day before had cost them more precious days while Jason arbitrated an argument between two brothers vying for chiefdom. Born on the same day to different wives of the recently deceased chief, each had their own faction to support them. Jason created another tribe to prevent bloodshed. He decreed that if either warred on the other, mercenaries would arrest both brothers and bring them to Ilorin. Long Ju Ju would then designate a new chief for each village, and the brothers would suffer the fate of slavery.

Inside his tent that same evening, an exhausted Jason sat on a mat in front of the low table and picked at his food. Tomorrow, late in the evening, they would arrive at Ilorin. Sarah had become too heavy with child to perform her daily chores. Protest, or no protest, Jason would definitely find her a maid to take over the household chores at Ilorin even if he had to threaten to shackle Sarah to a chair. Behind him, he heard his wife piling the much needed animal skins for warmth on their makeshift bed when she suddenly called, "Jason!"

"Do you need some help making the bed?" he asked, finally putting a piece of lamb in his mouth.

"No, Love. Jason…it's time," she plainly stated.

"Time for---oh great Ifa! No!" he shouted, jumping to his feet and upsetting his plate.

Sarah nodded, grimaced and grasped her abdomen. Water cascaded between her legs wetting the animal skins as Sarah slowly dropped to her knees.

"Guard! Guard! Jason bellowed in panic. Two men responded with pistols ready. The confused soon-to-be-father shook clenched fists by his head and yelled, "Put those away you fools. Go get the shaman."

"No!" Sarah screeched over a contraction and waved an open hand side to side at the guards to emphasize her point. Two immobilized mercenaries stared at the woman breathing through her mouth and awaited further instructions. Who held precedence now--the high priest or his pregnant wife? "No!" Sarah said in softer tones. "There is nothing he can do. It is up to me now." She extended her hand toward Jason in a plea for him to take it. "And my husband, of course. Wait outside. He will give you further instructions on what we'll need." Jason confirmed the order with a nod and a curt wave of his hand and took his wife's outstretched one with the other.

After the guard's departure, Sarah pulled off her sarong with the help of Jason. "Sarah, love, let me get someone in here who knows what they're doing," the frightened man pleaded.

Jason wished he had listened to his intuition and insisted Sarah have female servants accompany her back to Ilorin, but the strong-willed woman would have none of it. She didn't want to demand a serving woman leave friends and family to accompany her unnecessarily to a strange city all of the way across Africa. She assured Jason they would arrive at their destination long before the birth. Wrong.

There were strong taboos concerning men at the birth of a child, but Jason had to revert to a less stringent ethos and rely on the little he saw practiced by doctors and veterinarians in America. With no women present in the entourage, he had to choose between the shaman and himself. Sarah soon made the decision for him.

After another contraction, Sarah panted, "The shaman will bounce around the tent rattling bones while I have to do all of the work. If you choose one of the priests, he would have difficulty in deciding which end of the incense to light, and if it was one of the mercenaries, he would probably shoot his foot at the sight of the baby being born. "She began to roll the wet skins into a pile. "Find some dry skins. These are all soaked." Sarah let out a moan and bent over almost touching her head to the ground. Jason rushed toward her, but she waved him off. "Hurry up!" she commanded in a no nonsense voice. Jason, totally unaware of his actions, seized skins from adjoining tents as the bewildered company looked on at the antics of the frantic priest. After returning to their makeshift home, he kicked the wet skins toward the rear of the tent and hastily placed the dry ones on their mat and helped Sarah to lie down.

Sarah lay upon the soft skins complaining of severe low back pain. She pulled Jason into a kneeling position beside her and held his left hand. The contraction had subsided now. Meaningfully, she squeezed her husband's hand. "We made this little one together, and together we shall bring it into the world."

The dumbfounded husband replied in a shaky voice, "Sarah, I don't know anything about this."

Sarah found his response almost comical. "Congratulations! Since this is my first, neither do I. Even as a child, the women use to push us young girls out of the way, so I never got to see a human birth. But, like me, you've seen plenty of animals born. It can't be too much different, and I listened well to what the women had to say about what to do. This should teach you a lesson. You should eavesdrop on the chattering of women," she said with a chuckle.

"Sarah, you're not a cow," Jason desperately reminded her.

Sarah became too busy in the throes of another contraction to respond immediately. She squeezed her husband's hand so hard Jason assumed every bone fractured. At long last Sarah breathed a long sigh of relief, released his hand and smiled. "Sorry!" She glanced toward the tent flap that concealed faces of the murmuring voices outside the high priest's tent. Word had diffused throughout the camp; the high priest's wife's labor had begun.

The tent flap suddenly pushed aside admitting an old, gaunt man sporting an assortment of gourds and fetishes. Between contractions, Sarah howled at the old man to get out in language that Jason never knew she had learned, let alone would use. Intimidated by the vehemence of the order, the shaman dropped gourds and feathers and made a hasty exit. After months spent with such a docile creature, a surprised Jason became awed at a demanding Sarah. In the future, he would never underestimate her prowess again. He had no choice but to comport himself as a reluctant midwife.

Well after dark, the contractions became more intense and frequent. Despite the frigid night air, Sarah's naked body became saturated. The lower back pain increased to the point of unendurability. Between contractions, Jason offered words of encouragement and sponged her writhing body with cool well water. Three hours after the desert sundown, Sarah rose from the animal skin bed and squatted. She pulled her husband around to face her and gripped him tightly by the shoulders.

Between pants and a series of pushes, she said, "Jason! The baby is coming. Look between my legs. You should be able to see it," she commented between grunts. Jason looked at the almost rounded vaginal opening and spied a circle of black, matted hair protruding. With a scream and final push on Sarah's part, a small head jettisoned through the opening and immediately faced right. Instinctively, Jason reached between Sarah's legs as she gave a final scream and pushed the new life into its father's waiting hands. The new father almost dropped the little wet, slippery newborn spotted with yellowish material.

Sarah's labored breathing began to become more regular. "Slap the baby on its bottom," Sarah gasped. Jason's eyebrows arched. Surely this fable contained some delusion associated with childbirth. No loving mother would demand such a sadistic act on something so helpless. He gaped at Sarah. "Do it!" she said harshly. Jason held the two small legs by the ankles, the only part of the wet newborn on which he could get a firm hold, and gave the baby a not too tender whack on the bottom with his right hand. The baby scrunched up its face, opened its mouth wide, and emitted a coughing-like cry. The baby's second attempt at crying produced a yell that awoke rocks. The world now had welcomed the little one.

Zombie-like, Jason ignored a large cord containing two large blue arteries and a large red vein encapsulated in a gelatinous substance connecting the baby's belly to the vaginal opening. He stood over Sarah still holding the crying infant by the ankles. Sarah arched her back and removed one of the animal skins and placed it on her abdomen as she lay back on the skins. "Place the baby here," she said patting the skin. Mechanically, Jason obeyed. Sarah balanced the baby just below her swollen breasts and took her finger and cleaned the baby's mouth. "Now go get three strips of leather and a sharp knife." Jason ran from the tent bellowed for the requested articles, once more setting the camp in disarray to find the articles. Sixty seconds had not elapsed before he returned to the confines of his tent. Sarah offered the newborn to its father. "Keep the head supported when you carry the baby." Jason accepted the gift as if he was transporting a soap bubble. "Now, put the baby between my legs just below my knees." Angel feathers would have received rougher treatment as Jason placed the squalling bundle between Sarah's legs. "Now two fingers from the baby's belly tie one of the thongs very tight around the cord. Make sure that it is extra tight and double knot it." Upon completion of the task, a slack jawed high priest stared at his wife for further tutoring. "Tie another one finger above that." With shaky hands Jason obeyed. "Tie the last strip two fingers above the last leather strip." Sarah stared down her body as Jason completed his assignment and sighed to himself with relief that Sarah's mini course in knot tying had concluded. "Now take your knife and cut the cord between the last strip you tied and the one next to it." Jason gaped at Sarah incredulously. This time she smiled. "No! You're not going to hurt the baby or me." Jason folded the cord and placed the sharp knife in the loop between the two thongs. With a slicing motion he severed the connecting link between mother and child. Some blood spurted from the sliced cord, but both mother and baby appeared unaffected.

"Give me the baby," she said in a tender voice. Jason once again lifted the now quieted bundle that made sucking motions despite the closed eyes. "Jason, you didn't even ask if the baby was a girl or a boy." Sarah snickered. Jason just nodded like a cork on water. Caught-up in the role of midwife, everything around him blurred. His body had reacted like a puppet to the vocal direction of Sarah to the exclusion of all else.

Suddenly he became aware that an heir might have been born. "It's a girl," Sarah said. Jason, never moving from his wife's side, again he nodded. Perhaps the next child would be the desired boy, he noted. Still, if his daughter possessed his wife's attributes, he considered himself the luckiest father on earth. Sarah looked up at her still stunned husband. "Now go get a jar," she requested.

"A jar," he echoed.

"A jar," she reemphasized. "As you clearly pointed out when all of this started, I am not a cow, so don't expect me to eat the afterbirth."

Like a mouse being chased by a cat, Jason ran from the hut and yelled for a jar. One of the priests brought an earthen jar that had been used for spices that now seasoned the ground. Jason ran through the tent opening holding the jar with outstretched arms as if it were some gift to Ifa. In the meantime Sarah made use of the dry upper portion of her sarong to clean the birth residue from their daughter. Satisfied most of the fluids no longer dotted the baby and not to expose the newborn too long to the cold night air, Sarah nestled the little one's head under her left arm and drew the animal skin over the baby. Soon, Sarah delivered the afterbirth.

"Sa-Sa-Sarah, there's another baby," Jason exclaimed, pointing at a large swelling below her naval.

Sarah suppressed her tiredness to explain, "That's the womb, silly. I have to keep rubbing it to keep it hard. It has to stay hard like that or I could bleed to death. Before the week is out, it will disappear. Now take the excess there, put it in the jar, and bury it. Oh, and have someone bring some warm water and old cloths so that I can better clean the baby and myself," Sarah mandated.

As if led by a nose ring, Jason complied. When he returned, Sarah held the baby to her right breast. The baby made suckling motions with her lips but seemed sound asleep. Making rocking motions with her body to the contentment of the newborn, Sarah said, "Now go get me some old clothing so that I don't get blood over everything. It will be just like my time of the month for a few days." A priest brought a basin of warm water and old clothing donated by members of the entourage. Sarah began gently to clean the baby. Finally, she diverted her attention from herself and the baby back to her husband. On the earthen floor with his head resting on the one of the clean hides lay Ifa's unconscious high priest. Sarah cuddled the baby closer, shook her head and mumbled, "Men!"

CHAPTER X

INTERLUDE

Long Ju Ju sat alone in the temple of Ifa staring at the god's wooden image behind the Golden Stool. He reflected not on spiritual musings but on Jason. Since Jason's return from the east coast of the continent, Konte discerned a definite alteration for the better in Jason's personality. Sarah had performed miracles not only with Jason but the people of Ilorin. Sarah. Konte loved her like the daughter he never had. Where did Jason ever find this gem amid beads? No other woman who inhabited the temple complex quite had her attributes. She had an air of ascendancy without arrogance. She exceeded the female rivalry pervading the compound and won friendship among competing female factions.

Konte smiled at the wooden statue when he thought of their daughter, Miriam. Since both parents had European names, they agreed to a non-African name for their daughter. From the moment of her arrival, the child became the real ruler of Ilorin. With only a coo, she stole everyone's hearts that happened within viewing or hearing distance. Even the most callous priests smiled and endeavored to hold her for a brief time. She would giggle, kick her feet, and stretch her tiny fists toward them. Her infectious innocence permeated that individual's being after her guiltless laughter overwhelmed them. Sarah asserted her maternal authority so she could see her daughter at feeding time, change of clothing, or a nap. Otherwise, if the people of Ilorin had their way, she would never see her bewitching daughter. Konte wondered if even Ifa had power over that precocious little sprite.

Konte reflected on how much Jason changed. Long Ju Ju noted that his second in charge still possessed some evil vapors of the panther in his soul, but Jason did return the young boy Konte once knew. Supported by an almost ideal home life, the younger man performed all sacred duties perfunctorily, but could still become short tempered and restless without provocation. Even Sarah had no control at certain times. Thanks to Sarah and Miriam, the citizenry of Ilorin had forgiven but not forgotten Jason's actions. Though they joyfully mingled with Sarah, they reserved a certain hidden distain for Jason. Jason noticed in their social contact aloofness in speech toward him which Sarah did not have to encounter. Although Konte had not discussed the problem with Sarah, he knew she was aware her husband's black nature had seeped back into their lives and began to stretch toward the temple due to Ilorin's citizens' failure to ignore his ugly past actions. The nightmares too had increased since Jason's return to the city. The panther refused to pack up and go away.

A little over a year had passed since the advent of the newlyweds at Iolin. Sarah's welcoming and supportive personality made her an instantaneous success at the compound, especially after she had recounted the anecdote of Miriam's birth. Even at his own expense, Jason delighted in the tale of his performance as midwife at the birth of his first child. But in the ensuing months, a dark shadow had begun to exert an increased influence over Ifa's high priest. The shadow did not have free reign as it did before Sarah intervened. It manifested more subtle ways to regain control. At first, it was just small things like a harsh word which became a brooding mood. According to Sarah, before retiring for the night pacing became almost ritualistic. As ever, she remained steadfast, but her solace became inadequate to stave off the beast's advancement in her husband's soul.

Konte fingered an amulet hung around his neck. For weeks, he prayed to Ifa for guidance. In the end, the stark realization of an aberrant, but necessary, action became evident. He heard the shuffle of footsteps behind him but didn't turn or remove his eyes from Ifa's statue.

"You sent for me?" Jason asked the lotus-positioned figure.

"Ah yes, my son. Come sit here," Konte said in a gentle voice, patting the straw mat on which he sat. Jason assumed the same position as his mentor, but minutes ebbed without an utterance. Jason presumed Konte at prayer as Long Ju Ju slowly turned his head and faced Jason. "I want you to leave Ilorin, my son."

"Where do you wish me to go?" Jason asked, conjecturing a tour paralleling the one which had blessed him with Sarah. She informed Jason one month after their arrival in Ilorin of a second pregnancy, but this time Jason determined she would remain in Ilorin to deliver the baby. Under no proviso would he duplicate his past performance in midwifery.

"No Jason! I don't mean on Ifa's business. I want you to leave the priesthood and Africa," Konte said with a constricted whisper.

A flabbergasted Jason stared unbelievably at his mentor. What exploit had angered Long Ju Ju? What crime had he committed against Ifa? What had he done to merit such punishment? Perhaps Konte wanted to enforce this banishment as revenge for Jason's treatment of Rebah? Jason acknowledged old conflicts had lately reared their ugly heads due to his lack of sleep, but he thought he had managed to keep his negative feelings under control and well hidden. Sleep only induced the pleas for mercy from Rebah with three stoic women standing behind the kneeling specter, but that private haunting did not become evident in his official duties.

"How have I displeased you or wronged Ifa? I'm quite willing to do any penance you may impose, but I can't think of anything I've done to warrant expulsion from the priesthood," Jason said softly.

Konte shook his head. "No! I fear I haven't made myself clear." The old man deposited his hand on Jason's arm. "Since that day I caught you trying to steal from me so long ago, I have loved you like a son. I watched the boyhood wounds begin to heal as you became a servant of Ifa, but your rash action to Rebah created new and irredeemable ulcers in your soul and reopened old ones. I freely forgive you but I shall never forget, especially my participation." A dark cloud permeated the temple as Konte's eyes became unfocussed as he reflected on the past. "Along with other guilty and innocent people, Rebah paid for his sins. You will have to answer Ifa for that harsh judgment, and so will I for allowing such cruelty in order to protect past rulings of Long Ju Ju." Again Konte lapsed into a silence, regressing them both to that fateful day of the burning of Rebah's effects and the violation of the traitor's family.

Konte continued. "What is done is done. There is nothing that you or Long Ju Ju can do to remedy it." The old man hung his head. "May Ifa forgive us? I want you to leave, not as a punishment, but to save yourself, because your future does not lie here."

"Konte, my whole life is here. I have never felt so at home. Sarah, Miriam and now the new baby that is coming. My work for Ifa. Haven't I done a good job?" he said with a lump in his throat.

Long Ju Ju gave a sad smile and placed his arm around the man's shoulder. "There is more to life than doing a good job for others. You also have a responsibility to yourself. I once told you that there was a beast within you. I saw it the moment you condemned Rebah. It feeds on your hate. Sarah has done much to curb it, but unless you can find a way to destroy it, it will eventually destroy you and your family." The old priest readjusted his position to face Jason. "I have watched you over the past months. It's trying very hard to regain control. Sarah sees it, too. She says nothing, but I can see it in her eyes. She's afraid of losing you, and so am I."

"Then let me stay and work this thing out," Jason pleaded.

"I prayed to Ifa to show me another way. I don't want to see you go. I need not tell you I love you as my son, but this is a thing you must do for yourself and your family. The answer to your healing is not here in Africa, but back in America. Retrace the dark one's steps and seek the wrongs committed along the way. Where you can repair the harm do so; where you cannot repair, acknowledge your faults and come to terms with them. For every wrong you right or acknowledge, the beast will lose control over you. Go back, Jason, and find those pieces of your life that were taken from you in hatred and anger and replace them with honor."

Konte broke eye contact and began to pick at a broken piece of matting. "Once, I believed you would die a lost, bitter man. I must confess I was looking for some pretext to relieve you from your duty as high priest before you left for Quilimane. You had become a person I came to both pity and revile. Your anger and revenge had infected the temple and the city and would have eventually led to great strife. Some of your suggestions, since your return, were wise. Others left much to be desired." Konte held up his hand for silence. "No! I don't believe that you were ambitious and striving to replace me, like Rebah." The old priest smiled. "Yes! I was aware of that, but Rebah had his uses, too.

Your troubles come from somewhere deep inside you. You didn't know that the beast controlled your life. Thanks to Sarah, you are aware of your dark side now. It cannot allow the Jason and Sarah I know and love to exist. Happiness, love, and respect are its enemies. Only one of you can survive. You or the beast. It's starving for your anger and hatred. Unless you win the war against your negative feelings, they will strike out at your family first and feed on your guilt to regain control. Allow those feeling to become predominant again, and your very presence will mean destruction of those around you whom you love. Retrace your steps, Jason. See the pain and agony you have caused. Deplete the fuel on which your panther feeds. Change what you can, and learn to accept what you cannot. I don't have the answers how to do that. They lie in your past. Go back! Find them, Jason. Go find your real life."

Konte rose from the mat. "I shall not force you to leave unless you become a threat to Ifa, and my personal preference is to ask you to stay, but search your heart Jason, as I have mine. It is out of love I want you to do this. You will realize it is the sole thing you can do if you wish to keep all you hold dear. For me it is my precious memory of a hungry lost lad in a green sarong. You don't have to leave right away. Talk it over with Sarah and let me know your decision." Konte patted Jason on his right shoulder and exited the temple, leaving a crestfallen man sitting on a mat in front of a wooden idol and the Golden Stool.

Jason did not know how long he tarried in the temple after Konte's departure. He mulled over the mind-numbing conversation again and again. Jason believed he had made great headway in his emotional control. Sarah had said nothing about any negative alteration of behavior. Customarily, Sarah was always the first to alert him of his need for a temperament readjustment. Still, recently he snapped at her and Miriam without motive. He performed the ceremonies with brusqueness and could hardly refrain from omitting certain rituals so they could terminate the liturgy quickly. He weighed judicial matters with less thought and sometimes lamented his settlements. Perhaps Konte and Sarah saw something he did not. No! He saw it too. One may tolerate lying to another person but lying to oneself becomes unforgivable. Ever since that first night with Sarah he knew about his dark side. Sarah kept it in front of his eyes; not with words but with looks and silence. She never pouted, but her soft voice and kindness cut sharper than any reproaching tongue. What did Konte say? The beast detested love and therefore the first ones it would attack would be Sarah, Miriam, and the unborn baby. Jason rose from the mat and went in search of Sarah.

She squatted outside their house weaving a sleeping mat. She looked up at Jason's approach and immediately comprehended something disturbing had transpired at his meeting with Long Ju Ju. She had become accustomed to Jason's dark moods, but this countenance had a distinct personal trait. Sarah controlled the anxiety she felt in her work and offered her husband a lead to talk about what troubled him with a questioning look.

"Where's Miriam?" He procrastinated.

Sarah continued her weaving. She had to wait until he wanted to discuss his concerns. "She's taking a nap before evening meal," she replied.

While pacing in front of Sarah, Jason rubbed his eyes with the palms of his hands and then drew his hands across his face. Hoping Jason ignored her shaking hands, Sarah gave the appearance of total absorption in her work.

"Are you happy here in Ilorin, Sarah?" Jason finally asked in a soft voice.

She looked at him quizzically. "Of course. Why?"

"Would you be unhappy if we had to live somewhere else and leave all of this?" he asked, glancing around the temple complex.

Sarah discarded her unfinished mat and stood. Taking Jason by the hand, she led him into the house. Just inside the door, Miriam lay asleep on a bed of animal skins. She put her arm around Jason's waist and pointed to Miriam and placed his right hand on her abdomen. "This is my home," she said squeezing his waist. "The rest of this--," she said waving her hand back and forth indicating the inside of the hut and beyond, "are only things. We can always replace them or get something better, but you, Miriam, and the one to come are more precious to me than life itself. You three are my real home." Reassuringly, she smiled at him. "Where does Konte want to send you? Back to Quilimane?"

Jason's heart almost burst with pride. "I can never thank Ifa enough for the wonderful gift he gave me in you and Miriam." He paused a moment to kiss her forehead. "We may have to leave Africa."

For an instant, Jason felt Sarah's arm tighten around his waist. "America?" she asked. Jason nodded.

Sarah released him and reorganized the little body squirming on the skins. "I always knew one day you would hunt the panther. I never realized it left such a long trail, but it must be done for all of our sakes." Sarah took his hand off of her stomach, kissed the back of it and held it to her right cheek. "Konte is a wiser man than I thought. He's right, you know. It's time you do the hunting instead of letting it stalk you." She paused. "When are we leaving?"

"I don't know just yet. I have to think this out carefully, and besides, I'm not going to leave until after the baby is born." In turn, he gave her a hug. "You're not going to trap me into playing midwife again."

Sarah roared with laughter. "And I had such a nice outfit picked out for you to wear."

Jason joined his wife's laughter and then grew serious again. "Besides, I think the beast's trail begins here." Jason hadn't hooded his eyes for a long time, and this time he did so against his black nature. "Once, long ago, someone taught me the first step in becoming a hunter is to start at your present location. Now that I think about it, I know just where the beast's trail begins. Dear Ifa, this is going to be very difficult, and it will take a while before I can act. I shall do nothing until the baby is born. Perhaps I am using that as an excuse, but I can't help it. When the time comes, I'll need you more than ever. The action I am about to take does not concern Ifa. I shall definitely need not only your support, but your help." Jason crushed Sarah to his chest and began to stroke her head. "Without you, I am lost. You have borne so much already, and, instead of the promise of happiness and security, I ask you to bear even more." For the second time in his life, Jason wept.

Sarah offered no comment as she held her husband tighter. This problem Jason had to resolve alone. She could only help implement and do his bidding if it did not lead down the path of the beast. Sarah prayed to Ifa that Jason made this decision without the beast puppeting events about to take place. With the baby due next month, it would grant her time to evaluate if the course Jason pursued originated from the beast or her beloved husband. Sarah resolved she would not desert her soulmate or allow the beast to win. "Great Ifa help both of us!" She silently prayed.

Miriam woke, rolled to her hands and knees, and began to crawl off of the skins. Sarah gently released her husband and, after swooping the gamin into her arms, proceeded to change her into drier clothing. Jason regained composure and retreated outside. The temple complex prepared for night with the closing of shops and the bustle of priests for evening service. Jason began to walk toward the temple to add his part to the ceremonies. He looked west at the sun's corona on the horizon. Did it signify the end of his old life or the end of the new?

CHAPTER XI

SUNRISE

Too big for her small frame, Makiba tightly folded and hugged the faded, flower-print robe around herself. More than three odious years had elapsed since the incarceration of her and her daughters in this wretched hovel. It was hard to believe that much time passed. In hell, minutes, hours and days have no significance. Rebah's wife constructed a crude palate on the floor as far from the loathsome bed as conceivable. So far the evening ended as a slow night. She serviced only three men -- two street cleaners and a coolie. Their alcoholic breath laced with vomit still permeated her senses. Thank the gods that Miama died. Her youngest daughter had succumbed to a plague that ravished the town last spring. At least one of the three women found peace, but Melika, her eldest still suffered under Jason's severe sentence. Younger and more beautiful than her mother, the helpless girl warranted a greater demand for her services. Other captive women held by Ali shared with them the secret of avoiding pregnancy as well as the combination of certain herbs which would result in an abortion if the previous methods failed. Ali didn't provide this anti-pregnancy service from the goodness of his heart. His customers didn't desire to pay for sex with a pregnant woman. Ali dismissed such a faux-pas woman to the street due to the loss of profit. Makiba wondered how much indignity they had to tolerate before blessed death would release their two tortured souls. Like the last two passengers on a sinking ship, the two women daily succored each other in this abysmal hole of filth.

The cubicle door flew open. No need to knock. Privacy became an alien concept long ago. Ali glanced toward the empty bed. Noting the absence of a customer, he immediately looked in the far corner at the forlorn figure crouched in a pile of dirty linen. "Get up. Gather your things and come with me," he ordered.

Makiba rose slowly and glanced at Melika clutching a small bundle of her personal belongings standing behind the pimp. "What is it? What is happening?" The mother asked in a trembling voice as she began to pack.

"You and your daughter have been sold," came the whoremaster's curt reply.

Sold? At least she and her daughter would have to service only one man, one household at the worst. Rarely did one whorehouse sell its wares to another. Makiba discarded the robe, donned a faded floral dress, and gathered the few shifts that passed as dresses, wrapped them in a bundle which she slung over her shoulder. She walked past Ali to join her frightened daughter in the hallway. The two women followed the short Arab down a flight of steps leading to his private apartment. He opened the door and, with the jerk of his head, ordered both to enter. As if doused by ice water, the women became petrified. Desperately they groped for each other and glowered at their new owner. Jason!

Another woman, foreign to both of them who held a baby, walked from behind Jason, placed a little girl in a nearby chair, and told Jason to watch her and tendered him the baby. Her approach to the distressed women radiated warmth to both wretched creatures as she greeted them like long lost relatives.

After she embraced each, she grasped them on their free shoulder and turned them around. "Let us leave this place, now," she said in a gentle voice that denoted she felt their suffering. Jason, who all the while stood by a wicker table, walked across the room, handed the infant he held to the kind woman, and went to retrieve the little girl, squirming in the chair.

His face showed great stress, but, as they recalled their last meeting with their nemesis. His wide eyes seemed somehow gentler now than the two women remembered. Mother and daughter could not rid themselves of suspicion. They allowed the strange woman to lead them into the noxious air suffusing the wharves of Dahomey where the seedy business of Ali thrived. Jason followed at a slower pace, due to the toddling steps taken by the little girl who examined everything within her reach. Once the door slammed shut, Ali returned his attention to other paying customers and his merchandise. No one spoke.

The entourage felt relieved to abandon the nightmarish wharves and enter the more socially acceptable part of the city. The two ransomed women put one foot in front of the other, their terror still paramount at the thought of what new tortuous scheme Jason might have in mind. Perhaps he escorted them to some unknown place produced by the worse demon in hell. The two bewildered women considered the possibility the woman walking between them protected her new recruits as any other madam of a house of ill repute would have. Had Jason procured his own whorehouse to epitomize their disgrace by advertising them his prize whores?

Makiba and Melika lost track of how many intersections or turns the weary troop traversed. They had no knowledge of this part of the city. After twenty minutes navigating the mud of the dirt streets, looming in front of them stood an inn called The Red Parrot. From its clean and well kept exterior, the inn obviously catered to business travelers. Perhaps Jason had sold them to a rich merchant.

When the party entered, a room to the left of the main desk contained the bar and a drinking area but had no paying occupants. The sound of someone preparing place settings came from behind shut double doors across from the tavern room that obviously housed the dining room. From the looks of the interior with its well-polished hardwood floor, this establishment catered to European clientele. A young boy finished mopping the floor and began to remove the bar chairs from their upside-down position on the tables in the bar. From somewhere inside the dining room, a grandfather clock chimed two o'clock in the morning as another hotel employee prepared the tables for breakfast. The innkeeper smiled at the party of six, nodded, and went about his assignments. With a wave of her hand, the unknown woman gestured for the nervous women to ascend the carpeted stairs at the end of the foyer leading to the inn's bedrooms. The moment of truth had arrived. Who awaited them up there? What new torment had Jason concocted? The two fearful women diffidently complied. Jason disappeared with the two children through a door at the top of the stairs. Makiba and Melika walked with the unimposing woman halfway down a narrow passage and stopped at one of the doors that had the number four nailed on the outside. She indicated by a wave of her open palm for them to enter. Resigned to their fate, both entered through the doorway and were surprised to find an empty room.

"Get some sleep. It's late and we can talk in the morning. If you need anything, there is a boy who sleeps at the end of the hall. Just tell him what you want." The stately-dressed black woman embraced mother and daughter again, gave Makiba a key, and left, gently closing the door behind her. Makiba waited a few minutes then bolted to the locked door. No. The woman had left the door open and Makiba had the key. She peeked outside and saw the nodding head of a little urchin crouched at the end of the corridor. Otherwise, the hall appeared deserted. Makiba pulled her head back inside, turned, and looked at Melika who merely raised her eyebrows and shrugged when her mother closed the door. Both women dropped their pathetic belongings on the floor.

"What's he up to?" Melika asked suspiciously. Makiba just shook her head.

"I'm quite sure he has the inn watched just in case we try to escape. Any escape attempt would be punished with more public humiliation. We'll just have to wait until morning to find out our fate. It's sad that one human can treat another like this." Makiba sat beside her daughter on the soft bed. Despite mutual vows of vigilance, both soon fell asleep sideways across the clean, feathered bed.

The women awoke with a jerk at the light tapping on the door. "My little ones have been awake for an hour already, and they are driving me crazy. I'll have the boy bring you some hot water. I'll meet you downstairs for breakfast when you finish," said the friendly female voice through the closed door. They heard a pair of footsteps retreat down the hall toward the staircase landing leading downstairs to the dining room. Three minutes later, another tap on the door announced one of the houseboys with a pitcher of hot water in a fern-designed pitcher seated inside a similar ceramic basin. He deposited it on the nightstand and left without a word. Both women luxuriated in the morning washing and the donning of clean clothes before descending for breakfast.

As Makiba and Melika came down the staircase, they glanced to the right and saw the now familiar woman sitting at one of the dining tables, grappling to get porridge down a little girl perched on a chair. The moppet had her concentration focused on other diners and everywhere but on the breakfast table. The baby cradled in the woman's left arm seemed indifferent to the jostling as the woman attempted to retain some of the porridge on the spoon between the bowl and the little girl's mouth. The suspicious mother and daughter approached the only known occupants of the room while a waiter, aware of the arrival of new guests, initiated breakfast for the shabbily dressed women.

"Where's Jason?" Makiba asked abruptly, refusing to sit. Melika peered over her mother's shoulder awaiting a response.

"My husband had some business in town and probably won't be back until late this evening," the woman replied while attempting to focus the little girl's attention on food and not on the new arrivals.

Husband? What kind of woman would want to marry such a degenerate? What plans did he have for them? Makiba stared at the woman wiping a mustache of porridge from the little girl.

"I'm sorry. Let me introduce myself. My name is Sarah, and this little demon is Miriam, and the one who minds me," she said rocking a baby cradled in her left arm, "is Alva. Please sit down and eat. We have much to talk about." Sarah released the squirming Miriam from her table prison. Immediately, Miriam let out a squeal of delight at her freedom and tottered off after a passing waitress who, with a twirl, scooped the child up above her head and rocked the devilish tot side to side.

"May I show her the chickens out back?" asked the waitress, whose cap became an object requiring careful scrutiny by Miriam. Sarah nodded assent, and the waitress, with one eye covered by her cap, disappeared through the kitchen door holding the squirming Miriam.

"Are you our new mistress, or is he going to sell us to someone else?" Makiba asked without formality as both women sat.

"Sell you?" Sarah said with astonishment. She sighed and continued. "Things happened so fast last night, and everybody was tired. We had just arrived from Ilorin, and Jason insisted your removal from that awful place could not wait. We went directly to Ali's after reserving rooms here. Jason owns a house here in town but thought you would feel more comfortable in an inn. I'm sorry we didn't have a chance to talk last night, but Jason agreed to let me do the talking, and the little ones were tired and cranky. Plus I thought you would enjoy a good night's sleep." Sarah abruptly broke off the explanation and laid her fork on the table. "Now it's time to clarify one very important thing. No one owns you. You are entirely free to come and go as you please." The two women stopped eating and looked suspiciously at Sarah.

Sarah lowered her voice. With sadness and anger she continued, "Not long ago a great wrong was done to both of you." She paused before adding, "And to two who are no longer with us." Sarah reached across the table and clasped Makiba's hand. "Ali told us of the death of your daughter. We're very sorry. There is no way to change the past or to right those wrongs. The only thing to be done is to offer a new road to travel and give any help we can along the way. The choice is entirely yours." Sarah released Makiba's hand and played with the porridge she had fed to Miriam.

"I don't want anything from that man," Makiba said bitterly.

Sarah once again reached across the table and took Makiba's right hand. "Think carefully before you say anything. It was a statement like that on Jason's part that caused this trouble in the first place. Don't allow hatred to destroy you as it almost destroyed him. Makiba, he can't correct all things, but he can stop some of the ugliness and perhaps offer something new. Give all six of us a chance. Yes, I said six. The path Jason, the children, and I must take is tied up with the path you will take. I ask you to show the mercy to us that Jason denied you, so all of us can learn to deal with the guilt and the pain and get on with our lives. I'm not asking for forgiveness or forgetfulness, only a chance to set these bitter things aside for now and start anew."

Makiba placed both hands in her lap and spoke directly to the woman on her left. "Start anew! Do you realize that every time that I walk into the street someone will whisper, 'There goes Makiba and her daughter, and they were once Ali's best whores.' What prospects does Melika have at a normal life? Or me? The daughter of a whore, and a whore herself. Every washer woman would shun us, thanks to Jason. What are we suppose to do? Open our own whorehouse? You say we are free? Free to do what? Become our own whores with the help of your husband?"

Sarah who had her eyes lowered during Makiba's tirade elevated them to lock on those of the hurt and angry woman. "No! The business that Jason is about now will free you from that type of life." Sarah allowed a pause before she offered a possible solution. "We want you to come to America with us."

A lightening bolt could not have stunned both freed women more. America? Makiba became as silent as her daughter.

"The harm done to you here can never be repaired by Jason or anyone else. What you say is correct. If you stayed here you would have to live a life of shame and ridicule. Jason and I talked about it at great length, and we want you to come with us. Nobody in America will know what happened here." Sarah paused and sat very straight in her chair. "I won't assume to speak for Jason, but I shall speak for myself. Until you say that you can manage on your own, and I know that there is no bitterness in that statement, I shall not desert you. We are not poor and are quite willing to make you part of our family until such time as you want to be on your own. You need not have any dealings with Jason but only with me, if that makes you more comfortable. For our sakes, as well as your own, I beg you to accept our offer. The future of six lives rests in your hands. If you decide to remain here a curse will follow us, not only because of the harm Jason has caused, but you will both continue to live a life of shame. Allow us to put this hideous part of all of our lives behind us and begin a new life in a new country without that stain."

"I have to talk this over with Melika in private," Makiba replied coldly.

"I would expect no less." Sarah shifted in her chair and dabbed her lips with a napkin.

The mother and daughter rose from the table and retired to their room. Makiba let out a long sigh as she plopped on the bed. "What do you think? Do you trust Sarah?"

Malika paused to consider her reply and she sat in the chair adjacent to the bed. "I really don't know. Certainly staying here is not an option unless we want to return to Ali's. On the other hand, what's to prevent Jason from selling us once we arrive in America?"

Makiba shook and lowered her head. "It's quite a problem. I still don't trust Jason, but Sarah seems quite different. What on earth did she ever see in Jason?"

"She doesn't seem like typical Masai woman that obeys a man without question. Do you think they both liberated each other?" Maliba mused.

"It could be she is no longer dominated by a tribe and she is helping free him from ghosts of the past. I can't see any deception in Sarah, but there is always Jason in the background." Makiba offered.

"Let's keep on watch, take our time, and see if she is trying to trick us, or is she sincere. We don't have to give a decision today." Malika concluded.

Makiba agreed as both women left their room to join Sarah and give her their decision.

Sarah sat in a chair in her room watching the two girls wrestling on the bed. Alva didn't have a chance as her sister kept tickling her. Sarah stood and welcomed her guests. "Alright girls, that's enough. Miriam, you and your sister make room for Malika and Makiba to sit down, and no roughhousing." After a final tickle, children moved to the top of the bed. The two women sat on the foot of the bed.

"Well have you decided anything?" Sarah asked in a hopeful voice.

Malika shook her head. "This is a very difficult decision to make. We need more time."

Sarah refused to abandon hope for a positive response.

"Jason hasn't been able to find a ship going to Mobile so there is time left. Meanwhile, whether or not you accept our offer, we must do something about your wardrobe. Those clothes are fit only for scrubbing floors, or should be burnt. Evidently none of us are hungry this morning," she added pointing to the almost untouched plates. The two women had not exactly banqueted at Ali's, but current events had quashed their appetite. Sarah rose and bent over as if whispering a secret in Makiba's ear, "I have a line of credit from Jason drawn on an account he keeps with the Aqua brothers here in Dahomey. Come on," said Sarah merrily as she rose and shifted the sleeping Alva into a more comfortable position, "Let's go bankrupt him!" After rescuing a flock of squawking chickens at back of the inn from Miriam's onslaught, all five departed for the market place.

Try as she might, Makiba could harbor no ill feelings toward Sarah. The company consumed the entire day going from shop to stall and back to shop to buy bolts of cloth for new clothing for three adult womenfolk and two children. The newly-liberated women began to relax in Sarah's company. Many years had passed since Makiba had the liberty to contest the outrageous prices charged by merchants as she had done in Ilorin or by accompanying Rebah on some of his business trips. She astonished Sarah with her expertise at bartering. Her taste in color, fabric, and discernment of cloth quality exceeded Sarah's.

Then, on to the dressmaker. The patterns for the latest European styles seemed a bit flamboyant. They approved some designs but discarded the chic bustles and tight fitting corsets. Instead, they opted for the unrestrained and graceful flowing illustrations of more comfortably fitting wear. Sarah bribed the dressmaker, by almost doubling the price, to have them fitted within the week. Then off to the cobbler. And who could resist the numerous bracelets, necklaces and earrings marketed on the way? An exhausted troop finally wended its way back to the Red Parrot as the shops closed for the night.

"I never want to see another bolt of cloth as long as I live," said Sarah exhaling a large puff of air as she threw an armload of packages onto the bed.

"Or another piece of leather," Makiba added as she sat in a chair by the window, still grasping her precious cargo.

Melika's assignment to baby sit on their outing proved the most difficult task of all for three women. The young girl had no difficulty with Alva, but the capricious imp Miriam had all but free reign as the women transverse from shop to shop. On return to the inn, all discovered that voracious appetites had returned. Everyone wanted an early supper and a soft bed but first some tea.

"I think I'll take the little ones to our room and wash them for bed," Melika proposed.

"Melika, you must be made of iron, especially after that little game of 'Catch-Me-If-You-Can' Miriam forced on you at the fruit vendor which finally ended at the pastry vendor. I'll have the innkeeper send their tea to our room when you are through washing them. You'll probably need a shovel just to get down to Miriam's skin. That girl can get herself dirty just standing still, which she never does. I'll feed them and put them to bed," said Sarah.

"Oh, there's no need. Let me put them to bed in our room. Have their tea sent there and then you can transfer them to your room later. I'm determined to see if this little monster actually sleeps," Melika volunteered as she gave the squealing Miriam a hug. With a smile of thanks and a nod from Sarah, Melika took the children to her room. Sarah opened her bedroom door and waved to the boy at the end of the corridor. "Bring tea for two here and for one to room four and make sure there is plenty of milk on the single tray," she ordered, closed the door flopped on the bed next to the packages.

Makiba gave a groan of tiredness as she rose from the chair. "I'll be right back. Let me get rid of these packages and let Melika know that tea will be served soon. I'll make sure Miriam drinks some milk, that is, if Miriam hasn't tied Melika up to a chair by now," Makiba laughed.

Sarah sat propped up on the bed by her elbows. "It's good to hear you laugh," she said with a lot of meaning.

Makiba paused in the doorway and looked at the smiling woman sitting on the bed. Thoughtfully, she replied, "It's good to laugh. I almost thought I had forgotten how." She closed the door and went in search of her daughter.

Later in Sarah's room, Sarah and Makiba sat next to the empty tea tray and reviewed the day. Anyone coming upon them would have assumed them friends for years.

"I still think the pearl-colored cloth with the seashell design will make a beautiful dress for Melika. It will highlight her features and make her skin glow," Sarah observed.

"How did you meet Jason?" Makiba surprised Sarah with the sudden shift of topic. For a long while, silence prevailed, both women lost in their respective thoughts. Sarah gave a sigh, relaxed in her chair, and began her tale. "I too was abused by him at first. Thank Ifa, I was able to see the good man struggling to survive inside him." Makiba sat quietly in her chair for over an hour listening to the chain of events leading to their current situation and Sarah's attitude toward those events, including the birth of Miriam which always brought laughter to whoever heard it. When Sarah had no more to relate, as she did earlier in the day, she placed her hand over Makiba's. "Help me, Makiba. I know it's hard for you to believe, but Jason truly is a decent man. This thing that happened between your husband and mine twisted all of our lives, but I believe that at least for Jason, it started long before that. The terrible things he has done I call the panther in his soul. It is no easy task to fight the beast, especially when it has had control of him for so long."

Sarah removed her hand and sat back in her chair. After a sip of cold tea, she said, "I have no idea what awaits me in America. What evil things has he done there that have to be repaired? I don't even know if he is capable of doing it. It's only by trying to do things and recognizing the wrongs he has done that Jason can destroy this beast. You and your daughter are the beginning of the path he must retread. The idea to take you with us was his, of which I heartily approve. Long Ju Ju agreed with his decision as well. Much to our disgrace, you have experienced the wrath of the beast. I want it stopped and destroyed. You and your daughter can help maim this thing even further by accepting Jason's offer." Sarah rose and walked to the window and stared down at the empty street. "You are the first he has repathed by removing you from that den of hell in which he put you. If you come with us, you will be a constant reminder of the positive that can be done and help strengthen his will to fight his dark side, not only for himself, but for all of us. I have no one else to turn to. If not for Jason's sake, then help me, Makiba, and help yourselves. The beast of hatred destroyed your husband and daughter, and it would love to come and live in you. Think back on the vindictive person you knew that I now call my husband. That can easily become you. Don't let that happen. For all of our sakes, I want to build, not destroy. Come with us Makiba," Sarah resumed her seat beside the silent woman.

"I still have to discuss this with Melika. Whatever she decides, so will be my answer," and on that notation Makiba rose to go to her room.

"Jason won't return until late. I know we're all tired, but will you and Melika have supper with me in about an hour?" Sarah invited.

"Won't we wake the children?" Makiba responded.

"I'll have one of the house boys watch them. If you choose to remain in your room, I'll understand, but I really don't want to be alone right now," Sarah admitted.

Makiba nodded and left and discovered her daughter neatly stacking today's purchases. She related that latest conversation with Sarah, but both women remained ambivalent.

Sarah sat a long while staring into the now empty teacup. Deep wounds like Makiba's could not be purged overnight. Sarah liked the woman and her daughter. From first contact, Sarah felt a bonding. In other circumstances, they would have cemented into instant confidants, but all of the women in Jason's life stood in the shadow of the beast. She startled as she felt a hand on her left shoulder. She hadn't heard her husband enter. "I thought you wouldn't be back until late," she said.

Jason sat in the chair previously occupied by Makiba. "I have to be back at the harbor in a few minutes. How are Miriam and Alva?" Jason asked.

"Oh, they're fine! They're both in bed now in the women's room. I'll be getting the little ones in just a few minutes. Alva was asleep before we came back, and Miriam could barely make it upstairs, which is unusual for her. I hope Melika got her to eat before she went to bed," Sarah commented.

"Melika? Is it wise to leave either of them alone with the children?" Jason asked warily.

"Jason, if they were going to hurt the children, they have had a hundred opportunities to do so today. If you're so doubtful, then why buy their freedom and ask them to come with us? Maybe they will strangle all of us in our sleep, or maybe they will throw us overboard on a dark and stormy night. Jason, this nonsense could go on and on. The road you have taken has a signpost---trust. Unless you can trust them, I suggest you give them gold and let them go on with their pitiful lives here," Sarah said irritably as she rose and removed the packages from the bed and placed them near their luggage.

"We have talked about this. You know we can't leave them in Africa. Wherever they go, they will carry the title of whore," he said.

Sarah paused and looked down at her husband. "They haven't accepted our offer as yet, but they have nothing to gain by hurting the children. I saw or heard nothing that would present such a danger. They were more afraid of their future than focus on revenge on the children. I wish you could have seen the patience that Malika had with Miriam." She stacked the last package and sat by her husband. She relaxed, smiled, and took his face in her hands. "If anybody knows what it's like to be innocent and suffer, they do." Jason flushed. "I don't mean to hurt you, but I can't alter the truth. There are four innocents in this affair, not two. Learn to place trust again, Jason. You did in me, and I hope I haven't disappointed you," she said as she crossed her arms and scrunched up her face in mock anger.

Despite himself, Jason laughed. "Hmmmm! I will have to think on that one."

Sarah playfully slapped his arm which brought about another round of laughter. "I really have to get back to the docks. There are two ships leaving in a week for America, but neither are going to Mobile. I'm going to see the Alba brothers about deeding over the house and its contents I own here to Long Ju Ju and to find out if they know of any ships going to Mobile. And I want to check with the captain of a ship that was docking when I came here. I won't be back until late."

"It doesn't matter. After that last remark of yours, you'll be sleeping on the floor anyway," she teased as she gave him a hug. She rose and accompanied him to the door.

"The way Miriam kicks the foot of our bed and you snore, that might not be such a bad idea," Jason chuckled. Sarah gave him a playful shake, a quick kiss, turned him around and pushed him out the door. Slowly she went to the window, pulled the white laced curtain to the side, and watched as Jason stepped out into the already darkened streets.

As the inn's maitre d' of the dinning room began to seat newly-arrived guests for the evening meal, Sarah resumed her seat at the dining table she had occupied that morning. She wished Jason could always hide his dark side and present to the world only his dutiful husband and father side. She hoped Makiba would accept their offer. Sarah didn't know if she alone had the strength to aid Jason in America in his fight against the beast.

The mother and daughter entered the dining room and sat. As they unfolded their napkins Melika began the conversation.

"How do you manage the baby and Miriam at the same time? The baby is no problem, but Miriam has enough energy to run three times around the town and still want to leap over all the houses. She is either a strong windstorm or totally passed out. There is nothing in between," Melika remarked, not thinking seriously about a word she said. Sarah merely shook her head and laughed.

The waiter brought a thick chicken stew with coarse brown bread and more tea. Until the end of the meal, conversation purled around the day's shopping adventures and the children. With their appetites sated, once more a pleasant tiredness permeated all the women.

"If I eat one more thing, someone will have to carry me upstairs," Sarah remarked. "It has been a long day. Is there a single merchant in Dahomey we don't know on a first name basis?"

"I don't think so!" Makiba replied, and then without preamble added, "We have discussed your offer."

"And?" Sarah asked, her heart skipping a beat.

"It's hard to reach a decision."

"I understand," Sarah said. "Is there something I can do to help? Any further information you need?"

Makiba said, "No. It's actually quite simple. We still don't trust Jason. He could turn on us in a second, and we would be in a strange land, not knowing anyone or where to go for help. On the other hand, if we stay here, wherever we go our past will haunt us, and we have no future. In short, we don't know." Melika kept her eyes lowered, and Makiba drummed the table with her fingers when the waiter interrupted the conversation with more tea.

After his departure, Sarah poured three cups and said, "You don't have to trust Jason. It seems as if I have had this conversation a little earlier with Jason."

"Jason? You mean he's joining us?" Makiba said with a little threat in her voice.

"No, he just stopped to let me know that he is still looking for a ship to Mobile. Makiba, he had to face you at Ali's, and, sooner or later, you're going to have to face him."

Makiba took a sip of tea from the trembling cup. "I don't know if I can," she forced herself to say.

"Odd! He said the same thing before coming here to Dahomey," Sarah countered as she, too, took a sip. She placed the cup back into the saucer and leaned on the table. "Look, I hope that you trust me, at least. I shall guarantee that he won't turn on you, and I personally will see you through this. I vow this commitment by the vengeance of holy Ifa."

"And if he does turn on us, would you be willing to side with us and leave him?"

Makiba had thrown the gauntlet to Sarah. Sarah sat back as if physically assaulted. She stared hard at the woman across the table. A long silence ensued as Sarah carefully phrased her response.

"Yes! Because then I shall know that I have lost him to the beast," she said in an unfaltering voice.

Still holding eye contact, and after a brief pause, Makiba replied, "I believe you. And because I believe *you*, we'll go."

Sarah gave a sigh of relief but could not contain herself. She rose and embraced each woman. She resumed her seat and began talking as if the tense previous topic of conversation had not transpired. "There is so much to do. We have a wardrobe, but we still have to purchase trunks. Even more important we have to start on English."

"English?" asked Melika.

"That's the language they speak in America. I suppose now's as good a time as any." Then, in English, she said, "Please pass the tea," pointing to the teapot.

Hours later, Sarah leaned lazily against the propped up pillows mending one of Jason's shirts when her husband returned. It was a little after midnight.

"The Aqua brothers showed me the pile of bills and documents that almost covered the top of their desk. Will Dahomey have to shut down and wait for a new supply of wares? With all you spent today, you won't have to do the job of clothes shopping again for the rest of the century," he complained with a chuckle.

"Oh, everything we bought is ours. If you want anything, you'll have to do your own shopping," she replied, as she snapped the thread of a recently turned collar.

He came over to the bed and gave her a kiss and then went to check on the children. Alva had her fist in her mouth, and Miriam's little bed at the foot of theirs presented itself as a pile of linen, demonstrating that, even in sleep, she had energy to spare.

"They will be coming with us," Sarah said without looking up from her work.

"I never doubted it," Jason remarked.

"There's more to it than that." She began to relate the entire conversation to an interested Jason.

"That was smart of you to make that promise," he said approvingly.

Sarah put aside her work and looked at her husband. "Jason, I meant every word I said."

"You mean that you would actually leave me?" he asked incredulously.

"No, Jason. You didn't listen. You are my soulmate. I shall never be anyone else's, but I shall not allow the beast to destroy all of us. I would grieve at losing my husband, but I could not bear to sacrifice my family to the beast even for him. Yes, I would take the children and go, but my heart would always be yours, and I refuse to allow the beast to have the smallest part of it."

Stupefied, Jason began to pace at the foot of the bed. He had never considered the contingency of Sarah leaving him. Women didn't do that. But Sarah was no ordinary woman. What about the children? She said she would take them too? So many things had changed in his life and all too fast. True, to date, his life had become better, but life held no sureties. For the first time in months, Jason felt dismay fed by his old standby--anger. If Sarah thought that little of him, then it was better to let the bi---. Jason paused in his pacing. What in the hell made him think like that? Sarah had warned him to sentinel his feelings against these very thoughts. Resolutely, the nervous man sat on the edge of the bed. "Then I shall have to see to it that I give no cause for any of you to leave," he said quietly.

Sarah laid aside her work, clambered off the bed, placed the finished shirt on the back of a chair, and prepared for sleep. As he watched her undress and climb between the covers, a new feeling took hold of him. He found it difficult to describe. It bypassed his sexual desire for her, ignited the deep love he already felt, and went endlessly beyond even that feeling. Quickly he undressed and crawled in next to her.

Three weeks passed, and still there was no word of a ship bound for Mobile. The women had received their dresses but carefully packed away the most beautiful ones and wore only those created for everyday use. Jason religiously avoided them. He always ate an early breakfast and absented himself for the remainder of the day. Sarah never inquired where he went or what he did. She felt the beast had something to do with his absences, but did not feel a threat to the women or her. Sarah dared not confront him on suspicion alone, but she had lived with the beast long enough she could sense its involvement in their lives. The intuitive woman could only watch and wait.

She appraised Jason's avoidance of Melika and Makiba, and, for the present, they needed to avoid him. Life rebloomed in the two women. They weren't strained around Sarah and accepted her company as a long lost familiar. Sarah responded in kind. They spent their days waiting for news by shopping together for nonsensical things. Once in awhile they returned to the market to barter over some bolt of cloth newly arrived from Europe or the color of some high button shoe.

Even though all purchases technically Sarah made, she would make some excuse to assure they went to the woman who admired the article. Either the cloth didn't look as nice in the sunlight, or the earrings made her face look longer. One way or the other, Melika and Makiba lavished in Sarah's "unwanted" articles and her kindness. Without an official declaration, Melika adopted the role of nanny. She acquired the knack of making Miriam obey. Well, at least once in a while.

To date the mother and daughter were lucky. No one during their shopping sprees recognized the women as employees of Ali. The clientele that frequented the whorehouse mostly remained in the seedier part of the city. The two women knew their anonymous status could not last forever. This fact proved to be prime consideration in their decision to accompany Sarah and Jason.

The women sat at one of the tables in expect the inn, as a busy waitress prepared the dining room for lunch. Alva cooed rhythmically in Malika's arms, while Miriam played tents with the tablecloth. Jason bolted through the front door of the inn and headed directly to his wife. The other two women stiffened in their chairs and lowered their eyes. Miriam crawled from under the table and seized her father by the leg. Without thinking he lifted her into his arms.

"There is a ship leaving day after tomorrow and is making a stop in Mobile. Can you be ready by then?" he asked breathlessly, keeping his back to Sarah's guests.

Sarah gazed at the table's other two occupants who did not move and remained non-committal. The time had arrived. Unfortunately, the future, good or bad, always has a way of becoming today. Apprehensive, Sarah rose and took Miriam. "We'll be ready." Jason required no other confirmation as he pirouetted and retraced his steps out of the inn.

"If you're half as scared as I am, we're all going to have to go change our undergarments," Sarah said only half- jokingly. The other two forced a smile, lunch completely forgotten.

"There isn't much packing to do. We have already done that. Perhaps we should buy some fresh fruit and vegetables to take with us," Malika offered. The other two nodded.

"Oh, and we had better get some extra toys for Miriam, or she'll have all of the sailors jumping overboard," said Sarah, trying to palliate the tense conversation.

All three attempted to assume the air of nonchalance but could not dispel the apprehension that permeated each of them. "Well, I guess we had better get started," Sarah finally said. "I have to go back to the room to change Alva, so I'll meet you downstairs in about twenty minutes." She pushed the chair back.

Each woman present knew it was just an excuse to be alone so all could absorb the shock reality suddenly thrust upon them.

An hour before sunrise on the second day of the tidings, the little band approached the passenger vessel, Sea Dragon. The entire craft, from crow's nest to the voices heard in the open holds, swarmed with activity. Jason, as the only male in the troop, walked ahead up the gangplank followed by Sarah holding Alva in her arms then Makiba and finally Melika with Miriam in tow. A sailor stood to the left of the plank waiting for the passengers to board, so he could load the last of the cargo. As Jason stepped on deck, the sailor grunted and yelled over his shoulder. "Hey, Grant! Come here and look at this. This nigger is moving his whorehouse to America. I hear that black poontang is really good. Maybe if we're real nice to him, he'll give us a free sample."

Before he could continue with his exposition, the sailor was facing up at the crow's nest with Jason on top of the surprised man, flailing fists. Jason felt strong arms pin him as two more sailors grabbed the man beneath him, forcing both contestants into abeyance.

"That's enough of that," screamed a third man.

"That god-damned nigger attacked me," said the confined sailor, attempting to lift his constrained arm to wipe the blood issuing from the corner of his mouth.

"Good! He saved me the trouble. I heard what you said. Now you listen to me, you stupid son-of-a-bitch. This man and his family are paying passengers, and, like all paying passengers, deserve respect. Now I know that word is foreign to you, but after this, I hope you have learned what it means. Now go below, get your things, and get the hell off of my ship," said the man, who obviously had some authority.

"You would take up for a nigger over a white man?" The injured sailor snarled.

"No. But I will take up for a man whose family has just been insulted by an asshole." The man, who hired on as first mate, thumbed over his shoulder. "Now take him below and get him off of this ship before he makes the bilge rats sick."

He then turned toward the sailors watching the altercation. "And any of you who think like this asshole can join him on shore now, because if I find out that any of you has shown any disrespect to our passengers, you'll be docked pay and spend the remainder of the trip in the brig on bread and water. Is that clear?" He yelled.

Heads bobbed like corks on water.

"What in the hell are you standing around for? I want this ship in motion in ten minutes. Fred! Come here!" The order resounded against a chorus of drumming bare feet slapping the deck in a scramble to return to their respective duty, except for the one called Fred who responded to the first mate's summons.

"Take Mr.," he paused and looked at Jason.

"Just Jason," Jason said in return, rubbing his jaw.

"Take Mr. Jason's luggage below, and show the ladies their cabins. Do it now, mister," he yelled.

So quickly did the luggage and the sailor vanish, the passengers thought Fred a magician.

The first mate turned and tipped his hat to Jason. "Sorry for the unpleasant welcome. They really are a good crew, but every once in a while we get a rotten apple. If any of them gives you any trouble, you just tell me. O'Brian's the name. Patrick O'Brian!" The freckled man offered Jason his hand.

He shook Jason's hand vigorously. "Now if you will excuse me, I have a ship to get to sea," and with that he turned, barking orders left and right. To Jason, the way the crew moved reminded him of a herd of antelope attacked by a lioness.

Jason turned to take Sarah's arm and saw that blank look on her face as she took charge of the children. That usually boded trouble. He waited until Makiba and Melika entered their cabin then went into his cabin to face Sarah. His wife busied herself with the arrangement of a cradle and linen for Alva, allowing Miriam to use the top sheet as a headdress. Jason walked over and rested his hand on his wife's shoulder.

"What is it?" he asked.

"What is what?" she countered, as she straightened and gave her husband her full attention.

Jason gave her a sad smile. "I guess we have lived together too long. I can always tell when you are upset over something. Now what is it?" he asked again.

Sarah picked up Miriam, sat on the edge of their bunk, and stowed the playful imp on her lap. "Jason, are we going to have to go through life fighting every time some person decides to make some slur? I don't like it any more than you do, but you don't see me jump on the first person who does that. I don't say we have to tolerate it, but there has to be another way to show up another man's stupidity besides violence. Look how Mr. O'Brian handled the situation. True, he had the authority, but sometimes the words themselves carry their own authority. Beating him up only confirms his belief; it doesn't change it. If a man uses his fists, then use your fists back, but if he is fighting with words, those are the weapons you use. Make your words show that him, and his beliefs, are of the gutter. Do that and you will gain a greater victory than you ever could with your fists?"

She removed the sheet from Miriam's head, picked up both the cloaks from the bed, and went to Jason to put her arms around his waist. "Now let's go get Makiba and Melika and go up on deck to watch the sunrise." She gave his waist a squeeze.

Jason absorbed the rebuke as they walked next door and tapped at the cabin door.

"Come in," responded Makiba's voice.

"No! You two come out. Let's go upstairs and watch the sunrise," came Sarah's response. Soon the little troop scuttled up the hatch and stood close to the port rope railing to stay out of the scurrying sailors' paths. Jason surprised everyone by addressing the group.

"It's time for me to speak. I won't insult you by offering an apology, because what I did was unpardonable. Just remember that I, as well as you, have to live with that fact every day. You may have to live with the shame, but I have to live with the knowledge that I was the one who caused it."

Jason continued, speaking in a low voice that could barely be heard above the shouts coming from the crew. "What I am doing is not atonement, but rather a new path for all of us to take. Some, or all of us, may fail. I can't guarantee you will be better off than staying here. I can't even guarantee that to my family, but the road I was traveling would have definitely destroyed my family, and the road I had forced you to travel led nowhere. Long Ju Ju knew I had to backtrack to America to find the right road. He and my wife also showed me the gateway to that road started with you two, who I believed to be three at the time."

Jason saw agony cross the two women's faces. He turned and stared at the fleeting shoreline in the predawn light. "That, too, is another thing I have to live with. Until you feel secure or ask me to leave, I shall be nearby to help in any way I can. Meantime, I shall be around you as little as possible. Believe me it's just as painful for me to see you as it is for you to see me. For the time being, I think it wise to be civil to one another, but for the most part please deal directly with Sarah. Anything she says is automatically approved by me.

"There is only one other thing. You are going to a new land. Leave this old land and its bitter memories behind. When I was in missionary school as a boy, I was told a story about two women who set out on an unknown journey and were just as unsure of its outcome as you are this moment. They were just as terrified as you, but they went anyway. Your African names will be very strange in America and will be a constant reminder of what I did to you here, so I will ask you to take the names of the two women from the white man's Bible. The oldest was called Naomi, and the younger, Ruth. Would you mind adopting their names?"

"I don't know. What happened to them?" Malika skeptically asked.

“At first, they had a hard, but happy, life. The younger eventually married a rich man, and both had an easy life after that,” he answered.

“Well, how do you like your possible new names?” asked Sarah.

“I don’t know about marrying a rich man, but I like the sound of their names. What do you think, Ruth?” Makiba asked.

“I like it, Naomi.” Both women smiled at Sarah, who nodded approval.

“Now we just have to work on English until we arrive,” Sarah reminded Naomi and Ruth. All turned and stared toward the fiery red tongue that had just appeared over the horizon.

The ship departed the delta and headed for the open seas, as the figures of four adults and two children briefly watched the flaming orb vaulting above the African shoreline in pursuit of the tiny vessel.

NAT

1873

CHAPTER XII

FANGS

Ever since Jason left on what he termed as business, a distraught Sarah paced the hotel room at The Beacon. Some unknown dark design reclaimed her husband. She reiterated to her secretive spouse, she would execute her promise to Naomi and Ruth to the letter if circumstance demanded it. Jason assured her his business had nothing to do with her or the other women. This affair concerned him alone and he refused to deny the beast's involvement or reveal what it entailed. His wife warned him that whatever he planned could possibly affect future decisions in the beast's attempt to regain control. Sarah became aware that if her husband continued down the same old path of the panther eventually the children and she would fall victims along the way. Fear permeated her very essence. She became aware some intrigue from her husband's past overruled his present effort to vanquish the beast. Sarah languished over the fact that Jason now accompanied the beast and not reform his family needed. She felt helpless. Before leaving for the afternoon he told her they would depart for Whispering Willows by Friday of the current week.

Sarah paused by Alva's crib. The cuddly human doll had rolled over on her stomach. So peacefully did the tot sleep that if Sarah herself had not placed her daughter on her back the loving mother would never have known the child had moved a tendon? The covers resembled a freshly made bed. Sarah then checked on Miriam who hugged Jason's pillow. Even in sleep

Miriam wore a smile on her face. Sarah swore her capricious daughter spent sleeping hours devising devilment for her waking hours. Lovingly the caring mother leaned over and kissed both children on the forehead. Alva did not move, but even in sleep Miriam's arms automatically went into the "pick me up" mode. Any attempt by Sarah to visualize Miriam's future husband other than the god of winds resulted in futility. The little vixen snuggled deeper into her father's pillow as Sarah turned toward the large overstuffed chair by the window on the left side of the bed. Her body ached as she plopped into the chair.

She pulled aside the white-laced curtain and stared at the saloon occupying the opposite corner of the street which housed the recent arrivals from Africa. Jason had gone there. He had frequented the bar daily for hours since the first day they disembarked the ship in Mobile over three days ago. Compared to the time spent in the saloon Sarah considered it odd that he always came back completely sober with only the slightest trace of beer on his breath. Sarah had inquired from the maids at the hotel the saloon's reputation. Factoring the white man's attitude toward blacks she worried about a black man drinking with white men. She feared a repeat of the boarding incident that occurred on the Sea Dragon. The staff related the tavern's dubious reputation that included numerous confrontations among its patrons of all races, some resulting in death. Anyone with money to buy the watered drinks whether white, black, or from another planet, could patronize the seedy establishment. She had expressed her concern to Jason, but he dismissed the information as woman's gossip and assured her of perfect safe attendance with his business drinking companions. Coupled with his secretiveness, Jason's restlessness only confirmed her suspicion of the beast's involvement. Her assumption that the beast's conspiracy began during their wait in Dahomey became validated by the panther's instant return on their arrival in Mobile. Jason plotted some infamous deed that would produce only pain and suffering during their extended stay in a city he detested. Sarah allowed the curtain to shut, closed her eyes, rested her head against the back of the chair and traced her current melancholy back to the day they arrived in Mobile.

That fateful day a travel weary but expectant group had sauntered down the gangplank onto the wharf in the port city. Jason quickly viewed the changes in the waterfront since years ago he had stood on the same levee awaiting transportation to hell. Though night concealed much detail, certain landmarks had burned into the ex-slave's memory.

Proclaiming world wide fame at their ability to weather all Yankee invasions until the very end of the war, the gray forts stood as ominous guardians to the harbor. The quay bustled like any other port in America or foreign country but the view beyond the waterfront displayed the most change. A new city rose amid the old. Everywhere Jason looked open wooden roof beams prayed toward the overcast sky. His limited knowledge of Mobile's geography traced a trail from the waterfront to Duval Street and from Duval Street north to exit the city all under the cover of night. Jason particularly noted the few white faces barking orders to the laboring blacks on the docks. In that particular quarter of labor and management little had changed. Jason made a mental note. When he saw Hunter he would attempt to interest him in the commodities' market and the possibility of more blacks in management. As he stared at the busy docks he became convinced that Hunter could make a lot of money by expanding his business to Mobile. Jason would resume his old position of bookkeeper and remain in the background with the title of silent partner. Sean would present no problem and agree to anything Mr. Wilkerson desired if large amounts of money resulted.

After his experience as a captive with other poor souls at Duval Street, Jason had a personal dislike for Mobile and loathed transacting any business in this city. If Hunter approved the business expansion to the import/export business then Jason's possible future boss in this venture would have to conclude all affairs in Mobile himself. Jason would only ply his bookkeeping expertise and just bank his share of the profits in the Birmingham bank he established under the advice given by Hunter which he almost depleted when he left for Africa. Hunter could supply the wheeling and dealing end of the business while Sean supplied the white skin necessary for southern entrepreneurs. Surveying his current surroundings from the dock only infused grotesque memories and affirmed Jason in his resolve to have nothing to do with Mobile after he completed his current business in that city.

"Are we going to spend the rest of the day on the wharf?" Sarah impatiently chided. Ruth and Naomi hid a grin behind their hands when Jason startled at the interruption of his train of thought while stacking of the luggage. On the voyage to Mobile Naomi and Ruth had mastered the basic necessities of the English language rather well as far as asking for food, drink, and a little general conversation. Even Miriam shocked Sarah with her ability to rapidly absorb the language in baby talk by mimicking the lower tones of the English language as compared to the higher pitch of Swahili. The women had forsworn Swahili on the crossing. Despite their heavy accent this immersion forced the new students to become fairly proficient in the language. However, the women's understanding became greater than their ability to communicate verbally in English. This ardent desire to master the language sometimes proved embarrassing to Sarah when her curious traveling companions made inquiries of certain colorful phrases used by the sailors.

In baby talk, while pointing at a stevedore passing with a bunch of ripe bananas on his shoulder, Miriam had complained to her father of hunger.

He responded by swinging the little girl up into his arms, "Daddy's going to find us a place to stay and then come back and get you so that we all can get something good to eat. OK?" Her giggle assured him she could stave off hunger for that period of time. Jason sat his daughter back down on the gray boards of the pier and turned to give instructions to a nearby sailor concerning their luggage. Miriam immediately toddled after a startled seagull and probably would have wound up in the harbor had not a vigilant Ruth grabbed her arm and pulled her back. After three weeks of chasing the little scamp around the ship, Ruth could sense the impetuous enchantress' impending antics most of the time, not that the self-appointed nanny could do anything about them. Alva, always entertained by Miriam's mischief, clapped her hands and giggled at the capture of her older sister.

"Now you stop that. You're just encouraging her," Ruth chastised while tickling the baby's tummy. This brought new squeals of laughter as Miriam stretched to grab another seagull that with one eye cocked looked quizzically at the little girl.

"For heaven's sake hurry up. She'll start a riot before we even get settled in," Sarah said to Jason as she handed Alva to Ruth and scooped the little girl into her arms to prevent further explorations.

"I won't be gone more than an hour. If you have any trouble, call for the first mate. He's seeing about unloading the cargo," cautioned Jason. Sarah had nodded assent while wrestling with the little tornado.

Jason disappeared into the milling crowd on the wharf. The three women sat on their clothing trunks that the crew had unloaded from their cabins. Each had tried to make chitchat to allay the disquiet brought about by a missing male figure that would have staved off so many strange and threatening male faces eyeing them. What seemed an eternity to the nervous women in reality totaled only forty minutes before Jason returned with a buckboard driven by a large black man grinning from ear to ear despite showing the absence of four upper front teeth.

"This is Joe. I'm sorry about the wagon, but it was the only thing I could find on such short notice," Jason apologized as he and Joe alit from the buckboard and began to swing the heavy trunks on the back of the vehicle.

"That's all right. I'm so tired after wrestling with this one," Sarah said gently, shaking Miriam's left shoulder and giving the tot a kiss, "that I could ride a cheetah to where we're going."

"Here. Let me take her," Jason offered after he and Joe secured the last trunk. African men usually avoided helping with child care but Jason's deep love for his daughter overrode that taboo, especially after his input into her birth. Unlike the other members of the company, Miriam immediately obeyed every command of her father without rancor. After Ruth returned Alva to Sarah two chubby little arms wrapped around her neck as Joe helped Naomi and Ruth onto the back of the buckboard. Naomi seemed quite surprised at the ease with which Joe had swung her up. After the ladies assured him their places in the vehicle would not cause them to fall off Joe then proceeded to the driver's seat and took hold of the reins. Sarah clambered up next to Joe with Alva tightly secured in her arms followed by Jason, who restrained Miriam after her attempt to ride bareback on one of the hitched horses and then sat quietly in her father's lap.

The cavalcade preceded eight blocks to one of the newer inns built to accommodate the sudden influx of seamen of various nationalities now Mobile had resumed its role as an active seaport of trade. The Beacon proved one of few hotels in Mobile that provided integrated residencies for their rooms. Because of the race factor construction in the fashionable part of the city became non-optional. The Beacon did offer a safe harbor in a rowdy part of town by having four burly bellboys on each shift just in case any ruckus occurred at the inn. The rooms, though small, provided all necessary comforts to transients. Most of the guests relying on busy shipping manifests rarely stayed more than three days but the proprietor enforced strict rules against hourly rentals and female room visiting. Joe assisted Jason with the trunks up a flight of stairs and the remainder of the luggage soon followed. As Jason and Joe lifted the first trunk off of the wagon he watched Miriam take off after the resident hound dog lounging on the veranda who by instinct dove for the comforting protection under the inn's porch. Ruth barely had time to secure an ankle of the little huntress preventing the hound's wrath to come into play due to the unwarranted attack by a squealing human. Jason grinned at Ruth. Without a doubt he had the better part of the assignment by handling the heavy trunks.

Naomi and Ruth retired to their room and collapsed across the clean brass bed unlike the unfortunate Sarah who had resumed responsibility of the whirling dervish, Miriam. Already the little imp had tilted the wash basin and pitcher at a very precarious angle much to the delight of the giggling Alva securely resting in her mother's arm. Sarah had rescued the endangered wash basin, plopped Miriam down on the bed, and placed Alva in the middle of the bed, until the crib arrived.

"Jason," Sarah entreated, "You keep her busy for a while. I'm going to try and get Alva to take a nap first and then it's going to be our little hurricane's turn," Sarah said turning down the covers on one side of the bed.

After a silent pause, in a low voice Jason said, "I would, sweetheart, but I have to go out for awhile. There is something

I have to do before supper. Why don't you take everybody downstairs for lunch and have one of the housekeepers watch the children?"

"Where are you going, Jason?" Sarah had asked in a strained voice sensing something amiss.

Suddenly his eyes became hooded and his jaw stiffened. "There are a couple of people I have to see."

"I thought that you didn't know anyone here in Mobile," Sarah stated suspiciously.

"I don't. There's an old friend of the Aqua brothers I have to look up," he replied. It was the tone of her husband's voice that had alerted her to something clandestine.

"Jason! Don't do it!" she had whispered in alarm.

"Do what? I haven't done anything," he had replied, too innocently.

Sarah remained silent while the babies gently wrestled each other on the bed. She stared long and hard into the hooded eyes. He simply broke eye contact and exited the room.

That confrontation had occurred last Friday. Sarah sighed and rose from the chair. Nightly since then Jason visited the corner bar the Aqua brothers had recommended for whatever those secretive needs required. He absented himself from Sarah most of the day and offered Sarah the lame excuse of avoiding Ruth and Naomi. Sarah became well aware that the panther plotted something malevolent.

A gentle knock interrupted Sarah's thoughts. Ruth peeked around the edge of the door and said, "Mother will be here in just a minute. She's trying on a new dress." Sarah held her index finger to her lips and pointed to the two sleeping children and whispered, "If you need anything I'll be in the dining room. Are you sure you don't want to join us? I can get one of the houseboys to watch the children."

"It's my fault I'm not hungry. I shouldn't have eaten all of the fruit that we bought at the market today but it was so delicious I just couldn't stop. You and mother go ahead and enjoy your supper. We'll be all right." With a dismissive wave of her hand Ruth entered the room and sat in a chair she placed beside of the bed.

Naomi and Sarah descended the steep staircase which emptied into the long hall leading to the reception desk on their left. A double door folded back faced the reception desk inviting any passersby to enter and taste the results of some of the delightful aromas exuding from the immaculate kitchen directly in back of a formal dinning room with well set up tables.

Sarah looked at Naomi with a painted smile as both women sat. Before Sarah's companion could make any inquires as to Sarah's tenseness, a waiter wearing a snow white apron appeared with menus. Naomi looked toward Sarah for help in meal selection. She had semi-mastered speaking some English but could not read it. Releasing her melancholy Sarah assisted the woman in the choice of food. Both decided to try a dish foreign to them. With the order given and the menus collected, the waiter scurried off to the kitchen to place the order. The table became silent. Sarah would tell her friend the reason for her doldrums in her own good time. Within minutes, the bustling waiter returned with heaping dishes of shrimp gumbo. From the first taste of the delectable selection the ladies' eyebrows went up and a moan of delight came from both. Conversation revolved around the delicious dish for the next half hour.

Dessert of pecan pie served with a pot of hot tea completed the scrumptious meal. The time now seemed appropriate for Sarah to reveal her concern. "I'm scared!" Sarah stopped mid-sip from her cup of tea and pushed her pie untouched to the side. "The beast is back," she said.

Naomi stiffened. "No! No! It doesn't concern either of you," Sarah reassured the alarmed woman as Naomi's facial muscles tightened. "Something is going on and Jason is not telling me. I can feel the wall between us. We were supposed to go directly to someplace by the name Whispering Willows. There is no reason for us to stay longer than overnight here but he has rented our rooms by the week. He says he has to see a friend of the Aqua brothers but I believe it's more than that." Naomi parodied her benefactress' act of reassurance by reaching across the table to place her hand over Sarah's. The reverse physical touch produced a wave of compassion for the woman who had always given support and now needed to receive some back.

Sarah looked sternly at Naomi. Hard resolve shot from her eyes. "I intend to keep my promise to you. If what he is doing hurts you in any way I shall leave him. I'll just have to wait and hope it isn't going to destroy everything we've built in our marriage." Since she gave the vow back in Dahomey Sarah never alluded to her promise given to her new-found confidants again, until now. Naomi became tense as she realized that her friend would truly enact this abhorrent but necessary choice and how that dreadful decision emotionally affected their patroness.

"We'll take the children over to our room for tonight so that you and Jason can talk. If you need us we'll be just next door," said Naomi. Sarah nodded her appreciation as Naomi finished her dessert and tea, rose and left the room. The despondent woman remained twirling a fork in a hardly touched piece of pecan pie and taking a bite now and then until the dining room had almost emptied. With a sigh of resignation Sarah rose and returned to her room. Still Jason had not made an appearance. No! Not Jason. The beast. Tears welled in her eyes as Sarah choked out her prayer, "Any god who will listen, how may I pull those fangs?"

CHAPTER XIII

VICTIM

For three days prior to the newly arrived troop's scheduled departure to Whispering Willows

Jason sat alone at the bar directly across the street from the inn where his family and his adopted family resided. Now, his beer had long gone flat as he unconsciously swirled the pale beverage resting on the table in front of him. Mentally, he reviewed the afternoon.

After leaving a much saddened and suspicious Sarah, he spent the entire day in Bailey's Bar. He found the whereabouts and sent for Victor Collins, an attorney well recommended by the Aqua brothers and noted for getting things done---for a price. The lure of three bars of gold brought Collins on the run as soon as the judge at the local courthouse ruled in favor of his client and released the wily lawyer from the courtroom.

Collins slunk past the swinging doors of the bar and leaned against the nearly empty bar. He stared at the pendulum clock behind the bar whose hands registered two-fifteen and checked the bar time against his pocket watch. The sun would descend much further into the west before the dock workers would start their evening revelry. His eyes swept the empty tables come evening, would fill with some of the rowdiest and questionable customers Mobile had to offer. At last, Collin's eyes locked on the sole occupant of a table in the rear of the barroom, who, with a wave of his hand, invited the new arrival to join him. Collins shifting eyes evaluated everything around him as he heeded the invitation.

"Mr. Jason?" Jason nodded. "I'm Victor Collins. Your note said you had urgent need of my services," he said as he placed his bowler on the table.

"May we have two beers?" Jason shouted to the bartender who was already headed for the tapped barrel. Jason shoved his flat beer to the side. Sitting across the table from his new client, Collins had a difficult time discovering a comfortable sitting position while trying to decipher whether or not a black man could afford his fee. Despite his obvious discomfiture, he asked, "What can I do for you? The letter of recommendation from the Aqua brothers that came with your note instructed me to help in any way that I could."

"I want you to purchase a piece of property here in Mobile." Jason's forthright response put the cunning barrister at ease. Considering the Machiavellian advocate had already received three bars of gold for his legal service, the request proved menial. Any first year law student could complete that assignment in his sleep. Collins felt relieved, especially after the urgency implied in the note and letter.

"Is the said property up for sale?" Collins asked, shifting his position for the fourth time.

"It doesn't matter. Offer the owner fifteen thousand dollars in gold. I don't care what reason you give him for the sale. That's up to you, but I want that property. If you can complete the deal within two days, you will have earned an additional two bars of gold." Jason watched Collin's eyes glimmer with greed. "Here is the address." Jason propelled a piece of paper across the beer-stained table.

Collins unfolded the crinkled piece of paper and read, "137 Duval Street. Hummm! That's rather a high price to pay for real estate in that part of town."

"It's my money," the prospective buyer growled. "There's only one stipulation," Jason added. Collins became more circumspect. He envisioned his gold changed to brass as he gave a shiver and stared into the hooded eyes across from him. "The deal must be signed here. I want to meet the owner personally."

"For that amount of money, I could bring the mayor along to witness the deal, but I still say that's a steep price to pay for real estate in that part of town." Collins gulped the last of his beer and rose to leave so that he could draw up the bill of sale that night.

"Another thing," Jason injected. Collins paused but could not guess the latest impediment to the deal. "John Aqua told me you know a Captain Boggs." Collins clearly started at that statement.

"You don't want anything to do with the likes of him," Collins hissed.

"Oh, but I do!" Jason retorted with a sardonic smile, "Have him meet me here in about an hour."

The counselor began wringing his hands. "I don't know if I can find him that soon. He's not the easiest man to locate considering his---" Collins paused searching for the correct phrase, "line of work."

Never taking his hooded eyes off of Collins, Jason reached into his coat pocket and produced a shiny bar of gold. He neatly placed it in the center of the table. After tapping the bar with his right index finger, he shoved it across the table toward Collins. "In one hour!" he repeated.

The gold bar melted into some hidden pocket on Collins' person. Jason received a nod as rejoinder. Jason became the lone occupant of the table who glared back and forth at two empty mugs, a mug of flat beer, a vacant chair, and swinging barroom doors leading to the darkening street and his inn.

Two-and-a-half hours elapsed, still no Boggs. Jason had no doubt Collins had located and delivered his message in the required time span. Boggs presumed his delay would implant the importance of his position in bargaining and create owed chip with his future client if Jason had further need of the service Boggs provided. The saloon began to fill as the day crew departed from the levee and paused for one cold one before supper. Jason's attention centered on a city employee igniting a gaslight just outside of bar. If necessary, Jason resolved to remain in attendance for Captain Boggs until closing.

Another hour elapsed before the swinging doors flew open and a bearded, barrel-chest man entered accompanied by two equally scurrilous-looking individuals. All heads diverted to the new arrivals and gave the new customers three spaces as well as an additional three empty spaces at the end of the bar. The middle man locked eyes with Jason and headed directly toward him while the other two huddled closer to order a drink at a now vacated end of the bar.

The man leaned on the back of the chair occupied earlier by Collins. "You Jason?" he asked in a raspy voice. Jason nodded. "Victor Collins said you wanted to see me. Well here I am," Boggs said in a threatening tone. The intimidation had no effect on Jason.

"Allow me to buy you a beer, Captain Boggs," Jason offered in his most amiable voice.

"Rum!" Boggs snapped, hoping again to intimidate.

"Rum it is," said Jason leaning back from the table and waving his arm to get the bartender's attention as Boggs sat. "A glass of rum for my friend and another beer for me," Jason bellowed. The bartender delivered the requested drinks and departed fast enough to pass a bolt of lightening. Jason reached into his pocket and removed yet another gold bar. Boggs' eyes became riveted on the shiny object. Jason shoved it across the table toward him.

"That's for keeping the appointment and listening to my business deal. If you accept the proposal I'm about to make there will be another three just like it when the proposal is complete." Boggs pocketed the gold bar and sanctioned Jason to continue.

"I'm about to close a real estate deal right here in this bar. I want you to keep in touch with Mr. Collins. After the deal is closed, I want you to pick up a package for me."

"A package?" Boggs asked suspiciously as he sipped his rum.

"Yes! John Aqua said you were very good at picking up packages and delivering them," Jason smiled ambiguously. "You come highly recommended."

"And just where do you want this—" Boggs paused smiled, emptied the glass of rum and said, "package delivered?" Boggs relaxed more now Jason made reference to John Aqua.

Jason grinned and realized that Boggs understood perfectly what he cryptically asked. "Bartender, another round for my friend here," Jason yelled at the barkeep. "Its destination is of no interest to me. You may leave it on any pier. I don't care. Just make sure that it is delivered far from Mobile as possible. There will be a considerable amount of money attached to that package. I don't want a single penny stolen. Make damned sure that instruction is carried out to the letter." Jason took a long drought from his mug and cleared the white foam from his mouth.

"I know a couple of mates that will remove the money and put it back when the trip is over. I can trust them. And just when will this package be ready for shipment? I have to find the proper vessel on which to ship it," grinned Boggs while sipping on his second glass of rum.

"In two days. Check with Collins as to the time and place. I shall leave your gold with Collins. He'll be instructed to give it to you when the package is on its way. Is that fair enough?" Boggs nodded. "Good! Then we have a deal." Jason offered his hand to Boggs who smiled, nodded, squinted one eye, and vigorously pumped Jason's hand.

Boggs gulped the remainder of the rum, pushed the chair back, and, with a final tip of his hat, headed for the swinging doors, followed by his two cronies who abandoned their half-filled mugs on the bar.

Jason had returned to the inn after meeting with Collins and Boggs to find Sarah sitting alone in the dark room. "Where are the children?" he asked.

"They're spending the night with Naomi and Ruth." Sarah paused for a moment. "You didn't come back for supper. Have you eaten?" she asked stoically.

"I'm really not hungry. My business took longer than I thought," he replied.

"What business Jason?" she asked gently.

"I really can't discuss it at this time. We'll be heading for Whispering Willows by Friday," he remarked, trying to change the subject.

Sarah did not become sidetracked but became austere. "If you do anything to hurt or disgrace Naomi and Ruth I shall keep my pledge. Even if I am in a foreign land, I cannot live with the beast I see before me. I don't know what you're up to but I see that one day you will have to make a choice, your family or the beast."

"Sarah, I---," he started to explain, but she had already turned her back on him and started preparing for bed. Jason leapt across the room, wrenched her by her right wrist, and spun her toward him. He looked into blank eyes that slowly lowered to the restraining hand.

Stoically Sarah said, "Tell the panther to release my wrist, Jason."

As if he seized a hot coal from a blacksmith's billows, Jason released her arm and backed away. "I'm sorry, Sarah." She stared at him a moment more, rubbing the wrist he had grabbed, and then continued preparing for sleep. Without further discussion, Sarah crawled between the clean linen and left room enough for Jason to come to bed but the bed did not possess the welcoming warmth it had in the past.

Why did he feel so dirty, he asked himself? Instead of following Sarah to bed he sat in the adjacent chair, staring out the window at the dusty street below. He must have dosed because an assaulting beam of sunlight invaded his shut eyelids to announce morning had arrived. He awoke with a start and immediately glanced toward the now empty bed. Ignoring his dishevelment, he fought to control the panic that consumed him as ran down the stairs to the front desk. The clerk on duty ceased separating the morning mail when Jason breathlessly asked, "Have you seen my wife?"

"Oh! She, the other two ladies, and the children had an early breakfast. They wanted to get some shopping done before it got too hot," the clerk replied, shoving another letter into a pigeonhole with the number 18 embossed in brass below it. Jason let out a sigh of relief. He left the front desk still covered in goose bumps and ascended the stairs to his room to clean up and put on fresh clothes.

The next two days cloned the previous one. Sarah remained empty to him. Courteous and motherly to the children, indulgent toward Naomi and Ruth, she remained formal and distant to Jason. Naomi and Ruth shunned him like plague, not that they ever demonstrated doting fondness toward him. Twice he reconsidered his course of action, but persuaded himself that his investment progressed beyond the point of no return. From somewhere far in the back of his mind came a gentle voice reminding him, "The worst sin of all is to lie to yourself. This may be stopped at any time." Like a dead leaf in an October wind the beast exited from his mind.

Jason encouraged the women to shop and sightsee. They complied without enthusiasm. On the third day, Jason received word from Collins he had completed the sale. The transaction required only the buyer's and seller's signatures.

Jason engaged the table in the back if Bailey's bar that he had occupied the first night. He borrowed the bartender's ink well and ink pen to complete the transaction about to take place. Jason had assiduously avoided the women during the past two days, except at night when he shared the same sleeping quarters with a cold unresponsive Sarah. It reminded him of their first meeting at the Masai village in Africa. Any sex with his wife at this time would have constituted a violation, an event he devoutly wished to avoid. He had overstepped his limits when he grabbed Sarah's wrist and promised himself he would not repeat any such attack or molest her in any way. She would have relinquished her body to him without any emotion which would have reproduced the agony of the past he had sustained before meeting Sarah. His wife said nothing when he crawled into bed next to her, but declined to offer any affection. Jason had prepared himself to accept a rebuff, but not apathy, which hurt worse than anger and he therefore avoided touching her even for a kiss. As if she possessed some internal alarm clock, Jason always found the bed and room vacant when he awoke.

His mind snapped back to the present as Collins came through the swinging doors, attended by a bald-headed, medium sized man with skin like hundred year old weather beaten leather and wearing a threadbare jacket a size too large. Both men approached Jason's table with deceitful grins. Collins kept glancing around. A few men dawdled at the bar before heading toward their respective homes or some clandestine affair for the evening. Only barflies begging a drink, or procrastinating husbands avoiding henpecking shrewish wives remained.

"Mr. Jason, this is Mr. Braxton, previous owner of the property that you have just purchased," Collins graciously commented, all the while circling the brim of his bowler through his hands.

Braxton extended his hand. Jason limply offered his in exchange. "My God!" Jason thought, "He doesn't even recognize me. I guess there were so many. Besides, all black men look alike to men of his caliber." Jason smiled back. "Allow me to buy you gentlemen a drink. Bartender! Bring over a bottle of your finest whisky," Jason called joyfully. Magically, three glasses and a brown bottle appeared on the table. Jason paid the barkeeper and poured a round to offer a toast. "To the sale." Three glasses clinked and the ten-year-old Irish whisky disappeared, supervened by sighs of satisfaction. As Jason poured the second round, the bar doors swung open, and three men went to the end of the bar. The sole customer at that end sauntered to the other end.

"Would you like to read the bill of sale?" Collins offered Jason the written documents while sipping his newly filled glass.

"No! No! That's not necessary. I'm quite sure that everything is in order." Jason turned to Braxton. "Have you read the terms, and are they acceptable to you?"

"Oh yes! Mr. Collins already has deposited the agreed amount of gold in my safe deposit box at home. I now have enough money to move to a better part of town. Where do I sign?" said Braxton anxiously, lest Jason have a change of heart.

"Here! Here! And here!" Collins replied pointing out three blank spaces. After shaking off some excess black ink back into the inkwell he offered the pen to the anxious seller.

Braxton's hand became a blur as the pen flew across the assigned blank spaces on the pages. Braxton then passed the pen to Jason with his right hand and shoved the legal documents toward the new proprietor with his left. Jason paused a moment and stared at the previous owner of 137 Duval. Braxton stiffened.

Had Jason reservations concerning the sale? Would he demand the return of the money? Suddenly Jason smiled, lowered his eyes, and scrawled five letters in the assigned spaces.

"Done!" shouted Collins, clapping Braxton on the back as he smiled across the table at Jason. "You are now proud owner of 137 Duval Street, Mobile, Alabama." Jason merely nodded.

Braxton downed the last of his whiskey and stood. "Well! I had better be getting back. I'll be out by the end of the week. Will that be all right?"

"Take all of the time you need," Jason replied, sitting back in his chair, tapping his fingertips together.

"Would you like to walk a ways with me, Mr. Collins?" Braxton invited.

"I have some further business to discuss with Mr. Collins. You understand," Jason responded to the overture that Collins never had the opportunity to reply. Jason never allowed the Cheshire-cat grin to leave his face.

Braxton nodded, once more displaying teeth that could have passed off as well seasoned white piano keys. "Of course. Then I'll bid you gentlemen a good evening." He felt the inner pocket of his jacket once more to appease himself that his copy of the deal still resided there. After another nod, the former slaver turned and exited the bar. He paid no notice of two men who followed him out. The third headed for Jason's table.

Captain Boggs sat down uninvited and poured whiskey into Braxton's empty glass. He pretended to study the light refraction in the glass as he said, "In four hours, your package will be on its way to Australia. Is that good enough?"

"Perfect. Make sure that his strong box goes with him. He'll need that to start a new life which is better than the choice he gave me. Tomorrow, after the ship has sailed give Captain Boggs these three bars of gold, "Jason added with a lot of bitterness as he tossed the promised payment of the notorious sailor toward Collins.

Captain Boggs downed the whiskey. Jason smiled and winked as Captain Boggs poured another drink, stood, tossed it down, tipped his hat at the two sitting men, and strode out the door to assure his cronies had completed their assignment. Collins gave a shiver despite the warmth of the bar.

Jason broke the silence. "Now as to my recent purchase. I want you to make arrangements to have the house torn down. Sell all of its contents, and you may keep the profit."

Delighted at this unexpected windfall, Collins rubbed his hands together and said, "A wise decision. As to the house, it was just about to collapse anyway. I know a very good construction company here that will build anything you wish at a reasonable price," Collins offered.

"I want nothing built on that site," Jason replied.

"Nothing?" asked an astonished Collins.

"Nothing," Jason affirmed. Collins leaned back in his chair. "For as long as I own that property, I want nothing built on it," Jason further ordered.

"But empty lots have a way of becoming trash heaps," an astonished Collins argued.

"That particular lot always has been. Now the people of Mobile can see it for what it really was." Jason finished his drink and rose to leave. He threw another gold bar toward Collins. "That's to cover the expense for the demolition. Leave the rubble on the lot. Years from now, when the people of this fair city brag about their forts, let them look at 137 Duval and remember that history, too."

A stunned Collins offered no verbal reply. He quickly poured himself another drink and downed it with one quick jerk of his arm.

"Take the bottle with you. It's paid for, and you seem to need a couple more. Please, be my guest," grinned Jason. He turned and exited through the door, crossed the street, and entered the inn.

CHAPTER XIV

PATHS

When Jason walked through the door of their hotel room, Sarah sat on the bed combing Miriam's hair. Sarah paused only momentarily to restrain Miriam from leaping from the bed with the comb still in her hair in order to get to her father. Nervously, she checked to see if Miriam's rambunctious behavior had awakened her sister sleeping in her cradle.

Jason sat on the overstuffed chair and, to his daughter's delight, assumed his wife's chore. "My business here is over. We'll be leaving for Whispering Willows on Friday. You still have one day to do some shopping," he commented hoping to break the ice.

"Have you seen about transportation?" Sarah asked, keeping her tone normal so as not to alarm Miriam of any tension between her parents.

"Joe seemed quite willing to part with his buckboard for a reasonable price. I know it will be a rough ride, but it's certainly large enough to hold us and all our things, except for a certain girl I'm thinking about leaving behind," he said tapping his squirming daughter on the head with the comb he removed which resulted in a delightful squeal and placement of a kiss on her father's cheek.

"Jason, please don't wake the baby! She's been cranky all day, and I just got her to sleep. I think she is beginning to teethe.

Have you had anything to eat?" Jason shook his head. "Give Miriam back to me or she won't go to sleep for a week." Sarah requisitioned the child.

Sarah finished undressing the tyke and helped her between the sheets.

"We have time for a late dinner. I didn't think you had eaten anything so I've asked Ruth to watch the children while we eat. God! I don't know what I would do without her," Sarah commented to no one in particular. Sarah rose from the bed and went next door to get the baby sitter.

On entering the room the women saw two large brown eyes peek over the covers as Sarah said; "Now you go right to sleep."

Miriam teased by squeezing her eyes tight, pretending to sleep.

"We won't be too late," Sarah said as she stood in the hallway awaiting Jason.

"Take your time. If she gives me any trouble, I'll feed her to the first wild animal I see pass by," Ruth said in a very serious voice as she sat in the chair. Immediately, a soft squeal came from the bed, and the little felon threw-back the covers and climbed into Ruth's lap, while Alva continued the sleep of the innocent. Sarah turned back into the doorway, but Ruth shook her head and waved Sarah out with her left hand, as her right hand went around Miriam's waist.

Jason and Sarah chose a table near the window that faced the bar across the street Jason had left not an hour ago. Only two other couples occupied the dining room at this late hour. More quickly than a genie from a bottle, a waiter appeared at their table with the menus and remained standing at the newly occupied table. In all probability attending to Jason and Sarah would conclude his tour of duty for the day. Anxiously, he lingered with pencil poised as they scrutinized the menu.

"I'm going to have the seafood gumbo. I had the same thing last night but I can't seem to get enough of it," Sarah said in a buoyant voice. A stranger could not have detected a rift between her and her husband.

"I'll have the same," Jason said pleasantly. The waiter vanished through the swinging doors to the kitchen. Conversation stalemated until the harried waiter returned with heaping plates of food and placed them before the latecomers. "Will there be anything else?" he asked, nervously wiping his hands in his apron.

"Not right now, thank you," Jason replied, picking up his fork. The waiter retreated through the doors again to persevere in the kitchen cleanup.

"I really don't know which is better, the good food or the beautiful woman I'm privileged to dine with," Jason said, attempting to keep the conversation light.

"It's a pleasure to have my husband back," Sarah replied, but, after a lull added, "I hope he tells me what the beast has done."

Jason returned a scallop to the dish and swirled it in the rich, brown gravy as he mentally concocted some innocuous response. He soon discarded that idiocy as he tasted the delicious food. He faced Sarah. Nothing but the truth would suffice. Besides, his plans had been finalized. Nothing could change them now. He allowed the ensuing silence to continue wishing Sarah would introduce another topic but she seemed intent on her meal. At long last he surrendered to her request. Slowly he told her of being held captive in the cellar of 137 Duval by a man called Braxton, who sold him into slavery to Hunter. He swore revenge then on the house and its owner. He proceeded to recount the episodes of the past three days. During the entire time, Sarah kept her eyes on the food and offered no critique. Only when he came to the part of his story about having Braxton shanghaied to Australia, did Sarah push her almost empty plate away and looked him in the eyes. Jason became mute.

Sarah trifled with the rim of her water glass, producing a bell-like sound. "I see that the beast has had a grand time. No wonder you didn't want to discuss this before now. Doesn't that sound a lot like what happened to you in Ilorin?" Sarah paused. "The panther is very clever. To help regain control it is using the same old tricks of the past that worked. Only this time it is proving how nice it can be by only kidnapping and shipping a man to an unknown land with people rather than isolating him at an oasis." Jason knew her too well. He fidgeted in his chair as he waited for the other shoe to fall.

"Not too long ago, I remember a man telling me about being kidnapped and sold into slavery. The person who did that heinous act paid with his life rather than live with the additional horror committed by you on his family, but that was the good part. Innocent people near that person had to pay an even higher price of lifelong shame that was created by you. Vengeance rarely has the desired end result. Is that what you wish for Miriam, Alva and myself if any of us cross the beast in any way?"

"Braxton has no idea that I'm involved. Everyone in Mobile knows about Boggs but can't prove it. He's just one more of Boggs's victims," Jason rationalized.

"Boggs' victim with that amount of money with him? Rationalization is the key to your dark side's decisions. It doesn't matter whether or not Braxton knows of your involvement. You know. When you grabbed my wrist last night what did you intend to do? Beat me? Toss me on the floor? If I defy your panther again are you going to ship me to China? Your lesson from the beast is well taken," Sarah said quietly. "Since this is going to be your choice in life maybe I should join you. Perhaps I should backhand you here in public for molesting me last night or, better still make you sleep in the cattle yard as you once did to me. But why stop my retribution there? While I'm enforcing my vengeance maybe I should go upstairs and yell loudly in Alva's ear all night as she has done to me in the past. Oh yes, and why not destroy some of Miriam's precious belongings to get even for all of the things of mine she has destroyed. Yes, that is the solution to everything isn't it, just destroy anything that displeases you? Discard all innocence and thought of possible outcomes and enjoy----now what did you call it ---ah yes, the empty feast?" Sarah gave Jason a big grin and leaned across the table toward him. "I know. I have a perfect way to do it. I'm sure the beast will be delighted if you can give me enough money to return to Africa like you did and hunt down the Arabs that killed my family and make sure they are fully punished. You're teaching me well, Jason. Shall I pass acts of vengeance on to the girls as a way to live their lives? Spite is a very easy lesson to teach. It is the back door frame of the beast. Let me make sure that I have the rules straight. A person should avenge any unkind or hurtful act regardless of who gets hurt in the process so long as my wrath is appeased and the accumulated interest on the hurt is paid. Destroy and don't build." Sarah paused long enough to allow the statement to absorb. "I'm very confused at this point. Would you please explain the difference between your kidnapping of Braxton and your sentencing of Rebah, or do you want to play with the words shanghaied and slavery? I really don't want to upset the beast's rationalization."

The waiter stuck his head out of one of the swinging doors and scanned the dinning room. Only Jason and Sarah remained. "Will there be anything else?" he worriedly questioned, observing Jason had scarcely touched his plate.

Sarah leaned back in her chair and smiled back at the concerned man. "No! It's really quite delicious. Unfortunately, my husband's appetite was satisfied much earlier in the evening."

The waiter shrugged his shoulders and reentered the kitchen.

"You trod a dangerous path, Jason. I'll stand by you through thick and thin, my soul mate, but I will not walk the path of the beast with you. I have lost this battle, and it has regained strength. Be very careful it doesn't destroy everything you love." She took his hand between hers, "And everything that I love too. I have to go upstairs. Poor Ruth must want to jump out of the window by now."

"I'll be up soon. I think I'll go for a walk," said Jason as if hypnotized. Sarah patted his hand and left the room. Jason sat a while longer before exiting the inn. He walked to destination nowhere in a night as black as his soul.

CHAPTER XV

GUILTY

Approximately three more miles, and the buckboard would turn off the main thoroughfare onto the road that leads to the plantation house known as Whispering Willows. Jason conjectured as to whether Sean, Hunter, or both men currently busied themselves at Whispering Willows or, if they had traipsed off to supervise some building project site. He also wondered if Lulu had made Hunter's life miserable after she presented the second set of ledger books to Sean. The beast began to stir as Jason set the scene for his intrusion into a witch's cauldron of delight for the panther. He assumed Hunter somehow had outmaneuvered Sean and still held the reins of power on the plantation. Lulu loved Hunter so much she would have forgiven her lover anything and would present no problem. By now she would have discovered Amanda never existed. Her long time beau would have probably married her in order to keep peace on the plantation and would assist the new Jason in regaining Lulu's favor.

Jason's relationship with the women on the buckboard, remained precarious. Sarah seemed more like her old self, but Jason knew she waited to observe his management of the next crisis. In less than three miles, Hunter, Sean, and Lulu would supply that test.

Notwithstanding the magnified rocking and bouncing provided by the potholes in the dirt road coupled with their knowledge of events in Mobile Naomi and Ruth voiced no protests or negative comments during the junket to the plantation. The children delighted in the bumping and considered it some entertaining repetitive game. Every bump provided a pretext to emphasize it even more to Miriam. If not for the restraining arm of Ruth, she would have been bounced out of the wagon at least a dozen times. Miriam never sustained any injuries but would not allow their threat to stem her unlimited curiosity and playfulness. Miriam's lack of prudence kept her surrogate nanny on alert and applied a careful restraint on the little pixy.

Jason brought the buckboard to a halt and stared down a dirt road lined with willow trees. Sarah reached over and gently grasped his arm. The two women in back pacified Miriam long enough to scrutinize the dappled road with its dancing willows.

"This is where I spent six years working for Hunter. That was a lifetime ago. I don't know how much things have changed but I'm quite sure that Hunter can find something for all of us to do," Jason said optimistically as he directed the horses into the shaded roadway. Like no other place, including Ilorin, Jason sensed that he had come home. He hoped Hunter would notice the changes in his old second in command and forgive the past maltreatment done by Jason.

Slowly the willows gave way to an immaculately manicured front lawn outlined with a graveled roadway. To the right side of the plantation house near the entrance to its library the well-trimmed hedge maze with a marble cupid perched on an orb in the very center that appeared to have raised his arm in a welcoming gesture to the little group. Further down past the maze the old slave quarters and the adjacent slave cemetery still appeared in good repair. In back of the manor house the sprawling cotton fields accented the scene with their puffy whiteness bobbing in the gentle breeze. More than the cotton fields Jason's mind arched beyond the slave quarters, the cemetery, and the reclaimed swamp area to the swamp itself. His mind zeroed on a small island about a mile inward into the dangerous marsh and wondered if Hunter had tapped into or moved the golden hoard buried there. Jason assured himself that despite all the trouble Sean caused regarding the Wilkerson account Hunter would never reveal that stash. Only he and Jason knew of its existence. He would have to discuss with Hunter if the portion of the gold he had not carried back to Africa still lay hidden there.

The main house looked well kept. Either Hunter must have just had it painted, or he had restrained Sean and his cronies from further abuse of the building. Jason could detect no servants wandering past the windows. Surely Morning Glory still reigned supreme in the kitchen and scuttled about preparing supper for Sean and his cronies. A lone female figure sat rocking on the front verandah watching the approaching buckboard with interest. Jason pulled the vehicle in front of the steps leading to the main entrance to the manor and handed the reins to Sarah. He removed his floppy hat and walked toward the rocking figure and stopped dead in his tracks. "Miss Ann!"

"Jason? Is that really you?" Ann said, rising and offering both hands to the stunned man.

"Yes ma'am," he stammered, taking both of her small cold hands into his and trying desperately to recover from the shock of seeing his old plantation mistress. Awakening to current reality, Jason said, "Let me introduce you to my wife, children and two friends of ours."

As Jason introduced the women he encouraged their small talk to allow him time to observe the changes in Ann. Snow-white hair framed a face that had retained much of its youth but nevertheless a touch of sadness still revealed itself. Her body had filled out more and she stooped slightly. Her black dress made her look much older but Jason felt as if the greatest changes in the all familiar persona had yet to surface.

"My! My! Where are my manners? Let me have Morning Glory make us some tea and I know she has been baking some cinnamon rolls. I'll be right back. Make you---" Ann never finished her sentence.

In the front door entrance to the manor stood a black figure with uncombed, matted hair. Lulu's faded dress hung from her left shoulder like a young schoolgirl at play. Her face contorted with rage as she flung herself on Jason. "You son-of-a-bitch. You killed my man," she screamed flailing her arms at Jason. Only after she had scratched his left cheek did he restrain her arms. Even thus restrained she attempted to bite him and kick him with her bare feet. The women and children froze in place with shock at the sudden attack. Except for Ann.

Ann walked over and removed Lulu's wrists from Jason's grip. She stepped between the two and gathered Lulu in her arms. Slowly she pushed Lulu at arm's length away from Jason. "Honey, it's Jason and his family come to pay us a visit," she explained to the panting, wild-eyed woman.

"I know who the son-of-a-bitch is," she shouted, leaning her head around Ann's shoulder. "Since you couldn't get me did you find yourself a whore who would put out for you?"

Jason glanced over at Sarah's perfectly blank face. Ann immediately looped her arm through Lulu's arm and walked with her toward the front door of the mansion. "Now honey, you let me handle this. You go tell Morning Glory to bring some tea and her cinnamon rolls for my guests. Then, why don't you go take a nap before you do my hair for this evening. It's in such a mess and I want to look especially nice. Mr. Andrew may come back early and I don't want him to see me like this."

Politely Lulu responded, "Yes, ma'am. Now don't be too long. I'll lay out your blue dress that Mr. Harrison likes so much. You'll have to make yourself extra pretty before he gets home. Oh, and I'll take out that cameo you like so well. I think that's the best gift he ever gave you. I'll tell Morning Glory to take out an extra ham just in case the Garrets come over to dinner." After giving Jason a look that could kill Satan Lulu went inside, making plans for the phantom dinner party.

Ann turned to face the astounded women and frightened children. "She usually isn't like this. I guess it's the excitement in seeing you Jason which unnerved her. She hasn't been the same since Hunter died," Ann sighed.

"My God! Hunter's dead?" Jason groped for the verandah steps as the effect of the news began to darken things around him. Ann and Sarah rushed toward the stunned man and supported him until he could regain physical control. Sarah remained with her husband as Ann ran to the well for water. After three gulps of the cold liquid Jason's anxiety subsided somewhat even though his hard breathing continued. After returning the dipper to the well Ann returned to the distraught man who now leaned on one of the Doric columns of the patio for support but sat again on the steps. "I'm all right now Miss Ann, thank you. What's happened here since I've been gone?" Jason asked, still reeling from the calamitous information.

"I thought you knew. We assumed the Klan captured you somewhere in the woods and killed you when they captured Hunter and Sean and hung them. When I saw you today I thought you escaped them and fled north. I didn't know you were unaware that Hunter and Sean were dead."

The front door flew open and portly black woman appeared. "Well as I live and breathe, if it isn't Mr. Jason. We all thought you dead. It's so good to see you again," said Morning Glory setting down on the table next to the cane rocker previously occupied by Ann a tray with a pot of tea, plates, teacups, and a heaping plate of freshly baked cinnamon rolls. Jason managed a weak smile for a friendly greeting as the cook gave him a hearty hug. "We all thought you had died in the woods when nobody found your body hanging on any of the trees near Hunter and Sean. Some of Mr. Sean's men even---"

"That will be all for now Morning Glory. Will you please see that enough food is prepared for our guests this evening," said Ann taking Morning Glory by the arm and ushering her back into the house.

The black woman stared for a moment longer to evaluate the situation and realized something radically wrong and perhaps she had spoken out of turn. "Yes, Miss Ann. I'm sorry. I didn't realize---"

"That's all right, Morning Glory. Now you go see if you can make something extra special for my guests tonight. How about some of your famous shoofly pie? I'm quite sure Jason hasn't had any like it since he left," said Ann trying to make Morning Glory feel better.

"Yes Ma'am," replied the retreating figure.

Ann allowed a moment of silence for the tension to lessen as she placed a single bun on three plates and invited Jason and Sarah to occupy two of the three straight back wicker chairs across from Ann. Ann finally spoke first. "Ruth! Why don't you take Miriam and Alva under one of those lovely trees and play? They haven't heard the sound of children's laughter for quite a while and it may make the limbs dance more."

Miriam let out a squeal of delight. Another adventure presented itself. Alva started to giggle, knowing that excitement displayed in her older sister would soon prove entertaining to her.

"Take the plate of buns with you and have a picnic. That's what we call eating outside. Why doesn't one of you see if Morning Glory could make some lemonade for the children? I'm sure they would like that better than tea." Ann offered.

Sarah started for the front door when Jason gently `clutched her wrist. "Naomi, would you please get the lemonade?"

The older woman had not missed the request for Jason and Sarah to have a private conference with Ann. "Of course," Naomi replied as she headed into the house.

"Stay with me. I want you to hear this. I really don't think I could bear this alone. I need you now more than I ever have. I know I keep saying that but each time it is truer than the time before this. How could I have done such things and ruined so many lives?" Jason pleaded grasping his wife's wrist tighter with his shaking hand.

Sarah gazed into Jason's eyes and saw only anguish. Her wrist pained from his grasp but the cause came from her disturbed husband and not the beast. With a slight nod of her head and an encouraging smile, she helped him stand and sit in one of the vacant chairs. She sat next to him and wrapped her sore arm through his. Ruth proceeded toward the willow trees trying not to drop the plate of buns after Miriam detected the sweet aroma that issued from the delectable confections on the plate. To pacify the over active gremlin she handed her a large warm bun. Miriam amused Alva by trying to cram the big bun in her mouth and talk at the same time. Finally the children and guardian disappeared under a willow's protective branches. With a sigh of someone bearing bad news, Ann resumed her seat on the porch rocker and addressed the couple sitting next to her.

"There really isn't too much to tell. I was still in Charleston with Gwen when things happened here." Ann paused and frowned. "I always felt like an intruder at Gwen's house. Oh,

Adam and Gwen did their best to make me feel at home but I always felt I was in the way and Whispering Willows was my real home, but that had been sold and I had only the memories of living here. Do you know that Gwen has made me a grandmother three times? I just wish that Andrew---" Ann stopped short and caressed a locket hung over her breast and gave a smile. "My! My! How I do go on! You don't want to hear about that." She paused a moment longer. "Most of what I know was told to me by Mr. Ellis when he came to visit me in Charleston. It seems as if Sean and Hunter went to Birmingham on some business. That was the last time anybody saw them alive. Lulu believed that she caused their deaths by taking some bookkeeping ledgers to the sheriff to try and get Sean and Mr. Wilkerson arrested and free Hunter from their influence. To this day I don't know why she did such a foolish thing when she knew how much Bubba hated both Hunter and Sean, but somehow she blames you for her decision. Ever since that night she went to see the sheriff she has had some sort of brain fever. Some days she's all right, but others---well I won't dwell on that. Lulu said she hoped they would find your body chopped into small pieces, but I'm quite sure that wish is part of her brain fever."

"I'm not quite so sure of that," Jason mumbled. Sarah closed her eyes and squeezed his arm tightly. The need for the beast's destruction became more evident to Jason with every word said by the woman in the rocking chair.

"What do you mean, Jason?" asked Ann.

Jason now had to face an ordeal greater than what he had done to Rebah. He could rationalize that Rebah had wronged him, but what of Hunter, Lulu, and Sean? His insides felt as if he had eaten ground glass as he said, "The ledgers were real. The night I left I taunted Lulu with lies about Hunter seeing another woman in Birmingham. I told her about the real and the false ledgers. I wanted her to take the ledgers to Sean, not Bubba."

The rocking chair ceased creaking as Ann leaned forward. "Oh my God, Jason! You knew how she felt about Hunter. What ever possessed you to do a thing like that?" Ann censured.

Jason finally came to the realization that he could not control the beast to exact revenge in the precise way he planned. Once unchained, it awakened the beast in others. Together the aroused beasts produced their own negative results regardless of the original plan. The innocent or guilty who suffered along the way became irrelevant as long as the panther and his cohorts could get any kind of hurtful results. The sweetness of revenge proved to have a bitter saccharine flavor of remorse attached. Excuses dissipated as he looked his former plantation mistress in the eye and replied to her query, "Blind, unfounded hatred of others that almost destroyed my life on more than one occasion," Jason replied and looked toward Sarah, "If it wasn't for this woman, Miss Ann, long ago I probably would have killed myself and left behind as much unhappiness as I could for others to suffer."

Ann s tared at her former slave and unwittingly pushed the knife of guilt in further. "But Jason, I never heard Hunter say an unkind word about you. You weren't the friendliest person on the plantation. Hunter tolerated you but I know for sure that Lulu would have nothing to do with you," Ann added sadly.

Jason buried his face in his hands and shook his head. "I had no idea what took place here. I didn't intend for those things to happen. I thought she would give the books to Sean, and he would see how Hunter had been cheating him all that time under the name of Wilkerson, and between Lulu and Sean Hunter's life would be made miserable."

"But why, Jason? What did Hunter ever do to you?" Asked Ann.

"Absolutely nothing, except treat me as a trusted employee, tried to be a friend, and wanted me to make a new start here in America. I reacted out of self hatred and found an excuse to blame him for my own unhappiness. He belonged to a people who I thought I despised. At that time there was little difference between Bubba and myself except skin color. Unfounded hatred gives no choices in life. Its absoluteness denies all options. My wife has since proved me wrong in that stupidity over a thousand times. It took that many times for me to finally accept the truth," another admission came to the forefront.

"I could understand if you were like our local sheriff who hates anyone who isn't white or disagrees with his opinions, but Hunter was black like you and I thought you both worked so well together," Ann observed.

"Color had nothing to do with it, Miss Ann. It was his tribe into which he was born that gave me the excuse to hate. At the time of which we speak I tried to blame everyone for my unhappy life except myself," Jason tried to explain.

"Color? Tribe? Religion? What's the difference? Why didn't you look for the similarities instead of the variances?" Ann asked in a quiet voice.

"Miss Ann, you're not the same person I remember. Even though what you are saying rips at my very soul I think I like this person sitting before me much better than the pampered mistress I once knew," Jason commented.

"Many things changed for me since Andrew died. A lot of things I believed I couldn't do I found out I could but I never had to do because Andrew did them for me and Papa before him. I began to notice the good and bad in people, no matter their background. Lulu looked after me for years like the loving sister I lost when she eloped with a frontiersman and Papa refused to allow me to keep in contact with her. Now it is time I repay some of that devotion Lulu gave me. Her color has nothing to do with it. It is a debt from one person to another that I am paying back with all of my heart. I love Lulu as my lost sister. She had always been just that and I couldn't see it because I was so wrapped up in myself. I recognize that relationship now and delight in being able to help a poor lost soul that is as close to me as Gwen. I have Lulu living in one of the old guest rooms upstairs. I told her I needed her there in case I had a bad dream or wanted something during the night. I've had a lot of time to think about my life while living with Gwen. I came to realize that individuals who shuffled in and out of my life were people too, and they weren't put on this earth just to satisfy my needs. It took a lot of years, but I believe I'm better at seeing things and people for what they really are. In short Jason, I finally grew up."

Jason felt a light squeeze on his arm as Sarah silently drove the point home. "How did you come back to Whispering Willows?" he asked, thoroughly confused. When Jason had retreated to Africa the plantation belonged to Hunter under the alias of Wilkerson.

"That brings me back to my story," Ann resumed. Before she could continue, Naomi exited the front door carrying a tray with a pitcher of lemonade and four glasses gave the three occupants of the verandah a cursory glance and headed for the willow trees whose branches hid the playful trio.

The three watched as Ruth parted the curtain-like limbs to allow her mother passage under the umbrella like trees. When the live curtain closed once more Ann poured some tea for her guests and for herself then continued. "As I told you Mr. Ellis came to see me in Charleston. It was about a month after Sean and Hunter were found hanging on a tree on the road to Selma. There were remains of a charred cross in a nearby clearing not too far from where they were found. Everyone hereabouts knew it was Bubba and the Klan but who was going to prove it? Mr. Ellis told me that Mr. Wilkerson and Hunter were one and the same, and that he had used that name because he didn't want any trouble with business deals from the white folks around here. He said Hunter had made a will and I was part of it. Ann took a sip of the cooling tea and encouraged the two still shocked persons next to her to do the same. After that brief intermission she continued with her narration.

"He left Whispering Willows to me and an account of ten thousand dollars in trust for its upkeep and an additional ten thousand dollars for my personal use. He left the construction company to the Wilkerson account after Mr. Ellis was suppose to have bought out Sean, but of course Sean was killed along with Hunter so the construction company went directly to the Wilkerson account. Mr. Ellis takes care of the running of the plantation and its payroll as well as the construction company. You could have knocked me over with a feather when he told me I was sole owner of Whispering Willows! I am now mistress of my own home again. Gwen tried to make me sell the plantation and stay with them but I wanted to come home. Home. I suddenly felt alive again. This is where I belong, not Charleston. Hunter always knew that." Ann paused for a sip of tea and said, "Do you remember how I use to hate to do figures, Jason?

Jason nodded and gave a little smile.

"Well! You should see me now! I can account for every penny I earn and spend and I'm living just on the interest alone from the gift Hunter bequeathed me. I'm no expert and Mr. Ellis manages everything concerning the plantation and does help me with my household figures. The profits from the cotton crops he splits in half after taking out his fee. One half goes to cover any expenses that may occur on the plantation such as the workers' salaries and new seed, and the other half goes into my personal account. That personal account is the one that has taught me the real value of money and how to manage it." Ann paused and sipped some tea. Jason could read the pride of that accomplishment in her eyes. Daintily she replaced the cup on its saucer and continued. "He also left ten thousand dollars to Lulu, but she refuses to touch it. She thinks its pay off money from Mr. Wilkerson for the death of Hunter." Ann folded her hands in her lap and sighed. "Try as I might, I can't make her believe they were one and the same person. Mr. Ellis petitioned the court and now has power of attorney over her account. She won't accept any money even from me. I try to buy things I think she needs or likes but she takes no interest in them."

"Did Lulu remain here after Hunter's death?" Jason queried.

"No. She remained in town," Ann replied in a whisper.

"How did she come back here?" Jason asked curiously.

Ann bit her lower lip as she dredged up the sad memory. "That's sort of tied up with my return. When I returned here the place was in bad need of repair and most of the servants except for Morning Glory were gone. Since he had no family, Mr. Ellis divided Sean's estate among his New York friends who returned there within a week after Sean's death. They took Sean's body back with them at the request of somebody named Tweed who was going to see about giving it a good Christian burial. Mr. Ellis hired a local man, Ted Withers, to oversee the construction part of the business and the profits still go into the Wilkerson account in Charleston. The only one who stayed was O'Reilly. He gave his share to be divided among the others in exchange for the saloon in town, which makes him one of the wealthiest men in Unionville. Mr. Ellis saw to it that Hunter was buried in the colored graveyard here at Whispering Willows, and had a stone marker placed over his grave. It's the only decorated stone marker there. Lulu takes good care of it and spends a lot of time there. Hunter loved Whispering Willows and it is only fitting that he rest in peace here. Whenever we can't find Lulu around the house we always can find her sitting by Hunter's grave. Usually that's the time when she is least affected by the brain fever. With the interest from the upkeep account I have restored the grounds and with what I get from the cotton fields after paying the help and buying supplies the place is starting to look like old times." Ann let loose with a hearty laugh. "Can you imagine? Me! A business woman! Well, sort of. Anyway, I went into town the second day here to hire a foreman to do the cotton planting. I was interviewing Josh Washington -- you'll meet him later -- when I spotted a group of children teasing this black girl. I went over to make them stop and we both recognized each other at the same time. Lulu looked worse than you saw her today. She had been living in the street and eating out of garbage cans. My heart went out to her. I immediately brought her with me back here to Whispering Willows where she belongs. Due to her brain fever, she treats me the same way she did before the war. Time has stopped for her. If I try to do anything for myself, she gets all flustered and sulks for days, so I just let her have her way. She's always planning for Andrew's return and grand dinner parties with the Garrets. Morning Glory feels the same way about her as I do. We try to make her life as pleasant as possible but something in her died with Hunter. She's had a hard enough life and if a little white lie here and there makes her happy then so be it."

Jason could not look Ann in the face. "Well at least you kept Morning Glory to help with Lulu," he said trying to change the painful subject.

"Lord, Jason! I didn't keep anybody. Hunter left her five thousand dollars in remembrance of her good cooking. She can leave anytime she wants. She stays of her own free will. I even tried to pay her a salary. She just laughed at me and said she couldn't even spend the money that Hunter left her and what was she going to do with more? All in all, between the three maids I've hired from town that come three times a week we're doing pretty well here." With that last comment, Ann fell silent and began to rock.

Jason thought for a while before he finally said, "Miss Ann, I came here to sit things straight with Hunter and ask him for work. It seems a little late for that now. I can't undo what I caused and am truly sorry for what happened, but I hope that one day I'll be able to offset what I have done. I don't know how, but the misery I have caused will always be in the forefront of my mind and I pray to the gods that I shall recognize a person in need and offer what help I may when I see it. In the meanwhile do you have any work my family and friends can do?"

Ann rocked a bit more than said, "I was just about to hire someone to come in and start fixing up the inside of the place. It badly needs painting on the inside. Some of the flooring needs replacing, and the staircase needs repairing before someone falls and breaks their neck. Every chimney needs cleaning and even rebricking in some places. I'm afraid to even look in the cellar. Lulu still believes she is the housekeeper she once was and takes the credit for the hired help's cleaning and I support her in that little white lie. She'll walk around the house for hours with a broom talking to herself, or she'll go to the kitchen where Morning Glory will give her some small chore to do. To be perfectly honest she messes more than she cleans. Miss Ann paused and tapped her right index finger on her chin. "Let me see now," she mused. Suddenly a bright smile lit up her face. "I can give your ladies the jobs of the hired maids. The ones I have now don't like coming all the way from town out to here, and we could use a kitchen helper. Though I know she'll deny it, but Morning Glory isn't as young as she used to be. I've tried to make her cook just for the three of us but she still cooks enough to feed an army and call it a small dinner. Cooking is the only thing she has to look forward to, so I let her. Needless-to-say, we have some pretty fat field hands from her leftovers." Ann paused and looked sadly at the mansion door. "Then again there's Lulu. Your little ones are so lively. Maybe they will help pull Lulu out of her doldrums." Suddenly Ann stopped rocking and leaned forward. "Of course I won't be able to pay you much, say a dollar a week for each of the women and a dollar and a half for you. You can fix up a couple of the cabins to live in and get your meals from the kitchen if you don't want to cook for yourselves. That should please Morning Glory. Is that a good enough offer?"

"Miss Ann, I hope I never have to cross swords with you in business," Jason chuckled.

"Oh but you will! Open a new building material account at the store in Unionville and I want receipts for all of the materials you buy, and this time I'll take care of the ledgers. The inside of the house repairs come out of my personal account," she said only half jokingly. "Now to celebrate your resurrection and the closing of our deal I want all of you to have dinner tonight here. It will be such a delight to hear the old dinning room fill with one old and five new friendly voices again. Let me go in and tell Morning Glory. She'll swear she's died and gone to heaven when she gets the news. She hasn't prepared what she considers a big meal since the Irishmen left. You had better warn the others not to wear any restricting clothing for dinner, not unless they want seams to start to rip. I wonder if I should have Josh keep the wheelbarrow outside the house tonight to get all of you back to your cabins. I know Morning Glory won't settle for you to have just one helping of her shoofly pie. Please warn the others that a second helping is a must or they will have to face a pouting Morning Glory for the rest of the month." Ann giggled and left to search of Morning Glory, but she paused at the door and looked at Jason. "My! But it's nice to have an old face around me again." She looked down at Sarah and said, "You have done marvels with this old grump. If he starts to act up again with his nonsense we do have a wood shed in back that has some pretty large hickory sticks in it that you can use anytime you want to teach him to mind his manners," Ann giggled again and went in search of Morning Glory.

Jason sat awhile staring at his feet. He could still feel Sarah's hand on his arm. If it hadn't been for its presence he would have raced across the lawn screaming to the top of his lungs long ago.

Sarah understood. "So this is where the beast had free reign," she said quietly. "Oh my love how bad you must have hurt to be so cruel without any provocation." Sarah put her arm around his waist and rested her head on his shoulder. "I don't know how but this is where the most difficult part of the path you must walk will be. What's done is done. You said that Miss Ann had changed. Well, so have you. Things have not ended. They are only beginning. Walk carefully, my love. Here lies the greatest temptation to walk the old path." With a final squeeze of his arm she rose from her chair and headed for the willows, not only to tell the two women the welcomed news of their employment, but to warn them of the huge banquet this evening topped off by at least two helpings of Morning Glory's shoofly pie and to prevent the tree from becoming a Wailing Willow as she spied Miriam swinging back and forth on an armful of willow branches.

Jason did not move as he watched his wife join the other women. A beginning? Yet, not three days ago. NO! He must not think about that but he had to think about it. Not only think about it but make damned sure that nothing like that ever happened again. Still? Where would the beast see the next opportunity to strike?

CHAPTER XVI

THE LETTER

Jason relished his tiredness and felt quite satisfied in all of his accomplished hard work. He stared at the horseshoe staircase leading to the upstairs bedrooms. Repair of the entire staircase enjoined over three weeks of tedious labor. He couldn't inconvenience Miss Ann by restoring and varnishing all of the steps at one time, so he had to reconstruct, stain and varnish one side of the staircase steps at a time. Miss Ann volunteered to temporarily move into the single downstairs bedroom to speed up the repairs, but Jason wouldn't hear of it. Lulu purposely stomped over the newly varnished stairs until Miss Ann asked her not to do it because she wanted it to look nice for Mr. Harrison when he came home. After that request Lulu carefully avoided marring Jason's work.

Ruth, Lulu, and the children went on frequent picnics, if for no other reason than to keep the little ones out of the kitchen where Morning Glory insisted on stuffing them with every sweet known to mankind, and to detain them from interrupting their busy father. It took Lulu a while to accept Jason and Sarah's offspring after the cruelty of the town's brood but Lulu discovered Jason's children could ignore her sickness and enjoy her company as she finally did theirs. It took a few weeks but Lulu joined Ruth and the children on their picnic outings. Miriam won over Lulu when the rascal wrapped her arms around the distraught woman, held her hand or planted wet kisses on her cheek.

Naomi begged Morning Glory to teach her some of her recipes and shared some of the African recipes with the most famous cook of Perry County. Morning Glory gladly obliged as she had not traded recipes since the Garret's cook, Sapphire, left the Garret's plantation and moved to Atlanta. The recipe for Morning Glory's shoofly pie still remained a well kept secret. After a while it became very difficult to discover whether Morning Glory or Naomi had prepared the meal as the aroma of new versions of old receipts that earned Morning Glory's approval saturated the reanimated manor.

Sarah, Naomi, and Ruth made the reclaimed cabins as comfortable as possible for the newly arrived plantation workers. Their current lodgings had long remained vacant and required extensive repairs to make them acceptable to the women. The new employees combined their wages to purchase cloth for curtains, and bed and table linens. The women sat by the fireplace in the evening and chatted about the day's events while cutting and sewing the cloth to make the cabins more home-like. The adopted family had learned to reluctantly tolerate Jason and even spoke to him now and then.

Unbeknownst to anyone Jason still had that large reserve of gold hidden on the island and money in an account in Birmingham also under the name of Wilkerson that Hunter made him open but had Jason's signature rather than Hunter's to access it. The entire troop including Jason decided to live on their wages paid by Ann. The plantation mistress grew close to her new employees and relished the tales they told about Africa. To make sure she understood the stories correctly Ann assisted Sarah in broadening Naomi and Ruth's knowledge of the English language. The real mistress of the plantation went by the name of Miriam. She began to talk and insisted on becoming the first walking encyclopedia with all of the questions she asked. No one could resist the coquettish smile and kiss that usually went with the questions especially Ann who always saw a young Lulu in the tot.

Jason avoided going to the swamp island. That money no longer existed to him unless a dire emergency arose. He had visited Unionville only once since his arrival at the plantation to set up an additional line of credit for repair material. After that one visit, he made a list of various components needed for remodeling and gave it to Sarah who did the shopping and she delivered Jason's list to Shamrock Construction for delivery. Though he didn't have to accompany the supplies O'Reilly, who had become quite a respectable citizen around town with his marriage to one of his former bar maids, Caroline Jenkins, accompanied the materials to the plantation to see how Ann restored his former residence and dispense a little blarney to the amusement of the mistress of Whispering Willows. Periodically Ann would even include a dinner invitation to the couple, much to the delight of Morning Glory.

Sarah became very adept at handling horses and driving the buckboard. The animals seemed to take to her. When not cleaning in the manor she helped the stable boy care for them. Early one spring morning, after seven months of settling down, Jason found her pitching hay and rubbing the horses down. He smiled at his busy wife and said, "Now don't go learning how to shoe a horse. I don't want to be married to any woman with arms bigger than mine." She had merely grinned and continued with her pitching.

The overseer of the cotton fields, Josh, proved a very pleasant fellow, and began courting Naomi. The amiable widow did not discourage Josh's advances but those closest to the once abused woman noted the agonizing memories of Africa had not healed completely.

Ruth began dating one of the supply drivers for Shamrock Construction by the name of Ulysses Brown, but, like her mother, needed a bit more time for past wounds to heal.

Jason heard the front door open and turned to see Sarah inspecting his current work of repairing and painting doorway trim. "I never knew you could do such good work," his wife complimented.

Jason grinned from ear to ear. "I almost forgot how to work with my hands. I had to learn the hard way when I lived here. I was so grumpy that nobody wanted to help me and if I didn't want to catch pneumonia in my drafty cabin I had to do repairs myself." Jason looked down at his now-callused hands. "This is a long way from my life at the temple of Ifa in Ilorin," he commented quietly.

Sarah came over and gave him a kiss. "Some material I ordered for new play dresses for the girls is due to arrive at the general store today and I wanted to dye the table linen. With such a nice breeze it will blow the smell away from the house and dry them very fast. Would you mind going into town and pick the supplies up for me?"

Jason cleaned the paint brush in a can of turpentine and dried it on an old rag. "Not at all! After all I don't have anything to do. The cellar has to be cleaned. I still haven't finished painting upstairs. I haven't even looked at the kitchen chimney, and now you want me to take the rest of the afternoon off and go to pick up material."

"It will do you good. You've been fixing this trim work from sunup to sundown everyday now for the past week aside from working on the two cabins. Take a little break and have yourself a beer while you're in town. From what I hear from Josh O'Reilly serves both black and white. If for no other reason, he does it to upset the sheriff who hates the Irish almost as he does the blacks. You don't have to finish all your work assignments in one day," she reminded him as she pinched his cheek and drew his face to hers for a quick kiss.

Jason began gathering his tools. "Make a list of things, and make sure you give me enough money for two beers. I just may meet one of the dance hall girls who could be thirsty." Sarah chuckled, turned, walked out the door and returned to their cabin.

After he put the tools away, Jason headed for the barn to hitch the team. Sarah already had the buckboard ready. She smiled and handed him a piece of paper wrapped around three silver dollars. "I wouldn't want your girl friend to go thirsty, so if the store bill is over two dollars, have it put on Whispering Willow's credit account.

Jason took the paper and climbed into the driver's seat. He leaned over and gave Sarah a big kiss. "If she's really pretty, I may stay all night."

"Oh good! Then I can have Ruth watch the children and I'll keep my date with Mose," she replied. Mose happened to be the ugliest man on the plantation. His lack of teeth gave him the appearance of a dried apple and made him look older than his sixty-four years.

Still laughing, Jason brought the reins down across the rumps of the horses. He looked back over his shoulder to see Sarah with her wrists on her hips and swaying her shoulders side to side. "I just may have to sneak back and keep an eye on you," he called back to her.

Sarah threw both arms in the air a waved him onward. Still laughing she turned to close the barn doors as Jason drove the team into the cool road between the willows. God! How he loved that woman!

Unionville had not changed much in the past seven years. O'Reilly's remained the only bar in town and did a booming business even if one side of the bar served blacks and the other side whites without a partition to separate the two halves. To date that unwritten rule limited the number of bar fights. Each side seemed to appreciate their own race for company but could mingle in the middle of the bar if they desired. In the beginning O'Reilly had to toss a couple of patrons from both sides of the bar out on their ear and warned them the next time they caused problems the bar no longer wanted their patronage. Bubba tried to stir up problems until O'Reilly informed him that sheriff or no sheriff the rule also applied to him. The single watering hole within forty miles bore the name, O'Reilly's. Bubba complied. The general store had the same owner, only the merchandise changed. With the end of the war many things that had been embargoed now occupied space on the once nearly empty shelves. Jason tied the horses to the hitching post in front of the store for easy loading. After throwing the bolts of cloth and supplies from Sarah's list in back of the wagon, he decided to walk across the street to O'Reilly's for a beer when he heard a voice call from behind him, "Jason! Is that really you?" Jason turned toward the caller and came face to face with Gregory Ellis.

"We all thought that you were dead. My God! Where have you been?" Ellis said just as surprised as Jason.

"It's a long story. I heard what happened to Sean and Hunter," he said sadly.

Ellis glanced around quickly. "I just got back from a few months vacation in Ohio and Italy. Is everything alright at Whispering Willows?" Jason nodded. Ellis wrinkled his brow and spoke in a low voice. "This is not the place to talk. Come on over to my office." He placed his hand on Jason's shoulder and directed him back across the street. No further conversation took place until they had mounted the steps beside the general store that led to Ellis's office above the emporium.

"One never knows who is or who is not a member of the Klan. Rumor has it that our illustrious sheriff is the Grand Wizard. Of course nobody can prove anything and anyone found asking too many questions is usually found unconscious in some back alley if not swinging from a tree," Ellis said opening the door to his office.

The small office contained two cabinets that appeared to be locked, a safe, two chairs, and a small desk with a swivel chair. "Have a seat," Gregory invited, tossing his hat on top of the desk. "I just returned to Unionville yesterday with my wife, Ann Blyth. You remember her. Sean rented a room from her when he first arrived here in Unionville. We spent the past year visiting my old home in Ohio. I hardly recognized the place. Then after a couple of days in Charleston we took an extended vacation to Italy to see the art work. Hard to believe isn't it? Me, an art lover. The vacation was really nice, but it's so good to be back home. It'll take me another year to catch up on things and review my son's work while I have been gone. He almost as good a lawyer as I am," he bragged while unlocking his desk drawer.

"As president of the Unionville bank, you know that I take care of the general management of Whispering Willows?" Jason nodded. "Miss Ann insists that she take care of the manor house expenses. I admit that I have to give her a little help with her bookkeeping, but she's only off a few cents one way or the other, and once in a while she's right on the mark. I never would have believed it of her. I wonder who ever put an iron rod on her spine."

Jason smiled and rubbed his nose. "Maybe it always was there but she never had to use it."

Ellis just chuckled, nodded and said, "I never thought of that."

Jason shifted position in the creaky chair and said, "While I'm thinking of it I meant to speak with you about my Wilkerson account in Birmingham. You were with Hunter and myself when we opened it. I think he planned to change the account name in Charleston and wanted another account opened under a different name. He also wanted my signature on the Birmingham account instead of his because he wanted me to maintain it for my own use after he retransferred the money to the new account. If anyone tried to trace the disappearance of the Charleston account and discovered Wilkerson had an account in Birmingham the signatures would have been different. Could you please close the Charleston one and transfer all of it to the Birmingham one?

"That shouldn't be hard to do. Since your signature is legal on the Wilkerson account in Birmingham and Hunter certainly will not be making any more withdrawals on the Charleston account, I see no problem," Ellis agreed.

Suddenly the lawyer rose from his creaking chair and pointed a shaking finger at the ceiling. "That reminds me. Lucky for you I'm a pack rat. There are two letter packets here for you." Ellis walked over to the two file cabinets to the right of the entryway and unlocked one of them. Mumbling to himself and after some studious examination of various files he had partially removed and replaced, he finally shouted, "Aha! Here they are!" Ellis removed two large slightly yellowed envelopes from a manila folder slammed the cabinet drawer shut and threw the letters on the desk in front of Jason. "You probably want some time to read them. At least I can use that as an excuse to go across the street to O'Reilly's for a quick beer," he said, patting Jason on the back. "I'll be back in about a half-an-hour's time." Ellis relocked the cabinet, took his hat and left Jason sitting alone in his office.

Jason's hand shook as he picked up the first packet with his name on it. The other envelope read: To be opened by Jason on request, and had Ellis's signature on the left lower corner of the envelope. Clearly the handwriting belonged to Hunter. Jason perspired despite the coolness of the afternoon. He felt he stared into Hunter's commanding brown eyes instead of the letter. Something in his mind frighteningly growled for him to put the letter back on the desk and leave. No! He had tried running from problems and unpleasantness in the past, and it only created more complications. The over-dried glue immediately released the envelope flap as if Hunter wanted freedom from his paper genie lamp. Slowly Jason removed the large packet of papers inside. Before reading he scanned various words for the identifying flourishes that Hunter once made to make sure that the handwriting really belonged to Hunter. Try as he might to declare them forgeries Jason had to admit the verity of the letter's author and could no longer find a reason to procrastinate in perusing it. Reading the letter demanded a return to his bitter past a task he must perform with much reservation. He flicked the pages back to page one and began to read:

"I know that as a legal document this should be very formal, but this is a legacy to my closest acquaintance. I can't use the word friend in the strictest sense because you would never allow it. Besides, I discarded that word along with many others on my voyage from Africa. You were the closest thing to being my friend whether or not you wanted to be. That is the reason I always treated you as my confidant and never deceived you. You were always a challenge to me from the first night we met in that hellhole in Mobile. I always felt that something had personally warped inside you that was not of my doing and it placed a barrier between yourself and me. If you are reading this, I must have died without knowing just what it was. I wish our relationship could have been closer. Perhaps, if both of us would have ceded a little in our stubbornness, we could have become much different people.

"I have tried to provide for everyone who befriended me. Miss Ann is now where she should be and always could have been had her husband not been so damned mulish. His death was totally unnecessary. Ancestral pride only displays an outdated mind. Never live on what others did but what you can do. Master Andrew and his kind belonged to medieval Europe and not in a developing, vibrant country like the new United States.

"I'm quite sure Sean can manage on his own without my guiding hand. He may not be as successful, but he'll manage. I have instructed Ellis to buy him out to Mr. Wilkerson and put the construction business under that account. When he learns that Mr. Wilkerson is withdrawing from the deal and investing elsewhere, Sean will want to sell too. He certainly won't want to remain a partner with a black man. To show that his heart is in sympathy with Sean Wilkerson will offer to buy him out first. That's when I'll transfer all of the money into the Birmingham account and create a new alias. If anyone tries to trace the money they will discover the signatures don't match and there isn't as much money in the account as they expected to be. With the money he'll receive from the sale Sean and his cronies will more than likely be heading back to New York. I don't want them within a thousand miles of Miss Ann when she repossesses Whispering Willows whether or not I am dead.

"I left Morning Glory enough money to start her own restaurant business if she wants. Of all of the things I hate to leave it's that delicious cooking of hers. I hope she prepared an extra special feast for my wake.

"The only one I'm not sure of is Lulu. She always saw me as her husband but at best I could love her only as a girlfriend and not as a wife. My goals were elsewhere besides a cozy cabin with a devoted wife and children scenario she tried to inflict on me. She could never understand this. I knew of your interest in her, but she has a one-track mind. Perhaps if you were just a little less forward you could have succeeded. Again, if-if-if. I really cared for her in my own special way. Now that I'm not there I want you to look after her. She's such a fragile thing. Miss Ann is the only other person I would trust her to besides yourself. If you can't win her affection, make sure that Miss Ann takes care of her. I have left both women financially independent so that neither will be a burden to the other or to you.

"Now down to business! You seem so blinded in returning to Africa. I say it again for the last time, I believe that you are disallowing yourself great opportunities here in America. With my death, I am going to make one last try to open your eyes and make you see your future is here. Despite your nastiness, there is a potential to excel even what I have achieved if you really want only in a different course in life then the vengeful, conniving life I chose. Whether or not you decide to eat yourself alive with your hatred or release that hatred and seek out all of the great or small happiness life has to offer, will be your decision.

"For a long time I have been in contact with John Garret who finally settled near a place called Cascade, Montana. He claimed there are large areas of fertile land that can be bought for a song. Ellis handled the sale of his plantation here, but John spent what little he had traveling, and the purchase of his new land. He wrote back to Ellis looking for someone to invest in a new speculation of cattle ranching. John worked very hard to maintain his plantation here and failed, but he proved to be a studious worker and never accepted failure as an end product. He wrote to Ellis that much of the land in Montana is used for cattle and sheep but a lot of the land can be made into farmland.

As Wilkerson I loaned him five thousand dollars at one percent interest. He not only thanked me but paid the loan off in three years. This perked my business interest and under the name of Wilkerson, I have bought five hundred acres next to John's ranch. There is another envelope I gave to Ellis's keeping that contains the deed. In two more years from the writing of this will I am going to send you there as my overseer to see if you like living in the west and could rid yourself of the panther I named you. With my death the land is yours. If you choose to take my offer the other envelope contains not only the deed to the property in your name but a letter of introduction to John Garret. Take the gold we have hidden on the island and make a new life for yourself in this new land. Whispering Willows is not your home. It belongs to Miss Ann. You will only have bad memories of that place. Leave and find your own life. I hope that you trust me in this. Your future does not lie in your past in Africa. Perhaps by going to Montana you can get rid of some of the bitterness that is consuming you. I don't know. I won't be there to see the final outcome, but you have trusted my decisions in the past. Trust me in this. At least try it. With the gold hidden on the island, you can always go back to Africa and live comfortably. I want you to go forward not backward and grow with this country. It won't be easy but you're a stubborn son-of-a-bitch, and if anybody can make it, you can.

"No matter what your decision is, I wish I could have been around to see the results and give you as much hell as you have given me in the past. Good luck!

Hunter"

Jason read the letter again and yet again. After the third reading he crumpled the pages in his hand, let out a long low moan, and buried his head in the crook of his arm on top of Ellis's desk. He had never felt so empty since the night he had cried himself to sleep in Sarah's arms. Every act of vengeance he had committed came forward in his mind. All memories displayed unforeseen consequences as they ripped part of his soul from within him. His malicious achievements had resulted only in death and self-torture. Jason searched his soul for the satisfaction this vengeance had brought. The silent reply? Nothing but more agony for himself. He saw no way to right the wrongs he had done. Hunter believed and trusted him and he had betrayed him but he could not restore Hunter's life. Remorsefully he realized Sarah had showed him the only course of action to take. Learn from the past and find ways to offset the horrible damages he has done. The beast must die. Filled with self-loathing, Jason leaned back in his chair and firmly pledged that never again would the beast destroy another life through him. Slowly he salvaged his tattered composure. He had to deliberate Hunter's offer. No! He had to deliberate the course of his life.

Land! Five hundred acres! But where in the hell could he locate this place called Montana? Due to the war Jason familiarized himself with most of the states but he had no concept of Montana. It could lie somewhere in the China Sea for all he knew. The sudden opening of the door made him start. Ellis entered and threw his hat on the desk. Compassionately he disregarded Jason's agonized face and stood in back of his desk.

Jason removed the second envelope from the desk. "Your signature is on the bottom of this second letter. Do you know what it contains?" Jason asked.

Ellis sighed and plopped into his swivel chair. "Yes! He insisted on it. Well? Are you going to take the other envelope?" he asked Jason.

"My God, man, I just found out he was dead not too long ago and now this," he said grasping the opened letter tighter and slung the unopened envelope back on the desk. "Besides I have a family now. I can't make this decision by myself. Let me think this offer over and discuss it with my wife," Jason pleaded.

Ellis replaced the envelope containing the deed and letter to John Garret back into a manila folder. "Look, I have waited this long to give you that letter, another week, another month, isn't going to make any difference in whether or not you take the land. Just let me know what you want done," he said.

"May I take this with me?" Jason asked, waving the first letter.

"Why not? It's yours," Ellis shrugged as he rose, walked over to the cabinets, unlocked the nearest one to the door and replaced the file.

Jason rose and headed for the door. "I'll let you know soon one way or the other," he said before exiting the office. Ellis just nodded.

Jason didn't even recall the ride home. Sarah discovered him still sitting on the buckboard in front of the closed barn door staring at the reins in his hands. She reached up and placed her hand on his left leg. "What's happened?" she asked with apprehension.

"I've always wanted to go back to the past, but now the past has come into my present and wants to shape my future." He reached down and pulled Sarah into the seat next to him and enfolded her in his arms. Sarah had never seen Jason cry as hard since the night he defied the panther in a tiny Masai village. Still holding each other tight Jason freed one arm and reached into his coat pocket, removed the letter and handed it to Sarah.

CHAPTER XVII

FRIEND AND ENEMY

Jason sat on a newly repaired chair and leaned his right elbow on the wobbly table separating him from Sarah and stared into the blazing fireplace.

"I'm sorry I didn't mention the gold before this but it no longer exists for me. It's tainted anyway. My part of the share I used to return to Africa and began all of this misery. Unless there is a dire emergency I never want to touch it again. You are the only other person that knows of its existence. What would you like me to do with it?" a disturbed husband asked his wife.

Sarah just stared and replied, "It's your gold. The decision has to be made by you. As for me, I have already erased it from my mind."

"Then it will remain there until doomsday as far as I am concerned," Jason finalized by slapping his hand on the table.

"As to the rest of the letter Sarah what should we do? We just got here. Should we just pack up and go to---God only knows where?" he asked dispassionately.

"Jason, I have followed you half way around the world. That was your decision, and so is this," she replied. Sarah went to the fireplace and added another log to the fire after using the poker to stir the glowing embers. She stood staring into the flames while Jason watched the firelight flicker in her eyes.

"Yes but this is different. If the land was in the East or near here I wouldn't hesitate for a minute to go, but I don't know anything about this place called Montana. From what little I've heard anything west of here is no paradise. Some people say there are savages who kill all strangers. The weather can go from scorching you like the Great Desert one minute to burying you under a mountain of snow the next. What the hell do I know about cattle, sheep, or any other farming except cotton, peanuts, and soy beans?" he said, presenting the negative side of going.

"It seems as if this John Garret did well for himself and you had to learn about the crops that are grown here too," she interjected proving that even an indulged southern gentleman could survive the transition.

"He's a white man," her husband responded, adding another negative credit.

Sarah strolled across the room and sat once more at the table. "From what you just described I don't think color counts as much there as it does here," she countered.

"But there are the children and the women to consider. That land is hard enough for a man let alone a woman." He rose, rubbed the back of his neck and began to pace.

Sarah gave a hearty laugh. "And just where would Miriam be if I had been the one who passed out?" She continued to chortle for a while recollecting the event. Even Jason joined with a harrumph. She walked behind him and began to rub his neck. "My love, you have many fine qualities but being a keen judge of people is definitely not one of them. You said that Miss Ann was a pampered thing at one time. She is certainly anything but pampered now." Sarah paused in her massage and kissed him on the neck. "It has only been in the last few years that you have discovered who you really are. As I have always told you, think this through." She led him back to the table and made him sit and then sat back down across from him. "Just how well do you think you knew Hunter?"

"I don't know. As he said in the letter I never allowed him to be close to me," he reminded her.

"Did he ever lie or deceive you in any way?" she queried.

Jason paused and carefully examined his relationship with his ex-boss. "Not to my knowledge. He did to plenty of others but he always seemed to treat me fairly," he finally responded.

"Do you know of any reason he would want to strike out at you from beyond the grave?" she queried.

Instantaneously Jason replied, "No!"

"Well then! That solves half of the puzzle. As for the rest of us, just because we are women we aren't made of glass. God help the savage that meets Miriam." She placed her elbow on the table and rested her head in her hand. "That also brings to mind something else. You once told me that you didn't know what a savage was. Each tribe in Africa looked on the other as savage because they had different beliefs and ways of doing things and only an individual tribe could claim to be civilized. Is it any different here?" Jason allowed the inquiry to go unanswered. "I would be very content to stay here and raise my family, but our roots are not that deep. I would be just as happy raising them in a new land. As always the decision is yours." Sarah rose and went outside to restock the wood box leaving Jason with his uncertainty.

The next four days Jason threw himself into the manor house repairs with abandon. So long as he was physically occupied he didn't have to dwell on the enigma that haunted his waking hours. Early afternoon on his fifth day of deliberation, Sarah finally made him slow down by invading his work sanctuary.

"You have done a month's work in five days. Enough is enough!" she chastised as she began gathering up his tools. "I got a complaint from the dance-hall girl that you didn't buy her a beer and Mose wants to meet me behind the barn in an hour. Today is an undeclared Sunday. You're going to go into town, and you better come home drunk. Otherwise I won't be able to nag you." She stopped long enough to take his face between her hands and give him a big kiss. "Now get out of here and draw a pail of water to wash up before you leave," she ordered before releasing him and continued gathering his tools.

Jason stared at his wife with a big grin on his face. He knew better than to challenge her like this, so he made a mock bow to her and replied, "Yes, your majesty."

Sarah dropped a chisel, shifted her weight to her left leg, and put her hands on her hips and looked at him with a silly grin on her face. "Well! It's certainly taken you long enough time to address me properly."

Jason ran over, grabbed his wife around the waist, and spun the laughing woman in a circle. "You be nice to me, or I swear I'll find a new gal in town who will."

Sarah stopped laughing and squinted her eyes. "You do that, and I'll make you take care of Miriam for a whole month while Mose and I go to town," she threatened.

"No! No! I'll be good. I promise. Anything but that," he laughed as he released her.

"I have some clean clothes laid out on the bed. You'll find two dollars on the table. Now go wash up before I change my mind. Besides, I don't want to keep Mose waiting," she said giving he husband a big hug.

It was a little after one o'clock when Jason hitched the horses to the post in front of O'Reillys. He kicked the dust from his scuffed boots and entered the swinging doors. For a moment the darkened room blinded him. Soon the dim light from the gas lamps behind the bar lit the interior and his eyes adapted somewhat to the altered lighting from bright to dark allowing him to continue his survey of the room. Few patrons lined the bar or occupied the tables this time of day. Most people had not finished their daily work. Only two bar girls sat in a corner table. Jason guessed that most of the patrons consisted of drifters and the town drunk. Even so that made only seven patrons, including himself. He stepped up to the bar. "Beer." Jason ordered and placed one of the silver dollars on the bar. The bartender filled Jason's order after he finished polishing a sparkling mug and sat the drink on the bar in front of him. The huge, beefy-red hand of the bartender covered the coin, and started to head toward the register for change.

"This one's on me, Ed," an all too familiar voice said, forcing the bartender to quickly turn and return the coin.

Jason still tried to adjust his eyes from the sunlight so he could discern details, but he knew very well by the voice who stood next to him. "Hello, sheriff! Thanks a lot for the beer," he replied tipping the glass toward Bubba and taking a sip.

"We all thought that you were dead," Bubba remarked with a hint of chagrin.

"No I've been away for a while," Jason replied, offering no more information.

The sheriff placed his right foot on the bar railing and stared hard at the man who just received his gift. "Too bad you didn't stay. We have a law-abiding town here now that the asshole Irishman and his ass-licking nigger are dead. Turns out they were a bunch of crooks but before the law could get hold of them the Klan did. Now isn't that too bad," Bubba seemed amused.

A seething Jason remained silent and continued to sip his beer. Seven years ago, Bubba had established himself as the town menace and bully to the populace. Since then he applied the law with his own interpretation. What the sheriff couldn't enforce the Klan could. With the passage of time that danger had only increased as the surly sheriff had consolidated his power base by fear and intimidation.

Bubba took Jason's silence as obeisance to his legal status of sheriff and his illicit status as Grand Wizard of the local CHAPTER of the Ku Klux Klan. All pretense of friendliness disappeared as Bubba grabbed Jason's vest lapels. "If you think you can come back here now and start that Shamrock Enterprises shit all over again I'd think twice. We don't want your kind around here. If I were you, I would finish my beer and take my black ass out of Unionville as soon as possible before somebody thinks it will look better decorating a tree limb."

Jason started to sling the mug of beer in the thug's face, but felt a constraining hand on his arm that held the glass.

"Now, now Bubba! The man just came in here to have a beer. I'm quite sure this is just a little misunderstanding among friends. Isn't it?" The newcomer placed an emphatic accent on the question. Bubba straightened up, squinted at the man, and released Jason but made no further move. The unknown black man continued, "Now! We're all friends here aren't we? Bartender let's have a round on me," he said, releasing Jason's arm.

"I'm not drin--" Bubba's statement suspended with a cold stare from the man, whose smile never left his face. The bartender nervously placed three beers in front of the disputants.

The stranger picked up his beer and saluted Bubba. "To your continued good health, sheriff. I'll guarantee the health of my friend here," he toasted, never taking his eyes from Bubba. Nervously, Bubba never lowered the mug from his lips until it was empty. "I have some paper work I have to finish over in the office. Both of you can go to hell," Bubba sneered.

Jason watched Bubba's retreating figure almost tear the swinging doors off of their hinges as he left the bar. In amazement, Jason turned to examine the black man able to make Bubba cower.

He was in his early twenties, a bit shorter than Jason, dressed as a drover, but nothing about him imparted a threat to anyone, let alone to Bubba. The fact he had made the Grand Wizard back off became of primary importance. Jason could not believe a black man had done it.

"Name's Nat. Nat Love." Nat continued to smile, a genuine smile, and offered his hand to Jason.

"How did you do that?" asked Jason still dazzled as he shook Nat's hand.

"Do what?" Nat clicked his tongue and waved his right hand. "Oh, him. Like all other bullies they run like hell when you look them in the eye. Don't pay him any mind. I always spend a couple of days here on my way back and forth from Texas to Tennessee. Bubba and I have gotten to know each other pretty well by now. We just try to stay out of each other's way. That's all."

Jason had the feeling that Nat was not relating the entire facts concerning the incident. Nobody, but nobody, ever provoked Bubba in his own town particularly a black man. Jason determined to borrow a page from Sarah and allow Nat to disclose his narrative in his own good time.

"I have friends I'm visiting in Tennessee. I've got to leave tomorrow. One of them is getting married, and I sure don't want to miss their wedding. Half of the state is invited." Nat took another sip of beer. "Are you married?" he asked Jason.

Jason felt he could talk freely to his newfound friend. "Yep! Two little girls to boot."

"Two girls? Have you got something against boys?" the cowboy snickered.

"We're working on it. Besides, you haven't met my oldest daughter. She would drive a drunk sober," Jason replied with good nature.

"Sounds like my kind of gal," Nat quipped. Both men allowed a moment of silence.

"Are you staying at the hotel here in town, or are you staying with friends?" Jason finally asked his new friend.

"Neither. I got a camp just outside of town. Can't get anything cheaper than that," Nat chuckled.

"You said you're leaving tomorrow?" Jason asked again.

"Right at sunrise," Nat responded.

"I would like to pay you back for the favor you just did me. How would you like some of the best food east of the Mississippi and a clean bed to sleep in tonight?" Jason suggested. "Besides, if you can scare Bubba maybe you can do something with Miriam, my daughter."

Nat responded with a laugh. "Is she really all of that tough?"

"Just ask anybody who's been within five feet of her," Jason said proudly.

"A good home cooked meal is just what I need now. Let's stop at my camp long enough to get my things and I'll take you up on your offer," Nat said, finishing up his beer.

"All right, but don't say I didn't warn you. I'm not to be held responsible for what happens when Miriam get her hands on you," Jason teased.

"I have always prided myself with my handling of the ladies," Nat bragged.

"Lady? Miriam? Boy, are you ever in for a surprise," Jason chuckled.

"I'll take my chances," Nat responded. He put his arm around Jason's shoulder and both walked out the door into the arid street.

CHAPTER XVIII

PROPOSITIONS

Miriam let out another squeal as Nat lobbed her into the air. His incessant and enthralling cowboy tales held the adults as well as the children captive. He recounted anecdotes about his military father, a Buffalo Soldier of renown. Buffalo Soldiers formed from a group of ex-slaves who attempted to bring law and order to the west no matter the ethnicity. Nat had inherited all of the persistence and ethos not only from his father but from the soldiers themselves. According to the self–congratulatory cowboy nobody could break a horse like Nat and with such speed and style --- with his accent on style. The key in subduing a horse relied mainly on one's ability to know what the horse thought and react accordingly. "Now that makes good horse sense doesn't it?" he claimed with a chuckle at his pun. "Sometimes I believe they have better sense than some of the people I've met."

For all Nat's prattle, Jason ascertained little personal history. Their most welcome guest could entice the birds out of the trees and more importantly Miriam into tranquility. Jason had never experienced his daughter's quietude for such a length of time. Nat enchanted Miriam, not only with the narrative, but the body language in which Nat personified the tales. Miriam anastomosed herself to him.

Alva found calmness in her big sister boring. She diverted herself with her playthings and, finally, a siesta.

Miriam always resisted bedtime, but tonight it took nine legions of soldiers just to broach the subject. No Texas storm could possibly produce the hullabaloo fabricated by Miriam on the announcement of bedtime. Only Nat had any influence to reduce the household storm to a mild hurricane with the assurance of one more story, and he would personally tuck her into bed. The entire household, Nat included, breathed a sigh of relief when her eyes finally slid shut and she rolled over to cuddle the pillow.

Nat finally joined Jason and Sarah at the table for cider and cake Naomi had made. "Whew! Jason you were right. Give me the good old bucking broncs any day. She's really a handful. How do you do it, Sarah?"

"Oh! She keeps me busy. Come to think of it, I don't remember if I have ever had a dull day," Sarah smiled proudly.

"Jason, you have a beautiful family. I wish you could meet my ma and brother. There's nothing like a close family. What I wouldn't give to spend more time with mine," Nat said, allowing the dying fire to crackle a bit before changing the subject.

"You were telling me about this land in Montana that was given to you. You would love it there." Nat's gaze reached beyond the crude cabin wall. "You feel as if you have to put up fences to stop from falling off of the edge of the earth. Just standing in one place I once counted fifteen colors of blue in the sky. That place is so big even the moose feel small." Nat paused and rubbed his nose. "It has its drawbacks too. The winters are cold enough to freeze the sun, and it can snow higher than a man. When it drifts it can even go up to the roof of a house. The wind can blow so hard sometimes it carries away anything that's not nailed down. Despite all of that it is some of the most beautiful country I have ever seen, not to mention some of the best grazing land. The mountains in the west are so high you would swear the sky would fall if you took them away. The rivers have a liquid clearness that lets you see the markings on a silver dollar on the river bottom. Some other rivers run so wild that only a trapper or an Indian can canoe on them. I did it once in a canoe with a friend of mine. It took me two weeks to work the soreness out of my muscles from all of the paddling trying to avoid hitting huge rocks. I have never experienced a thrill like that since then.

"Well, I could go on and on. Like every place it has its good points and bad. You have to figure out if the good points outweigh the bad." Nat leaned forward and rested his chin in the pocket between his right forefinger and thumb.

"It's not just me. I have a family to consider and two other ladies," Jason amended.

"Jason, except for children, everybody is responsible for themselves," Nat shot back.

Sarah couldn't contain herself and discharged a loud whoop. "It seems as if you've learned in a very short time what I have been trying to teach my husband for years." Jason scowled.

Sarah had the perfect lead to drive another point home. "Jason, we are equally responsible for the children. I'm not telling you to go but don't use us as an excuse to stay. We came all of the way across the ocean to a strange new land. We had no idea what to expect here. How would a trip to Montana be any different? I admit. I like it here. Miss Ann is good to us. In a very short time we have become most comfortable but I could be just as comfortable in Montana or any other place you may choose to go. As always the choice is yours." Sarah poured more cider in the men's cups.

"I just don't know," Jason mused.

"I'll tell you what," Nat drawled. "I'll be back this way in a couple of months. I'll stop back by and if you want to go to Montana you can come with me back to Texas and see if we can find a herd to take to Montana and take advantage of all of that grazing land you inherited. Perhaps you may decide on farming instead. Wheat and corn seem to do well there. So you have your choice of what to do with your land. How does that sound?" Nat offered cheerfully.

"And what if I decide to stay?" Jason offered the other side of the coin.

"So what? At least I have some new friends to visit whenever I'm in the territory not to mention a warm bed and good cooking. By the way since Miriam is too young do you think Morning Glory would consider a proposal of marriage?" Nat chuckled a bit and then continued. It would certainly be better than spending time in town with Bubba. Even if I had to do it I don't think Bubba could cook as well as Morning Glory and his prejudicial company couldn't equal your pleasant house. Yep. You just think about it. No matter what you decide I still win. Hell, I won't be back through here for two months if Jeb throws a proper wedding. That gives you plenty of time to think. Now, if I'm going to make any distance tomorrow, I had better get some sleep. Thanks Sarah, for the warm welcome and for letting me meet your daughters. If Miriam was fifteen years older, I'd still marry her," Nat said, rising from the table.

"If she were fifteen years older, I'd hold you to that promise even if I had to buy a shotgun and force you to the preacher," Sarah said with a big grin on her face as she continued to clear the table. "Oh, I forgot to tell you. I put a couple of extra blankets at the foot of your bed just in case it gets cold during the night. There's a sack that Naomi gave me beside your saddlebags for you to snack on during your journey.

"If I know Morning Glory I'll still be eating those, so called, snacks on my way back." Nat turned and shook Jason's hand. "It's nice knowing you. Now you think about what I've said, and I'll see you in a couple of months. Good night, folks." Nat picked up one of the two candles on the table and was gone.

"Nice guy," Jason commented.

Sarah nodded her head while cleaning the last crumbs of cake off of the table. "He must have had a hard life to have done so much so young. I wonder just how much he said tonight is true. Some of it must be true for him to make Bubba back off."

"I don't know, but Miriam certainly believed him." Jason paused. "Sarah, what do you think about his offer?"

"I think he meant it. No matter what you decide, the girls and I are ready to stay or go," she responded.

"What about Naomi and Ruth?" he asked.

"I don't know. Just like we did when we came here we can only make the offer," Sarah responded.

"Do you think they would go?" he asked.

"Jason, you haven't even made your mind up whether or not you're going. Isn't it a bit early to ask them?" she pointed out.

"I guess so. Oh well! Let's sleep on it." He stood up, winked, and smiled at her.

As Sarah put the dishes in a pan of water, she glanced at Jason and returned his smile. "Sleep? I don't think that's what you have in mind. But these dishes will wait until morning." Sarah wiped her hands on her apron, blew out the candle, and with the dying fire illuminating the passage, headed for the bedroom in back of the cabin, separated by a curtain which contained their two sleeping treasures on the other side.

CHAPTER XIX

CATALYST

The sway of the horses' rumps mesmerized Jason as they cantered down the dusty road from Unionville on the way back to Whispering Willows. The sheriff's fortunate absence in Unionville made this trip more pleasurable. Jason didn't fear Bubba but had learned the avoidance of confrontations made life easier.

Jason had not reached a resolution to Hunter's offer and petitioned Ellis for at least a month to resolve his dilemma. Ellis agreed and requested if Jason decided to go the lawyer would need at least a month's notice before departure to inform John Garret of Jason's arrival and get Jason's Wilkerson's bank account in order. That would provide an easier transition for settlement to a pioneer, black family.

Ellis's demeanor had radically altered since the previous business transactions with Jason. He now had scruples about the desecration of the destitute Southerners and their estates. After he had settled in Unionville, he began to notice the damage done from him and his fellow Carpetbaggers. Once a relentless pursuer of money Ellis now become the town's staunchest defender for those in need of legal protection. If anyone had a large input into this change the local bigoted sheriff could take credit. People from every walk of life in the town that questioned the sheriff's actions discovered Bubba's unique brand of justice which included a beating in some alley to a hanging on a tree outside of town. The townspeople became cautious in openly denouncing the sheriff and his Klan bullies by their inability of identifying them as the culprits. Somehow the Klan always received word of any possible infractions as interpreted by the sheriff. A suspected individual's religious beliefs, country of origin, or skin color became the criteria for most reprisals by the tyrannical sheriff. Such actions sickened the lawyer and made him carefully examine his own part in the terrified community in which he lived. On finding his houseboy hung after caught getting ready to throw a rock at the bullying sheriff for refusing to move aside into the muddy street and allow Bubba to pass, the angry lawyer visited the sheriff's office and said, "By God! If you're going to rob or murder people, at least do it legally." Ellis began to fight back. He had too many Carpetbagger friends throughout the South for Bubba to take any action against him. Bubba didn't want any intervention from anyone outside of Unionville in the running of his town. Bubba knew better than to challenge people who appealed to the lawyer for help and had to tolerate Gregory's interference in local CHAPTER of the Klan's business. Ellis's legal sense prevented any legitimate action against the sheriff who made sure that no damning evidence remained after a cross burning or the immediate squashing of any threat of insurrection against his terrorism that may prevent a cross burning and unquestionable obedience to his hold on the town.

Jason's mind wandered back to Nat. What dominance did Nat have over Bubba? Not discovering an explanation to that enigma, Jason embraced the premise that any enemy of Bubba's could spontaneously call Jason a friend.

The horses automatically veered from the main road into the welcoming willows. Jason became aware he neared home as one of the small branches blown by the wind lashed his face. He continued down the shaded path until the manor appeared. He encouraged the team to a canter as an idea for a solution to his problem presented itself. If Sarah would not help in his decision-making, perhaps Naomi and Ruth would. He halted the buckboard in front of the house and bounded up the stairs to the manor.

The excited man looked at the grandfather clock whose constant rhythm could only add depth to Miss Ann's afternoon nap with its syncopation. Jason heard movement inside the dining room and pulled the sliding doors open to reveal Ruth and Lulu polishing silver. The gaze Lulu gave him would have withered stone. By her lucid eyes, Jason assumed the sick woman experienced a good day.

"Miss Ann said I was to avoid you, you bastard," Lulu hissed as she threw a spoon on the table and began to wipe her hand on the rag she used for polishing.

Ruth calmly laid her work to the side, rose, and walked behind Lulu's chair. She placed her hands on the frowning woman's shoulders, leaned near her left ear, and said in a gentle voice, "Now honey, don't go upsetting yourself. Let's go to the kitchen and start making tea for Miss Ann for when she wakes."

Jason realized another crossroads had presented itself. He positioned himself in the doorway as to block any egress. "No! Wait! Ruth, you and Lulu come with me down to the graveyard. There are certain things that must be said, and I want to say them to both of you and I want Hunter to hear them too," Jason pleaded.

Ruth had grown fond of the disturbed woman and gave Jason a contemptuous look lest he tries to hurt her friend again, but she acquiesced to his request.

Jason could see the Ruth's protectiveness in her eyes. "I promise not to say anything to hurt her, Ruth but I want her to know my side of what happened," he said with great resolve.

On arrival at the graveyard Lulu plucked some weeds away from Hunter's headstone and sat down next to it with Ruth. Jason sat on the other side of the marker and tried to gather his thoughts.

After a few moments Jason took a deep breath, exhaled, and continued, "Lulu you blame me totally for Hunter's death and though I had a very important part in it many of us including Hunter were involved in what transpired. I lied to you when I told you he had another woman. It was vicious and wrong. I was trying to get you into bed that time you gave me lemonade while you were ironing. I did that just to try and turn you against Hunter for no other reason than to cause him pain because I knew what you meant to him. As to the lies about Amanda I wanted to make you jealous and have you take the books to Sean. Sean would have taken all of the money and you would have made Hunter's life miserable. I did all of that because I was a miserable person and wanted to make everybody around me just as miserable as I was."

Lulu raised accusing eyes from her lap and locked them on Jason, still accusing, still full of hatred.

Jason refused to offer excuses. "You must wonder what he did to me to make me want to get even with him like that. The truth is --- nothing! He did absolutely nothing. I was so full of hate and self-pity I wanted to strike out at anybody. Hunter was of the African tribe that had sold me into slavery, and I blamed him for what others had done. I hated him for being Masai. Though he had questionable dealings with others, he always treated me fairly but my prejudice blinded me to that fact."

"You're a damned liar. You just wanted to get me in bed and you were jealous of Hunter," Lulu accused.

Jason shook his head. "No, Lulu. I wanted only to take you away from him to hurt him. You were a wise woman to resist me and threaten me with bodily harm like you did on my last night here. All three of us could have been hurt more if I had succeeded."

"Jason, another person died in Ilorin and another in Dahomey thanks to your rash action and even though Lulu didn't give in to you she was nearly killed too. You spread death wherever you go," Ruth added, putting her arm around Lulu's shoulder. "You have brought nothing but death to friend and foe alike."

Jason flinched. "That's true, and there's nothing I can do about that except give my promise it will never, I repeat, never happen again." he sighed.

Jason stared directly at the frowning woman. "Lulu, please believe me when I tell you I didn't want Hunter to die. I wanted him to suffer, yes, but I had no wish to see him dead. His death could not have satisfied the unwarranted hatred I had. I wanted him alive to hurt as I was hurting. I am just now learning that the problem with creating an evil is that it takes on a life of its own and doesn't necessarily follow the prescribed passage of its creator."

"It doesn't matter the reasons. I'm still without my man," she chided.

Jason leaned his back against the headstone and rubbed his forehead. "The reasons are very important," he answered. "I admit I was wrong in what I did. I can't change the past and, as of now I can't mend the wrong I have done to both of you women," he gestured to include both Lulu and Ruth, "but, Lulu I can't go on torturing myself with my past actions. The best I can do is hope not to repeat them in the future. Even that is not guaranteed. Whatever the future brings I refuse to devote my entire life to grief and atonement. That way I'll become useless to the people I've hurt, my family, and yes even to myself. I can't remain here at Whispering Willows. From the grave, Hunter steered me into a new course which I now intend to take. Remaining here would only lock both of us into grief and retribution. The wisest course for all concerned is for me to take my family and leave. This time though I am not leaving with hatred or guilt but to help ease your burden if I can and to seek out the life that Hunter saw as a good future for me. If in the future you have need of me and I have the power to do it just ask. For now I am helpless here and I have to go forward with my life." Jason now focused on the woman that provided such empathy to the injured soul of Lulu. "Ruth tell Naomi about our conversation and take tonight to think about whether or not both of you would like to come with us. Come to the cabin after breakfast and we can discuss it.

Ruth nodded, gave a gentle shake to Lulu. "Come on, honey. Let's go to the kitchen and make some tea. Miss Ann should be down soon and we can surprise her with some of those turnovers that Morning Glory made."

Ruth and Lulu rose, and the latter stared coldly at Jason. "I still don't believe you but thank you for telling me anyways." Lulu said with some doubt in her voice.

Surprisingly Jason's defense came from Ruth. As the two women walked past Jason Ruth turned, looked directly into his resolute eyes and said, "I believe you, Jason, and in time so will Lulu."

Jason watched the women leave. He had won a small victory, not over them, but over himself. Jason slowly rose from the ground. He gazed at Hunter's headstone and said, "That's the best I can do," he paused and added, "Friend." He rubbed his hand over the headstone and ambled toward his cabin in search of Sarah and the comfort her presence gave him.

CHAPTER XX

REVELATIONS

Jason stared at the retreating figures of the two women spotlighted in the morning sun. Both Ruth and Naomi had opted to remain at Whispering Willows and they had plenty of reasons to do so.

"Miss Ann needs help in running the house. Lulu thinks she's helping but makes more of a mess and leaves things undone," Ruth said.

"Morning Glory is getting arthritis in her hands and needs some help in the kitchen, though she would never admit it," added Naomi. "Miss Ann has been extra nice to both of us. We've been through enough adventures to last a lifetime. I want to put down some roots. Besides, Josh has been courting me and Ulysses has been getting awfully sweet with Ruth and has asked her to marry him. I think she is going to accept. Josh knows very well I don't love him at the moment but a little companionship is just fine and he is willing to accept that for now. He is such a gentle soul and who knows how I shall feel in a year or two."

Ruth had more to add. "You have your family and we sort of adopted one here. Lulu is just like Miriam. She's such a child. Some days she is as normal as you or I but others --- well, she needs a lot of help. She almost drives Miss Ann crazy with attention. I've learned how to keep her busy enough so that Miss Ann can get some rest. I couldn't go even if I wanted to. I'm needed here. Besides, I've fallen in love with Ulysses and want to start a family of my own."

"I made a promise to both of you aways back. I just wanted you to know that I still intend to honor it," Sarah remarked. Jason winced.

"You're released from that promise as of this minute. This is a decision we have made on our own. Good or bad after today events are of our own choosing," Naomi reassured.

"I can't release myself. Though there is miles between, if either of you need help in the future I still bind myself to that promise," vowed Sarah.

Jason placed his arm around Sarah and looked both women directly in the eyes. "And I include myself to that vow. Whether or not you accept me as part of it I promise that I shall be there if you are in need," Jason said to the shocked assembly.

After a moment's silence, Naomi said, "For the first time I believe you, Jason. There is no doubt in my mind you would be the first to come to our defense, and we thank you for it. As you can no longer live in the past, neither can we. This path is of our choosing, and you are walking down another. We offer the same promise to you both." Both women rose from their chairs, walked around the table, and hugged Sarah. To his surprise, both women gave Jason a hug, too, and left without further comment.

Jason closed the door and went to sit at the table again. Sarah reached across the table and took his hand. Words proved useless. Sarah and Jason could have passed the entire afternoon in that position, but the door suddenly opened. Miriam and Alva came rushing through.

"Kitty smell bad. Mama give kitty bath for Miriam," their daughter asked, holding the animal by its tail. Alva stood by her sister with a scrunched face and holding her nose. Sarah and Jason froze.

"Miriam! Get out of this house with that skunk this instant and let it go," her mother ordered as she and Jason jumped from the table to throw open the shutters.

A confused and smelly child retreated with her sister in tow and did as ordered. Sarah approached the door and gazed into the innocent brown eyes of her youngest daughter and took a sniff. "Good lord! You too, Alva? I'm surprised at you." Sarah turned just in time to see Jason wipe tears of laughter from his face. Sarah glowered at her husband. "Oh funny huh? In that case you can get the washtub from up at the manor and ask Ruth to give you a bar of lye soap. Sarah then turned on the little delinquents. "And you two stay just where you are and take off every bit of your clothes. Miriam, you give your sister a hand and don't either of you move until your father gets back."

Jason returned in ten minutes carrying the washtub with a bar of soap inside. By this time Sarah had recovered from the initial shock from her daughters' antics but she couldn't allow Jason to get off so easy. "Don't you start with me with that, 'She's your daughter' nonsense," she commented to her husband over her own laughter. "You keep an eye on these two while I get some hot water." Sarah shook her finger at the older naked girl staring up at her mother in all innocence. "Just you wait until you smell good enough so that I can get near enough to your backside." Jason convulsed in another round of laughter. "All right. You have just volunteered to do the honors," Sarah said, handing Jason the bar of soap as she went inside to get some hot water she kept at all times in the fireplace. After adding the correct amount of hot and cold water Sarah stood in the doorway with her arms crossed as a signal for Jason to begin.

"Come on, sweetheart! Let daddy give you a bath." Jason picked up his youngest, held her at arm's length and placed her in the tub. Miriam held the tub and tried to jump in but the rim was too high for her. Her father had to perform the same service for Miriam as for her younger sister.

Sarah watched intently as her husband smeared the soap generously over every part of their bodies. "Make sure you wash their hair well. The stink seems to linger there the most. I swear if the next one is as bad as the oldest one, I'm going to make you build two cabins and bar the door to mine," Sarah threatened with good humor.

Jason allowed Alva to help in the medicinal application of the soap but suddenly came to an abrupt halt. He turned and looked at his wife. "What do you mean 'next one'?"

Sarah walked over and examined her daughter, all the while sniffing. "I'll show you sometime next February," she said, taking the soap from Alva and starting the process over again.

Neither parent had inkling to discuss the forthcoming addition to the family at that moment. Sarah thoroughly scrubbed both of her daughters a third time before she dried them and allowed them to don clean clothes. Sarah threw up her hands in defeat. "Oh Jason, it's going to take at least a week for her to get that stink off of her body."

Miriam sniffed her arm. "Still smells bad but it didn't hurt."

"No! But your bottom will, if you try that trick again," assured Sarah, kissing her daughter on the forehead. "Now, both of you go play, Sarah said with a wave of her hand. "And don't pick up any more animals," she admonished as the two tots disappeared around the corner of the cabin.

"Well, I guess I had better get back to my chores," Jason laughed.

"Not yet you don't. Dig a hole down to China and bury those clothes. I'll never get the smell out of them no matter how much they're washed," she said resting her chin in her hand and shaking her head. I have to get busy and make the girls a new set of play clothes. I'll clean this mess up here while you do that and then you can return the washtub after I have scrubbed it out."

Jason still had a smile on his face as he followed Sarah's instructions. He heard the shearing of scissors when he came back for the tub and decided not to disturb his wife who chuckled to herself as she cut the pattern for the girls' new outfits.

The remainder of the day passed without incident. Come evening the girls ate at the far end of the table. Sarah felt relieved when she announced bedtime. Surprisingly Miriam didn't offer her usual bedtime battle, but willingly toddled off and jumped into bed beside her sister.

Sarah tucked them in as two little arms wrapped around her neck. "Night, mama. Love you," said the little truant.

"Night Miriam. I love you too although at times I don't know why. Night, Alva. Thanks for helping wash your sister." Alva merely smiled as Miriam snuggled next to her sister as an invitation to accompany her to more adventures in dreamland.

Sarah pulled the curtain isolating the children's bedroom from the common area. "I worry about her. She isn't afraid of anything, and when she gets hurt she seldom cries."

"I once asked her about that. She said that crying didn't help the hurt," Jason replied. "Then I asked her why she did the things she did and she said she wanted to know all about them. When I warned her that things could hurt her, she said more things make her feel good than hurt and besides she knows what will and won't hurt her. She evidently hasn't quite got that last part of that statement down yet if today any indication is," he chuckled.

"That stubborn curiosity and refusing to give in to life's lessons must come from my side of the family," Sarah sighed, thinking back on a little girl tossing a clod of dirt at a slaver.

"I would like to agree and take the easy way out but I'm afraid I have contributed my half as well," said Jason, remembering with pain a little boy refusing abuse by an adult.

Sarah rose to see if there was any coffee left in the pot hanging in the fireplace. "I guess that makes her OUR daughter," she chuckled. Jason joined his wife in laughter nodding his head in agreement.

Sarah returned to the table with two cups. "There was only enough for a half of a cup apiece," she said.

"That's fine. We'll be going to bed soon anyway." Jason took a sip of the rich chicory blend then looked across the table at Sarah. "Are you really pregnant, or were you just striking out in anger."

"Jason, women never joke about something like that. Of course I'm pregnant. I was going to wait another week before telling you but it just came out," Sarah countered, also savoring the black brew.

"Maybe we should put off going to Montana until after the baby is born," he offered.

"We're not going through that again are we? The baby isn't due until February, that's almost seven months away. Heaven's Jason! We could go to Africa and back in that time," she censured.

Jason furrowed his brow. "I remember we had just about the same amount of time when we left Quilimane for Ilorin. I don't care what you say. I'm not going through that experience again. We don't know what we'll find in Montana. We don't have a house built; we don't have any workers. There is a lot to be considered," he said with concern.

Sarah relaxed in the chair across from Jason and said, "Somehow I feel Nat wouldn't just take us there and abandon us. I'll wager he knows a lot of people out there. If the baby is about to come he would find a midwife, and don't wrinkle your nose.

I don't mean you. He would start to think of a lot of midwives along the way just in case I'm early. We can pay him to hang around until we get some hands and get our house built before winter. With the money from the Wilkerson account we can at least last through the winter and with the cattle or crop---"

Jason interrupted her, "I've been thinking about cattle. I've had enough of farming to last two lifetimes."

"Jason, that means you have to take a herd with you when you go to your property," Sarah said with a little fear in her voice. "You don't know anything about cattle. I don't want to see you get hurt. Food crops never trampled or gored anyone to death," Sarah said with concern. "It is your decision but you have a family that's growing. Think carefully."

"I really don't want to do any more farming. Would you rather that we remain here? We certainly could lead a very good life without the headache of cattle," he responded.

Sarah took a long sip of coffee and stared at the dying fire for a while. "No, my love! From what I have heard of Hunter he seemed to have known you as well as I do despite your defenses." Jason lowered his eyes and slumped back into his chair. Sarah sat down her cup and reached again for her husband's hand. "I didn't say that to hurt you, love. It was a very positive statement. I'm just siding with Hunter. It seems as if we were the two people in the world that saw through your pain and had your welfare at heart. You made the decision to go. Let's not change it now. One way or the other I'll make sure what money you have left after buying the cattle will hold out until our place can support itself. If things get rough we can always apply to Ellis for a loan."

Jason sat erect and placed his cup on the table. "Sarah, go see if the girls are asleep."

"What is it, Jason?" Sarah asked with concern.

"Nothing bad. It just time that I share with you Hunter's last legacy. Go check on the girls. After today's antics I know they'll sleep sound. We'll have to take the chance they won't waken. We'll be gone for about three hours," he reassured.

Sarah rose and peeped around the curtain into the girls' bedroom. "They're sound asleep. I think they'll sleep all night. Do you want me to get Ruth to watch them?"

No. The less people who know what I'm about to show you the better," he answered.

"Where are we going?" she asked.

In response, Jason lit two lanterns, handed one to his wife and beckoned Sarah to follow, and said, "To the swamp."

The couple walked over the reclaimed swampland to its soggy edge. The people who still lived in the old slave compound followed tradition and kept a boat in readiness for alligator hunting in the swamp. Superstition prevented the field hands from going too far into the boggy area and never at night believing the swamp haunted. Any lights or voices heard would confirm that rumor and discourage any exploration and make any listener cover their head in bed.

Jason helped Sarah seat herself in the stern of the dinghy and shoved the vessel into the stagnant water. Sarah started to speak, but Jason quieted her. He began examining various trees within sight of land. "Ha! Here it is!" He waved Sarah to carefully join him in the bow. He held the lamp next to a huge limb of a cypress tree. "Look at this," he told her.

Sarah squinted her eyes and peered at the underside of the limb being illuminated by the lantern. "It looks like a dipper," she observed.

"It is," Jason confirmed. "This was the marker used in the Underground Railroad to help slaves escape to the North. Mark them carefully because they are very difficult to discover unless you are looking for them. Always follow the direction the dipper handle is pointing. It's a zigzag route, and you can easily get lost if you're not paying attention. Help me look for the next one. It's been a long time since I've been to where we are going." Sarah picked up the lantern while Jason began to slowly row in the direction the dipper handle indicated.

After five minutes of slow rowing, Sarah beckoned for Jason to pause. "I'm not sure, but I think there's one here under this limb."

Jason withdrew the oars from the water and went to examine where Sarah was pointing. "Yep. That's one of them. If I remember, there're about eight more. Keep looking," he said, as he manned the oars once more and directed the bow to where the dipper handle pointed.

An hour of slow rowing elapsed before the search revealed the roofless cabin. Even the remainder of the structure didn't look too secure. Jason moored the boat in front of the edifice and gestured for Sarah to bring the lantern and follow him.

Jason made no effort to enter the shack but hurried to the back. He took the lantern from Sarah and placed it beside him on the ground next to a huge stone chimney. He searched for a broken cypress branch and began scraping the soil from the chimney. "I want to make the hole as small as possible." Jason paused and looked up at his curious wife. "What I'm about to show you tell no one not even the children unless it becomes necessary," Jason warned. "Bring the lantern over here," he directed after about three minutes of stabbing the dirt.

Sarah held the lamp over the foot-long desecration of the cabin's foundation. She saw nothing but mulch mixed with island dirt. Jason ceased digging when both heard a dull thunk. "Bring it closer," he breathed excitedly. Sarah knelt beside him as he discarded the stick and began to dig with his hands. Sarah had a sharp intake of breath as the black soil began to change color. "Oh my God, Jason! It's a chest of gold you spoke of!"

Jason stood and slapped both of his hands together to remove the soil. He then helped a stupefied Sarah to a standing position. "From the corner of the cabin to about three feet on the other side of the chimney is the gold Hunter accumulated during the war. He always added to it, even when he was partners with Sean. He called it his insurance policy. The corner on the other side of the chimney to here belongs to me." Jason paused and thought for a while. "I guess it all belongs to me now. That's what I'm going to use to start our new life if the Wilkerson account depletes but I don't think so. The company seems to be doing well and monthly deposits are made regularly. Ellis handles that end and has no idea of the gold here. Hunter and I were the only two who knew of this place. When I returned to Africa, I took only about a third of what Hunter had placed here for me. He paid me half of my salary in Yankee dollars to save for my return trip to Africa but insisted that half of it be placed in "insurance" like he did. That gold came from ruined lives, and it almost ruined mine. I vowed on my return never to touch the rest of it but Sarah I beginning to believe that it isn't the gold, it's the way the person uses it."

Sarah, still stunned by the amount of gold, said, "What do you intend to do with all of this?"

"If in the future the family is in great need the gold is here but I want us to resolve our problems without it if we can. Ellis has combined both Wilkerson accounts and there should be enough money in the Birmingham account to meet our needs. I'll open an account where we are going and have Ellis transfer money as needed. None of Hunter's gold will be touched but it is here if needed."

"He was rich beyond belief," she stammered.

"No, my love! It wasn't his greed for gold that destroyed him but his greed for power. This," Jason said, pointing to the ground, "was only his means of getting it. I believe he knew that I would be a richer man than he one day because he never had room in his life for a Sarah. Even with her simplicity Lulu would have made life good for him but that isn't what he wanted. With his ability to control people he could have molded her into a great asset and her unreserved love would have given him a peace he never achieved. His loss is my gain. That's why he had great patience with me. He used me for his own ends despite his offered friendship. But I think he also saw that one day I would have a life he never could have and he was curious and just a bit envious about that."

Jason had Sarah hold the lantern while he refilled the hole. He paused and looked up at her. "It's really funny. I hated him for what he was and he must have envied me for what I could become."

Sarah smiled down at Jason and stroked his cheek. "Though I never met him I like this Hunter of yours. He was a wiser man than you knew at the time. Let's let Hunter and his insurance rest."

Jason nodded in agreement "One other thing, be sure that if ever you have to come to this island, bring only things that you need and cover all traces of any living being having been here."

Husband and wife spent the next hour destroying all traces of their visit and then stepped back into the boat. As the cabin disappeared into the cypress trees, Jason stopped rowing for a moment and went to the bow to give Sarah a kiss. No more secrets separated them. Jason's had bared his soul. With a light heart, Jason rowed back to Whispering Willows.

CHAPTER XXI

BACKFIRE

When Jason apprised Ellis of his decision to relocate to Montana Ellis received power of attorney and an executor fee of $5 a month. The lawyer immediately posted letters to John Garret to expect settlement on the land adjacent to his and to give the new family help in settling in their new home. Ellis left the date of Jason's arrival open but estimated they would be there by late summer. Gregory suggested Jason keep John advised of his progress north so that they could rendezvous in Cascade.

Toward the end of the first week of June a brown mare came bounding from between the willows and headed toward the old slave quarters. Miriam who had been assisting her mother with the wash by handing her clothes pins dropped the bag and ran toward the rider screaming, "Nat! Nat!"

Nat rode past the little girl and swooped her into his arms, placed her in the saddle in front of him, and galloped around the open encampment bordered by the cabins. Miriam placed her small hands on the reins just below Nat's and feigned control of the steed.

Sarah picked up Miriam's scattered pins and placed them back into the laundry basket. "Nat! You're as bad as she is. Both of you stop that before you break your necks, she scolded. "Miriam, you get back here and help me finish hanging these clothes or I swear you'll eat supper tonight in your bed." Nonetheless, Sarah smiled at the mounted cowboy. "Nat Jason's up at the house fixing a broken hinge on the cold cellar door. Go on up there and visit so that Little Miss Tornado can complete her housework," she smiled.

Nat reined his horse two feet from Sarah and unceremoniously plopped the squealing Miriam into the laundry basket with a wink. Sarah shook a finger at the rider and said, "If you get this laundry dirty again both of you are going to spend the night scrubbing it clean." Sarah turned and grabbed Miriam by the arm pulling her out of the basket. "Now get your pins and help me hang these clothes." Turning back to the cowboy, she said, "As for you," but she conversed with air as the horse and rider already disappeared around the back of the manor.

As Nat rounded the corner he saw Jason screwing a new hinge on one of the cellar doors. Jason ceased work and offered his hand to the horseman. "I heard you arrive. Miriam screamed your name loud enough to be heard over in Texas."

Miss Ann poked her head out of the door and looked at the two men. "I wondered what it was that bolted past the house."

"Miss Ann, I would like you to meet Nat Love. Nat, this is the owner of the plantation, Mrs. Harrison, but all of us call her Miss Ann," said Jason who played the part of host.

Nat repositioned the horse so he could face the lady, partially rose in the stirrups tipped his weather-beaten hat toward the mistress of Whispering Willows and said, "Miss Ann." She, in turn gave him a gracious smile and curtsey.

"I'll wager those hinges were on there since the house was built. You're lucky the doors haven't fallen into the cellar. Make sure somebody keeps them well oiled," Jason cautioned her.

"I'll make sure Josh makes a note of that," Ann responded. "Well. You have company. Go get cleaned up. That's enough for one day." Ann then addressed the rider. "The best handyman I ever had informed me when you arrived you would be taking him to God only knows where," she said with some sadness.

"We're going to Texas first, then to Montana, ma'am," Nat responded tipping his hat again.

"Well I'm going to miss him and his family. Now remember we're all going to have a farewell dinner at the manor the night before you leave, Jason. You come, too, Mr. Love," Ann reminded.

"You just try to keep me away if Morning Glory is doing the cooking, Miss Ann. I'd be much obliged," Nat responded, tipping his hat for the third time.

From behind Ann came a cheerful voice. "Miss Ann! Miss Ann! Has Mr. Andrew come home? Don't let him see you yet. Come on back in here and let me make you look pretty for him. Lord! You are standing in the door chatting with the field hands while the master is waiting. Come on back inside while I find the curling iron. I don't want Mr. Andrew seeing you look like some poor white trash. He'll sell me off to Texas for sure." The exuberance of Lulu's voice made Ann's hand wrap around the locket over her breast.

"I'll be right in. You go look for the curling iron," Ann ordered in faltering articulation. "It's going to be a difficult evening," she sighed.

"Is there anything I can do?" Jason asked with concern.

Ann closed her eyes and shook her head. As she reentered the house the two men heard the mistress call, Ruth! Ruth!"

Nat sensed something was amiss. "What was that all about?" he asked.

"It's a long story. I'll tell you about it while I wash up," Jason said in a depressed tone. Jason and Nat headed for the shed to dispose of the ladder he had used to examine the back of the house shutter hinges and tools for repairing the cellar door. Jason began to relate to his friend his involvement in Lulu's current condition as he rolled up his shirtsleeves and headed for the water pump.

The sun was still high in the early summer evening sky when the two men entered the cabin for supper. Miriam immediately ambushed Nat from behind the door. "Miriam! The men just got cleaned up for supper and you're going to get Nat all dirty rolling on the floor," Sarah reprimanded as she began to place the food on the table. Nat rolled over on his back and raised the squealing Miriam at arm's length over him and rocked her from side to side. Alva, not to be ignored body-slammed Nat's abdomen which produced a grunt from the besieged man. Nat finally wrestled a girl under each arm and sat them down on either side the bench next to him at the table.

"Now if you don't clean your plate like I intend to do I won't tell you the story of how Rattlesnake Pete escaped from being scalped by Apaches," he threatened. Miriam began to inhale her food. "Whoa! Slow down little lady. If you finish before the rest of us, you're just going to have to wait. Let's see if we can all finish together and all of us can enjoy the story," Nat laughed. Mump-like cheeks smiled up at the cowboy and nodded. The remainder of the meal Nat interlaced with tales of the Tennessee wedding and the month-long reception that followed.

The summer sky shone bluish-white on the western horizon by the time Sarah had washed and stowed the dishes. Nat had related Rattlesnake Pete's tale for the third time when Sarah announced bedtime for the girls. Miriam ran right for the bed because Nat had promised to take her riding tomorrow. She surmised the quicker she slept the quicker tomorrow would arrive. As the last vestiges of day surrendered to the black mantle of night the three adults settled at the table to talk.

Jason lit a lamp, and Sarah placed three cups of coffee on the table and offered Nat pound cake. "No, thanks. Morning Glory is one dangerous woman. I want to avoid her cooking as much as possible. She would have me fat as a pig in three weeks if I lived here," he replied taking a sip of the hot brew. "Well. According to what Miss Ann said you have decided," Nat said lacing his fingers behind his head and leaning back.

Jason leaned forward on the table and clasped both hands. "Sarah and I have decided to go to Montana but we're going to need help getting there. I don't want to do a lot of farming just enough to feed ourselves and I want to purchase a herd of cattle to take with me. I've certainly ridden horses around the plantation but I have no idea on how to drive cattle. Miss Ann is willing to sell me a buckboard and two of her finest horses. The two ladies who came from Africa with us have decided to remain here. It will be just Sarah, the girls, and myself but I'll need an experienced crew to herd the cattle north and to teach the new owner of a cattle ranch a trick or two," Jason joked.

Nat scratched his chin. "That shouldn't be too hard to do. I have a good friend I'm meeting in Dallas who owes me a favor but I think he would want to go Montana just for the experience. The buckboard will be all right for now but it's worthless on the trip north."

Jason thought that he had made good provisions for the trip. "Why's that? We can load a lot of things on it," he said.

"The roads north are no more than trails. There can be some serious storms on the plains this time of year, and the sun can cause heat stroke if you're not careful. What you need for the trip is a Calistoga Wagon. In fact, you'll probably need two of them," Nat advised.

"Why so many?" Sarah asked.

Nat also leaned his arms on the table as he tried to explain. "Well, the first one you'll need for yourselves and your belongings. The second will have all of the supplies we need for the drive:

food, water, and ammunition. The cook can drive that one. You can only drive the herd no more than ten miles per day and even that's stretching it. The cook drives ahead of the herd and sets up camp so that when the cowboys arrive at the end of the day the food is ready."

Jason now took his turn in rubbing his chin. "Gee! I didn't think this would be so complicated."

Nat leaned back in his chair. "It really isn't if you leave well prepared for anything that might happen along the way. Don't bother yourself with what you need. Will and I will take care of that in Dallas. If you're willing to spend the money, we'll get you there safe and sound with only a few bruises on your bottom," he chuckled.

"I saw a couple of Calistoga wagons during the war being used by the army. You're right. They are much larger than a buckboard, can hold more supplies, and provide shelter for all of us and the supplies," Jason agreed.

"Besides, there will be room for the girls to play and nap during the day without the danger of falling off of the side. When he was alive Pa, taught me how to pack one of those things. If it's done right, you could get everything in this cabin in there, and still put the cabin in," Nat joked.

Sarah said, "Except for the clothes and linen, everything here belongs to Miss Ann. We thought we would buy everything we need in Texas before we left to go north. We'll take the buckboard there and stay at inns along the way to Dallas. Once there, we'll sell the buckboard and buy the wagons." As an afterthought, she added, "We have enough money laid aside, so don't worry about the cost of the inns."

"Well, it seems you have everything covered." Nat's tone became very serious. "Jason, I have another request. Whether you know it or not, I think you have one of the best cowpunchers already."

"Who?" Jason asked.

"Miriam." Nat replied.

Sarah rapidly replied, astonished, "Nat, she's nothing but a baby."

Nat refused to change his mind. "Babies have a way of growing up. Yes, she too young now, what is she, about seven? But with her quick mind and energy she could make any man in the west seem like a city slicker by the time she's fifteen."

"She can't steady herself on a horse yet, and she'll break her neck trying if she got wind of what you just said," Sarah warned.

Nat smiled and said, "I thoroughly agree with you, but, knowing her, do you think that's going to stop her? What I want to do is take her under my wing. Let her ride with me and get the feel of a horse and how to control it."

Jason's brow furrowed as he addressed the cowboy. "That will only encourage her to try on her own, Nat."

Nat never lost his smile. "She's going to do it whether or not we want her to. It will be all but impossible to drive the wagons, watch the cattle, watch for danger around the next bend, AND keep an eye on her. If she rides with me, I'll keep an eye on her at all times. If I'm needed in a dangerous situation, I'll drop her off at the wagon with the promise to come back for her. That should keep her from getting into trouble. And, I always have my ace in the hole to keep her in line."

Sarah shook her head and looked dubiously at Nat. "I don't think I'm going to like the answer, but I'll ask anyway. What ace in the hole?"

Nat's smile broke into a large grin. "Her pony."

Sarah gaped at the cowboy. "Pony? Nat have you lost what little sense you have?"

Sarah could not daunt Nat. "Think Sarah. You have to agree that she is going to ride the first chance she gets. That way she could really get hurt. If we teach her how to control the animal and be responsible for its care, but most of the time ride with me, our lives are going to be much simpler. If she rides her pony away from the wagons then I'll take it away from her and I won't take her with me for a couple of weeks. That threat should keep her in line. I'll teach her the proper way to mount and ride and take care of her animal. Without knowing it, she will be under twenty-four hour supervision, not hold up the drive with some antic, and learn to be the best damned cowgirl west of the Mississippi. If I know anything about Will Pickins and his hands, she'll have some of the best teachers that ever lived. I'll bet a five dollar gold piece that by the time she's a woman, she can outride any cowhand for three hundred miles around."

Jason looked over at his wife. "What he says makes a lot of sense. With Nat, Will, and his crew watching her, she would be less likely to get hurt. If we left her alone in back of the wagon with Alva, she could get both her and her sister hurt. You and another have to drive the wagons while we herd. I want to ride with the others to learn what I have to do to become a capable cowboy and unless you have eyes in back of your head you can't keep constant watch on our little windstorm and drive the wagon at the same time. With all the cattle and horse hooves, not to mention unforeseen dangers, we don't need the added burden of curbing her energy. Nat's plan has merit."

"I hate to admit it but you're right," Sarah grumbled. "But if she gets even a broken fingernail you'll answer to me, Nat Love," she threatened.

Sarah's threat made Nat laugh. "Sarah, she's going to get quite a few bruises and scrapes. That's part of the course, but none of them will be serious I promise you. There's one whole lesson on how to protect yourself from a fall from the horse. By the time I leave next spring, you're going to be proud of your little cowgirl."

Nat closed the argument once and for all. "Sarah, I love the little demon almost as much as you do. Do you really believe that I would do anything to hurt her? If anything I want to protect her from hurting herself."

Sarah stared long into the cowboy's eyes. Finally she slammed both hands on the table and rose to make a new pot of coffee. "If we were talking about Alva you would have a fight on your hands--- but Miriam? You're right, Nat. Just take good care of her."

Nat pretended desperation. "That's not the problem. Who's going to take care of me at the end of the day?"

Laughter suffused the cabin as Sarah took the pail and went to get water for the coffee. "Well Nat, you can't say I didn't warn you that day back at O'Reiley's," Jason snickered.

Jason waited until Sarah returned and placed the brewing coffee over the fire. With the problem of Miriam resolved Jason asked, "How many men will we need for the drive north?"

"How large of a herd do you want to buy?" Nat countered.

"That's where you come in. How big of a herd do you think?" Jason replied.

"That all depends on the acreage, if you want them strictly for dairy, or do you want to breed beef cattle?" Nat asked.

"I was figuring on beef cattle for about almost five hundred acres. I want to use some of the acreage to plant vegetables for the family and grow hay for the cattle." Jason stammered.

"You had better be damned sure. Both are a lot of work, but beef cattle can be even more difficult than dairy. The secret to them is selecting the correct bulls. I don't know too much about that, but my friend does. He has a crew of eight men working for him. If the pay is good enough, he'll take your herd north," Nat reassured.

"I'll give each man $5 a week. How's that?" Jason asked.

Nat gave a whistle. "That's a lot of money to trail herd a bunch of cows. I figure you could start with five hundred head. Not all will survive the trip. That will be enough to get started and breed a larger herd. A small herd will allow you time to learn the ropes of the cattle business."

"Are you sure that only nine men can handle that amount of cattle?" Jason asked dubiously.

Nat burst out laughing. "Hey! I'm going along, too. Between Will, his boys, and myself we could drive every cow south of Kansas north. You do have a lot to learn about being a cowboy. If anybody can teach you my friend, Will, can. When we arrive in Montana he'll make damned sure you have good cowboys to take the place of his crew and you'll be a decent straw boss before they return to Texas. It wouldn't hurt to hire two or three men as extras while in Texas. Will can work with them and groom your new foreman along the way. By next spring, the foreman should be pretty good at selecting your new crew."

"Can they help us build a cabin before winter?" Sarah asked.

Nat rubbed his chin again. "Hmmm! Let's see! If we leave in the next couple of days we should get to Dallas in a week and a half, two weeks tops. Another two weeks to select and round up the herd, buy supplies, and pack the wagons. Another month to move the cattle to Montana." He paused in his evaluation and studied the ceiling. "That means that we should arrive in Cascade sometime in late August or the beginning of September. Whew! That's cutting it mighty close to build the cabin and the bunk houses before the snow sets in."

"I'm willing to pay them the same wages as they had during the drive if they remain until spring. By that time I hope to be a seasoned cowhand, and Will should have selected my crew," Jason offered.

Nat draped his right arm over the chair back and began circling a coffee cup ring on the table with his left index finger. "It's not the money. Some cowboys, like Will and myself have an itch we can't scratch. Staying in one place too long makes us feel caged. I can't speak for Will, but I'll stay with you until spring. I've never known Will to let down a fellow in need. We'll just have to wait and see what he has to say."

"We'll go to town tomorrow and buy what we need for the trip to Texas," Jason said rising from his chair and tossing the coffee grounds in the bottom of his cup into the fire making it hiss.

Nat ceased his abstract drawing on the table and rose. "It will have to be in the afternoon. I have a date with a lady to go riding in the morning," he smiled. Both parents laughed.

Sarah rose and removed the now empty cups from the table. She handed a taper to Nat and informed him that she served breakfast at six.

Nat walked to the door, and then turned. "If I know Miriam she'll be outside of this door at five demanding the sun rise.

"I promise to keep her in tow until you wake up. Goodnight Nat," said Sarah.

"Goodnight Sarah. Jason." Nat tipped his hat and left.

Alone in the cabin, Sarah encircled her husband's waist. "I wish there were more people like him in this world," she commented.

Jason agreed, blew out the remaining candle and directed his wife to the solace of their bedroom.

Miriam parked herself outside Nat's door half-an-hour before dawn, waiting for Nat with a promise to Sarah not to make a sound until he came out of the cabin. All through breakfast she questioned him about horses. After the last drop of coffee had been consumed Miriam's date with heaven finally arrived.

Nat convinced Miriam not to gallop until she had firm command of the horse. Before mounting he gave her pointers on checking the horse for any injuries and showed her how to saddle. Once in the saddle Nat showed her how to use her legs, heels, and reins for control. A desert could not absorb water with such rapidity as did the little muffin did the riding lesson. She constantly complained to Nat about the horse inability to respond to her commands because she was so small. That being expressed by her, Nat made her promise not to ride a horse alone until her head reached the top of the horse's front leg. After two hours of galloping around Whispering Willows together on the same horse Nat and Miriam rode by Jason's cabin where Sarah sat darning clothes and Alva played with a doll at her mother's feet. As they rode by, Miriam gave her mother a big grin while Nat let out a whoop and raised both hands in the air. To Sarah's chagrin, Miriam was in complete control of the reins of the horse.

Sarah stood dumping the darning basket on the ground. "Miriam! You come here this instant. Your father will be back any minute now from the manor to go into town with Nat. Nat, you should know better than to let a little baby try to control a horse." Even Alva looked with surprise at her bigger sister riding by.

Nat laughed. "If she can control an animal as well as she does people, God help the wildlife. She's a natural born rider, Sarah. I've been around horses all of my life, and this animal likes her. She could ride by herself in a year or so."

"Nat! You get those foolish ideas out of your head. Next you'll have her galloping a horse around the dinner table," Sarah said with just a touch of anger and fear.

"If anyone could do it she could and I'll bet five dollars she wouldn't break a cup or a dish on the table," Nat added.

Sarah walked up to the lathered beast, gathered her daughter in her arms and placed her on the ground. "Run up to the manor and tell your father that Nat is ready to go," Sarah smiled giving her daughter a motherly pat on the bottom.

Miriam, still excited from her ride with Nat, let out a whoop like Nat and pretended she was galloping a horse, as she ran to do her mother's bidding.

Nat burst out laughing at the little girl's capers. Sarah just smiled "Lord! I'm going to be gray before we get to Montana. Remember no horse riding alone and don't mention that pony until we're in Texas. If you tell her now we'll all have to take the next boat back to Africa you included if we want any peace." Sarah returned to her work area, picked up Alva, and gave her a kiss.

"If you were like your sister I would leave home," Sarah said giving Alva's belly a tickle which produced the usual cacophony of giggles.

Nat rested his arm on the saddle pommel after wiping the sweat from his brow. "They're a good balance, Sarah. Think how dull your life would be if Miriam was just like Alva," Nat teased.

"I don't have to worry about that with you around to spur her on. I'll give your horse a rub down. You get ready to go," Sarah countered.

"That is going to be my next lesson. I can put her on a box to help with the rub down," Nat countered.

She looked around the back of the horse to see Jason coming down the path with Miriam galloping circles around her amused father. As Jason approached his wife, Sarah squinted one eye and said, "One word from you, Jason and you do the dishes for a month."

Jason couldn't restrain a hearty laugh as he gave Sarah and Alva a kiss then turned to Nat. "Just as soon as I have the team hitched we'll leave. For some unknown reason my wife is threatening to punish us beyond belief." Sarah gave him a friendly cuff on the shoulder. Both men headed for the barn while Sarah placed Alva on the ground long enough to attempt to corral her little human filly.

Provisioning required only a short span of time. Jason intended to purchase most of supplies in Texas. Nat assured Jason he would require ample armament in the form of small arms and rifles with ammunition to match. Even law enforcers considered most of the South still lawless territory and even if the trip proved uneventful the group would still need the armament for protection and hunting on the trip north. Jason purchased few food supplies since Sarah would prepare only light meals during the day on their trip. The inns would supply the main meal of the day. Hoping to keep the children occupied he added a few toys to the purchase list. They would suffice for Alva, but Miriam---well?

Having completed their tasks early Jason and Nat headed for O'Reilly's for afternoon libation. They headed toward the back of the saloon to diminish the effects of hot, dusty air coming in from the street. Nat propped his feet up on an empty chair he requisitioned from the table next to them.

"Well that should hold us until we reach Dallas. I would never have thought to buy rock candy to take on the trip for the girls," Nat said as he took a swig of beer.

"That comes with being a father. Whenever you're in town the girls always expect a treat when you return. I'll take out a couple of pieces for them now but you hide the rest in your saddle bags so we'll have something to sweeten their disposition on the trip," Jason said.

Neither men paid particular attention to the two figures that entered and positioned themselves at the bar near the swinging doors. Only when one of them placed an order with the bartender did they hear a voice that made them take heed.

"Good afternoon, sheriff," Nat smiled, tipping his hat at his nemesis. Instead of the usual grunt, Bubba smiled and tipped his hat back.

"I didn't know that you were so chummy with uppity niggers, sheriff," said the stranger.

Alarms went off in Nat's head. "Stay here and don't move," Nat said to Jason, never removing his eyes from the stranger. Nat made no comment but rose and took his beer to the other end of the bar away from the stranger and the sheriff. Jason scanned for the bartender who had disappeared along with the two dance hall girls that had been seen playing cards at the gambling table.

"You really think you're some hotshot. Don't you nigger?" The stranger walked around the bar away from Bubba and pushed his frock coat back on the right revealing a Colt .45.

Nat leaned against the bar staring at the man. He took a sip of his beer but never broke eye contact.

"'Deadeye Dick' they call you. Right?" the stranger said with a chuckle, "Is the eye of your dick really dead. Can't even get it up. Huh, boy?"

Nat didn't move from his leaning position on the bar or offer any comment but he kept strict observance of the stranger's movements.

"What's the matter nigger? Too damned scared to speak? If you piss your pants for me, I may just let you go with a bullet hole through your balls." Both Jason and Nat could hear Bubba's chuckle mingling with the stranger's. Nat still hadn't moved.

The stranger spread his legs about two feet apart, and hooked his thumbs beside his silver belt buckle. His gray hat was upside-down on the bar next to where Bubba enjoyed the show and sipped his beer.

Nat guessed the stranger in his late twenties or early thirties. The scarecrow-like gunfighter had a youthful face marred by heavy lines across the forehead and crow's feet around the eyes when he smiled. He looked Nat up and down with a sneer of contempt. Suddenly he removed his right thumb from his belt and the fingers of his hand pointed toward the floor. They twitched just once as he moved for his gun. A shot resounded through the bar and a look of shock and disbelief covered the stranger's face before he slumped against the bar and sank to the floor. A red stream trickled from underneath the body whose gun still rested within its holster. Jason, numb with fear couldn't move.

Instead of placing his gun back into its holster, Nat slowly walked to the opposite end of the bar, past the bleeding corpse and paused directly in front of Bubba.

"I thought that after that little picnic we had a year ago when I left three of your men dead and two crippled for life that we had an understanding. I see I was mistaken," Nat said in a low voice. Bubba backed away from Nat until he was flat against the wall of the bar. He was smart enough to keep his hands at chest level and never lower them below his belly.

Nat continued his advance on the terrified man. He placed his pistol at the bridge of Bubba's nose where the sheriff's eyebrows almost met. Sweat cascaded from Bubba's head, his pants became wet with urine, and his hands shook as if he had palsy. Nat never took his eyes from Bubba's.

"If ever you pull a trick like this again the first bullet will be right here," Nat whispered and he pushed the barrel of the gun against Bubba's forehead. "Then I'm going to knit a sweater before I send the second one through the one you hired to kill me." As if to emphasize his point, Nat pushed the gun so hard against the sheriff's forehead making a red mark that made

Bubba look like a Hindu. "If you haven't the nerve to kill me yourself then stay out of my way or it could mean your own death. If ever my friend and I come in here for a drink I want you to leave immediately. If we are in here already and you enter I want you to turn around and leave. I'm giving you this advice for your own protection. Do you understand, bastard?" Nat growled.

Bubba didn't reply.

Nat cocked the hammer of his gun. "I asked you a question, asshole."

Bubba's head rapidly shook up and down. The sheriff's chattering teeth and shaking hands made Nat smile. "Now go get a couple of your Klansmen--" Bubba's eyebrows arched. "Yes, I said Klansmen, and get this piece of shit out of here so that my friend and I can finish our beer without the stench of you or any of your hired morons around. And send the damn bartender back in here. These beers are flat," Nat said in a more pleasant tone as he removed his pistol from Bubba's forehead, uncocked the weapon, and placed it back into his holster. Nat allowed the nervous sheriff to exit and signal two of his sadly disappointed men waiting on the saloon porch to remove the gunslinger's body.

The bartender and the dance hall girls reentered. Ed resumed his position behind the bar. The girls nervously returned to the gambling table. Nat walked past the two men carrying the stranger's body out the swinging doors and walked to the front of the bar. "I suggest that you spread saw dust over there," he said pointing to the spot where the body had lain. "Blood leaves an awful stain in wood. But before you do that my friend and I want two more beers." Nat flipped a silver dollar that landed on the bar with head's up. "Keep the change."

When Nat returned to the table, Jason's hands shook as much as Bubba's had. "Deadeye Dick! Why didn't you tell me you were Deadeye Dick. Everybody west of Atlanta knows you," said an amazed Jason.

"Now, don't you start? I don't know who gave me that damned name, but I can't seem to get rid of it," Nat looked at the shaken black man with compassion. "Jason, I don't enjoy killing people but I'll be damned if I'm going to allow the Bubbas of this world to push me or people I care about around. If I have to blast a hole in a few of those idiots heads to make the rest of them learn then so be it." The bartender arrived with the new libations and hastily departed to obtain some sawdust heaped in back of the saloon.

"Don't mention any of this to anybody back at Whispering Willows. I want all of us to leave on a happy note. Let's not let Bubba spoil our trip. OK?" Nat asked. Jason nodded agreement, but it took over an hour of conversation with Nat before Jason's hands stopped trembling.

CHAPTER XXII

FAREWELLS

Ann stood in the doorway of the dining room and stared at the black faces seated there and two white faces at the end of the table. Smiling, she took her place at the other end but remained standing. Clasping the heart-shaped pendant hanging above her rose-colored dress, she surveyed her guests.

Jason sat to the right of the hostess with his wife opposite him. Next to her sat Ruth holding Alva in her lap. Across from her sat Naomi with Nat and Miriam beside her. Under Nat's tutelage, the little girl exhibited the best of quiet behaviors at least for her. Next to Ruth sat a quiet and observant Lulu facing an empty chair. At the furthermost end of the table sat Gregory Ellis and his wife.

Ann tapped her water glass with her knife and the face of Morning Glory appeared around the serving door to the dining room.

"Tonight is a special occasion. Morning Glory, would you please wheel the food cart in and join us at the table? Tonight is a semi-buffet and each person will have to serve themselves." Ann said.

Jason could not resist a barb. "At long last we'll be able to see Morning Glory groan as she struggles to get up from the table after eating her delicious cooking. I did it for years."

Morning Glory grinned from ear to ear. "You be good Mr. Jason or I won't give you a little something to see you along the road."

Jason placed his hands on the side of his head and shook it. "Lord, Nat! We'll have to leave right after supper and see if we can buy another buckboard." The entire table erupted with laughter.

The next hour passed with pleasant conversation to match the luscious cuisine. Nat managed to have Miriam clean her plate. Sarah made a mental note to ask him how he did that.

"I'll go back to the kitchen and get the dessert," Morning Glory said as she rose and emitted a slight groan. Immediately she glanced to her left and saw a smiling Jason with arched eyebrows nodding his head at her. Morning Glory burst out laughing as she exited through the serving door taking the food cart with her.

In five minutes, she returned with the dessert cart in tow. All looked at the shoofly pie that occupied center stage. Surrounding Morning Glory's specialty hungry eyes despite the abundant dinner ogled a plate of peach tarts and a three-tiered chocolate cake. All heads turned to the end of the table that resounded with the chime of a water glass.

"Before we have our dessert and coffee, I would like to offer a toast to Jason and his family. You'll be sorely missed and if you or yours are in the area Whispering Willow's doors are always open for you." Ann lifted her wine glass as did all other adults, who now stood, and toasted the departing family. As the guests sat back down, the hostess remained standing.

Ann clasped her hands in front and looked at each individual before speaking. "This room has not heard such laughter since before the war. For that I thank you.

"Ten years ago this dinner would have been impossible. Even I would never have believed that I would see Negro faces sitting at my table. Even now Andrew would never have approved and I seriously doubt that he could have learned the lesson I did: trust, love, and devotion can come from many directions. When we receive it from a non-white we felt it is only our due. How arrogant we white folks can be at times. I learned this bitter lesson in Charleston.

"Living with Gwen gave me a lot of time to examine my life. I realized I had been pampered and molded into a person both Papa and Andrew wanted me to be not what I could have been. I resigned myself to playing with my grandchildren when permitted, shunted to the corner at parties, and left to my own devices so long as it didn't interfere with Gwen's daily running of the household. I was no longer the primary focus of attention which gave me a lot of time to think.

"With the help of Gwen and Adam I considered moving and getting a house of my own. I encouraged Gwen to teach me the real running of a household. No longer fluttering and helpless I took active interest on how she managed things. I know there were many times Gwen wanted to strangle me for asking so many questions. It wasn't easy but I learned.

"My life had been one of subjection but not entirely. I defied Papa when I married Andrew. I helped Hunter save Whispering Willows when the Yankee army marched through. I did have strength. I just never had used it much. I lived in a dream and Andrew loved that dream.

"When the South as we once knew it died Andrew's dream died and I was a part of that dream. I tried to pretend the dream could go on but Andrew knew better. Though I didn't know it at the time, I couldn't tell the difference between dreams and memories. I now realize I live in memories. Andrew could never have done that. God rest his soul."

Ann paused, took a sip of water and dabbed her eyes on her napkin. Lulu rose to go to her mistress but Ann shook her head and waved the former maid back to her seat. After clearing her throat, Ann continued, "I still had some money left over from the original sale of the plantation, and I felt it time for me to move on. I told Gwen and Adam of my plans and they finally surrendered to my wish to move.

"I had just returned from my first day of house hunting, when Gwen informed me I had a visitor. It seemed strange to me after all of the frequent callers to the house for Gwen this one was for me. After I hung up my cloak and bonnet and entered the drawing room, I was bowled over seeing Mr. Ellis sitting there." Ann pointed her arm to the end of the table where the grinning lawyer tipped his wine glass toward his hostess.

"I was shocked to discover that Hunter had bought Whispering Willows under the name of Wilkerson. Gregory explained to me that Hunter had stored a lot of Yankee coins in a Charleston bank during the war, and all from the sale of peanuts, beans and vegetables from the reclaimed swamp land. I remembered him constantly advising me to receive all payments in Yankee currency and not Confederate money but Andrew held to his dream. Had Andrew listened to Hunter, Whispering Willows would never have been lost. But my darling did the best he could according to his beliefs.

"I almost fainted when he told me that Hunter was dead and had bequeathed the plantation to me with an escrow account for its maintenance. I almost fainted again when Mr. Ellis told me I had also inherited a personal dowry."

Ann again looked at the end of the table. "Mr. Ellis, you went on and on with the 'party of the first part' and 'the party of the second part.' I didn't hear a word you said. Only one thing was going through my mind: I'm going home." Ann paused and took another drink of water.

"My heart was in my throat as I drove up the line of willows and the house came into view. Home! I swore to God that I would never leave it again. The last tenants had left two days before my arrival and the inside was wrecked. The only thing that remained the same was Morning Glory puttering around her kitchen. We spent most of the day and long into the evening discussing what had happened to Whispering Willows during my time in Charleston.

Determined to restore the manor, I took the buckboard into Unionville the next day to look for help to restore the manor. Mr. Ellis agreed to oversee the day-to-day running of the plantation but I insisted the manor was strictly my concern.

I interviewed and hired three local women to help clean up the house and then to come three times a week to maintain it. Jason doesn't know it but just before you all arrived one girl told me her and her husband were moving to Georgia in a month and the other just had another baby, her eighth and just couldn't be here very much. Had I let Jason know that he would have driven a harder bargain," Ann received a nod and smile from Jason for that statement.

"Anyway as I left Mr. Ellis' office I heard a group of children yelling. I didn't pay much attention at first until I heard an adult voice screaming at them. When I looked, I saw a woman standing in the middle of a circle fending off rocks. I rushed over and shooed them away and, much to my surprise there was Lulu."

Ann lowered her head and looked at the woman at the end of the table. She bit her lower lip trying to make her lower jaw stop quivering. In a cracked voice she barely whispered, "Like me she came home, too."

"On the ride home I began to think about all of the kindness she had given me. Not just the personal care that was required of a slave but all love and charity she gave of her own free will that I had never noticed or said 'thank you' for. I won't bore you by enumerating them but, take my word there were many.

Many times, in my silliness I thought she could have been my sister except she was Negro and a slave. On the way back here I realized color and status had nothing to do with the devotion and companionship she had given me. She was my surrogate sister. I began to see Morning Glory as more than just a Negro cook but a person with a heart as sweet as her shoofly pie. I found myself seeking her company and asking for her help in caring for Lulu. I learned more in running a household from Morning Glory than I ever did from Gwen. She taught me simple recipes like how to make biscuits and buttermilk pancakes. I took an interest in and could account for everything in the larder down to the last cup of flour." Ann looked toward the cook. "But she still won't teach me how to make that shoofly pie," she grinned.

"No ma'am, Miss Ann. You don't get that recipe until my death," Morning Glory chuckled.

"Well it looks like I'll have to wait another hundred years," Ann replied.

"Since then I have had one or two suitors at the door. They really don't want me but the plantation." Ann shook her head. "I want to go forward not backward. I like being my own mistress.

"Before we have our dessert I have one more thank you and that's to Jason." Ann now focused her attention on the man to her right. "You may be leaving tomorrow but I thank you for leaving behind the wonderful gifts of Ruth and Naomi. I feel as if Lulu had invited her sisters to come and live at Whispering Willows. In the short time they have been here a new life has taken hold of the house. I must confess it is good to be surrounded by women who share things rather than by men who demand things. My life is much fuller since their arrival as I hope theirs are. And on that sweet note let's have dessert," Ann said, clapping her hands together in front of her mouth.

"If everybody doesn't have a piece of everything, I'm going to sit on them and make them eat one piece of each," Morning Glory threatened.

"All right! But that goes for the baker, too. I may be small but I know there are seven other people here who will make sure she follows her own rules," Nat countered, followed by a 'Here! Here!" from the other diners.

With a raucous laugh, Morning Glory admitted defeat. "All right! All right! Have just a small piece of anything you want."

Nat rose from the table and removed the pastry knife from the cook. "You give me that. You have no idea as to what the word "small" means." Nat went to the table and cut a two-inch square of the shoofly pie, a slice of chocolate cake and one tart and put it on his plate, then returned the knife to Morning Glory.

"Now that's the sizes I was going to cut for you," she defended herself.

Nat arched his eyebrows and stared into the sparkling eyes of the best cook he knew. "Yes and I'm a tightrope walker for the circus." Once more laughter filled the room.

Another hour elapsed. Alva had fallen asleep in Ruth's arms. Miriam became restless despite the attention she received from Nat. Sarah walked around the table and relieved the cowboy of his welcomed burden. Ann stood by the door and spoke to each individual as they left.

Ruth and Naomi offered to help Morning Glory with the dishes and to clean up the kitchen. Gregory Ellis thanked Ann for the invitation and promised to continue to do his best for her and Whispering Willows as he went to his buggy parked just outside. Jason held a sleepy Miriam on his left shoulder while Sarah carried Alva and they thanked Ann for the dinner before heading back to their cabin. Ann stared back at the table at the lone figure sitting there. She walked over to the back of Lulu's chair and placed her hands on her shoulders. "Come on Lulu. The party's over and it's time to go to bed."

Lulu tilted her head back and looked up at Ann. "Oh Miss Ann I have been such a bother to you but some days---" Lulu paused and stared at the bare table in front of her. "I miss the old way of life but most of all I miss my man." Tears began to stream down Lulu's cheeks.

Ann seated herself beside the sad woman. "Honey, that's all over and done with. We both lost the man we loved but we have to make the best out of what life has to offer us." Ann reached across the table and took Lulu's hand between hers. "I thank God that He gave you back to me. Aside from Papa, Andrew, and Gwen there's not a person on earth that I love more. No one can fix my hair or take care of my things like you. You're the only one here who knows all of the secrets that Andrew, you, and I use to share. I can't talk about them with anyone but you. Now we have Ruth and Naomi to tell all of those delightful stories about Africa. But my memory isn't what it use to be. I forget so many of the little important things about Andrew and myself and I need your help remembering." Ann patted Lulu on the shoulder.

"Come on, honey. After that big meal I need some fresh air. I'll walk with you to say goodnight to Hunter." Ann rose and helped pull Lulu's chair away from the table. In silence both women paused on the verandah and watched the swaying of the willow trees in the moonlight. One visualized a tall man with a shock of brown hair, dressed in a gray uniform emerging, and the other could feel the brush of lips on her cheek from underneath their protective branches.

"Where did it all go, Miss Ann?" Lulu whispered.

"I really don't know, Lulu. Sometimes, I wonder if all of it really wasn't a dream." Ann linked her arm with Lulu and the two silently stepped out into the night.

Will

1875

CHAPTER XXIII

FLATLAND

Jason wiped dust from his eyes and stared at the black dot in the horizon that began to take the shape of buildings. In another hour the little band of travelers would enter Dallas. Sarah sat by her husband treating Alva to some rock candy. At the side of the buckboard a wide-eyed Miriam heeded every word Nat spoke

concerning sensing a horse's disposition. He allowed the little girl to hold the reins by herself and placed his hands over hers if they changed directions as he rode further ahead of the wagon. After ten days riding in Nat's charge Miram knew as much about his horse as he did but realized her tiny body could not yet assume control. After a day in the saddle with Nat Miriam related all she learned at the supper table. The adults could not believe how rapidly Miriam absorbed basics of horses' needs and riding techniques. Reluctantly Sarah admitted she had made the correct decision allowing Nat to spend most of the day with Miriam. With the threat of not returning to the saddle for the rest of the day, afternoon naps became less hectic to enforce. Alva sat quietly playing with the toys her father had bought back at Unionville or observing the scenery around her. She became crotchety when hungry or wanted to nap. With these needs met dolls or waving at her sister trotting merrily beside the wagon with Nat pleased her. Sarah could not believe how Miriam maintained the restrictive rules imposed by her mother and Nat. No antics. She did not want to lose her riding privileges.

Leaving Whispering Willows proved more difficult than Jason assumed. At dawn Ann, Ruth, Naomi, and Morning Glory appeared on the verandah. As she hugged Jason for the last time Naomi whispered, "Thank you for bringing us here, Jason. It is a new life and it's good to be here. Whatever debt you owed us has been paid. Let's start again this time as friends." Jason had held her closer to prevent her from seeing the tears that welled in his eyes.

Ruth gave him a hug and said, "Now don't forget to write and let us know how you're coming along. Miss Ann will read the letters to us."

Jason promised. It felt good having one wrong of his past righted.

Ann gave him a big hug. "Now if things don't work out in Montana remember you always have a home here. Keep in touch. If ever you're in the area you're welcome to stay here."

Jason thanked Ann and headed to mount the wagon. One voyager absented herself. "Where's Miriam?" he asked his wife.

Sarah looked for her wayward daughter. "Miriam. Miriam. Come on. We have to go," her mother shouted.

A tiny head peeked over the upstairs balcony railing. "Right down, mommy. Saying good-bye to Lulu."

"Tell her good-bye from all of us," Jason yelled. His daughter disappeared back into Ann's bedroom.

Nat helped Sarah onto the buckboard. Jason turned in time to see Miriam bursting through the front door and rushing into Nat's arms as Jason handed his youngest to his wife.

Nat gave Miriam a big kiss, swung her into the saddle and settled behind her. The blossoming cowgirl looked across to her mother and father on the wagon. "Lulu said good-bye."

Jason flicked the reins and started the horses down to the row of willows. Miriam kept leaning around Nat and waving at the assembly on the verandah and the lone figure on the balcony. As they entered the willows, Jason waved a final time. Even Lulu continued to wave at the departing caravan. Eventually, only the protecting willow branches of the plantation waved at the departing company. Sarah leaned over and rested her head on her husband's shoulder and looped her arm through his. Both knew another CHAPTER in their lives had concluded.

Sarah interrupted Jason's reverie. "Have you decided where we're going to stay in Dallas?" "Goodness! I haven't really thought that far ahead. I want it to be the best. I have a feeling it will be the last luxury we're going to see for a long time," he said.

Jason signaled to Nat to return to the buckboard. With Miriam holding the pommel of the saddle the cowboy's horse cantered next to the vehicle. "Something wrong?" he asked.

"No. We wondered where the best hotel in Dallas was. Sarah and I agree this will probably be the last of soft beds for quite a while," Jason grinned.

Nat shoved his hat back on his head and rubbed his chin in thought. "It's been a while since I've been in Dallas. I'm supposed to meet Will at the Silver Dollar Saloon between five and seven. That's the time he said he would be there until the end of the month. By the looks of the sun we should arrive just in time. Let's ask him. I'm more use to camping. I think you two would spoil me with inns and hotels if I had to travel with you another month." Nat handed Miriam to Jason. "Now you behave yourself young lady while I'm gone or no story tonight before bed." Miriam nodded. He then turned his attention back to Jason. "I'll ride on ahead to see if Will arrived. Just keep straight on this road and you'll see the Silver Dollar three blocks down on entering the city. My horse will be right outside so you can't miss it. I know Will knows of some place." Nat turned his horse toward the town and galloped away.

It's been a long day so why don't you and Alva take a nap now," Sarah said.

"Alright mommy but go a little faster so we catch Nat," the youngster replied

Jason watched the cowboy disappear as town's buildings began to take shape. He still had an uncertain feeling about his decision to leave Alabama. He glanced at his wife and said, "Honey do you think we made the right decision in leaving Whispering Willows?"

Sarah put another small piece of candy in Alva's mouth and waited for the little girl to eat it before placing her next to her sister. Sarah then looked at her husband and smiled. "Jason it's very difficult to determine if any decision is right or wrong. The trick in life is to make the best results from the decisions we make. Even wrong decisions can be shaped to right decisions. Don't doubt yourself, love. The good things in life are there for us to enjoy but our failures are there to teach us. We're going to make great ranchers. It's going to be tough but we'll succeed." Sarah gave his arm a pat.

Jason remained silent for a moment before he said, "Sarah I have often wondered why you refer to me as your soulmate and not your husband. At long last I have the answer. A wife or a husband can be obtained with a piece of paper but a soulmate is worth the entire wealth of the universe. You are my very reason for being. I am honored to be your husband but it is a privilege to be your soulmate. My God woman, every time I think I can't love you anymore than I do you make me multiply that love by a thousand, and that happens every day. I can't think of a man, woman, or animal that would stick by me after some of the things I have done, but you have always been there for me.

Sarah, if I haven't told you in the last five minutes, let me say it now---I love you!"

Sarah scooted closer to her husband, and kissed him gently on the cheek. "I had a suspicion you did," She teased, "but it's still nice to hear you say it."

The wagon left the barren flatlands and passed into the main street of the town of Dallas. The center of town had more than just a main street but four parallel streets with several cross streets with construction beyond that scene. At the present rate of growth, Dallas would soon compete with Mobile in size.

Jason continued down the center main street until he spotted a building with the sign *Silver Dollar Saloon* perched above the overhang of the wooden walkway. Tied to the hitching post outside of the establishment, Nat's horse waited patiently for its owner. Jason pulled the wagon to a halt and started to descend when two men exited through the bar doors.

Nat approached the wagon followed by a medium-height, wiry cowboy. Jason's traveling companion smiled up at the seated couple and said, "Folks. I want you to meet a good friend of mine, Will Pickens."

Will smiled and extended his hand to the adults. Miriam suddenly appeared from inside the wagon she would never accept a simple handshake but leaned over her father and gave Will a hug. Nat burst out laughing. "See Will. I warned you but don't you go getting any ideas about stealing my gal." Miriam let out a squeal and leapt into Nat's extended arms. From inside the wagon another child's head appeared as smiled up at the two men.

"Meet Alva. She's the one who is a lady," Nat remarked.

Jason grinned from ear to ear. "I guess Nat told you we were looking for a good hotel to stay in until our business here is complete."

Will looked at the man and shook his head. "The best is the Cattleman's, but they're rather selective in their guests if you know what I mean. I suggest Mama Rosa's. It's not as fancy, but the rooms are clean and a lot of nice people stay there."

Jason looked at the man. "Mama Rosa's will be just fine. Let me get my family settled and I'll meet you back here in about an hour to discuss business."

"Great. Just go to the end of the block and make a left. You'll see Mama Rosa's at the end of the block. We'll be waiting for you," Will said giving a semi-salute. He and Nat turned and entered the saloon as Jason went in search of Mama Rosa's.

CHAPTER XXIV

PREPARATIONS

Jason entered the Silver Dollar. In the center of the barroom sat Will and Nat. As he approached Will placed his beer back on the table and again extended his hand which Jason vigorously pumped. Jason gave the bartender his beer order and sat. Will settled back in his chair and pointed his thumb toward Nat. "Nat tells me you want to take a herd north."

Jason gave a sigh. "Will, I don't know the first thing about cattle."

Will gave a soft chuckle and said, "I could say that about every new cowpoke I've hired. It really doesn't matter. Just when you think you know all there is about cattle, some damned cow, steer, or bull comes up with something new."

Will leaned on the table and nodded his head toward Nat. "Nat says you're in a hurry to get north before winter sets in. That eliminates rounding up strays. I know a couple of reliable ranchers that will help us put a herd together, though we'll have to spend some precious time branding them. What brand do you want?"

Jason scratched his head. "Can't we just drive them without a brand?"

Both Nat and Will laughed. "Not unless you want to wind up in Montana with nothing but dust. There will be other herds going north on the same trail and we'll cross some ranchers' land.

If any of our cows stray and get mixed in with another herd without a brand, they're fair game. You can bet that the drover who discovers a cow without a brand will soon have theirs on its rump. Besides, that will be lesson number one lesson for you: how to rope, wrangle, and brand."

"Is a week enough time to get all of the branding done for a thousand cows?" Jason's voice denoted concern.

Will snickered. "A thousand cows? It better be less than that or I'm going to get some new cow hands and I hope you own at least two thousand acres."

Jason sat back despondently in his chair. "I guess I really have a lot to learn."

"You'll learn pretty fast. I'll have you work with the segundo and myself. By the time Nat and I leave in the spring the segundo will take over as your foreman," Will explained.

"What is a segundo?" Jason asked.

"That's the guy who is second in charge after me. I would like to hire him and a couple other cowpokes here. After I train them, they'll be able to hire quality help in Montana. You and your new foreman will have to work together to know what to expect from each other. I'll supply the wrangler for the remuda and old Jake has to come as cook or it will take me two months after I get back to sober him up."

Jason quizzically shook his head. "Here we go again! What in the hell is a remuda?"

Will smiled and rubbed his nose. "Sorry! I forget you're a tenderfoot. That's the herd of horses we take with us."

Jason became thoroughly confused. "I thought that each cowboy had his own horse. Why a whole herd?"

Nat couldn't resist contributing to the conversation. "If you were a horse, how would you like to herd cattle going from a trot to a gallop and turning back and forth every minute for hours on end, day after day? Besides, some horses can do certain things better than others. Maybe one doesn't get spooked in a lightening storm but hates to go back and forth across a river. Another doesn't mind the river but hates rocky terrain. What if your horse goes lame, is killed, or drowns? Trust me; you don't want to be on foot around cattle on the move. That's why we'll pick up at least eight horses for each cowboy. He has to take care of his eight, but there is another cowboy who has to herd them with the drive."

Jason took a sip of his beer and thoughtfully lowered his head. "Boy! There's more to this expedition than getting a herd together than shooing them in a certain direction."

Both cowboys laughed at the understatement. "We had better go across the street to the general store and buy clothes more fitting for you and your family. Make sure your women folk have long brimmed bonnets. The sun can get pretty brutal on the plains," Will said.

Nat corrected him. "You'll never get Miriam to wear a bonnet. I suggest boy's cowboy hat for her. We can teach her how to move it around on her head to protect her from the sun and rain."

Jason was aghast. "Miriam? In the rain?"

Nat scoffed at Jason's concern. "She won't be near the herd. I'll have her ride beside the wagons 'protecting' them. A cowboy's life is done in all types of weather. If she is going to be any help to you she has to learn. Riding beside of the wagons gives her the option of coming out of the rain any time. That's more than the other cowpunchers. With her personality I would like to meet the person that will keep her inside the wagon when she thinks she could help."

Once again Jason had to yield to Nat's logic. The big problem now became convincing Sarah. "Aside from the hat like yours, what size chaps do you think I'll need to go with it?"

Both cowboys almost doubled with laughter at that question. Will said, "You won't wear chaps unless you want to fry yourself. I may let you wear them when we wrangle and brand but otherwise I suggest you pack them away until we're in mesquite country. They're meant for preventing sharp branches from tearing you apart or to stop rocks and dirt from ripping your clothes off you when you wrestle a steer to the ground. I'll teach you how to wrangle a calf or two, but certainly not a full grown cow---not yet. You'll also need a good kerchief to keep the dust out of your lungs and buy the tightest burlap pants you can find. After a while, you won't know that you're wearing them."

As a man who once wore priestly robes, Jason didn't relish the thought of wearing so tight of clothing. "Couldn't I wear them just a little more loose and comfortable?

Will leaned his elbow on the table and rested his chin between his thumb and forefinger. His smile almost went from ear to ear. "That's fine by me but after riding all day and maybe getting bucked by a bronc who has seen a rattler I hope you won't mind singing soprano for awhile."

Jason's eyes widened. "Oh!"

Wiping tears from their eyes, the two cowboys roared with laughter at Jason's look.

"Jake will purchase all of the foodstuffs along the way, and Nat here will see to it that we have all of the guns and ammunition we need for the trip. He may even teach you how to shoot. You don't have to hit anything. It's just to turn a stampede and help others locate you if you're lost," Will guffawed. "Oh! One more thing. Can you get a letter of credit to cover any unforeseen expenses along the way?"

"I'll send a telegram to my lawyer this afternoon," the new rancher replied, and crossed his hands over his crotch. That act by Jason prompted the cowboys to leap from the table and rock with laughter.

Jason removed his hands from his lap. After taking a sip of beer he joined the laughter.

Nat wiped the tears from his eyes for the fifth time and said, "Don't worry about them, Jason. Will and I promise to save you an extra pair when we geld some bulls." That was the final straw. All three men headed across the street to the emporium, periodically pausing to gasp for breathe between bouts of laughter.

During the remainder of the week everyone had assignments. Sarah sighed with relief that she wouldn't have to cook for so many men, but she still had to drive one of the wagons and do the washing, mending, and care for the children. Miriam spent the day with Nat who explained to her the different personalities of the cattle. He pointed out to her certain cows that would determine what the rest would do and pointed out other animals for her to watch and why. She rode point with him in transferring forty to sixty cattle to the rope corral Will had built outside of Dallas. Will combed other ranches around the town for strong cattle that could make the trip north, and then his boys cut them out of the rancher's herd and took them to the rope corral, which gradually began to fill. Jason chased down two Calistoga wagons. Though a little weather beaten, Jason's foreman pronounced them fit for the trip. Jason's legs and arms had many black and blue areas from his herding experience, but he refused to surrender to the pain. Will encouraged and corrected his roping and cattle driving. When Jason became more proficient in roping, Will would allow Jason to rope cows. Now the worse lesson presented itself--- learning to brand and geld. One more week remained before the agreed time to start the trek north. Jason could not decide what brand to use. Will pressed him to decide in the next two days.

Will and his crew helped Sarah transfer their belongings from the buckboard to the wagon. The buckboard overflowed with their personal articles, but, the way the cowboys stowed them in the Calistoga, the wagon seemed half-empty.

Jake, the cook, confiscated the second wagon for himself. In Jason's opinion, he purchased enough supplies to feed an entire army for the complete trek. When Jason made that remark, Jake looked him up and down before he said, "I see you're new at this. After spending twelve to fourteen hours a day with the herd, a cowboy builds a big appetite. I only hope I've bought enough to last to the next depot. Oh! By the way, are you getting oxen or mules to pull the wagons?"

Jake's question baffled Jason. "I thought some of the horses from the remuda would do that."

The old cook's mouth flew open and his eyebrows arched as he stared at Jason in total disbelief. "Man don't you know that every damned horse will be needed by the cowboys for the drive? You're not taking these wagons to settle in Oregon. You're driving a herd of cattle. Now damn it go tell Will I want a good team of mules and I'd advise the same for your wagon." Jake shifted a bag of salt on his shoulder. Mumbling to himself he leered at Jason with disgust and left the store.

At the hotel that evening Jason sat despondently on one of the two chairs by a writing table and watched Sarah prepare Miriam for bed. The constant war to make Miriam go to bed had ceased. On some occasions, Sarah considered herself lucky if she got Miriam undressed before she fell asleep. Antics had decreased to such a degree that Sarah questioned Miriam's health. Nat had wrought miracles with her. The threat that she would have to spend the remainder of the day at the hotel made the little demon sprout wings and produce a nimbus around her head. Even mealtime astounded Sarah. The concerned mother considered herself fortunate to have Miriam consume two peas. Now, the girl asked for seconds all around. Sarah got around this by heaping Miriam's plate and ordering adult portions in a restaurant for the young cowgirl.

Jason watched as Sarah tucked the covers around the little girl who could barely stay awake. She finally dropped down next to him a vacant chair and smiled. "Since Nat that girl has gotten more like Alva. I sort of miss the nightly fights to get her to go to bed." Sarah glanced over at her silent husband who rested his elbows on his legs and stared at the floor. "What's wrong, Jason?"

Jason raised his head, shook it, and then looked at his wife. "I feel like such a fool. Will's men keep asking me if I want this or that in forming the herd and I don't know how to answer. Repeatedly I've told them to ask Will, but he always sends them back to me." Jason rocked back and forth in the chair shaking his head to emphasize his worry.

Sarah rose, sat on the arm of Jason's chair, and put her arm around his shoulder as Jason straightened himself into the welcoming comfort of his wife's arm. "Will is a wise man, Jason. They are moving your cattle. It's going to be your ranch not Will's. You'll have to get use to making decisions. It's Will's way of teaching you to deal with the hands and assume responsibility as a ranch owner. I'll bet that if you tell any of the men something wrong they'll immediately make a suggestion that makes more sense." Jason nodded. "You may be a tenderfoot but you're still the boss and the men are showing you proper respect. When you're at your own ranch you won't deal with just the foreman alone. The more the men ask you things the more you'll learn not just from the boss' point of view but from your hired hands." Sarah gave his shoulders a little shake. "Come on let's go to bed. I have a little wrangling I want to teach you."

Jason reached over and patted his wife's hand. "You go ahead and get ready for bed. I have to think about some sort of branding iron. I don't think even Mumia had a decision as tough as this"

Sarah jumped up from the arm of the chair. "Jason! I've got it!"

He stared at his wife in puzzlement. "What are you up to now?"

"I'm not up to anything. I realize the answer to our brand," she said excitedly.

"And?" he led her on.

"The Lightening M for Rancho Mumia," she replied enthusiastically.

Jason rose and hugged his wife. "Sarah, you've done it again. I'll wait until morning and have the blacksmith make four Lightening M branding irons." He gave his wife a kiss. "How does it feel to be married to the owner of the Rancho Mumia?"

"I still prefer ol' Mose back at Whispering Willows but I guess you'll do for the time being," she teased.

"I knew I should have accepted that dance hall girl's offer to run away to Georgia," he countered.

"That wouldn't have bothered me at all---if you took Miriam with you," she said hugging him back.

Oh dear! In that case, it looks like we're stuck with each other," he giggled.

Sarah looked into Jason's loving brown eyes and ran her hand across his cheek. "In that case, let's go to bed and see if we can work out a compromise."

Jason walked over and blew out the lamp, which ignited a spiritual fire stronger than the sun.

CHAPTER XXIV

BIG BOY

Jason met Nat and Will at the Silver Dollar the following morning and told them about the brand.

Will rested his arm on the table and placed his thumb over his lips and thought for a moment. Finally, he sat back and shook his finger at the ceiling and said, "Let's go over to the blacksmith and draw it out for him. He'll have them ready by tomorrow, and we can start branding. I want that herd moving in five days.

"There's a rancher near here that owes me a favor, so we can use his chute and corral for branding. That will save a lot of time and energy and cut down on the wrangling."

Nat agreed, "That's good. It will give me time to teach Jason how to use a gun without shooting himself in the foot. It also gives him an opportunity to practice his roping and it will be his first experience at herding when we drive the cattle to the ranch. With four branding irons and a chute we'll be on the move in no time. Come on let's go see the blacksmith now."

The three men headed to the blacksmith's shop on the edge of town. The blacksmith, who had arms as big as his largest anvil, greeted them at the door. After three sketches, all concerned agreed on the design. The forge man promised to have at least two of the four ready late that evening so that branding could begin early the next day.

Will left the group to ask permission of his rancher friend, Perry, to use his chute and corral. If the rancher agreed, Will would ride to the herd with Jason and have his crew start moving the herd for branding. It would take the remainder of the day to slowly drive the herd from the rope corral to the ranch. Everyone felt elated as if the drive north had already begun. True to his word the blacksmith had two of the four branding irons ready that evening. Jason praised the work done and could hardly wait to see his brand on the rump of some cattle.

The next day when the Will, Nat, and Jason arrived back to the hotel from a morning of branding Jason went upstairs to get his anxious daughter, Miriam. Nat would keep her busy while her father accompanied Will back to the ranch for an afternoon of branding. Sarah looked up from the bed where she and Alva played at rolling a ball. That game bored Miriam. Due to the absence of Nat she almost felt punished by having to remain in the hotel room all morning. She ran directly to her father from her place at the window. Perhaps he could release her from her prison. Jason lifted the girl and gave her a hug.

"Where's Nat?" Miriam asked looking over her father's shoulder.

"He's downstairs waiting," he answered. Jason looked over at Sarah and winked, "Would you and Alva like to come downstairs and watch Miriam begin her riding lesson?"

Sarah rolled her eyes heavenward and shook her head. She still hadn't quite accepted Miriam's horse back riding. She picked up Alva and followed her husband who held Miriam's hand.

There, standing by the hitching post in front of the hotel, stood Nat holding a pinto pony complete with bridle and saddle. Miriam never doubted to whom the beast belonged. She began jumping up and down clapping her hands demanding to know its name.

"His name is Big Boy," Nat said as Miriam ran toward the pony. He picked the little girl up but instead of placing her in the saddle he began to explain a few rules. "Now listen to me, little missy, first of all, you are not to ride him without an adult around. If you do you can imagine the consequences. Second he's yours now and you are responsible for his grooming and upkeep. I know you're too little to spread hay but you can make sure he's watered and help me brush him. When you're a little bigger, you'll be taking more responsibility." Miriam's eyes sparkled as she agreed but Nat continued, "If you break any of these rules, your father will sell him immediately, and I won't take you riding anymore. Do you understand?"

"Make sure you understand the rules," Will added.

At that point, Miriam would have agreed to walk around the world backwards but before placing her in the saddle Nat made her repeat every rule and its consequence.

Nat had adjusted the stirrups to fit her legs so little space existed between the saddle and the stirrups. Instinctively, Miriam settled into the saddle. "Can we go for a ride now? Please Nat?

"Well, I guess that's one less cowpoke I have for the day," Will said with a smile on his face.

Nat placed a lead on the halter handed the reins to eagerly awaiting hands. "Now, no galloping. We're just going to walk him around town for a while." Glowing with pride and glee, Miriam nodded.

Without being told, Miriam drummed her small knees into the pony's shoulders, placed her weight on the stirrups, and began to synchronize her movements to the pony's gait. Nat smiled with pride that his ward had absorbed and could execute all of his past instructions as Big Boy, Nat, and Miriam trotted down the street. Miriam kept turning back waving at the three adults.

Sarah put her arm around Jason's waist and held onto Alva who wanted to go after her sister. "It's going to be your job to tell her the pony can't sleep with her and she can't sleep in the stable with it. Bedtime's going to be a lot of fun tonight. You'll find me down at the train depot waiting for the first train to anywhere," Sarah laughed.

Jason hugged his wife back and watched his daughter and pony disappear around one of the street corners. "Oh shush! You're just as proud of her as I am." Sarah smiled and nodded assent.

"Mr. Jason?" a voice behind him asked.

Jason turned his head and looked at a cowboy of medium height, good musculature, sharp green eyes, and mop-like brown hair protruding from under his hat. "My name is Hank Fenchack. I spoke with Will Pickens over at the Silver Dollar last night, and he said you were looking for a segundo to take a herd to Montana and stay as foreman. I would like to talk to you about the position."

Will stood innocently next to Sarah. Jason knew better than to drag Will into the conversation because he would just refer the matter back to him. Jason shook Hank's hand and said, "We have an hour or so before going back to branding. Why don't you join Will and I for lunch and a few beers. I'd like to find out a little about you and you can come with us for this afternoon for branding if you're free. I'll pay you for your time. When we're done for the day, I'll let you know if you're hired.

Hank nodded and said, "Fair enough." Will paid close attention on how the dude rancher handled the hiring situation. Jason could have sworn he saw a slight smile cross over the old cowboy's face.

Sarah picked up Alva, "I still have a lot of socks to darn. If I know Nat and Miriam, those two won't be back before sundown.

I'm quite sure Nat will see Miriam gets lunch. Alva and I will go upstairs after having lunch here at the hotel. Enjoy your lunch."

Jason kissed his wife and daughter on the cheek and stepped into the dusty street along with Hank and Will. On the way to the saloon, Jason told Hank about his daughter's new pony while Will commented on her riding ability. Entering the saloon, the three men stood at the bar rather than sit at a table and ordered a beer and some stew. After wrangling all morning, Jason had strong reservations about sitting on the hard wooden chairs. Jason wanted to celebrate the latest exploit of his daughter and insisted they have a shot of Red Eye to go with their beer. A true cowboy never refuses a shot of Red Eye.

"Well, Hank, what did Will have to say? "Most of the time I trust his decision." Jason said trying to give an appearance of a knowledgeable ranch owner. Will kept a blank face.

The cowboy turned toward Jason and propped his foot on the shiny rail. "He asked me a lot of questions about my past experience in driving cattle, and if I had any personal reasons that would prevent me from remaining in Montana. We talked quite a while about cattle, stampedes, different trail bosses I have worked for, and my knowledge of the trail north. He told me he couldn't make any final decision without your approval and sent me to see you."

Jason slowly sipped his beer and ordered another round of Red Eye as a thank you to Will for doing the preliminary interrogation and thereby saving him valuable time. The warming whiskey gave Jason the needed courage to continue the interview. "I'll get Will's point of view later but I want to see for myself. I'm paying high wages to get the herd to my ranch before winter sets in and I want to make sure you are what you claim. We'll have to build a small ranch house and a couple of bunkhouses in addition to driving the herd. In the spring I won't be able to continue paying the same wages. Will and his boys intend to head back then. The same wages I'm paying Will will hold for you until spring, then I'll have to put you on a monthly salary of---oh let's say---forty dollars a month as foreman, and any good hands you can recruit will receive an additional five dollars after they have had a month's tryout."

Hank grinned ear to ear and offered his hand to Jason. Jason shook it and said, "You still have to prove yourself at the branding this afternoon, then maybe I'll put you on the payroll."

"Bartender!" Hank yelled. "Three more Red Eyes over here and another mug of beer on me."

"This is definitely the last Red Eye and then we get some hot grub in us. One more Red Eye and the cattle will be branding us," Jason laughed.

Jason returned to the hotel late in the evening. His first experience at herding and branding proved difficult. Sarah sat in one of the chairs mending socks while Alva played at her feet. "You're back late. How did it go?" she asked.

"The new segundo seems a pleasant fellow, and he must know his stuff, or Will wouldn't have sent him to me. As for me," Jason grunted and eased himself on the edge of the bed. "Don't even think about any hanky-panky tonight. If you even touch me, I'll fall into a thousand pieces." He glanced around the room. "How did the day go with Nat and Miriam?"

Sarah looked at her husband with amusement as she picked up Miriam and sat her on her lap. "This is her first day with her pony. Except for lunch and supper she spent all day with Nat. I think that now is the time for some other new experience for our little cowgirl." Sarah laid her work aside, and after a big hug, released Miriam to her father and picked up Alva. "Why don't you come with me over to the store before it closes? I saw some children's books they just got in, and I thought it about time Miriam learn something else besides horses."

Jason emitted another groan as he rose from the bed. "Come on Miriam let's go." he said, following his wife out of the door.

That night a new restriction lessened the amount of time Miriam spent in the saddle. After experiencing a day with Big Boy Miriam would have agreed to hanging by her thumbs. Sarah employed good timing in beginning to teach the child to become literate without another revolution on her hands.

That same evening after supper, Jason headed for the Silver Dollar. Nat, Will, and Hank sat at one of the tables and waved at Jason to take an empty chair. Nat started the conversation.

"Your daughter has done it again. If I'm any judge of horseflesh that damned pony will follow her to hell and back. She walked me over every square inch of this town and guided the pony herself. I felt foolish just holding the guide line which I never had to use. I'll tell you, Jason, she'll be riding that pony by herself in less than a month. When I feel the time right, I'll let her ride alone beside your wagon. That will keep her out of the way, and Sarah can keep an eye on her. It will be easier on the pony, too. With his short legs, he would never be able to keep pace with the remuda horses. Give her another ten years, and she'll be running your ranch. You have one hell of a daughter there, Jason," Nat said.

"And don't think she'll let me forget it," Jason replied proudly and turned his attention to the other occupant of the table. "How'd it go today, Will? Did Hank pass mustard?"

The wrangler sat back in his chair and folded his hands across his chest. "I don't think you're going to have any trouble by hiring Hank. As to the branding, Frank Perry, the owner of the ranch, agreed to allow a couple of his hands to help with the wrangling if you pay each of his men five dollars. With them helping, we can finish in three days and be on the trail. Frank and three neighbors agreed to sell you enough horses to make your remuda. We'll have about forty-eight horses, all told, plus eight mules for the wagons. Then I stopped by the blacksmith, and he has one more iron to finish. He promised it to me this evening. Damn! He's really done a good job. With that fourth branding iron the work should speed up," he paused and took a drought of beer. "Nat tells me you're getting pretty good at roping and shooting. At least the lasso goes in the same direction you point it." Will had to hide his grin. As he settled back again, he said, "I think I'll assign the branding of the calves to you. That way, you'll be able to break in those new chaps,"That reminded Jason of their first conversation. "You stick by Nat, and he'll show you how to herd and cut. I still want you to wrangle calves rather than chute the cattle. That way, you'll get some experience without too many bruises and what it's going to be like on the trail and at your ranch. You'll eventually have to do it with your own cattle in Montana. Before we get there I'll have you wrangling the big ones with the rest of us. "

"I can hardly wait,"Jason remarked sarcastically. "By the time we get to Montana, I'll be able to out-wrangle you, Will."

Will chuckled. "Oh, I think my career is pretty secure, Jason." He leaned over the table pretending to whisper to Nat. "Don't forget that extra pair we promised to save for our boss." The sound of raucous laughter filled the saloon as the four men enjoyed the remainder of the evening.

When Jason returned to the hotel room, he found Sarah reading to a sleepy Alva. Sound asleep in one of the two beds, Miriam hugged a pillow. Sarah rose and began to prepare Alva for bed. She pointed to her sleeping daughter and said, "She went to bed without a peep right after supper. If Nat can guarantee me that every night, I may consider divorcing you and marrying him."

Jason laughed, walked over and gave his wife and daughter a kiss. "So she didn't give you any trouble about the pony sleeping here?"

Sarah put a nightgown on her little daughter, Alva, who began to play with a ball atop her parent's bed. "No! After her ride, Nat took her back to the stable and showed her how to brush down her pony and make him comfortable for the night. She polished off a large bowl of stew and three slices of bread. If I didn't know better, I'd swear she was feeding a dog under the table. When we got back here, she insisted on undressing herself and putting on her own nightgown, claiming she wasn't a baby anymore. She said she had to get to bed early because she had to feed the pony early in the morning when Nat would come to pick her up on his way to feed his horse. She gave me a long hug and a kiss and said to tell daddy 'Thank you', and there she is."

Jason looked down at his sleeping daughter. "There's not a thing on earth that can make you feel old except when you discover your child is no longer a baby," he said to his wife.

"And there is nothing on earth that makes you feel younger than when you keep the heart of a child in your soul," she replied as she gave him an affectionate hug.

From in back of the couple came the plea, "Daddy! Play ball?" Despite his tiredness Jason sat on the bed and began to roll the ball back and forth with his youngest daughter as Sarah moved one of the chairs closer to the window.

"Did everything go all right with Will, Nat, and Hank?" she asked relaxing from taking care of the children.

Jason continued his game with Alva and said, "I definitely hired Hank, but I had to play the big boss role tonight. Everything that Nat has been teaching me came into play today. I just hope I didn't make too big of an ass of myself, but I have to start sometime."

"Never an ass. You need bigger ears," Sarah said with a laugh.

Jason looked at her curiously. "You know I've never done any ranching."

She assumed a surprised look and said, "Oh! You were referring to ranching."

Jason stopped rolling the ball and smiled at his daughter. "Daddy will be right back after he has taught momma to mind her manners. He rose from the bed and started to tickle his wife sitting in the chair. "Now you take that back or I'll tickle you so hard you'll wake Miriam."

Sarah fought in vain to make Jason stop. "All right! All right!" she said in a whisper as Jason ceased his attack.

The couple locked eyes and laughed at each other's nonsense. Sarah rose and put her arms on Jason's shoulders. "That abuse will cost you a new dress I saw at the store today."

Jason put his arms around his wife's waist and said, "What? You insult me and then I have to pay for it?" Both parents turned to look at the giggling girl on the bed.

"Mommy and Daddy! Funny," the little girl said clapping her hands.

Jason released his wife and headed for the bed all of the while wiggling his fingers. "Oh, you think so. Do you?"

Alva let out a squeal which made Sarah look toward the other bed. Miriam frowned in her sleep and rolled to her other side.

"Both of you stop it. You almost woke Miriam," Sarah ordered.

The guilty parties shushed each other. Alva then crawled to the edge of the bed. Jason scooped up his daughter and swung her in a circle.

Sarah returned to her chair and watched father and daughter play horsy for the next half-hour.

"That's enough for today, missy. Now it's time for bed," she said taking her daughter from her husband's shoulders.

Jason sat his tired body in the chair recently occupied by his wife. He had to succeed in ranching. He lovingly looked around the room at the three good reasons and another reason on the way. Doubts and fear could not dampen his spirits. Life was good.

CHAPTER XXV

BRANDING

The next morning, Will walked away from the branding chute and headed toward Nat and Jason standing right of the corral. Thanks to the chute, branding proceeded at a more rapid pace. He slapped his hat against his chaps causing a halo of dust to surround his lower torso.

"How's it coming, Nat?" he asked.

"Jason's getting better with the rope, but I still don't think he's ready to tackle any cattle yet," Nat replied.

"I've roped that fence post four out of ten times," Jason bragged.

"You'll have to increase those odds if you want it to go around the neck of a running steer," Nat replied. He placed his arm around the disappointed ranch owner and added, "You'll get all of the practice you want on the trail. Will, the boys, and I have been doing this for years. You really don't believe the first time we had a lasso in our hands we roped cattle do you? I remember wrapping the rope around myself a hundred times, and the first time I roped a cow I was foolish enough not to be on a horse, and she must have drug me half-way to California until my stubbornness lost out and I let go. It took over two months for all the skin to grow back and the bruises to go away."

Will added a word of encouragement. "The first time I roped a calf I was on a horse. I thought there was nothing to it. My horse was new to wrangling, and I headed to tie the calf's feet. That damned horse just stood there and allowed the rope to go slack. That calf gave me kick that knocked me out for ten minutes. Even now, I don't catch the critter every time I throw the rope. Remember, I told you once when you think you know all there is, the damned cows think up something new and sometimes it's your fault when things go wrong?

"On my last drive we were just loping along at a nice pace in the Indian Territory when my horse got spooked by a rattler. If there is one thing in the world I hate its snakes. I blocked out everything else except, 'Kill the son-of-a bitch.' So, I drew my gun and blasted the bastard's head off. Big mistake! It took the boys and myself the rest of the day chasing that herd all over Oklahoma before we could get them to mill and round up strays. Stupid! Yet I did it!

"Now, I consider myself a professional and a damned good cowboy, but I still do stupid things. So don't be so hard on yourself. Until you pass those pearly gates you can't have everything just the way you want. Put up with the missed roping and being knocked on your ass like the rest of us. As you do it more and more you'll your skills will increase but you're still going to make rotten decisions and do stupid things now and then. Now get back to work or I'll have Miriam replace you," Will said giving Jason a friendly punch on his left shoulder.

Miriam delighted in all the activity. She would leave her pony only when necessity demanded. Due to the abundance of help, somebody constantly walked her on her pony well away from the chute, in case a maverick acted up. The men taught her how to rein and turn quickly. She had learned from Nat how to control her mount. That came naturally to her even on her second day in the saddle. She astounded the cowboys that one so young could have such control. They even gave her a small length of rope to pretend to lasso. Heaven could not provide more joy to Miriam.

Will introduced Hank to the crew. They immediately accepted him, and, like Will, he deferred to Jason for decisions. Will approved of Jason's choice for Segundo. He felt secure he could leave Hank as top hand at the new ranch. The two other hired hands needed some tutoring from the seasoned cowboys but Will declared they would be as good as his men by the time they reached Montana.

Jason proudly had taken the branding irons to show Sarah the evening the blacksmith had them ready. No art work in any museum could compare with them according to the happy couple. The branding iron looked like three lightening bolts supporting two archways. Jason could not resist a "Yippee!" as the first cow exited the chute wearing the new brand. He asked Will to have her branded on the other haunch to mark her as the first and never to be sold. Jason determined that she and her first calf would always wear the double brand as the mascot breed to his new ranch.

Jason glanced around at the working cowboys and asked, "I don't see Hank. Where is he?

Before answering, Will yelled at one of the cowboys manning the corral, "Cut that one out for a steer. Sorry, Jason! Jake took the wagon out to the remuda, and Hank went with him. I wanted him to check out the horses. Did you have an assignment for him?" Jason just looked at him and shrugged.

Will turned to Nat and asked, "Nat, will you take over here for me. Jason and I want to go for a walk. OK?" Nat nodded and took Will's place by the chute as the owner and his foreman walked away from the corral.

"It's about time we had a little talk before we hit the trail," Will said to Jason as both men walked by the fire containing the branding irons. "Jason you have to stop doubting yourself, especially in front of the men. It only encourages them to slack off. Be firm, even if you make a mistake. Correct it later, but make the decision. During the drive I want you near me. I'll ask your permission to do things I think is right, but you must say yes or no. You don't have to agree with everything I say. I told you earlier, I make mistakes too. Tell me what you want and if I disagree I'll give you my reasons not to do it. If you believe your idea is better overrule me. If it's wrong you'll find out soon enough and we'll try something else. The hands know you are new at this but you always have the final say in things. Another thing, as owner you don't have to ride herd day or night, but I want you to volunteer to do both. Pair up with Hank on the nights when you do late watch. I want this order to come from you and not from me. On those days you do night watch, I want you to sleep by the campfire."

"Why can't I sleep in the wagon with my family?" Jason inquired.

"You can if you want, but you may wake the children and your wife when it's time to do your shift. That's why all of the cowboys are paired at the campfire. You wake a pair and not everybody else," Will explained.

"Now all I have to do is convince Sarah of this," Jason chuckled.

"I'm glad you mentioned Sarah," Will said. "That brings up two more points. Nat and the boys feel that Miriam has learned so fast that she can ride her pony at a loping pace alone, even after just a few days. We're all going to be busy with the herd to watch her and if we try to force her to stay in the wagon God only knows what would happen. We think we would like to have her ride beside the two wagons. Jake is an experienced rider if anything happens he'll be there and she can be under the eye of Sarah."

"Won't she be tempted to ride out and herd with the cowboys?" Jason asked with concern.

Will smiled at his boss. "Jason, the wagons rarely stay with the herd. After breakfast, Jake moves ahead of the herd about five or six miles and starts to prepare the afternoon meal. After the afternoon meal, he moves ahead again about another five miles and starts supper. If the chuck wagon moved with the herd a lot of time would be lost. Besides, that should keep Miriam well away from the danger of the herd. Tell her since the cowboys are busy we need a scout to watch the wagons until they arrive. Just give instructions for Jake to give her things to do in help preparing the meal and I'm sure Sarah can find other things to keep her busy until the herd arrives."

"Right! Sarah bought some learning books in Dallas. Now is as good a time as any to make use of them. Miriam agreed to study lessons and with her pony tied to the wagon she'll be forced to ride with Sarah. Good idea Will! So you really think she'll be all right to ride alone?" Jason asked for reassurance.

"Sure! So long as she doesn't try to gallop or race. Sarah and Jake will see to that," Will reaffirmed. "We all agree that we have never seen any man, woman, or child take to riding like that little heart stealer. Give her another ten years, and she'll have you branded, hog tied, and she'll be running things."

Jason and Will started to head back to the cattle chute as the proud father said, "You certainly don't pay much attention to things Will. She already does."

CHAPTER XXVI

NORTHWARD

With the branding complete the long trek north became reality. After treating his entire crew to a farewell supper in Dallas, Jason and his family spent their first night in the wagon. The herd advanced only twenty miles north of Dallas and two of the cowboys left the feast early to ride north and relieve those watching the cattle. Finally all said farewell to Dallas and settled down in their first camp. Though it had all of the comforts one could wish the Calistoga could not compete with luxuriating in a hotel. On the second day out Jason announced that he would sleep by the campfire and actively participate in the herding. Jason and Sarah made the best of the separation. Both had spent nights together and apart in worse places.

Jake aroused the entire camp about an hour before sunrise for breakfast. Miriam insisted on dressing herself and Sarah dressed a sleepy Alva in no time. Jason helped his family out of the back of the wagon and all headed toward a low burning campfire outlining the red bar illuminating the sky in the east.

Today's breakfast resembled a feast. Jason insisted that the crew have scrambled eggs, bacon, and biscuits. Will had told Jason that cowboys loved eggs but they were impossible to transport. So, Jason decided that the second as well as last day of the drive the crew would have that treat.

The line of men at the chuck wagon gave way as Jason and his family approached. Jason insisted that the line reform. He and his family would wait their place in line with the rest. From the pile of food Jake had made no one would go hungry. Each cowboy's plate received what would equate to a triple portion of hotel dining food. Jason assumed the cowboys would waste at least a third of their portion and could hardly believe his eyes when empty tin plates clanked into a wooden tub by the chuck wagon without a morsel discarded.

Will, Nat, and Hank walked over with their plates of food and sat on the ground in front of the family enjoying their first taste of Jake's cooking. Sarah and the children occupied the only seat an overturned log.

Will took a large bite of the eggs and savored them. "Until the drive is over, the cowboy lives only for good food, sleep, and an occasional whoop-up at one of the cow towns along the way. Thanks to Jake I make sure they get a lot of the first, but I can't guarantee the second or third. You didn't eat much this morning, but give yourself two or three days and you'll be right up there with the other cowboys," he said.

The conversation took an abrupt turn. "Miriam ride with Nat," the eager girl volunteered. Nat and Will had prepared for this confrontation the night before.

"I really wanted you to ride with me, honey but Will makes the assignments and he selected you to do a very important job," he informed the crest-fallen girl.

Will stood and picked up the little girl and walked about five paces from the gathering. He turned his back to the crowd gathered around Sarah and Alva. Though he spoke in a low tone he assured that all could hear the conversation.

"Honey I've got your parents' consent to let you ride your pony by yourself because I need you to do something very important for me," he said to the sad moppet.

"What is it?" she barely mumbled.

"Well," he began as he shifted her weight in his arms. "I'm in an awful situation. I've assigned all of the cowboys to the herd and I forgot all about the wagons. I don't have a single soul to take care of Jake, your mother, and your sister. They'll be riding ahead of the herd and if anything happened to them why I wouldn't be able to forgive myself. I know it's a lot to ask a little girl--"

Miriam cut him short. "I'm not a baby," she informed the cowboy.

"Of course you're not! That's why I'm asking you to help me out," Will said. "Would you ride with the wagons and make sure that nothing happens to Jake, your mother, or sister? I know it's a big responsibility but do you think you can do it?" Miriam smiled and vigorously shook her head up and down. "Now let's keep this to ourselves. I don't want to worry the others but you keep your eyes open and take care of them for me. Will you do that?"

Bloated with the pride of responsibility, Miriam again shook her head as the two returned to the circle of people intent on the breakfast. Will placed his index finger on his lips followed by a wink, smile, and nod, and Miriam did the same.

"Jake. Sarah. Miriam will be riding with the wagons. She's a big girl now and can ride her pony beside you," Will informed the grinning adults. "When you pass the herd, ride on the far side of the wagons. The pony isn't experienced with cattle and is likely to spook them and I know you wouldn't want to cause a stampede." Miriam heartily agreed.

That crisis averted Will got down to other serious business. "We should be at the Red River day after tomorrow. Jason and

Hank, I want you to ride with me to look for water and bed ground for tonight. Sarah, you follow behind Jake and Miriam you ride beside you mother where you can see her all the time and keep an eye on her." Inclusion into the adult assignments made Miriam assume a serious face as she acknowledged Will's directives. Nat, you ride right point. I'll have Aaron ride left point. Charlie will be in charge of the remuda. He'll know what horses to rope for you, Jason. Just remember Jason, keep your saddle blankets dry and clean. We don't want anything to happen to the horses you ride." Will now turned his attention to his segundo. "Hank I want the two new men to ride rear. Let's see what they are really made of," he chuckled.

Jason couldn't resist asking, "Is riding rear dangerous?" All three cowboys broke out in laughter. Finally Will replied, "No! That would be point riding. If that herd takes off, you're right in front of them, and you better get the hell out of the way. When you ride rear you take half of the state of Texas with you in your nose and lungs and all over your clothes. I've yet to have a cowboy volunteer to ride rear. Well we'll never get to Montana sitting here. Let's get going," Will said as he turned and headed for the herd.

Everybody placed their empty plates in the tub and headed for their assigned places. Jason gave Alva, Miriam, and Sarah a final kiss and hug and said, "Watch out for Miriam."

The three men saddled their horses and made a circuit of the herd to assure that all the cowboys rode in place. Satisfied, the three headmen rode forward and gave the signal to the two points to begin the drive. Shrill whistling could be heard down the line on both sides of the herd as quirts lashed out at the lead cattle. They began moving north. Will, Jason, and Hank galloped well ahead so as not to interfere with the cattle's slower progress. About two miles down the Texas trail; the three men paused and looked back at the cloud of dust headed their way.

"We'll have to send the crew back with picks and shovels to find the men in the rear," Jason commented.

"I'll reassign them tomorrow. Everybody has to take a turn riding rear. You're the boss so you don't have to. Neither do I or the segundo. That reminds me. The segundo always stays with herd and is in charge when I'm not around. I appointed Nat since Hank is with us. If ever I'm away from the herd, and you have to take Hank with you somewhere, always appoint a segundo." Will turned his horse north. "Now let's scout," he said as both men followed his lead.

After riding about twenty miles, Will spotted what he considered good bed ground for the herd. Will paused and explained to Jason the reason for his choice. "There's good watering and grazing and see those little mounds over there." Jason looked in the direction his trail boss pointed. "It doesn't look like much to us but the cattle will think they're sleeping on top of a mountain and can see all around them and feel safe. If they get spooked during the night they'll run back to where they came, but I don't think that's likely. Come on let's see it at closer range," he said as the trio galloped toward the stream.

After careful inspection, Will seemed satisfied. "Last lesson of the day Jason. Always start to water your herd downstream so the leaders don't muddy the waters for the ones in the rear. Now let's get back to the campsite. Jake will have the noon meal ready by now," he concluded as he turned away from the stream and headed back toward camp, followed by the two other riders.

Jason discovered he had an increased appetite as he settled down next to Sarah who sat in the back of their wagon. "How are the kids doing?" he asked.

"Alva seems to be able to amuse herself and the rocking of the wagon puts her to sleep. As to Miriam, she takes her assignment very serious and watches Jake and me like a hawk would chickens. I tried to help Jake with dishes this morning, but he shooed me away. It was a perfect time for Miriam to begin her lessons so we sat here and started one of the readers." Sarah savored some of Jake's delicious food and commented. "Too bad we couldn't introduce him to Morning Glory. Those two would have been a perfect match. It would have been interesting to see which one would have thrown the other out of the kitchen first."

Jason shoveled a large spoon of beans in his mouth followed by a healthy piece of corn bread. The food tasted good but that didn't explain his hunger. Miriam appeared around the left side of the wagon holding Nat's hand.

"Nat said I'm doing a good job. If I keep it up and learn my lessons he'll give me a silver dollar when we get to Montana," Miriam said excitedly.

"Oh! And what job is that?" her mother asked.

Miriam put her index finger to her lips and said, "It's a secret."

"OK!" her mother replied, "Climb up here and take a little nap before we move out."

Nat swung the little girl up into the back of the wagon. "Don't forget to wake me mommy," Miriam reminded as she quietly lay down next to her sleeping sister.

"How did things go so far?" Jason asked Nat after Miriam had settled in.

"Not bad. Not bad at all," he responded.

"Couldn't we move the herd a bit faster?" Sarah asked.

"Not hardly. You would have walking, tough-meat skeletons by the time we get to Montana, and I don't think the other drovers on the trail in front of us would appreciate running our herd into theirs," Nat replied.

"It just seems like such a long trip," Sarah sighed.

"It is." Nat said, "But there's no way we can make it shorter."

The group continued eating as Will approached. "Good afternoon, Sarah. How was the trip?"

"Nothing much to tell. In fact it was a little boring," she replied.

"Let's hope it stays that way. When things begin to become unraveled you'll wish for the boredom," Will warned. "Jason, I want you to out-ride to the middle of the herd with Hank as your bunk," he said.

"That's fine. If anything happens I can just ask Hank," Jason said elatedly.

Will rubbed his chin with his thumb and forefinger. "Well if anything happens you better yell loudly. He'll be on the other side of the herd. Bunk mates ride opposite each other and the herd between. Make sure that none of those cows breaks free and goes off on their own. Keep them in line. Change your horse every two hours so as not to tire them. Just do as you see Hank do and everything should be OK. I'll be riding around the herd. If you have any questions just ask. Now finish your meal, and I'll see you at the remuda." Will turned and headed for a group of cowboys lounging on the ground.

That day the remainder of the drive progressed tediously. Jason swiftly learned how to turn his horse to prevent a maverick from going on his own. Tiredness overwhelmed him at day's end. He could imagine how the horses felt. The cowboys watered, bedded, and posted watch for the night for the herd. Jason took his heaping plate of food to his wagon and joined Sarah.

"I'm hungry enough to eat a bear," he said taking a large bite of meat. He looked over and noticed Sarah did not have a plate. "Aren't you hungry?"

"Jake fed me with the girls earlier so I could get them to bed," she informed her husband.

"Are they doing all right?" he asked taking another huge mouthful of food.

"They're doing just fine. I wish I could say the same for myself. My tail is so sore from bumping up and down that I'll sleep standing up tonight," Sarah complained.

"Speaking of sleeping, I won't be able to sleep in the wagon tonight. I have third watch with Hank and have to sleep by the campfire so as not to disturb anybody when I get up."

"It looks like I'm going to have to send somebody back to Whispering Willows for Mose," Sarah teased.

"I don't think he would be too interested in a pregnant woman," Jason countered patting Sarah's now expanding abdomen.

Sarah rested her head on her husband's shoulder. "I'm going to remind you of that statement when you get off watch," she teased.

Jason finished his meal and said, "Let's go over by the campfire and see what the boys think about today." Sarah glanced back into the wagon at the sleeping children and had Jason help her off.

"Let's go," she said.

As the couple approached the fire, the crew greeted and invited them to join the lounging cowboys. "Aaron here was just going to tell us the story about his adventures in Mexico. Here Sarah sit on my saddle. I'll sit on the saddle blanket." Nat rose and offered the only woman in the crowd a seat. "Go ahead Aaron. Tell us the story," Nat requested.

Aaron lay on his side and poked a dry stick into the campfire. "Well, as I was saying. I was courting this little senorita I met in a cantina in Mexico. She was the prettiest thing I ever laid eyes on and I think she kind of liked me too. We use to sit at a table in the back of the cafe holding hands and talking. I was real serious about that gal. After three evenings I was going to ask her to marry me but my Spanish ain't too good."

"Wait a minute Aaron! You just said that you sat and talked. If your Spanish wasn't too good what did you talk about?" asked one of the cowboys.

"I don't want to get into that. There's a lady present, and there are certain phrases you don't want me to repeat. Now can I get along with my story?" he asked the interrupter who grinned and shook his head.

"As I was saying before I got rudely interrupted I was just about to ask this gal to marry me when this big ol' vaquero comes through the door shouting 'Juanita! Juanita!' That gal must have jumped a foot off of the floor.

"Well. He spotted us in the corner and headed right toward me as Juanita ducked out the back door. He was one mean hombre. He had a mustache at least a foot long, and his sombrero was four foot wide."

"A four foot sombrero? Really Aaron!" said one of the cowboys as the others groaned and rolled their eyes heavenward.

"OK! OK! So maybe it was only three feet," Aaron conceded which produced another groan from the crowd.

Aaron sat up and threw the stick into the fire. "Now do you want to hear this story or not?" He seriously scanned the smiling faces before continuing.

Jason finally spoke up. "I don't know about the rest of them here but I want to know what happened."

Aaron put on a hurt visage. "I'd stop right now if it wasn't for you asking me to finish Mr. Jason," he replied with just a hint of pride. He settled back into his prone position and continued.

"Well! He grabbed me by my vest with a hand as big as one of Jake's frying pans and lifted me off of the floor. I knew I was a goner if I didn't do something quick. I reached over on the table where Juanita and I had been drinking tequila and grabbed the bowl of salt and slung it in his eyes. He let out a yell and began rubbing his eyes as I headed for the door.

"Outside was his band of fifty banditos surrounding my horse. I yelled that their boss needed help inside of the cantina and they all jumped off and ran inside to help him while I leaped on my horse and headed out of town."

"Wait a minute!" another cowboy yelled. "You spoke Spanish pretty well for them to understand you," he noted.

Not to be daunted, Aaron replied, "That shows how smart you are. I didn't speak Spanish. I used sign language." This sparked another round of groans.

"Now will you guys shut up and let me finish my story?" Aaron said with a little irritation.

Jason again came to the rescue. "Never mind them Aaron. I want to know what happened," he chuckled.

"Well Mr. Jason I was high-tailing it out of town and heading for the border when I heard a bullet whistle by my head. I glanced over my shoulder, and there was that vaquero rubbing his eyes and his entire gang behind me, but I wasn't worried. I had a faster horse and had only a mile to go. Bullets were flying all around me, but they were poor shots and I knew I was perfectly safe.

"I had a quarter-of-a-mile to go, and I'd be across the border, when my horse stepped in a gopher hole and threw me to the ground. I abandoned the horse and ran like the devil for the border. I heard the thunder of horses and cussing in Spanish which made me run even faster. Not even fifteen feet from the border, they surrounded me." Aaron reached over and poured himself a cup of coffee from the pot that rested on one of the hot stones surrounding the fire.

"How did you escape?" Jason asked.

"I didn't. They shot me dead," Aaron replied in all seriousness.

The entire campfire occupants roared. "Aaron, I have been wrangling for over twelve years and I have to admit that's the biggest cow-pie I ever heard," said one of the cowboys during bouts with laughter.

Will stood and addressed his crew. "That's enough for tonight boys. It's almost time to change the watch and you know we have to get an early start." Men rose from the fire and began to pair off as bunk buddies.

Jason gave Sarah a good-night kiss before she returned to the wagon. "I'll see you at breakfast," he said. Sarah gave him a final kiss on the cheek and headed for the wagon. Jason copied the other cowboys and made a makeshift bed with his saddle, horse blanket, and his oil slicker as a cover and settled down next to his bunk buddy. Jason thought it would take him hours to fall asleep on the hard ground. He listened to the occasional lowing of a cow and heard the two cowboys on watch alternate verses of a song as they circled the herd in opposite directions. Cowboys like to sing because it allows his bunk to know exactly where he is. Soon he drifted into peaceful sleep. The second day of the drive ended.

CHAPTER XXVII

SURPRISE

Four days elapsed since the herd started out from Dallas. The late dry spring weather and the Red River cooperated in getting the Rancho Mumia herd across it. Will told Jason that this calm river could become a torrent and had claimed the lives of cattle and cowboys alike. "Never trust the Red River," Will warned. "One minute you're only wetting your ankles, and the next you're swimming for your life." Between the watering and the crossing, an entire day expired. Will seemed relieved when the last cow crossed.

The herd has just entered Indian Territory when the first mishap occurred. Try as they might, Jake and Sarah could not avoid every single rock in the trail. The chuck wagon ran over a particularly large one and cracked two spokes on one of the rear wheels. The two wagons came to a halt as Jake climbed down to inspect the damage. Sarah, carrying Alva, walked up behind the cook. Miriam followed on her pony. "How serious is it?" Sarah asked the cook.

Jake reexamined the damage and remarked, "It's not too serious yet, but, if I don't do something about it, the wagon won't make it across the South Canadian to the Camp Supply."

Jason and Will, who just returned from scouting, galloped toward the stranded wagon. "What happened, Jake?" Will asked.

After Jake explained the situation, Will agreed with his assessment. "It would have to happen on the South Canadian. That damned river has a quicksand bottom. We're going to have a hard enough time with bogged down cattle without bothering about the wagons. We'll have to unload that wagon so we can lift it and remove the wheel for repair." Sarah assigned Miriam to watch her sister so she could assist the men in unloading the wagon. The two children crawled under the undamaged wagon to play in order to avoid the overbearing heat inside of the Calistoga.

During that time, the herd passed on its way to the bed ground. One cowboy riding rear couldn't resist a jibe at the cook. "What happened Jake? Did you run over one of your biscuits?"

"Yeah. The one you're going to eat tonight, if you want any food," growled the cook.

The cowboy could not accept defeat. "Pass the word! We'll have an extra two to three hours to live before Jake poisons us tonight."

The cook paused and shook his fist at the passing cowboy. "Why in the hell don't you go bite and poison a few rattlers to tide you over until you can taste some good food?" By the time Jake delivered the last remark, the cowboy had galloped ahead out of earshot.

Jake searched amid the supplies for wide rawhide strips and strong pieces of wood used for cooking fire to use as braces. "I'll soak these for about fifteen minutes," he said waving the rawhide strips. "That way, when they dry, they'll make a firmer binding."

"Look!" Jason said pointing to a spot about a mile on the other side of the passing herd.

Another herd outlined the horizon heading in the opposite direction. The adults standing by the stranded wagons immediately noticed the difference. Soldiers escorted that line which consisted not of cattle but human beings. Men in blue uniforms galloped toward them. The dust kicked up by the Rancho Mumia herd had just begun to settle when the horses' hooves enfolded the approaching riders in a cloud of brown dust.

The lead soldier reined his horse by one of the wagons and dismounted, followed by the other two. "Good afternoon, ma'am, gentlemen," he said tipping his hat toward Sarah as more of a sign of respect for her gender than her color. "I'm Captain Landwher in charge of transporting some Indians to their new reservation. We had a little skirmish a couple of miles back, but don't worry about it. We shot the young bucks who were the troublemakers but I have to scout the area to see if any escaped during the scuffle."

"Well I haven't seen any strangers around here. We've been here for about two hours trying to repair this splintered wagon wheel." Jason pointed to the offending wheel to emphasize the validity of his statement. Will and Jake nodded in agreement.

"Do you mind if we have a look in the wagons? They're a tricky lot," the captain requested.

"Suit yourself," Jason said with dismissal. "Have those strips soaked enough?" he asked Jake.

"Better give them another minute or two. I want to make sure the splint is real tight," Jake replied.

Two soldiers walked to the back of Jason's wagon as the captain climbed up on the driver's seat.

"Well? What have we here?" said one of the soldiers.

Jason glanced under the wagon where the children had been playing and saw three pairs of brown eyes staring at their father. He walked to the back of the wagon to see what the soldier had discovered. Huddled in the back were an Indian man, woman, and under the wagon, a boy slightly older than Miriam. The three stared at Jason, and in that instant a library of information passed between them. Quicker than lightening, Jason's mind recalled a similar incident many years ago.

"So there you are," Jason shouted. "Thank you for finding him," he said to the captain who had joined the group. "God-damn it! I didn't relieve you from the herd for you to visit with your squaw. Now get the hell over there and help Jake fix that wheel. If I catch you lollygagging again I'll kick your ass clear back to Texas."

"Texas?" the captain asked.

"Yep. I hired his wife to take care of the children and ease the workload for my pregnant wife. I really didn't want the man and boy along but my wife claimed another woman on the trip could help on our trip to Montana. That's where we're headed." Jake and Will remained silent.

"So they have been with you since Texas?" asked the captain.

Jason looked at the ground and shook his head up and down. "Take my advice and never hire any lazy-assed Indians. If I'm not after him all day he'll sneak off to see his squaw or curl up somewhere to sleep. The squaw wouldn't leave without the other two. I had no choice after two nights listening to my wife bitch about needing help. Which reminds me---Sarah!" he yelled.

"God-damn it woman! You talked me into hiring these lazy son-of-a-bitches and you guaranteed there wouldn't be any trouble. That's all they've been since this drive started. Even though they don't belong to the ones the captain is escorting, I have half a mind to ask him to take them with him."

Sarah walked directly into her husband's face. "Go right ahead. I hope you enjoy sleeping outside, hot sun, rain, and all. I've gotten use to her help. It's not bad enough I have to drive this stupid wagon all day but I have to put up with the yelling and screaming of the kids. You go around the campfire at night and listen to those filthy cowboy stories while I have to stay with the kids." Sarah turned on the captain. "Go ahead and take them and, while you're at it I hope you have some room for me." Sarah than addressed the squaw. "Get down from there and take care of the children. We're leaving."

The soldiers grinned at Jason's dilemma. Jason approached his wife with outstretched arms. "Now sweetheart we can talk this over."

Sarah pushed the two little girls toward the squaw who wrapped her arms around them. Both girls, never having seen their mother irate began to cry."

"Sweetheart ,my foot! Now look what you did," she said pointing to the crying children. "It'll take hours before they stop. I'll be ready in just a few minutes captain."

Captain Landwher cut off Sarah's entrance into the wagon. "Ma'am, I'm sorry but this is a military expedition. I can't take any civilians with me especially a woman. Besides, we don't have any provisions for you. I suggest you stay here and straighten things out with your husband."

Sarah rounded on Jason. "Well? May they stay or not? I don't care if they leave with the captain or not, BUT if they leave, I leave. I don't care if I have to walk back to Texas," she threatened.

"All right! All right! They can stay." Jason drew the captain to the side. "I was hoping to get rid of them, but as you can see my wife will think of new ways to make my life a living hell. I hope you understand."

Captain Landwher tried to conceal a smile as he nodded. "Perfectly! And I thought my wife was bad. I don't envy you your trip with a nagging wife and lazy Indians. Once you reach Montana maybe you can get rid of them and find better help," he suggested.

"God knows I can't find worse," Jason assured.

Sarah, who had climbed into the wagon with the squaw and the crying children, poked her head out of the front. "Jason, stop jabbering and get that wheel fixed." She pulled her head back offering complaints about the worthlessness of her husband and yelling directions at the squaw to get the girls stop crying. Jason despondently shrugged his shoulders as the three smiling soldiers mounted and headed back to the shambling line of poor wretches entrusted to their care.

Will and Jake stared at their boss approaching. Both realized the performance that just took place saved the family from rejoining the marching hell. Jason placed his hand on the Indian man's shoulder and said, "They're gone now. I'm sorry I was so hard on you and your family, but I couldn't think of anything else.

The man stopped weaving the rawhide around the stout sticks and stood. He towered a good foot over Jason, but presented no threat. His face displayed a life of suffering. His wife and son jumped from Jason's wagon and ran toward him with Sarah in pursuit.

"Let me introduce everyone. This is Sarah, my wife." The Indian nodded. "And these are my daughters, Miriam and Alva. Both girls after their experience with an angry mother reduced their shock to sniffling. Sarah went over to the girls and gathered them in her arms while trying to explain to them her pretend bad mood. This is Will, the head drover, and this is Jake the cook," Jason finished.

"My name is Gray Cloud, and this is my wife Laughing Water, and my son, Little Fox. We are very thankful for what you have done for us."

"This is not the first time something like this has happened to me. I could not stand idly by and allow them to take you back to that miserable marching line," Jason said.

"We've wasted a lot of time. Jake and I can finish up here. Why don't you people get out of the sun and go sit by the wagon," Will offered.

Without comment, the small band headed for the afternoon shadow of Jason's wagon. Jason surrounded Sarah with his arms and gave her a kiss. "Thank you so much for being nasty," he laughed quietly.

Sarah responded by giving him a gentle shake and saying, "Oh, it was all my pleasure. Perhaps I should try that more often."

"What happened out there?" Jason asked as the little group settled in the not-too-cool shade of the wagon.

Gray Cloud gave a shrug. "A group of soldiers rode into the Cherokee village two days from here and told the chief he had one hour to prepare for relocation on reservation land west of here. What couldn't be taken was burnt to ensure they did not return. Today, five young braves who had protested leaving their homes attacked the soldiers and tried to escape. I could see the dust trail of your drive and thought if I put the herd between the soldiers and my family, we would stand a better chance of escape. People were running everywhere trying to get out of the way of the soldiers' horses and bullets, and the gods blessed us. We were overlooked. Once on this side of the herd, we made a wide circle away from the cattle so the cowboys wouldn't see us. I saw you repairing the wheel and knew it would take you some time and decided to rest in your wagon until you were almost finished and then leave you in peace."

"But before you could make your final escape the soldiers arrived," Jason stated.

Gray Cloud nodded. "The rest you know. I wish the blessings of the gods on you for what you have done for my family. Otherwise we would have been returned to the line of relocating Cherokee."

"I know what it's like to be forced to go where you do not want to go," Jason said bitterly.

Sarah felt she had to distract Jason's association with slavery. "You speak of your tribe as if you don't belong to them," she said.

"We don't." Gray Cloud said proudly. "They are Cherokee and we are Lenni Lenape. The Cherokee were kind enough to adopt us when the white man forced us into their territory. Some of my brothers and sisters who were forced into Apache territory were not so fortunate," he added with lowered eyes.

"What do you intend to do now?" Sarah asked.

"I shall head south and search out some of my people in Texas. Perhaps they can find me work," Gray Cloud proposed.

Jason looked toward his wife who gave him a smile of encouragement. "If that is what you really wish we shall give you supplies for your family until you can reach a large town but there is another way," Jason offered.

"We are fugitives. Until we leave Indian Territory, we shall be hunted," Gray Cloud reminded Jason.

"True! But why not make a lie the truth? My wife is pregnant and has no woman around her in whom she can confide. Laughing Water can be her paid companion and help her drive the wagon as well as watching the children. I can assign the boy to help the cook. He can search for firewood and help with the serving and clean-up.

"You can be of special service to me. I was discussing with Will last night how to get the herd out of the territory without having to pay half of the herd to various tribes for passing through their land. While Will and I search for water and bed ground you could search for villages so that we can avoid them," Jason offered.

Gray Cloud stared at Jason. "What you say makes sense but if it wasn't for the passing herds, many people would starve. The white man kills the Indian's food for hides and pleasure and allows the meat to rot under the sun. He has promised us we can live the undisturbed life of the gods and instead has given us a bowl of dust. We are an honest people and take our oaths seriously. The white man takes our land and promises to leave us in peace if only we move on the other side of the river. Once he has filled his side of the river with his people he demands we move further toward the setting sun so more white men can take the land he had promised us. When we refuse he kills our women and children and forces us with his guns to obey. He breaks the treaty and calls us savages for defending what he agreed we could have." Gray Cloud stared into Jason's eyes. "The people here do not take the cattle for vengeance. They only want to do the one thing the white man does not want---survive with dignity."

Jason now lowered his head and stared at the ground. "It seems to be the white man's pattern. He is doing the same thing in my homeland. The difference is that we don't have to go through the sham of treaties. Only one man I knew almost beat the white man at his own game but they destroyed even him," Jason said with resignation.

"I am sorry," Gray Cloud empathized.

"All is not lost. He passed his legacy on to me, and though I probably will never become a great man as he could have, I will not fail him in proving that I am as good as any white man," Jason vowed. "Now! Will you accept my offer?"

Gray Wolf rose and helped his wife to her feet. "We had better get that wheel fixed and the wagon reloaded or the drovers will have no supper tonight. Laughing Water you can help us load and then help Sarah drive the wagon. Son, you stay with the other children and make sure they stay out of the way and do not get hurt." Gray Wolf offered his hand to Jason. Jason informed Gray Wolf about Miriam's special assignment.

"It is odd that so small a squaw is free to act like a warrior," Little Fox observed.

"For heaven's sake don't let Miriam hear you say that and don't be fooled by her size," Jason informed the boy. "She's more of a squall than a squaw but you'll find that out for yourself," he added.

Little Fox seemed to accept the advice but with much reservation.

Gray Cloud resolved the issue by saying. "Why don't you join the other children and start your observation?" Reluctantly Little Fox obeyed his father. Gray Cloud turned and faced Jason. "We really have no tribe near but the soldiers will have scouts looking for any of us that escaped and the ranchers around here are not friendly to the red men. I am familiar with some of the tribes and the lands north of here. Perhaps I can repay you for your kindness to me and my family. I shall return North with you and perhaps escape to Canada. It shall be as you say."

"You shouldn't have any problems with the men on the drive. Their boss is a black man, like me, and some of the cowboys are Mexican. It would be difficult to pick on a man because of his color or nationality," Jason added. "Welcome to the drive."

The children remained in the shade of the wagon as the adults headed to assist the cowboys in reloading. Jason walked beside Gray Wolf pondering. "Lenni Lenapi! I've never heard of Will, Nat, or any of the cowboys mention that tribe."

Gray Wolf had a sad smile as he replied, "It is no wonder. Those of us who the white man couldn't kill, or get our more fierce brothers to kill us, tried to erase my tribe by forcing us on other tribes, hoping that we would be absorbed and hide his crime from history, but we are a strong race. Our name means 'real people' but perhaps you know us better by the name the white man gave us."

"And that is?" Jason asked.

"The Delaware."

CHAPTER XXVIII

DARE

Another two weeks elapsed and the Rancho Mumia herd grazed just outside Dodge City. The herd zigzagged through the Indian Territory because of the numerous Indian village encampments along the trail. Gray Wolf's reconnaissance prevented a great loss of cattle. The drove had to surrender only three steers during the entire trip through Indian Territory.

Sarah enjoyed having a woman companion. Though she enjoyed the tales of the company of the cowboys she relished talking about feminine things that would interest only another woman. Laughing Water shared the care of Sarah's children with great care, but she preferred the company of Alva over Miriam. "Miriam has a woman's body but a man's spirit. It is a man's job to care for the girls and the woman's to care for both males and females in our tribe. That way the child learns both man and woman's point of view. Miriam takes on both responsibilities. Little Fox goes with his father fishing and hunting, but it is my word that is final in things concerning Little Fox way of life in the tribe's camp." Sarah realized she had much to learn from her new companion.

The cowboys offered no comment on Gray Wolf's sudden appearance. Jason could hire and fire anyone he desired, and they looked forward to Gray Wolf's stories at the campfire.

Jake had to make some adjustment having a new helper but Little Fox's amiable personality soon won over the cantankerous cook.

Accompanied by the cowboys off herd duty Jake drove the chuck wagon to Dodge City to restock supplies and mend the damaged wheel. Jason decided to remain camped outside of Dodge for three days and allow the men to let off steam in the cow town. Hangovers and black eyes could not prevent Will's men from their assigned watch except for the four Jason had to bail out of jail for shooting out street lights.

Will, Nat, and Jason went into town on the last night before breaking camp. He had certainly improved his wrangling and roping. Will even considered allowing Jason to rope a cow. For Jason, the experience of the drive so far over-awed him. He had to add the experience of the first cow town. The only rule that seemed to exist in Dodge was: There are no rules. The rowdiness and repeated gunfire alarmed him until Will informed his boss cowboys used this method to let off steam. Jason seemed calm until Nat said, "Yeah! No more than five men are killed during a night. Jason sat with his men in The Gilded Lily praying his companions would tire, and the night of "festivities" would soon end.

Nat placed his elbow on the table, leaned toward Jason and said, "If you think this is bad, wait until you see Ogalala." The light became blocked as a strange pair of hands rested on the table. The trio looked toward a wavy, gray-haired, stocky cowboy of medium height.

"Name's Lawrence Cousins with the Flying Double X out of Amarillo. Are you the nigger drovers driving the Rancho Mumia herd?" he asked.

Will placed his hand over Nat's, gave a slight shake of the head, and stood. "My name's Will. This is Nat, and this is Jason. What can we do for you?"

"My herd just arrived this evening. You have the best grazing area around here and I wonder when you were leaving," Lawrence informed the men.

"We figured on crossing the Arkansas tomorrow," Will informed him.

Lawrence wrinkled his brow and stood erect. "Damn! I would have to come in behind a bunch of stupid nigger drovers," he said to himself. "It'll take you a week to get that herd across. I sure would like to have the grazing area, so I tell you what I'm going to do. I'll loan you some of my top hands to help you get them across," he generously smiled at Will.

Will sat back down and offered Lawrence the only vacant seat at the table. "May I buy you a beer Lawrence? You don't mind me calling you Lawrence do you?"

The white cowpuncher plopped in the chair, ignoring the other table occupants and directing his attention to Will. "Not at all. My men will be there right after breakfast to drive your herd across. We'll have you on your way by afternoon."

Will smiled back at the foreman. "Oh, I don't think that's necessary. We can manage on our own."

Will's reply seemed to upset the drover. "Damn it man! I'm in a hurry and I don't have a week for you niggers to chase cows on both sides of the river. My crew is the best damned cowboys east of the Mississippi."

"Oh, I don't doubt that, but I think my crew can handle the herd. They have so far," Will said.

"Damn it, man. I'm in a hurry to deliver my herd to the ranch outside of Denver. I've never met a nigger yet that you didn't have to tie in the saddle. Now I have been nice about this and I'm going to ask you one more time: will you let my men drive your herd across the river? Once you're across, I'll stay here for two days to give you enough time to get a couple of miles down the trail. If you need any help we'll be right behind you until we turn for Denver. You can't get a better offer than that." Lawrence said with disgust.

"I really appreciate your offer but I think we can handle things just as well as your men could," Will replied.

"WHAT!" Lawrence shouted. He turned in his chair and yelled at a cowboy standing at the middle of the bar. "Mike!" The man called Mike turned his head and took his foot off of the railing of the bar. "Mike!" Lawrence repeated, "Get over here," he ordered waving to Mike.

The cowboy sauntered over to the table still holding his beer in his hand. Lawrence redirected his attention to those seated at the table. "I want you to meet Mike Dutton. He's in charge of the remuda and best damned wrangler in the south. There isn't a horse born that can't be broken by Mike. He can make a horse stop on a grain of sand and have a calf branded before it knows it's on the ground," Lawrence said proudly. He looked up at the tall, dark haired cowboy standing beside him and tapped him on the hip with the back of his hand. "These niggers think they can wrangle better than you."

Mike burst out laughing. "Boy, you better go back south and do what you do best, pick cotton.

"If we were staying longer I'd make you back up those words, Lawrence," Will said.

Jason surprised everyone by speaking. "Oh, I think we could arrange to stay an extra day or two. What did you have in mind?"

"And just who in the hell are you to speak for your foreman?" Lawrence asked snidely.

Nat couldn't resist getting into the conversation. "Don't pay any attention to him. He's just the ranch owner," Nat laughed.

"Where did a nigger get so much money to stock a ranch?" Lawrence demanded scornfully.

"Let's just say I got tired of picking cotton and eating watermelon," Jason countered. "Now was that all talk or do you mean to back up those claims," Jason challenged.

"What did you have in mind?" Lawrence asked.

"Will this is your department. What do you suggest?" Jason asked.

Will took a sip of beer and relaxed in his chair. "What about you and I see which one can stay on a bronc the longest? Each of us can get two tries at it."

Lawrence turned and waved four more men to join him at the table. When they arrived he said, "This nigger has just challenged me to ride bronc against him. What do you think about that boys?" The foreman's question brought laughs from the Flying Double X crew. "You're on! I'll choose the bronc you ride from my remuda and you choose the bronc I'll ride from yours. Fair enough?" Will nodded in agreement.

The bar became buzzed with the prospect of the forthcoming contest. Mike felt his ability as top wrangler also suffered under the challenge. "You get to have all of the fun of beating his ass, and we have to just stand by and take his insults if you lose," he grumbled.

Will pushed his chair from the table and stretched his legs across the floor. "I wouldn't think of leaving you boys out. How about choosing three teams of your best ropers against three of mine? Same rules as for Lawrence and me. OK?"

Mike's eyes lit up. "It's a deal!" he snapped at Will.

Will sat up straight and pulled his chair back toward the table. "Not quite yet. What do you say we make it more interesting with a little wager?"

Lawrence seemed eager to pick up that gauntlet. "I've got a five dollar gold piece that says I'll win."

Jason intercepted the wager. "Gentlemen! Let's have a real purse that can be divided among all. Let's say five hundred dollars. I'll guarantee the two hundred and fifty. You put up the other two hundred and fifty."

"God! I would like to take you up on that offer, but we don't have the owner traveling with us and that's a little too steep for us," a crestfallen Lawrence remarked.

Jason shrugged dismissing the plan. Will slammed his palm on the table. "Wait a minute! I have an idea." All heads turned toward the grinning man. "That's a mighty fine belt buckle you're wearing there," Will noted.

"Pure silver. This is Mr. Dyck's reward for us working at the Flying Double X for five years," Lawrence said proudly.

"How many of the trail men have buckles like that?" Will asked.

"Seven of us. Why?" Lawrence responded.

"If it's all right with Jason we'll let you put up the seven buckles as collateral for the two hundred and fifty dollars," Will offered.

By now, the entire attention of the bar focused on the table where the final details of the challenge hung in the balance.

Lawrence bit the knuckle on his hand and considered the proposal. The Flying Double X cowboys rallied around their boss.

"My god Lawrence why are you hesitating. Anytime I can't out-rope a bunch of niggers I don't deserve to wear the Flying Double X's buckle. Here is mine," Mike said removing the buckle from his belt and tossing in front of the trail boss. "And mine! And mine! And mine! And mine!" echoed the other four cowboys. Lawrence removed his and added it to the pile of silver.

"And mine," he finalized.

"Bartender!" Jason yelled. A man in a white apron immediately appeared. "Bring me paper and a pen. I'll write a draft for my lawyer to authorize the removal of two hundred and fifty dollars from the local bank back home and send it to the bank here." Jason wrote out the check, but could hardly concentrate due to the various wagers the customers of The Gilded Lily shouted at one another. Jason took a second sheet of paper and wrote where to send a telegram to Gregory Ellis for authorization. He handed it to the bartender saying, "Send this off first thing in the morning, and lock that check and these buckles up in your safe until the contest has been decided. You will have the other buckle brought to the contest tomorrow?" Jason asked Lawrence.

"It better be. One of the team wranglers will be wearing it when we come back here for the money and our buckles," Lawrence responded.

The entire bar set up a cheer as the bartender removed the buckles and check from the table. Will waved them to quiet. "Now, where are we to do this? Your camp or ours?" he asked.

Before Lawrence could reply, a voice from the crowd yelled, "How about outside of town here?" A sea of voices inside the bar roared approval.

"I don't have any objections? Do you?" Will asked.

"None at all," came Lawrence's reply.

"Then outside of town it is. One o'clock. You bring three calves, and I'll bring three," Will finalized over the roar of the crowd.

"Everybody who logs a wager with me gets a free drink," the bartender declared. Pandemonium broke loose as the bar patrons split into two separate camps, establishing odds and amounts to bet.

The next day, for the first time since the town came into existence, Dodge City looked like a ghost town. Bartenders, dance hall girls, merchants, drovers, even the "respectable" citizens attended the spectacle at the end of town. The Gilded Lily erected a nearby tent to quench the men's thirst with beer.

Nor did the proprietor overlook the ladies and children. He had sarsaparilla available for the non-alcoholic drinkers. No county fair could have generated more excitement. The Flying Double X crew of eight arrived first driving three calves and leading a large brown stud horse. They drove the cattle into the makeshift corral of rope and then tied the stud at the first watering trough in town.

The cowboy with the silver buckle dismounted, removed it from his belt, raised it above his head, much to the delight of the Flying Double X's constituency, and delivered it to the bartender of The Gilded Lily.

Lawrence addressed his crew. "The drinks are on me until our competitors arrive." A loud cheer and slaps on the back preceded the Flying Double X cowboys to the tent.

Only two men received their foamy libations when the sound of hooves came from the opposite direction. Three Rancho Mumia calves milled with those of their opposition. Nat led a black stallion with a white star to the next watering trough down from the horse Lawrence had brought.

Will dismounted and walked toward the men enjoying their refreshing beer. "Did you bring the other buckle?" he asked.

"It's right here," the bartender replied waving the shiny article in the air, causing another bout of shouts and firing of a few guns causing the calves to charge the unstable corral. Cowboys from both camps leapt into the corral to calm the nervous calves.

The bartender stood on one his barrels of beer and addressed the crowd. "Enough of that. Let's give everybody a fair chance. No more shooting." The bartender reached under his apron and pulled out a huge pistol. "Or the second shot will assure that the person who shot the first one won't do it again. Understand?" he yelled waving the pistol in the air. Some in the crowd mumbled dissatisfaction, but the crowd got the message.

Will and Lawrence met in front of the makeshift chute built by the good gambling citizens of Dodge that morning. Lots had been drawn, and three judges sat on bar chairs brought for that purpose. Chicanery ran rampant at all times in that cow town, but for reasons of their own, all had declared this event devoid of all underhanded acts.

"Do you want to go first, or should I?" Will asked.

"Let's flip for it," Lawrence responded, removing a shiny silver dollar from his pocket. He locked eyes on Will and said, "Call it."

"Heads," came the response.

Lawrence flipped the coin in the air. Even the nearby bystanders' necks craned backward to watch the shiny coin rotate in the sunlight.

"Tails. Stand aside, boy, and let me show you how this is done," Lawrence grinned as he picked up the coin that had landed between his feet.

The team that accompanied Lawrence retrieved the assigned horse brought by Will and placed him in the chute. Lawrence climbed one of the railings and studied the snorting creature before he swung his leg over the saddle. The horse began to show his disapproval before the gate opened by whining and rocking back and forth.

"Let 'er rip!" Lawrence told his crew as one of his men opened the gate and hastily got out of the way.

Immediately the bronco showed his displeasure of the cowboy on his back by lowering his head and kicking his hind legs high enough to fell a giant. He followed this with three successive hops and a swift turn to the left. Lawrence hung on. The beast, his previous strategy having proved ineffective, reared on his hind legs and came back down on his forelegs with head lowered almost to the ground. That tactic worked as Lawrence came tumbling over the creature's head.

"Six seconds," one of the judges yelled.

Lawrence rose from the ground and waved to the cheering crowd, showing he had not sustained any serious injury. Both Will's crew and the Flying Double X ran after and subdued the still-bucking horse.

Will approached the chute and repeated the actions of Lawrence. Once the chute gate had opened Will's mount also did a high rear kick, started to buck to the right, but went into a spin, galloped four paces, and lowered his head as he came to a sudden stop. Like his predecessor Will did a swan dive over the horse's head.

"Eight seconds!" the same official yelled. Like Lawrence, he rose and waved his hat at the cheering crowd to show he looked forward to the second mount by each contestant.

The judge who counted the time came toward both men. "I think we had better let the wranglers compete to give you fellows a rest," he said. Both men nodded in agreement. The judge announced the decision to the enthusiastic crowd resulting in loud cheers but no gunshots.

The next contest required a pair of cowboys. One had to rope a calf's head and the other had to rope a rear legs and one front one. While the calf lay sprawled on the ground, the cowboy in charge of the head had to keep the rope taunt and the calf prone until his partner could tie three of the calf's legs together. City slickers might suppose it would take three to five minutes to accomplish such a feat but to experienced cowboys five to eight seconds was considered a poor showing.

The Flying Double X crew learned to show proper respect for the black cowboys of the Rancho Mumia. When the dust cleared on the second roping and the scores tallied, the Rancho Mumia had won the event by two seconds. Lawrence turned livid.

The Flying Double X foreman stomped over to the chute for his second ride. He turned on his gathered crew. "What in the hell is wrong with you boys? You allow a bunch of tin-horn niggers to get the best of you? If I didn't have to get that herd to Denver, I'd fire your asses right now."

"It's sort of up to you now. If you win, we call it even. If you lose, then you had better use some of that rope to tie up your pants," one of his hands reminded Lawrence.

"Get the hell out of my way," Lawrence growled. "When this is over, I'll see if I can get you women's jobs at a dance hall in Denver," he added maliciously.

Lawrence lowered himself into the saddle and nodded for one of his hands to open the gate.

The beast had dismounted his rider once and saw no need to change his tactics, but Lawrence had learned from the first ride and held on tight. Sensing his old tricks didn't work, the bronco smashed his rider against to chute gate, throwing him off balance. Feeling the shift of weight, the steed went into a spin to increase the cowboy's slide. Lawrence realized he could no longer remain mounted and slung his left leg over the horse's neck and dismounted.

"Twelve seconds!" the judge yelled. Bedlam broke out as many in the crowd rushed forward and raised Lawrence on their shoulders and paraded him in front of the citizens of Dodge.

Will watched as his crew led his mount into the cute. The creature had a mean streak and could prove very tricky. Jason walked over and put his arm around Will's shoulder.

"You're doing the best you can, Will. It's no shame to lose. The shame comes from not trying. No matter what happens, I want you to know I'm very proud of you. If nothing else Lawrence has learned a black man can be just as good a cowboy as a white man. That's good enough for me," Jason reassured Will.

"I still have one more ride and the day isn't over yet," Will replied.

Jason rejoined the Rancho Mumia crew as Will headed for the chute. The cowboy climbed the railing and examined his mount for the last time. With determination, Will mounted the bronco and signaled for the gate to open.

Like Lawrence's mount, Will's bronco attempted the tried and true tricks that had success in ridding him of his rider. This time Will had time to prepare and the horse seemed annoyed the cowboy didn't catapult over his head. The bronco attempted more bucking and spins but the rider refused to dislodge. With a constant jerk of the reins, Will wouldn't allow the horse anywhere near the chute. More time elapsed and the bronco attempted every trick to dislodge his rider. Finally the horse tired and did a skittish gallop in a circle. Will gave him free rein to gallop and slowly applied pressure on the bit to bring the horse to a halt. Having succeeded at that Will kneed the horse and made him trot toward the Flying Double X gang.

"Nice horse you have here," Will said to Lawrence as he reined the horse and dismounted. "If he's for sale I'll be willing to buy him. He has nice spirit. Let's all go over to The Gilded Lily and have a drink on me while I pick up the prize money and the buckles and discuss the price of this mount."

Lawrence stared at the ground and shook his head. "Well there's no use to be spoilsport. You bested me fair and square today but I bring a herd up from Texas at least once a year and I want a rematch to win our buckles back," he said.

Will smiled at the man and said, "I'll give you a rematch any time you say. I won't be back in Oklahoma until late spring or early summer. If you're passing through, look me up. The buckles are ours now but I'll have the silversmith make another one up just for the upcoming occasion and we'll see who wins that one."

Jason came running over toward the two foremen followed by the tumultuous crowd from Dodge. "Congratulations Will," the owner of the Rancho Mumia said as Will was lifted on sturdy shoulders to be carried back to the bar for his prize and some serious drinking.

Jason finally caught up with his foreman after elbowing his way to the bar. Will and his crew sported the Flying Double X silver buckles around their waists as they received their share of the prize money. He sidled up next to his foreman who stood beside Lawrence.

"This is only a temporary victory. Will's promised to give me a rematch next summer. The boys and I will be saving for our share of the purse. Will said he would match it, and the winner will get a special silver buckle for the occasion. It isn't over yet," Lawrence assured Jason with good humor.

"Will you have given new meaning to the word rodeo," Jason commented.

Will leaned on the bar and stared into the mirror behind it. "I just may have done that," he said lightheartedly. "I just may have done that," he repeated in a more serious tone.

CHAPTER XXIX

STORM

After the victory over the Flying Double X crew Jason allowed an additional day in Dodge to celebrate. Most of the Rancho Mumia crew spent their prize money on new clothes, guns, drinking, and dance hall girls. By the time the herd moved, Jason doubted if ten dollars could be found among all of the cowboys, and that ten dollars rested securely in Laughing Water's pouch. Jason felt pride in the generosity of those individuals who participated in the challenge. The six men and Will felt an obligation to divide the purse with those left at camp including the newest male adult member to the Rancho Mumia crew.

Will reserved the right to dispense the buckles. Only he and those who wrangled earned and wore them. No matter how needy the recipient, pride prevented the sale or pawning of those articles. Each wearer had campfire tales of how he came by it and those tales of the individual's prowess grew in magnitude with each telling.

Sarah used the delay at Dodge as an opportunity to purchase her new found friends necessary objects to initiate a new life when they arrived at their destination. Gray Cloud and Laughing Water humbly accepted the pots and other household goods but gracefully declined any purchase of clothing. Laughing Water considered it her responsibility for the upkeep of the skin-clothing worn by them. She assured Sarah that Gray Cloud would hunt once they reached Montana and provide her with skins to produce a second set. Until then, what they wore had to suffice.

Time passed. Sarah swore she felt the fetus move in the small bulge below her naval. Laughing Water had examined Sarah's belly and pronounced definitely a baby boy.

Miriam made no complaints about her studies and seemed absorbed with her lessons as well as riding. Nor did she abandon her sister and delighted in the childish games with both Alva and Little Fox but her true love of riding never took second place to anything. Her control of her pony amazed Nat and Will. Her tender age became the only thing preventing her from participation in the drive. Sarah and Jake ceased their brooding and felt secure in allowing the young lass to trot beside the wagons. Miriam honored her pledge and kept in sight of one or both adults the entire time she rode her pony. She felt so proud of her accomplishment that she even allowed Little Fox to periodically ride her pony and even gave him some riding instructions she had learned from Nat.

Jason resented the inadequate time shared with his family, but the inordinate amount of time spent with the cowboys and herd provided the only way to learn ranching. Even periodic saddle sores could not keep him from his assigned watch. He felt he was beginning to earn the respect the cowboys as owner. The orders issued thanks to Will, Nat, and the crew had purpose. He no longer felt like a tenderfoot.

Two weeks elapsed since the Rancho Mumia crew left Dodge. Due to lack of rain, the Smoky Hill, Solomon, and Republican rivers offered more of an inconvenience than an obstacle. Gray Cloud and Will proved invaluable in finding water and bedding ground between the rivers. This formidable task took all of both scouts' energy. A severe drought blanketed the open range. Will remarked he had never seen the Republican so low. The foreman hoped the Northwest Territories did not suffer from the drought.

The hardship of the trail would ease tomorrow. The Rancho Mumia crew would reach Ogalala. Traveling through the dust storms of the plains had earned them this respite, and campfire discussions centered on their future activities in the town. Jason and Hank left for the third watch on the last evening before entering Ogalala. Both looked forward to the refreshments the town had to offer. The drovers talked about the dance hall girls and the boss about spending more time with his semi-abandoned family.

"Sing your lungs out tonight," one of the day cowboys ordered the new arrivals. "They smell a storm in the air," he added pointing to the herd.

Jason and Hank looked around at the starry sky. "It won't happen until tomorrow at the earliest," Jason said.

The cowboy grinned. "If you say so, Mr. Jason. I see you never ran into a plains' storm. They can come up quicker than a rattlesnake can strike. Anyway see if you can keep them calm. Sing opera if you have to. Just let them know you're there." The cowboy galloped off after his bunk buddy to get some much needed rest.

"I'll see you on the other side," Hank remarked as he headed his horse north at a slow pace. He started to sing The Little Black Bull to the top of his lungs. Jason headed south at the same pace and waited until his partner had finished the first verse before offering his rendition of the second. At least three cows' hearts fluttered, believing they had heard the bellowing of a strong bull.

After the third circle of the herd, Jason reined his horse beside Hank. Taking a sip of water from his canteen, he said to Hank, "They do seem a little restless tonight. Do you want to make up your own songs now, or would you rather do a few verses of Yellow Rose of Texas?"

Before Hank could reply, Jason jerked his head to the west and frowned. "I could have sworn I saw a flash of lightning." He then stared up at the starry night. "I guess it was my imagination," he finalized.

Both men stared west as the far horizon lit with another flash. "Nope. It's a storm, and a big one at that, headed this way. It should be here in about an hour," Hank estimated.

"Thank God. We really need the rain," Jason said with relief.

"Not like this," Hank replied. "It pours like mad and doesn't sink into the ground, but runs off and floods the rivers, making them very dangerous to cross." Hank stared at Jason's person for a moment. "Take off all of the metal you can. Get rid of your spurs. Put your pistol in front of your pants. Get rid of your gun belt and any change you have in your pocket."

In the distance, and rapidly moving toward the Rancho Mumia herd, lightning clearly punctuated the sky. The stellar dots in the west disappeared as if some giant blew out candles. Both men heard horse's hooves approach. They turned their attention away from the oncoming storm and greeted Will.

"I've been expecting this all evening. It looks like a bad one. Give me your metal, and I'll take it back to camp. Just to be on the safe side, I'll wake four of the boys to give you a hand." Will took the men's metal and placed it in his saddle bags.

Will said, "You've still got your gun, bullets, stirrups and shod horse, and you're the best lightening rod around. More cowboys are killed by lightning than any other way. I don't want you to be one of them. Keep a good eye on the herd Jason. The next couple of hours can get pretty touchy." Will turned his horse and headed toward camp. Within fifteen minutes, four other crew members joined Jason and Hank and began circling the herd at an equal pace. No two sang the same song.

The dangerous black aerial beast began to eat the stars overhead and began to vociferously thunder its displeasure at their limited number by illuminating its huge under belly and hurling jagged thunder bolts at the earth. All the cowboys donned their oil slickers and pulled the brims of their hats low in preparation for the onslaught. The cattle began lowing and glancing around for instruction from one of their kind on what to do. That decision became conclusive as a muley the cowboys had named Agnes rose, kicked the cow next to her, and started a chain reaction.

The rain began in torrents, and the cattle began shifting in a circle created by the cowboys. Will roused the remainder of the crew at camp and had them lend a hand. Despite the heavy rain, flashing lightning, and sonorous thunder, the Rancho Mumia crew managed to contain the herd.

Without warning, a forked flash of lightening struck down not twenty feet west of the herd. "Oh shit," Jason heard Hank yell as two of the cowboys guarding the south rode to the side of the herd and formed a funnel for the stampede. Both rode hard to the side of the lead cattle, using their quirts on the cow's noses in an attempt to get them to mill. The beasts felt nothing. They had but one thing in mind: return to the safety they had back down the trail. Three successive forks of lightning near the herd confirmed the herd's decision and encouraged them to run faster. The cowboys realized they could only allow the herd to tire. Then the most disheartening thing occurred.

The muley realized an inexperienced cowboy kept her in check and worked her way to Jason's side. She broke past Jason taking about twenty cattle with her. "Clem. You and Jason follow them and get them calmed down. We'll take care of the rest," Will yelled as he brought his quirt across the nose of another steer who believed he could do the same thing. A sore nose persuaded the beast of the wisdom of not running in the downpour with that particular herd.

The muley led the small herd at full pace for about a mile in a south-easterly direction. Jason used his quirt without reserve to prevent further division. He strove to drive the herd to veer right. Clem gave way.

The storm passed as rapidly as it had approached. Large flashes of lightning lit the east, but the horrific rumbles of thunder decreased to growls. Jason watched as the muley lowered her head to sample the wet range grass, not only for its nutritional content, but to slake her thirst with rainwater. Another, then another, cow followed suit. Jason yelled across the herd to Clem, "I swear tomorrow I'm going to be the first to have a steak from that god-damned muley even if I have to cook it myself."

Clem laughed and said, "I'll help you cook it if I can have the second steak." Jason nodded agreement as Clem said, "Will probably has the rest of the herd under control by now. Cattle are not meant for running and usually stampede no more than a mile or two before milling. These aren't going anywhere now. I'll keep an eye on them, and you ride back and tell Will where I am."

Jason waved at his partner, turned his horse, and headed back in the direction his small herd had run. It wasn't difficult to discover the trampled path taken by the frightened animals. Scarcely five minutes elapsed before Jason spotted the main herd.

A lone rider rode out to greet him. "Did you keep them together?" Will asked Jason.

"Yep. Clem stayed with them and sent me to get help to get them back," Jason said.

"Good man, Jason. I had better start looking after my job. You're becoming a regular cowboy," Will smiled at Jason.

Swollen with pride the ranch owner replied, "Thanks. Coming from you, it means a lot, but I wouldn't exactly sell your saddle just yet." Will gave a throaty chuckle, reined his horse toward the main herd, followed by a more secure rancher.

In the bright morning sunlight, Jason rode toward the breakfast campfire. Sarah and the children sat around the fire eating breakfast. Jake greeted him as he rode in. "It's a good thing we're at Ogalala. We're almost out of supplies, and I would have had to cook a mule tomorrow for breakfast."

Jason rubbed his eyes with the palms of his hands. He hoped he had enough tears to wash the encrusted dirt from them. Heavily he plopped down next to Sarah who supervised Alva's eating. Jake approached with a heaping plate of bacon, biscuits, and what the crew referred to as "coffee on a stick." Jason took a big mouthful and savored the taste. To him, it tasted like a gourmet meal prepared especially for him by the greatest of New Orleans' chefs. He called Jake back to him as the cook headed back to the chuck wagon. "Jake, there's a muley the boys call Agnes. I want her on the menu. No one gets to eat until I taste my first steak from her," he said.

Jake looked down at his boss and laughed, "Will has been telling you for weeks that muley has been causing a lot of trouble for the herd with its nervousness. It's about time you got rid of her. I get the second steak," laughed Jake as he put in his bid.

Jason vigorously shook his head as he cleared his mouth of food. "Sorry, you'll have to settle for third. Clem has first claim on number two."

"Doesn't matter. There's not a cowhand that liked that muley. I have a feeling we won't have any trouble getting rid of that side of beef, and all of it won't be from hunger," Jake said.

Jason surprised himself by finishing his breakfast during the brief conversation. As he handed the empty plate back to the cook, he added, "Skin her and give it to Laughing Water. Grey Cloud won't be hunting for some time and I'm quite sure

Laughing Water could use the hide. When are you going into town for supplies?"

The cook rubbed his scraggly beard and replied, "I thought about going right after the noon meal. Will or Gray Wolf would know the bedding ground by then."

Jason reached inside his vest pocket and removed the bill-of-attainder used to purchase goods needed along the trail and handed it to the cook. "I want you to purchase eggs for the men for tomorrow and see if you can get a supply of oysters for tonight's meal. Agnes can wait until we're on the other side of the North Platte."

"I don't know so much about the oysters this time of year, but I sure in hell will get the eggs. Mr. Jason, you're going to make Eastern Gentlemen out of these trail rats if you keep treating them like that," Jake smiled.

"You don't have to worry about that until you hear me tell Sarah to start making swallow-tail coats," Jason replied as he felt Sarah's arm loop through his.

Jake quickly headed back to the chuck wagon when he heard the gallop of the hungry Rancho Mumia crew heading toward the wagon to sate their hunger after a long night's work.

Laughing Water climbed out of the back of the wagon after having straightened up the sleeping quarters. Since both Jason and Gray Cloud spent most of their time with the Rancho Mumia cowboys, Sarah had invited the woman and her son to occupy the vacated sleeping area. If nature called one of the children during the night, Laughing Water tended to the need and allowed Sarah to sleep. She helped Sarah during the bumpy drive to make the next camp and became a nanny to the children. Though not as good as Gray Wolf in telling tales, she could mesmerize the children for long periods of time with tales of the Delaware. In return, Sarah included Little Fox in the lessons she gave Miriam. The Indian woman squatted on the opposite side of the campfire to Jason and Sarah after having obtained her breakfast from the chuck wagon.

Jason informed her of the impending hide and ordered her to make good use of it for her family. A grateful woman thanked him. Laughing Water expressed her opinion to her rescuer about the friendly competition that had developed between the two children. Alva seemed quite content staying with her mother.

Miriam proved the quicker of the two at book lessons but Little Fox equaled her with his knowledge of nature observation. Both children had a lot to learn from each other. Miriam's sharing her pony with the boy proved beneficial. He taught her about the spirit of the animals they encountered and how to look for the spirit in different members of the herd. He even described the spirits of the creatures of the wild that Miriam had not yet seen but he had learned their traits from his father. At no time did Miriam dismiss Little Fox's lessons as nonsense and considered them as important as those taught by her mother. A strange respect developed between the two children.

"How did you manage last night?" Jason asked his wife.

"Laughing Water helped keep the children calm by telling stories," Sarah replied. "What about you?"

Jason related his experience to Sarah. When he finished he put his arm around his wife and said, "You know, Sarah. I'm beginning to believe that I can do anything."

Sarah looked over at her husband mischievously. "Don't ever let Miriam hear you say that, or I'm moving back to Alabama."

Jason chuckled and gave his wife a squeeze. "The gods have been very kind to me, Sarah. You are my strength; Miriam my courage, and Alva my calmness and love. All of the rest are just things. If I lost everything this minute and still had you three, I would be content."

Sarah stared lovingly at her husband than gave him a hug. “Go on to the wagon and sleep. I’ll wake you when the herd is ready to move again. If Will, Nat, or any cowboy goes within five feet of the wagon while you’re sleeping I swear I’ll find a new use for the branding iron. Go on now. You look like one of the cattle.”

“First, why don’t you get Laughing Water to watch the children and help massage my aching bones,” he hinted.

Sarah splayed the fingers of her right hand across her breast, arched her eyebrows, and stared down her nose at her husband.

“You nasty, old reprobate. Are you trying to ruin a modest lady’s reputation?”

In response, Jason called to Laughing Water on the other side of the campfire. When the woman joined the couple he said, “Laughing Water would you please watch the children for a while. I have to bring my arrogant wife down a peg or two.” With that, he stood, swooped his wife off of the ground and headed for the wagon leaving an amused Laughing Water to assure the children would not interrupt the lesson.

CHAPTER XXX

OGALALA

Jason's unexpected bounty of scrambled eggs the next morning took the cowboys by surprise and certainly bolstered morale. After their hearty breakfast the cowboys drove their herd to the bedding ground outside Ogalala. Jason had the experience of Dodge City and knew well what the upcoming visit to this northern cow town would bring. He advanced his crew ten dollars apiece to be deducted from their final payment for the drive.

If Dodge defined lawlessness, Ogalala defied any definition. Shootings in the gambling houses occurred hourly and therefore warranted little recognition by the patrons of those establishments. The removal of a gambler's body by someone who caught him cheating presented a small annoyance as opposed to the gunshots into the ceiling by a drunken patron. Main Street resembled a brawling arena which became a maze for any horseman attempting to avoid trampling on the inebriated contestants. Respectable citizens went about their daily affairs without giving any credence to the turmoil taking place around them. All ignored the honorary title of sheriff, a currently vacant position. Each saloon, brothel, or business formulated its own definition of law.

On the second day of their arrival, Will, Nat, and Jason opted for their turn in the hell town. After reviewing the booming businesses along the main street the four agreed on the less rowdy Smart Ox as their watering spa.

The interior resembled any other bar. The distinguishing difference demonstrated itself in the patronage. It soon became manifest to the new arrivals that the clientele wanted only two things: to get reeling drunk and to fight. The four men sat at a table furthermost from the bar and the entryway. They wanted only to slake their trail thirst, watch the interaction of the customers, and return to camp.

"We're going to have a hard time getting those cows across the North Platte tomorrow," Will said.

"You mean because of the storms we've been having?" Jason asked.

"They're the cause of it. That damned river will be worse than its sister river to the south. Silt builds more rapidly in it. It creates quicksand, and if a damned cow stops to drink she'll start to sink, and her bellowing will upset the rest of the herd crossing and with all the rain that river will be running faster than a bullet. We'll have to start the crossing well west so by the time the cattle reach the opposite shore, it will be at the right spot to bed them down," Will explained.

"The first thing we have to get across are the wagons. It's going to take every cowboy's lasso to hold them steady going across. I sure as hell am not looking forward to tomorrow."

A shadow crossed the table as a voice yelled, "What in the hell are you god-damned niggers doing in here. Isn't it bad enough we have to put up with Mexicans? Now we have to drink with god-damned niggers."

Nat rose and pushed his chair back for clearance. "We're just having a few beers at no cost to you and having a conversation that doesn't concern you. If you don't like our company, then get the hell back where you belong," Nat replied.

The intruder staggered back from the table and stared at Nat. "If there's one thing I hate worse than Mexicans it's a big mouth nigger," he replied.

Jason looked across the table for help from Will. Jason's hope that the confrontation would resolve itself without bloodshed faded rapidly. Jason didn't want a reoccurrence of Unionville. He looked at the black gunfighter who refused to unlock his eyes from his antagonist.

Another cowboy approached the intruder from behind and nervously called, "Luke. Luke. Forget about it. Let me buy you a drink," he said. The new arrival inched his way between Luke and Nat. He leaned forward and whispered something in Luke's ear. Nat's adversary clearly paled at whatever information the cowboy had imparted to him. As the cowboy put his arm around Luke's shoulders to turn him toward the bar it became plain to all that Luke's gun hand no longer challenged the experienced gunfighter. Luke still complained about having to drink with minorities as he permitted himself to be led back to the bar. Nat resumed his seat but kept his eyes locked on the drunken cowboy.

"Let's go somewhere else. It's awful stuffy in here," Jason said.

Nat shook his head and said, "No. These beers aren't half finished. I think I want another after this one. Will would you mind getting a second round for us?" he said throwing a fifty cent piece toward Will.

"Not at all. I think I see a space just to the right of the fellow who was just here. I can place our order there," Will smiled.

"Nat, do you think that wise?" Jason asked in a frightened voice.

"Jason nobody tells them where to stand, sit, or how long they can stay. If they don't want to give us the same privilege then we have to prove to them we have the same rights and we will take them. He knows who I am and doesn't want any trouble. Sometimes my reputation can prevent a fight as well as finish one. We have to leave early tonight for tomorrow's wrangling. In the meantime I don't know about you but I intend to have a good evening right here," Nat said as he pushed his hat back on his head and stretched his legs under the table.

Will returned carrying two foaming mugs. "I would have liked to carry one at a time but that would have stretched a point; don't you think, Nat?"

"Yep. We've won. I don't want to act like that stupid idiot. Just go get the other one and let's forget about them," Nat waved a dismissal. As Will left, and Nat turned his attention to Jason. "The sooner we get the herd across the better. I hope we reach Fort Robinson in three days. I don't think the White River is going to be a duck pond to cross."

Jason recognized Nat's desire to change the subject and offer reassurance that the crises had ended. "It all depends on how many cows we have to pull out of the quagmire. If all goes well, we should be in Cascade the first or second week of September."

Will returned with the other beer and the conversation for the rest of the evening centered on the drive. Before dark the three comrades left the Smart Ox and soberly wended their way back to camp. Mention of any confrontation would likely upset the ladies, so the men related only their observations of the lighter events of their visit to Ogalala.

That evening, Jake discussed the wisdom of waiting until the wagons crossed the North Platte before restocking. The lighter wagons would abet the cowboys in reeling the vehicles across the North Platte like harpooned whales. The team could bring the supplies across afterward wrapped in their oil slickers. Jason agreed but refused to revisit the town even though the crossing would cost an extra day.

"Well I have second watch,"Jason said as a hint for the others to retire for the night.

The men rose to head for the campfire. The two women remained seated as Sarah expressed the thought Laughing Water refused to verbalize. "Tomorrow I hope one of you tell us what really happened in town."

The men tried to make light of the situation as Jason replied, "What? And lose a chance to see that dance hall gal again? Never."

Sarah gave her husband a doubtful look as she and Laughing Water rose and headed for the wagon to check on the sleeping children and prepare for bed.

The cowboys ate breakfast slowly. A heavy fog blanketed the landscape and they couldn't move the herd until at least an hour after sunrise. During that time each, cowboy volunteered for a specific space on either side of the river so that each individual's expertise could be use to full advantage. The ladies and children had to cross first with their husbands. This required they strip to bare essentials and wrap their dresses in oilskin to keep them dry. Laughing Water said she had no problem as the skins are better protection than cloth and dry quicker than a multitude of petticoats stretched out on the grass. After a small tantrum Miriam ceded to her father that she could not ride her pony across and agreed to let it cross with the remuda while she would cross with her father.

The mules became Hank's responsibility under the heading of remuda. Two cowboys remained with the herd. The rest of the crew split in half. Will took charge of those cowboys on the south side of the river and Jason those on the north. Each of the cowboys tied his lasso in a strategic area in front, back, and side in order to maintain proper balance for the wagon's crossing. After securing his lasso to the pommel of his saddle Jason felt as if the pressure of the current against the wagons would pull the saddle from the horse but both wagons crossed without incident. Jason had the wagons moved a mile north of the crossing to allow privacy to the men who either stripped to their undergarments or became naked to make the transverse back and forth across the river easier and not to embarrass the ladies who may or may not appear from inside the wagon.

A better part of the day elapsed without incident. Eight cattle had become bogged in the quicksand. Some so deep, it required tying up the tails to free them. When the beasts gained shore, they bellowed their disapproval of the treatment by charging at the nearest cowboy before joining the herd. The seasoned men had performed this task many times in the past and took it in stride. Then the unforeseen occurred.

One of the cowboys known as Barry screamed for help. His horse's legs had become cramped in midstream. Both rider and horse disappeared under the rushing water. Quicker than can be told Gray Cloud wrapped the loop of his lasso around his waist, threw the other end to a nearby cowboy and dove into the water just below where the struggling man had vanished. Two other men ran over and also grabbed the free end of the rope.

Barry's bunk mate allowed the twenty cattle they escorted to find their own way to the shore as the naked man directed his mount toward where Gray Cloud swam.

Gray Cloud treaded water and took a deep breath before diving. What seemed centuries, actually only seconds, the Indian's head and chest appeared above the water. "Pull. Pull" he shouted to the men on shore.

As they had for the wagons, the men began the tug-o-war with the angry river. The men on shore saw a man's head cupped in Gray Cloud's left arm. "Bring a saddle down to the shore," the swimmer yelled to Will who had just arrived on the scene.

Without acknowledging he had heard Will leapt from his mount and frantically began to loosen his saddle strap. After removing the saddle, Will ran to the river shore and dropped it. When Gray Wolf and the unconscious man came within five feet of land Will and two others rapidly waded into the water and lifted Barry out of the river and headed for shore. The four cowboys manning the rope kept tugging Gray Cloud toward shore.

"Throw his belly over the saddle and turn his head to the side," Will ordered when the men reached shore with the human flotsam.

Barry's skin had a blue tint. Will knew he had to act fast. He sat on the naked man's thighs and placed his hands on the lower part of Barry's back, and, with a rocking motion, placed all of his weight on his rigid arms.

At first, only a small trickle of water came from Barry's mouth, but after the tenth push by Will Barry took a deep breath and vomited a copious amount of fluid along with breakfast. Then he lapsed into dry heaves.

Will rose and looked down at the now conscious, prostate man.

"You'll be OK. But from now on, if you want a drink of water, please use your canteen." Barry smiled and nodded weakly.

The danger now passed, all eyes turned toward the stoic soaked Indian standing in their midst. If a single cowboy had a doubt as to Gray Cloud's worth on the drive it melted like dew in the desert sun.

Will walked toward the man and placed his hand on the wet shoulder. "It will not end here. Every man present will spread the word of your courage. There will not be a cowboy west of the Mississippi who would not consider it a privilege to be your bunk mate. If you have need you have only to ask it of any man here. I liked you from the first time you joined us but you have earned something even greater---respect. On behalf of all of us thank you." Will patted the man's shoulder and left. The void immediately filled with the Rancho Mumia crew wanting to shake Gray Cloud's hand. Barry weakly struggled to his feet and approached the man. Words would not come. Instead he gave the Indian a crushing hug.

All heads turned as they heard a rider coming ashore. Jason rode at a fast pace toward the gathered group and reined to a quick halt. "I heard a man was down. What happened?" he asked. After being briefed on the incident Jason approached Gray Cloud. "Words are useless at a time like this, but deeds aren't." Jason elevated his voice just loud enough for all to hear. "When we reach Cascade, I'm going to have my lawyer draw up a deed to ten acres to be given to you near where my house will be built. I want to keep a person like you near to me at all times. I don't want you to wander anymore. Now you have your own land and your own home if you wish to take it. Of course if you wish to continue on to Canada that is your right but that land will always be there for you whether or not you settle on it." The cowboys released a cheer and returned to their mounts to complete the crossing.

Left alone with Jason, Gray Cloud stared at the ranch owner and said, "I shall give you gift serious consideration and talk it over with my family. It will not be easy to live with the white man if I do decide to accept. Besides, I tried only to repay a life for a life."

Jason smiled and slowly shook his head, "I don't believe that. I have come to know you too well. If you had been under Army escort with a rifle pointed at you, you would have done the same thing. You are too much a man of honor to allow even an enemy to perish if you could prevent it. For reasons you couldn't understand this is a path of life I cheerfully walk so it's not being over generous. As to living with the white man I don't know if you had a good look at my skin lately," he said with a snicker as he held up his right arm for inspection. Jason placed his hand on the big man's shoulder and gave it a playful shake. "Most importantly, I would be proud to have you as my neighbor." Jason removed his hand and offered it to Gray Cloud. The Indian stood proudly erect and firmly clasped Jason's hand.

The rest of the crossing went almost without incident. The cowboys had to pull three more steers from the quagmire, but no one sustained an injury. Jason sent Jake back to Ogalala to purchase supplies and more eggs to celebrate the rescue. The Rancho Mumia crew could not recall better treatment from another trail boss.

Sarah received the news of her new neighbors with delight. Laughing Water remained stoic and deferred to her husband for a decision. Gray Cloud told his wife that the two "men" would discuss the offer on the trip north.

The next two weeks mirrored the previous ones. Will and his crew spent a dangerous time fording rivers and removing cattle from quicksand. Two more stampedes happened but no life threatening experiences occurred. At long last after nine weeks on the trail, the herd arrived at Miles City. On Will's advice, Jason left his family and the drive in Will's charge and headed west toward Cascade to find John Garret and his ranch land.

JOHN

1877

CHAPTER XXXI

A NEW FRIEND

Jason became adept at camping, foraging, and hunting. True, it required more than a single shot to down an animal but that would improve with time and practice. As he rode across the central part of the territory the flatness of the grassland amazed him. Like huge giants the mountains in the distance seem to guard some unseen treasure. The undulating waves of grass proved dangerous to the unsuspecting due to the spider-leg coulees that frequented the traveler's trip. Some had large pools of water and offered many animals a refuge from the hot sun. A careless traveler could easily get injured in the dark as the rims of these cracks could come upon one without much notice. Carefully, Jason took five days to travel to the western part of the territory. He allowed his curiosity to wander on many side trips and explorations.

On the sixth morning of his trip he encountered an elegant white house in the middle of the plains. Like a welcoming beacon it stood out from the few out buildings surrounding it. Jason had observed a few ranch houses on his travels mostly built of log. This particular one had an elegant colonial design. The pounding of his horse's hooves must have alerted the inhabitants of his approach. A woman stepped onto the porch and two more female faces appeared behind a screened door. Not to frighten the ladies Jason remained on his horse tipped his hat to the lady standing on the porch and said, "Good morning, ma'am. May I speak with your husband?"

Jason tried hard not to stare at the two Indian woman behind the screen door dressed in the latest eastern fashion as the lady replied, "My husband is in the north range. If you ride that way," she pointed, "you may ask any of the hands where he is."

Jason gave the ladies his best smile, tipped his hat, and kneed his mount in the direction the lady had pointed. He rode for about fifteen minutes when a cowboy herding about ten cattle came into view. Jason rode toward him. "Can you tell me where I can find the ranch owner?" he asked.

Before replying the cowboy had to mill an especially active steer who objected to obeying the cowboy. He galloped back toward Jason all the while keeping a keen eye on the moving cattle. "Mr. Granville is with the main herd. Just ride around that hill over there," he pointed, "and you'll see him. He's riding a strawberry roan." Jason thanked the hand and headed in the direction given by the cowboy who returned to the herd to prevent any more of the maverick's antics.

A man with black whiskers and eyes that could pierce stone watched as Jason approached. Discarding all protocol the man said, "I can always use an extra hand during fall roundup. What's your best---droving or branding?"

"Neither Mr. Granville, but thanks for offer. I'm looking for a rancher named John Garret. Have you ever heard of him?" Jason responded.

The thin ranch boss rubbed his chin. "Garret. Garret. Hmm. Can't quite place the fellow. Wait a minute." Stuart Granville rose in his saddle and yelled over at the busy cowboys. "Teddy. Teddy. Come here a minute."

A man with an oval-face, wide-forehead, wide round eyes, and a waxed mustache placed his lariat on his saddle horn and responded to the call. "Yes, Mr. Granville."

"This here gentleman is looking for a man called John Garret who owns a ranch around here someplace. I can't seem to place him. Do you know him?" Stuart asked.

Like Granville, the cowboy named Teddy stared at Jason for a moment while trying to remember. Suddenly Teddy's eyes lit up and he smiled. "Oh yeah. I remember now. He has a spread northwest of here between the Blackfoot and the Idaho border. I helped drive some cows there once. His ranch is called the Dusty Trail. It's a little over a half-a-day's ride from Cascade. After you reach Cascade, strike out north and follow the mountain range and you'll run right into it. You could make better time striking out across the Blackfoot territory but I wouldn't advise it. They get touchy about strangers crossing their land."

"Thank you, Teddy. You can go back now, "Granville said. Teddy nodded, removed his lariat from his saddle horn and rejoined the other cowboys. Jason sensed Granville would not waste more time with him now that he had his information.

"Thank you Mr. Granville. If you're ever up that way stop by the Rancho Mumia which is the name of my ranch and have supper with us," Jason offered.

"Mighty kindly of you. I might just do that. Now I have to get back to the branding," Granville replied.

Jason tipped his hat, turned his mount and headed back toward the ranch house and the dirt road in front of it. As he galloped past the front of the house he waved thanks to the three ladies sitting on the porch. He realized he had one more night of camping before he reached Cascade.

By late afternoon of the following day Jason spotted the town of Cascade. As he rode into it he noticed it appeared like any other cow town except for the unusual number of soldiers from nearby Fort Shaw. Though rowdy, the town did not exhibit the unbridled lawlessness of its more southern counterparts.

After long nights of camping and droving on the way to Montana, Jason treated himself to a hearty supper a few drinks, a hot bath, a trip to the barber, and a feathered bed for the night. Long after sunrise Jason breakfasted and prepared to continue his journey. He decided to make a final jaunt around town to familiarize with the main street since Nat had informed him this would be the nearest settlement to his spread.

Jason felt a slap on the back that almost knocked him down and a voice saying, "Howdy stranger. Saw you last night over at the Silver Spur. Looking for the whore house?"

Jason just stuttered, "No, I--I--I"

"Never mind. I doubt you could find a whore that's not busy now with all of the soldiers in town. Let me buy you a beer. Mary's the name. Mary Fields. What in the hell is yours?" she brusquely demanded.

"Jason," he replied.

"Jason what?" she pressed.

"Just Jason," he again stuttered.

Mary roared laughter toward the blue sky. "Well Just Jason at least I don't have to stumble over any god-damned foreign names. Come on let's get a beer and you can tell me about yourself," she said throwing her arm around his shoulder and directing him toward the Silver Spur.

"Don't you think it's a little early to start drinking?" he asked never breaking his stride.

"Early? My God, man, it's probably after midnight in China. Now there's a lot of Chinese folks that live in these here parts. You sure in hell wouldn't want to insult them. Now would you?" she smiled patting his shoulder.

In spite of himself, Jason liked this good-natured black woman dressed in men's clothes. He smiled, shook his head and said, "Well when you put it that way I guess I wouldn't."

“I thought you’d see it my way,” she grinned back as she ushered him through the doors.

The bartender busied himself stacking glasses and cleaning the mess left by the customers at closing. Mary walked to the center of the bar and said, “Frankie give my friend here and me a beer.”

“Mary, I haven’t even opened yet. Can’t you wait another hour?” Frankie requested.

“God-damn it Frankie. I didn’t ask what you had to do. I asked you to get us a beer.” Mary pulled her gun from her holster and aimed it at the glass Frankie held.

A human streak stepped in front of the beer tap. “OK. OK,” he replied as he filled two mugs with the foamy brew. He walked over to Mary and placed them in front of her in exchange for a dime. “I swear to God Mary, you’re going to be the death of me,” he moaned.

“Only if I can catch you in my bedroom without an invitation. Of course then you’ll be the one holding the shooter or is that thing only a pee shooter.” Mary’s laughter echoed throughout the empty saloon. Even Jason and Frankie couldn’t resist a hearty laugh.

“Come on Jason,” she invited, picking up her mug. “Let my busy bee finish his work.” She turned to Frankie and winked. “If you’re a good boy I may just give you some honey tomorrow night when I get back from my delivery.”

“Mary you’re the reason cowboys wear tall boots,” Frankie said dismissively and returned to work.

The two lone customers seated themselves at a table beside the entrance and took a sip of beer. “You up here for the roundup?” she asked as pulled a chair near from a nearby table and rested her feet.

“No,” Jason responded, “I’m looking for a rancher named John Garret.”

Mary reached inside her shirt pocket and produced a cheroot. "Cigar?"

Jason wiped some beer foam from his upper lip. "No thanks. Do you happen to know him?"

Between puffs of lighting the cigar Mary said, "Yep. Owns the Dusty Trail about a six-hour ride from here. Too bad you just missed him. He left yesterday. He was in town buying supplies. Had to leave before noon. Roundup time you know."

"Well, I have to go. I want to get there before it's late," Jason said finishing his beer.

As he stood to leave, Mary grabbed his shirt sleeve with her right hand and motioned him to be seated with her left. "Sit down. It's your turn to buy the beer. After that you can go over to the store and help me load a couple of sacks of sugar and flour and a few other things I have to take to the Dusty Trail. John couldn't fit all of his supplies on his wagon so he hired me to bring the rest out today. It's a long drive and I could use a little company. Besides, there's nothing to drink between here and there but water. Now go get these refilled," she ordered with a winning smile.

Jason went to the bar and asked Frankie to refill the mugs. When the bartender came back Jason asked in a low voice, "Would she have shot that glass out of your hand?"

Frankie grinned ear to ear. "Hell yes she would. You should see her shoot the cigar from a man's mouth when a stranger who doesn't know better pisses her off. Just about everybody around here loves her and we've learned it's best to stay on her good side." Frankie smiled, waved at Mary, and added, "If she's got one."

"Thanks for the beer," she said as Jason returned to their table, "You going to go work for John?" Mary asked taking another puff of the cigar and sip from the new mug.

"Not exactly." Jason began to explain his reasons for coming to Montana.

When he finished explaining she said, "If your ranch is the one I think it is, it's one of the most beautiful here. It nestles right against the mountain range, and the grass is green and tall. You're going to have the fattest cattle in the territory. It runs into John's ranch and is surrounded by a lot of free range. You have to watch out for the wolves and cougars though, especially after a good winter. Light snow allows their meals to run fast and sometimes get away while a heavy snow slows them down. Believe me you would rather deal the animals than with heavy snow. I've seen it snow so bad that a cowboy has to raise his horse's head to allow it to breathe. A lot of cattle can freeze or starve to death in weather like that. Your spread has a good winter pasture like John's but even that doesn't mean much when Ma Nature dumps twelve to fourteen feet of snow on you and the wind starts to howl. Sometimes it snows so hard I can't get over the mountains to St. Peter's Mission. That's where I work." Mary paused at that picture and angrily puffed on her cigar.

"Do you go to St. Peter's often?" Jason inquired.

Mary stared at him as if he had asked a stupid question and then replied, "I see you don't know anything about people around here. Jason, I'm one who takes care of the mission's outside work so that Sister Amadeus and the nuns can pray and teach the Indian children. I also deliver goods for people along the way who don't have the time to come to town."

Jason's jaw dropped. "My God, Mary, aren't you afraid of getting bushwhacked?"

Mary seemed to enjoy Jason's shock. "I'd like to see the son-of -a bitch who would try it. After I got through kicking his ass all over the road I'd cut off his balls and hang them on his ears for earrings."

"Believe me. She could do it too," Frankie added from his eavesdropping position behind the bar. "She fears only God and the Devil. One's her father and the other's her husband. So, she doesn't fear anybody," he chuckled.

"You're asking for one good ass-kicking Frankie. Remind me to give it to you when I get back from the Dusty Trail," Mary bantered as she finished the last of her beer and tossed the stogie into one of the spittoons lining the bar. She rose from the table and said, "Come on Jason. Let's go over to the store and load." As they started to depart, Mary could not resist a parting shot at Frankie as she pointed her finger at him and said, "Thanks to that last remark that's the last time I let you win at poker."

"Let me win?" Frankie squeaked. "Ol' George Grimes plays a better game and he's blind, you old horse thief," he volleyed at the swinging doors and the laughter coming from the street.

Jason and Mary spent the next hour loading Mary's flatbed. With great agility, Mary tossed the huge bags of flour and sugar on the back of her vehicle. Even when Jason assisted her in loading a barrel of nails he could tell she carried her weight in loading. At long last, Mary closed the flatbed's back. Jason tied his mount to the tail-gate hitch and climbed on the wooden seat beside Mary as she slapped the reins on the horse's haunches and began their trip.

Jason perspired profusely which matched his labored breathing. Mary looked as if she had just come from a Sunday picnic. Once again she removed a cheroot from under her rawhide vest. "Want one now?" she asked.

"No thanks. Somebody may think I'm a train puffing coal smoke with the way I'm breathing," he huffed.

"Hmm! I understand. I got a lot of training in loading and unloading the flatbed and carrying bricks to rebuild St. Peter's. Mary gave the reins another flick. "Look under your seat, Jason. I always keep a little something under there to make the dust taste better." Jason reached under his seat and removed a brown jug.

"Go ahead. Take a swig. It'll help you regain your strength," she smiled.

Jason popped the cork and rested the jug in the crook of his arm and took a swig. "Whew! What do you make that stuff out of, turpentine?"

While holding the reins in her left hand, Mary reached over and took the jug from Jason. "Why waste good turpentine, when we have perfectly good sulfur all over the place?" she teased and upended the jug. "Whew. You're right. This is some of the best ol' Tom ever made. I'll introduce you to him. His stuff is some of the best and his price is reasonable too." Mary recorked the jug and Jason stuck it back under his seat.

The warmth of the drink permeated Jason and gave him enough courage to ask, "Mary, how in the hell did you ever become a deliverer?"

Mary scrunched her nose and rubbed it against her wrist. "I'm not good for much else. I do a little washing and sewing for the cowboys to tide me over between trips, but mostly I work at the mission. I love the feel of the reins in my hands," she said waving the reins at Jason. "I thought about becoming a cowgirl, but I don't feel like fighting those horney sons-of-bitches for hundreds of miles on a drive. Besides, I'm a pretty good poker player and those bastards are always broke thanks to me. That gives me a lot of time to spend with the Cascade baseball team. It's a great game some Northerner invented and the kids love it. At long last you guys figured out something really entertaining to do with your balls."

Jason bent double with laughter.

"I like my independence. I just can't see myself with a kid puking down my back and another one shitting and pissing in my lap while I'm stirring stew for some asshole who comes home complaining about how hard he worked all day. Horses don't give you half the trouble of a husband. Besides, you can shovel the shit the horses give you." Jason roared with laughter again, reached under the seat and removed the jug. He offered it first to Mary who took a long draught and handed back to Jason who took another swig and replaced the jug.

Jason and Mary spent the remainder of the trip cementing a friendship. Jason discovered that Mary's brusque visage and intermittent colorful adjectives made an attempt to conceal a warm, caring person.

Miriam! How would his daughter react to Mary? Mary's individuality linked with Miriam's unpredictable personality would probably force Sarah, Jason, and most of humanity to seek a way to leave the planet. Still---Nat had only a positive influence despite his reputation. Perhaps Mary might do the same.

The wagon jolted along the rough road as the two occupants shared the jug and tall tales. They ignored the bright sunshine and waving grass. The open range rang with their laughter as each tried to tell a tale taller than the other one. Jason felt he had always known Mary.

CHAPTER XXXII

HOME

The six-hour drive seemed like only a few minutes to Jason and Mary. Good company mixed with white lightening ignores time. As the wagon approached John's ranch house, a slightly stout woman ushered forth, stepped off of the porch, and shaded her eyes against the low western sun. "Mary did you bring a bolt of cloth with you? It wasn't in the things John unloaded yesterday, and he's so forgetful when it comes to anything that doesn't concern a cow."

"It's in the back between two sugar sacks," Mary responded.

"Who's that with you? Don't tell me you've saved enough money to bribe some deaf, dumb, and blind man to marry you," the neatly dressed woman taunted.

"Nope. I found a couple of men with those fine qualities but none of them owned a still. I still haven't found a man worthy of me. I even offered to become a damned nun. I don't know why in the hell they wouldn't accept me. Anyway, this guy here is looking for John," Mary said jumping down from the flatbed. She unhitched Jason's horse and tied him to the hitching post in front of the house so she could open the wagon gate.

Still blocking the sun with her hand, the lady of the house made the same mistake Stuart Granville had made. "I'm sure my husband could use an extra hand for a couple of days. He's almost through cutting and branding the cattle but they still have to be driven to their winter pasture."

Jason stared down at the robust woman and smiled. "Miss Amy don't you know that as time passes you're supposed to get older, not younger."

Amy slowly lowered her hand and stared quizzically at the man who addressed her by name. "How do you---oh, my God---Jason? As I live and breathe, I don't believe it. I know John said you would be coming, but I didn't expect you so soon." Amy paused in her diatribe, brushed her dress to gain time to overcome the surprise, and said, "Come on in and have some coffee. John should be back in another hour or so."

"I'd love a cup, but let me help Mary unload first," he said.

"Well it's about damned time somebody realizes that there's work to be done," Mary grumbled over a smile as she removed the bolt of cloth from the wagon and handed it to Amy.

"One more word from you madam, and I'll make you sleep in the back of your wagon tonight so a cougar can eat you," Amy threatened.

Mary climbed aboard the wagon to drive it to the storage shed. "Don't bother me none. All the wild ones know if they ate me they'd only get indigestion. If you weren't the best cook in these here parts I wouldn't even bother spend the evening," she replied good-heartedly. Jason climbed aboard the wagon as Mary flicked the reins and headed for the storage shed.

An hour elapsed as Mary and Jason rearranged things in the supply shed to make room for the newly purchased stock. After securing the lock on the shed Mary drove the wagon to the side of the ranch house. She and Jason alit from the now empty wagon and entered the cottonwood structure.

Everywhere Jason looked warmth and utility met his eye. A low, polished ceiling with two round holes in cross opposing end corners allowed the fireplace to heat the upstairs and capped the single large room. The far left corner off the door belonged exclusively to Amy. Pots, pans, and cooking utensils of various sizes decorated two walls. A low cooking stove with an iron shelf in front interrupted the line of cookware on one wall while a handmade breakfront containing Amy's good china and silverware occupied the other. Amy's work table, between the breakfront and the corner contained immaculate canisters filled with various seasonings ending with a butter crock. All neatly lined up and within near reach for the cook.

The remainder of the room melded into a dining/living room accented by a long, polished handmade table with three chairs and a matching bench all with a heart pattern carved in their backs. Covering most of the right entry wall stood a stone fireplace with two cushioned chairs, a rocker, and two small tables containing coal oil lamps. In the two corners outlining the fireplace wall, two additional chairs rested for use by guests who might wish to join John and Amy by their warm hearth. Two highly polished rifles rested upside down over the fireplace mantle which displayed precious knickknacks Amy carried from Alabama. In the center at the back of the room, John had erected a staircase with crude banisters which led to the upper floor containing a master bedroom and two guest bedrooms.

Both Jason and Mary sat at the table as Amy placed three mugs on it. As she retreated to get the coffee pot she asked, "How's Ann?"

Jason offered his hostess his cup and replied, "She's doing just fine. I never thought she---that's fine thank you."

"Milk and sugar?" Amy asked.

"No, thanks. It seems as if I have learned to drink it black on the trip up here. It's nice to drink it instead of eating it off of a stick," he commented as he took a sip of the strong brew. Amy filled Mary's cup then her cup, returned the pot to the stove, and joined her guests at the table. "As you were saying," she cued. Mary remained silent enjoying her coffee hoping to pick up any bits of information that would give her a better insight into her new found friend.

"She turned out to be quite a business woman with Gregory Ellis's help," Jason informed.

Amy clasped her mug in both hands and stared at the black liquid. "I only met the man once when he delivered the tax bill to John. Never in a thousand years would I believe that he would become Ann's champion," she said in an unbelieving voice.

"He also married the widow Blyth and they have a son. People change Miss Amy," Jason commented.

Amy looked up from her mug and stared at Jason for a moment. "So I see. I remember you as a very bitter and unpleasant man. I never saw you smile or say more than two words to anybody except Hunter."

Jason winced. "God, how I wish I could deny that Miss Amy," he said regretfully.

"You can stop calling me Miss Amy. Just Amy will do. Formal titles are a thing of the past around here especially since you're going to be our neighbor," she added. Jason nodded agreement.

"You'll meet the reason for my change in a couple of days," Jason said gleefully.

"More coffee?" she asked.

"No thanks. I've had enough." Jason placed his empty mug on the table.

"How about you, Mary?" she asked, turning to her other guest.

"No thanks. I think I'll go see about the horses," Mary answered as she rose and went out of the door.

"When the door had closed Amy said, "Don't let Mary's gruffness fool you. She would give you the shirt off of her back.

Everybody would take advantage of her good nature if she wasn't so gruff. I guess you'll discover that some of Sister Amadeus has rubbed off on her when you know her long enough," Amy snickered.

"On second thought, I think I will have another cup of coffee, if you don't mind," said Jason.

"Sure." Amy rose and headed for the stove.

"Who's this Sister Amadeus?" he asked.

Amy poured both another cup of coffee for both and returned the pot to the stove before replying. "Mary was a slave to the Dunn family in Tennessee. She hated cotton but when she was old enough she used to hitch the mules and plow the fields. She always loved horses and mules. The only thing she loved more was Dolly Dunn, the owner's daughter. The two were about the same age and, as children, established an undying bond of friendship that has lasted until today. When the Dunns sold their plantation after the war and moved to Ohio, Mary went with them. Dolly went off on her own, but Mary remained with the Dunns. One day Mary received a letter saying Dolly needed her here in Cascade. Both of them received a shock when Mary saw a Carmelite nun waiting for her. Dolly, who had become Sister Amadeus, saw a tall, black woman in men's clothes smoking a cigar standing in front of her. But nothing could break that childhood bond. Fact is that Sister Amadeus developed pneumonia soon after Mary's arrival and Mary nursed her back to health. Nobody worked harder in restoring St. Peter's Mission than Mary. The men resented a black, ex-slave woman giving orders, and one challenged Mary to a duel and she killed him. After that people both black and white began to show her respect. Sister Amadeus berated her for the man's death but Mary brushed it off by saying the only thing that guy could shoot off was his mouth and God didn't have time to listen to that nonsense to get His mission rebuilt. She still works for them and has caused many of the nuns to go to prayer with a red face when things don't go her way. Did she tell you how she got the delivery job?"

Jason shook his head which brought a slight snicker from Amy.

"Well a few years back the job became available and Mary wanted it. The local sheriff at the time didn't want to give it to a woman, especially a black woman. He considered it strictly a man's job because it also included mail carrying for the United States Government. Mary left the sheriff standing in the street as she climbed up on the stage coach, knocked the driver off, grabbed the reins, and drove it to the other end of the street. She turned it around and headed full speed toward the sheriff and stopped the rig about ten feet from the sheriff. 'Now do I get the job or do we do this again?' No problem. She got the job."

"If it was anyone else but Mary I would say you're telling a tall tale," Jason responded.

Jason heard a horse approaching. "That must be John," Amy said as she rose and headed for the breakfront to get another cup and check on the delicious aromas emulating from the stove. Jason heard John's voice shout to Mary, "Did you bring Amy's bolt of cloth?"

"Yeah. You're going to look cute in bluebell longjohns," she countered.

"Maybe Amy will have enough left over for a pair of bloomers for you," John shot back, stomping his boots and entering the house. John spied the man sitting at his table sipping coffee. At long last," he said and extended his hand to the rising man. "I didn't expect you for another week. Is your herd behind you? Amy, may I have some coffee, please?"

Amy half filled John's cup with enough left over for both other cups. "I didn't expect company. I'll make a new pot," she said and went to outside to the pump to wash the pot and get more water.

"I left the herd over a week ago. I wanted to see the layout of the land before they arrived. They should be here in a couple of days," Jason replied.

"How's Ann?" John asked.

"She's just fine and runs Whispering Willows with a tight fist in a velvet glove," Jason responded.

"God, I'd give the world to see her. As soon as we get a little ahead here I want to go back for a visit, but it's very hard to find time to get away. When you start your ranch you'll find that out." John crossed his arms and leaned on the table. Both men ignored the sounds coming from the kitchen as Amy prepared more coffee and rechecked the evening meal cooking on the stove.

"I'll ride you out to your place tomorrow morning. There's a wonderful spot that would be ideal to build the ranch house and will protect you against the snow drifts and the wind," John volunteered.

"Mary warned me that the winters can be pretty bad," Jason added.

"You can't describe them until you've been through one. You and I have some of the finest grazing land up here but an especially bad winter negates that fact. When your herd arrives I advise you to take them directly to your winter pasture. You have some nice land that runs up a mountain side. That should take care of them for the winter. How many did you bring?" John asked.

"About five hundred head. Of course we lost some along the way," Jason answered.

"Whew! That's a lot of cattle for the winter range after that long drive," John said.

"My ranch is pretty big," Jason reassured.

John looked down at the table and shook his head. "For now you'll be able to manage, but what about down the road? I use the free range too. Then there's the Blackfoot's cattle, the bison, moose, deer, and elk to share the range with our cattle, and you have to lay away hay for the winter."

Jason stared at the swirling coffee in his cup. "I guess when you put it that way my spread is pretty small."

"It's your ranch Jason. You can do what you want. You can make a lot of money fast or a good profit over a longer period of time. The choice is yours," Jason's neighbor said.

"Which did you choose?" John's guest asked.

The seasoned rancher sat in silence for a while before replying. "I'm not the man I once was, and by our conversation I don't think you are either. I believed firmly at one time it was my duty as a white man to instruct the other ignorant races. Before I answer that question let me ask you one. Can you guess who helped me build this house?" Jason shook his head. "Mary," John said proudly. Jason's eyebrows flew up and his jaw dropped.

John continued. "Amy and I stopped in Cascade to replenish our supplies before coming here. Mary stopped and watched us loading our wagon." John laughed. "The first words she said to me were 'Keep lifting like that, and you'll have your balls hanging around your ankles." Both men laughed.

"That sounds like her, and I've only known her only a few hours," Jason chuckled.

John said, "Anyway, I've never met a person who could load a wagon so fast. During the loading she told us she worked for St. Peter's Mission and the bishop was visiting. Sister Amadeus thought it wise if Mary would absent herself for a while. She volunteered to show us our ranch and came along for the ride. She seemed very bossy to me at first but I began to see what she told me was an aid and not a criticism. She selected this site for the house after considering other sites. She taught me how to choose and mill the proper trees for the construction of the house. The cowboys who arrived with the herd I had bought in Dodge City were amazed at the amount of the ranch house Mary, Amy, and I had completed. I kept that crew for another month to watch the herd and build the bunkhouses and sheds. Three of them are still with me today. Mary, Amy, and I finished the ranch house. Mary assigned me the project of planning the rooms and polishing the wood while she returned to St. Peter's to do her assignments there.

"We offered to pay her what we could afford. 'Did I ask you for any money?' she said. After that Amy and I had ringing in the ears for a week from her response to the supposed insult. Since the day we met she has always remained our closest friend. So much for teaching the Negro race," John said with great pride.

"I guess you wonder what all of this has to do with my choice. Well, the answer is everything. Mary introduced me to some of the Blackfoot." John's demeanor became thoughtful. "After that, things I would have never noticed became important to me. At one time a beaver dam was an annoying pile of wood in the middle of a stream. I spent an entire day with the Blackfoot watching one dam. When I saw how many creatures large and small took advantage of the dam I could hardly believe it. The braves explained the importance of the dam to every creature that approached and how that fit in with the balance of nature.

"I had heard from many of the soldiers in Cascade that the Blackfoot were savages and not to be trusted. In all of the time I have known them and shared the range with them they have never broken faith with me. They taught me that if I respect the land my reward will be abundant. Thanks to Mary and the Blackfoot I try to live with the land and not on it. Five hundred head is the top limit of cattle I keep. So much for teaching the ignorant Indian," John ended.

The door flew open and Mary demanded, "Don't you damned people ever eat? What in the hell do I have to do to get fed around here? I've been working my ass off and you people just sit there jabbering while I starve."

The remainder of the evening the new friends spent reminiscing. John and Amy spoke about the dinner parties and their relationship with Ann and Andrew Harrison. Jason revealed his puzzled relationship with Hunter and told the listeners about his family especially the tale about Miriam's birth. Mary also lightened the conversation with the antics of her and Sister Amadeus as children. The table lamp burned low and dawn would come early. Mary and Jason headed off to the bunkhouses, now empty because of the roundup and John and Amy headed upstairs to bed.

Mary had everybody out of bed before sunrise. She wanted breakfast before leaving for Cascade. John, Jason, and Mary left for the stables to hitch the team and saddle their mounts for their trips while Amy made breakfast.

After a breakfast of buttermilk pancakes with huckleberry syrup, sausages, hot biscuits, and freshly churned butter, and two pots of hot coffee, Amy made thick ham sandwiches for Mary and the men to take with them on their separate journeys.

"If you need me for anything tell John. He knows where to find me. Oh and Amy you must have John model those bluebell long johns," Mary yelled back over her shoulder as she waved a goodbye and headed back to town.

John gave Amy a kiss before he and Jason mounted their horses. As they headed toward the newly-created Rancho

Mumia ranch Amy grabbed the milk pail and went toward the barn to begin her daily rituals with the farm animals.

The crisp and bright morning warned of the change of seasons. John proudly pointed out vague boundaries to his property in the far distance as the pair headed north. After gently loping along for a half-an-hour, John reined to a halt. "See that group of rocks over there surrounded by range grass?" he pointed.

Jason squinted his eyes. "Uh-huh," he replied.

"That's where everything around here comes together. East of there is Blackfoot and open range. Where we are is my ranch and if you look straight ahead and left to the mountains, it's the southern and western part of your spread," John said.

"What about the northern boundary?" Jason asked.

John removed his hat and scratched his head and replaced it. "Oh, the Canadians will tell you all about that if you go too far north," he smiled.

For the next three hours, the two ranchers rode back and forth across Jason's new ranch studying the topography. Periodically they stopped when they saw small herds of bison grazing in the green ocean of grass. In the dark green cover of one of the mountains that created the western boundary they heard the bleat of a moose. Another hour elapsed before John and Jason reined to a halt.

Jason stared at the scene and saw tall pines gently swaying in the breeze. A small stream wended its way toward its mother river. Nature had created an inviting alcove in the trees about a hundred feet from the stream. "I think Montana has been expecting my arrival," Jason said almost religiously.

"I was going to suggest this as your building site, but I see you have a keen eye for beauty and utility," John remarked.

Jason looked at John and smiled. "I married Sarah. Didn't I? Welcome to the Rancho Mumia John," he said extending his hand.

"Well, howdy neighbor. Welcome to Montana," John responded with a hearty shake of the hand.

The men enjoyed eating lunch at the prospective building site. Jason glanced south and commented, "Your crew must really be driving that herd hard to their winter pasture. Look at all of that dust."

John stood and shaded his eyes and looked toward where Jason had pointed at a huge dust cloud. "That's not mine Jason. That's your drovers bringing your herd home." Jason jumped up, let out a whoop, shook John by the shoulders, leapt into the saddle and headed for the dust cloud.

"I'll see you and your family tonight at the ranch," John yelled to Jason's back as the new rancher waved his arm in acknowledgment to John's invitation and spurred his horse to the growing cloud.

Sarah. Miriam. Alva. Nat. Will, Hank, and the boys. The scenery became blurred. Being by himself Jason allowed his feelings to vent. He became aware of the sweet smell of the range grass. The warm afternoon sunshine permeated not only his body but his soul. A moderate breeze fanned his flushed cheeks and made him aware of the pines dancing back and forth in delight at his happiness. In front of the dust cloud rode two wagons side by side on the right side of the herd. A little girl held by the waist by an Indian woman crawled into the wagon seat and began to wave. The woman holding the reins leaned over the side and spoke to another little girl riding a pony who received a nod from the driver. The little girl looked in Jason's direction let out a yelp and galloped toward him. "Thank you, Hunter," Jason whispered. He realized in that brief moment love had established itself as the most important thing in the world---and the second most important---home.

GREGORY

1878

CHAPTER XXXIII

ANTICS

True to their word Nat and Will remained until late spring at Rancho Mumia. Hank assumed Will's role with great proficiency. With Jason's consent he hired four more cowboys. Two of Will's original team opted to remain in Montana with the two cowhands Will had recruited in Texas. Will and Nat promised to return to Rancho Mumia and check on how Jason ran his ranch. With the assistance of some of John's crew the ranch house two bunkhouses, a barn, and a storage shed dotted the landscape before the first snow fall in late October. John allowed his new neighbor to occupy his two spare bedrooms until the skeleton of Jason's house nestled in the pine clearing.

Once again, with the help of Mary and Gray Cloud the timing for the completion of the ranch house met Sarah's schedule. Jason kept his promise by ceding ten acres of land to Gray Cloud. He employed him for hunting, building repairs, helping Sarah with the farm animals, and periodically helping Jason's other staff. As Laughing Water had predicted, in February Sarah gave birth to a baby boy which she named Seth. The Indian woman had exiled the perspective father to a bunkhouse and posted Little Fox as a sentinel to the main house. To pass time, and much to the amusement of the Rancho Mumia cowhands, Jason related the story of the birth of his first daughter. At last the bunkhouse door creaked open and

Little Fox's head appeared around the corner. "Mother said it's all right for you to come back to the house."

The final word had not left the boy's lips when Jason rushed past him sprinting toward the ranch house to get to his wife.

Sarah lay sandwiched between fresh bed linens holding a small bundle in her right arm. Except for the baby there was not a sign that a birth had taken place in the room.

Jason leaned over the bed and gave his wife a kiss. He didn't want to remain long because he could see the tiredness in her eyes. Sarah smiled up at him. "Seth, I want you to meet your father," she said handing the small bundle to Jason.

Jason cuddled the new baby like a soap bubble. "Seth?" he inquired.

"After God's fiasco with Cain and Able, the hope of mankind was placed in Seth. I thought it appropriate. I remember a lot of the names taught by the missionary after my parents were killed," Sarah explained.

"I like it Sarah." He kissed the baby's head, and rocked the newborn in his arms. "Yes. I definitely like it." He handed his precious son back to his mother, gave her another kiss and said, "Now you get some sleep. I'm going to spend the night in the guest room so as not to disturb you." Once more, he leaned over the tired woman, kissed her and said, "I love you, Sarah.

Sarah kissed him back and replied, "Well if you didn't, I can show you three good reasons why you should."

Laughing Water finally broke up the reunion with a quiet command, "That's enough Jason. She needs her rest. I'll be here the rest of the night so you go get some sleep." Jason hugged, and thanked the Indian woman then obeyed.

During the construction of the ranch house Jason showed some foresight. Due to the size of his expanding family the ranch house had a combined kitchen and dining room but a wall with an archway separated the living room with its huge fireplace from the rest of the downstairs. The low ceiling with the four inch holes in the polished ceiling dominated the lower structure. Upstairs boasted of four bedrooms. The parents occupied one. The girls shared the one next to their parents. The nursery which could easily be converted into a full-sized bedroom across the hallway from the parent's room awaited its occupant in a couple of weeks. The bedroom next to the nursery Jason reserved for overnight guests like the Garrets or Mary.

Jason no longer acted the role of ranch owner. Thanks to Will and Nat he had become one in reality. If any of the hands made suggestions to him he would pause to give their advice serious consideration before making a final decision.

Gray Cloud, Laughing Water, and Little Fox refused the comfort of the spare bedroom during the finishing of the construction and insisted on sleeping by the fireplace in the living room. Gray Cloud told Jason of the Delaware's tradition of five to seven families occupying a single log house room during the winter, but come spring, each family went on its own. The two Indian males had decided to accept Jason's offer to remain in Montana and concentrated on buffalo hunting in late winter to construct a teepee on their land. Came summer he and Little Fox built a small log cabin and used the teepee as a place of meditation. For his home Gray Cloud had chosen ten acres about three miles and a half up the mountain stream from Jason's ranch house. If Gray Cloud wanted he could raise some live stock as his own. Laughing Water busied herself making soft deerskin clothing for the oncoming winter. She even made a set of clothing for both Jason and Sarah which both insisted on wearing on the ranch. The softness of the deerskin almost made them feel naked. Before the appearance of the first snow flake the Native American family had prepared their new abode for whatever winter had to offer. Jason made his Native American neighbors promise that if winter became too difficult they would move into the main house. Gray Water merely smiled and reminded him of his heritage.

Much to the relief of Sarah Alva became a surrogate mother to her younger brother. She spent hours playing on the floor beside her male sibling's crib keeping him company and retrieved her mother when Seth needed changing or was hungry. Meanwhile, Miriam had graduated from pony to a full-grown horse. Her pony she treated like a special pet and it became a favorite of Little Fox who insisted on riding it bareback. Sometimes the two playmates spent the entire day galloping in the range and appeared only for meals. To the older children's credit they delighted in caring for the horses and the ranch's riding equipment. They received praise from the busy cowboys for their effort as well as a nickel a week for each child. The horses' coats, halters, and saddles never received such meticulous care from their owners as they did from the conscientious children.

The arrival of the second week of June of the first year saw Alva laid low with a summer cold. Sarah dosed her with blackstrap molasses mixed with a teaspoon of sulfur and put her to bed. Sarah could scarcely believe that her oldest had reached the age of seven and her sister five.

Amy and Mary wended their way through mounds of old clothing piled in the living room as Sarah returned from checking on Alva and brought Seth downstairs to his playpen. The three women busied themselves boxing old clothing for Sister Amadeus's summer clothing drive. Since Jason and Sarah preferred the deerskin clothing a huge wardrobe became unnecessary. Sarah kept six dresses and accessories to wear if she went into Cascade or visited John and Amy but she packaged the remainder of the wardrobe for Sister

Amadeus. Jason tried to limit formal dress code for special occasions only. The deerskin felt much better against his body than the burlap in which he spent most of the day. After they had paused in their task to eat lunch and relax over a cup of tea Sarah drafted Miriam to wash and dry the luncheon dishes. Her normally cooperative dishwasher laid low by a cold forced Sarah to seek the help of Miriam. Sarah had to keep an eye on Seth cheerfully playing in his playpen and had to finish boxing the clothes.

"But ma, Little Fox and I are suppose to go fishing," pleaded the caged victim.

"Not until every dish is washed, dried, and put away," the house warden ruled and returned to her charity helpers. "We should be able to pack everything else into two large boxes and that is the end," Sarah assessed.

"Good," said Mary. "If I leave right away, I should make St. Peter's by midnight. I promised Sister Amadeus I would fix the chicken coop fence by tomorrow. So, I have to get back tonight."

The women put the final touches on one of the boxes when a loud crash came from the kitchen. They ran rapidly to the kitchen to see Miriam still perched on a low stool surrounded by shards of some of Sarah's best china. In her haste to complete such an onerous task Miriam had stacked them haphazardly on the edge of the table with disastrous results.

"Go to your room this very minute," Sarah said in a low, over-controlled tone.

"Little Fox and I are supposed to go fishing," Miriam reminded her mother.

"You will remain in your room for the rest of the day," Sarah affirmed.

"Let me go fishing now, and I'll do my punishment tomorrow," Miriam wistfully offered a possible solution.

"Tomorrow the punishment wouldn't have the same effect. Those dishes meant as much to me as fishing with Little Fox does to you. Go on now," her mother ordered.

The little girl jumped from the stool and ran to the staircase and tearfully looked at her mother. "Damn it. You don't love me anymore. If you did, you wouldn't be so nasty." After her final diatribe she ran upstairs and slammed the door to the girls' room.

Sarah cleaned up the mess finished the dishes and rejoined her friends. "Sometimes, I fell like I could strangle that girl, and she is picking up some of your more colorful speech patterns Mary."

"I think I can share the way she speaks with some of the cowhands. She's just letting off a little steam. I use to be the same way as a little girl," Mary commented.

"Use to be?" Sarah looked toward Amy, rolled her eyes to the ceiling, and added, "Now let's get the rest of this stuff packed. We've only about another half of a box." The trials of Sarah's daughter faded as the ladies completed the packing and put the boxes on Mary's flatbed.

Mary had become a good friend to Miriam. She even taught the little girl how to play poker along with a few more adjectives that her mother constantly censored. Miriam found it hard to understand that no one corrected Mary so why can't she say the same things. Sarah tried to explain why those words belonged only to Mary and the cowboys. She explained that a lady didn't use that type of language. Miriam would merely smile and remind her mother that Alva held the title of the lady in the family. Modifying Miriam's speech pattern became an ongoing battle for Sarah.

Sarah looked at the well placed boxes and said, "Well, that's that. Let's have a final cup of tea before you leave, Mary."

"Sounds good to me. Tie your horse to the tailgate, and I'll give you a ride back to the Dusty Trail," Mary offered Amy.

“Thanks just the same but I’m to meet John here and we’ll ride back together. I would like to get back to the ranch in one piece,” Amy laughed as the women went back into the ranch house.

Mary gulped down her tea and departed for Cascade while Sarah and Amy took their time and chatted about the success of Sister Amadeus’s clothing drive.

Sarah suddenly jumped from the table and said, “Heavens. I forgot all about Alva during that to-do with Miriam. Keep an eye on Seth, Amy. I’m going to make a tray to take up to her.” After another five minutes, Sarah entered the girls’ room with a sandwich and a glass of milk. Alva slowly stirred from beneath her covers and pulled herself to a sitting position.

“Mommy, I feel much better. I can come downstairs and eat,” she assured her mother in nasal tones, followed by a sneeze.

“I know you do darling, but this is mama’s treat to her little girl. You can spend all evening in bed and mama will do all of your chores. And if you’re real good, I may let you stay in bed tomorrow, but no more because mama needs her little girl’s help.” Sarah kissed Alva on the forehead, straightened her covers and pillows, placed the tray on her lap and headed for the door. She turned in the doorway and turned. “You can stop pouting and come out from under the bed Miriam but you still can’t go fishing,” Sarah added to her wayward daughter.

“Miriam isn’t under the bed, momma,” Alva said over a mouthful of a egg salad sandwich.

“Then where is she hiding?” Sarah asked.

“I don’t know, mommy. She came up here madder than a bee, and then she said she had to go to the toilet and I haven’t seen her since.”

“How long ago was that?” Sarah asked suspiciously.

“It was before I took my nap,” Alva innocently replied.

"Thank you, sweetheart. Just leave the tray on your stand when you're through and I'll take it away when I bring you supper," Sarah instructed.

"All right mommy," Alva replied taking another bite of the sandwich as Sarah closed the little girl's door. "That girl won't leave this house again until the termites eat it to the ground," Sarah threatened as she hurried down the stairs.

"What's wrong?" Amy asked.

"That daughter of mine disobeyed me and went fishing with Little Fox," Sarah replied. She opened the door and called for her daughter. On receiving no reply she checked the outhouse. Nothing. As Sarah rounded to the front of the house, Amy stood in the door.

"She isn't there. I'm going to check the barn. If any of that riding equipment is gone, I'm going to tan her hide," Sarah threatened as she headed toward the barn.

"I'll check the bunkhouses," Amy volunteered.

As Sarah approached the barn she saw Little Fox polishing a saddle. "Have you seen Miriam?" the still angry mother asked.

"No ma'am. She was supposed to go fishing with me but she never showed up," the little boy said as he kept polishing the saddle.

Sarah turned and headed back to the ranch house, meeting Amy returning from the bunkhouses. "She's not there," Amy informed Sarah. "I'll bet she's off sulking somewhere," she added.

"I'm going to sulk her behind when she comes back. I have to start supper. You and John will stay of course. Perhaps the three of you can stop me from killing that girl," Sarah grumbled as she entered the house.

Supper time neared and still no word of the little reprobate. Sarah felt somewhat relieved at hearing the arrival of horses accompanied by John and Jason's voices. When the men entered,

Sarah rushed to her husband and said, "Jason, Miriam's missing." She then proceeded to relate the events of the day which led to the disappearance of her daughter.

"John and I'll search the stream to Gray Cloud's. You two search near the woods in back," Jason instructed. After an hour of frantic searching, the adults convened at the ranch house; this time with the additional help of the Gray Cloud family.

"She could be hiding in the range grass. I checked the barn, and none of the horses are missing. She couldn't get too far on foot," Jason assessed. "I'll get the boys from the bunkhouse to help and we'll search the range." Jason gave his wife a hug. "Don't worry, we'll find her. You and Amy stay here in case she returns," he tried to reassure his distraught wife.

"It'll be getting dark soon. That's when every hungry thing comes out looking for something to eat." Sarah clung closely to her husband. "You've just got to find her, Jason." As a reply, he patted his wife's back and left to recruit more assistance from the bunkhouse crew.

Unceasingly the sun hurried on its way west allowing sequined night to take charge. The lack of any moon distressed Sarah even more. Most animals can see in the dark and Miriam couldn't. She kept a pot of coffee brewing on the stove for the various cowboys who checked in at the ranch house to see if Miriam had returned. Midnight came and went; still no word of the missing girl. Sunrise found Sarah dozing by the fireplace in the living room beside an equally tired Amy. Lunch came and the four adults gulped down tasteless sandwiches with a minimum of conversation. Supper time neared and the two women if for no other reason than to keep themselves busy began to prepare supper. Approximately six o'clock, Jason and John entered the ranch house still with no news.

Moping figures sat around the dining table, not paying attention to the food before them. "Maybe she fell asleep in some cave, and is too scared of being punished to come home," Jason suggested.

"Yes. And maybe that cave was a bear den," Sarah added. The gloomy cloud hanging over the table became darker. All residents heard the clatter of Mary's buckboard and then her voice as she tied up her team. No one felt like tolerating Mary's good humor. After knocking on the door, Mary's head appeared through the crack. "Anybody home?" she asked.

"Come on in, Mary. None of us feel very good right now. Miriam is missing," Jason informed the new arrival.

"Oh," Mary replied, swinging the door open wide. "Does this belong to anybody here?" she asked.

All eyes went to the doorway and Mary holding Miriam by her hand. "Miriam," the chorus shouted.

Sarah immediately took control. "Young lady, your father and I have been worried sick about you not to mention everybody around here. You have every ranch hand in these parts looking for you along with Gray Cloud and his family, John and Amy, and your father and I. You have pulled some pretty odd stunts in the past but this tops them all. Now you go right upstairs and don't you dare come down until I call you," Sarah said, pointing to the staircase.

"I'm sorry, mommy," mumbled the little culprit.

"Not half as sorry as you're going to be when I call you down here again. I should tan your bottom until the redness blocks out sunlight," Sarah said to the retreating girl. Miriam plodded up the stairs with the entire weight of the world on her small shoulders. Quickly Sarah turned to Mary. "OK. What happened?"

"How about giving me a bowl of that stew?" Mary asked, "It's been a long trip for me and it smells delicious." The hungry woman plopped down on the bench as Sarah shoved her untouched soup bowl and plate across the table. Mary took a big mouth full and kept pointing her spoon at the bowl. “This is better than Amy’s. You had better be careful or I’ll start to be eating over here all of the time. Amy you should--”

“Maaarrry,” Sarah said, crossing her arms across her chest.

“Oh, all right. I just don’t want to get the little one in any more trouble,” Mary responded. Sarah sat back in her chair next to her husband pinched her lips tightly and gave Mary a deadly stare.

“All right. All right,” Mary repeated, laying her spoon to the side of the half-finished bowl of stew. “When I left here I drove straight through to St. Peter’s. I got there about one o’clock this morning. It had to be about then, because the nuns were still singing and praying like they do every night at midnight. I can’t understand why they do it. Surely even God’s asleep at that hour.” Sarah glowered harder at Mary’s comment. “Damn it. OK. OK. I decided I wasn’t going to get any sleep until they finished so I started to unload the wagon. I picked up this one box and wondered if you gals had packed a tree trunk? I sat it on the floor and began to rummage through it, and---” Mary paused and pointed her right arm toward the staircase. After four more spoons full of stew, she continued, “I took her to the chapel where the nuns were just leaving. I told Dolly, I mean Sister Amadeus, what happened and she put her up for the night. She told sister that no one at home loved her anymore and that she ran away to become a nun. At breakfast this morning sister made me hitch the team before sunrise while she had a private talk with Miriam. When I came back from the stable both of them were laughing like Dolly and I use to do as kids. Sister gave her a kiss and told her not to forget what she had told her. I tried to get it out of Miriam but she said that it was a secret between Sister Amadeus and herself. She slept most of the way back here. The rest you know. Pass the damned cornbread.” With a feeling that she had betrayed the little girl Mary finished her tale and realized she had also finished the stew. She rose and headed for the kitchen for a second helping. Sarah also rose and went to the foot of the staircase. "Miriam, come down here," She ordered.

Enough time had elapsed for the little girl to add the weight of the entire universe to the guilt she already felt. A frozen snail could have descended the stairs faster. Sarah waited patiently until the culprit stood before her. She took her daughter by the hand and brought her to the table where both sat. Still angry Sarah furrowed her brow and stared at the little penitent.

"You know I should give you a good spanking don't you?" Sarah asked evenly. Still keeping her eyes down and her head lowered, Miriam nodded. "Alva just told me I was in for it."

"Well she was right," Sarah confirmed her youngest daughter's observation. "The trouble with giving you a good thrashing is that it would only satisfy my anger and not be a good punishment. No, I'm going to do something even worse." Tears began to freely flow down Miriam's cheeks. "You took something away from me that I like; so I'm going to take something away from you that you like so that you will know how I feel.

"Miriam we all here love you Daddy and I included, but that doesn't mean that we like the things you do sometimes. You should have been more careful with my dishes and you know it. But you should have also been more careful with our hearts that still hurt by your latest antic.

"Just because we are grownup doesn't mean we can do anything we want. When we do good things we have a lot of happiness, but when we do bad things we are punished just like you are going to be. The only difference is that the older you get the worse the punishment becomes. Your daddy and I don't want to see that happen to you. I'm going to punish you now, but I hope that it will prevent a big punishment in the future."

"What's my punishment?" Miriam murmured.

Sarah readjusted her daughter's weight on her lap and said, "Starting today, you will be confined to your room for a whole month. The only time you will be allowed to leave is to go to the toilet, eat, and you will have to do all of the dishes for all three meals without any help from Alva."

Placed on the scales of justice, Miriam would have preferred a good thrashing. Her loss of freedom proved the worst punishment Sarah could have imposed. "Can I just have a good switching?" she pleaded.

Sarah realized she had selected the correct punishment as her anger dissipated and she chuckled at the request. "I don't think so. The pain would be over in a short while and all would be forgotten. This way you have plenty of time to think about what you did and perhaps learn to think of others before you try any trick like that again."

Miriam wrapped her arms around her mother's neck and gave her a wet kiss on the cheek and hopped off of her lap. She ran to her father and climbed on his lap and did the same. "I promise I'll be a good girl from now on," she smiled at him. "I'll go upstairs right now and start thinking about what momma said." When she leapt from her father's lap, her arm caught the plate holding his soup bowl which went crashing to the floor. The little moppet could have outrun the speed of light in her race to the staircase. Sarah buried her head on her folded arms on the table and let out a moan which blended into the uncontrollable laughter of the other adults at the table.

CHAPTER XXXIV

SETBACK

The ensuing month proved as much a punishment to the jailer as to the prisoner. Sarah demanded Miriam use the chamber pot in order to prevent the half-hour trips to the outhouse. On the third day of the sentence Sarah had to place a pitcher of water in the girls' room so that she didn't have to climb the stairs every fifteen minutes. Even those precautions couldn't prevent the questions about misplaced objects or the explanation of her school lessons. At the end of the thirty days, both mother and daughter heaved a sigh of relief.

The two middle weeks of August produced neither rain nor any comfort to the sweltering heat. The mountain stream near the ranch house became a trickle. Most watering holes had almost dried up. If relief didn't come soon, Jason considered driving the herd to an early winter pasture in the mountains. The once green range now vied with the color of the ground beneath it. The first week of September paralleled the Fourth of the July in heat and dryness. Periodic lightening storms brought no relief as the rain never reached the parched earth.

Jason sat at the table finishing his breakfast when he heard a frantic galloping toward the ranch house. Without formalities, John burst through the door and yelled, "Range fire." Jason dropped his fork and rushed out of the door behind John.

"Where? I don't see any smoke," Jason noted.

"It probably has just reached the outskirts of my ranch by now. The way the wind is blowing, it's headed in this direction and should be here in a couple of hours. Get your men from the bunkhouse, and I'll get the men that are herding and meet me by the rocks that divide our property."

"If you take all of the drovers to digging, who will herd the cattle?" Jason asked.

"Jason, if we don't stop this thing, you won't have any cattle to herd. Tell the men to bring picks and shovels," John replied as he turned his horse and headed for the open range and Jason ran to the bunkhouses.

Forty-five minutes later, the small band of volunteer firefighters gathered at the appointed locale. "Where are your men?" Jason asked John.

"They are digging a fire line toward here. Let's hope we meet up with them in time," John said nervously. The band glanced southeast and could see a pillar of black smoke in the distance. John continued, "We have one hope to stop this fire from reaching the mountain range. If it gets in there it could burn all of the way to Flathead Lake. We've got to stop it here. We don't have much time. Your men should start digging a bare area about six feet wide now. Never mind how deep it is. Just make sure the earth is bare. Keep digging until you see my men digging their way here. Once you meet start back fires and watch them closely so they don't jump the dug area." John and Jason both joined the cowboys in rapidly digging the bare area. Periodically one or another would glance up to see the progress of the fire. What had appeared as a single black column now widened into a distant black veil.

When adversity rears its ugly head men can perform impossible deeds. All of Jason's firefighters' muscles ached and each should have collapsed from exhaustion long ago but the six-foot wide bare area snaked its way southward to join its twin. In just under an hour, the two teams came in sight of one another.

This had a tonic effect on both teams. With renewed energy the frenzied teams rushed to complete the project. Once joined, John gave the instructions to light the backfire and not a moment too soon. The orange, flickering tips of the hungry flames appeared in the horizon searching for more nourishment.

The cowboys scattered along the bare line and soon quenched any hot ember that crossed the manmade barrier. The backfire rushed toward the range fire like a child toward a parent. Desperately running in front of the range fire were herds of animals. Predator ignored prey running side by side. Only escape from the inferno became paramount. The cowboys could almost feel the shock of the fleeing animals as they encountered the backfire blocking their escape. In panic, they turned and raced up the small alleyway between the two fires. Even the most seasoned cowboy winced as the two walls met and encased the helpless animals in fiery coffin. All of the men tried to block out the cries from the cremation taking place in front of them but the firewall held. Denied of further fuel both fires angrily shook their fiery fists at the heavens and searched near the soil for further nutrients. Both crews rode the trench for the next three hours searching for hot spots that could become a problem.

At sunset both crews met at the boundary rock. "Look's like we put a stop to her," John commented.

"Yes. But at what cost?" Jason countered.

Everyone looked across the scorched land littered with blackened carcasses. Gray wisps of smoke peppered the landscape like damned souls attempting to escape from hell. "We'll keep watch throughout the night for any flare-ups. Tomorrow we'll have to start burying the carcasses or we won't be able to live in our houses for the stench," John said.

"You and Amy come over for breakfast tomorrow, John. We have a lot to discuss," Jason said. John nodded and started to head back to his ranch house when he paused and held out his hand. A wet drop circled in his palm, followed by yet another. Soon the wet pellets dropped everywhere in sight. "Now it rains," John commented with disgust and kneed his horse forward. Jason remained a moment longer to enjoy the cool wetness surrounding him and then headed for his own home.

Two despondent men sat at the breakfast table the next morning. Sarah had just given them their third cup of coffee as the girls escaped out the front door to go with Little Fox exploring for any damage done to the forest and winter pasture. Sarah kept Seth occupied on the floor by her feet with one of Alva's dolls while she kneaded bread for the evening meal. Gray Cloud soon joined the men while Laughing Water and Amy helped clean soot covered objects and helped Sarah with the cooking.

John leaned his elbow on the table and stared into the cup, all the while stirring its hot contents. "I've lost almost my entire herd. What's left is going to take me weeks to find. It will take me another ten years before I fully recover," he said.

Gray Cloud offered to assist in recovering the scattered cattle for both ranches. His few cattle had not suffered from the fire. His offer didn't make the two ranchers feel much better.

Jason also leaned on the table and stared to his right at the melancholy man of the Dusty Trail. "Maybe things are not as bad as they seem," he said. John quizzically gazed at his host.

"John, I've lost almost as much as you have, and I have an idea that may benefit both of us," Jason hinted.

John leaned back in his chair took a swig from his cup and asked, "What do you have in mind?"

"I'm not a poor man. This ranch is not my only source of income. Gregory Ellis has made some very wise investments for me, and I have a reserve of cash if the ranch ever becomes threatened. Here's what I propose." Jason shifted in his chair so that he could look directly at his neighbor. "I have a family to look after, and I don't want to go on another cattle drive. With your and Gray Cloud's help for a new drive I'll stake you for new stock. Say, five hundred head for you and five hundred for me. You can pay me the current going price of fifty head of cattle for a period of ten years at one percent interest.

"You can take most of my hands for the drive as well as your own. Gray Cloud can be your Segundo. Most of the cowboys are useless here with no herd to tend. Leave behind four cowboys, two from your ranch and two from mine. We'll search for all of the strays from both ranches and herd them together until you return. That will be my job. I'll pay each man ten dollars a week to get the herd here before the passes get snowed in.

"I don't think it's necessary to go all of the way to Texas for a new herd. I hear there are a lot of short horns for sale in Oregon. They may not be as sturdy as long horns, but I hear the meat is much tenderer which should bring a higher price when we sell them. What do you say? Will you go over to Oregon and bring back our herds?" Jason said anxiously.

"I don't want any charity," John said emphatically.

"Charity hell. I intend to collect every single penny you owe me with interest. I don't see how you can call that charity. I need new stock as much as you do, and I can afford to pay you to get them for me, if you will. If you refuse I'll make the same offer to some other rancher who is hurting as much as we are, but you being my friend and neighbor I thought it only fair to make you the offer first. One way or another this thing has to be done if either is to survive," Jason said firmly.

"Well. When you put it that way, I guess I'll have to accept. When do you want me to leave?" John said.

"I'll go into Cascade today and wire Gregory to transfer two thousand dollars to the bank here. That should be enough for the time being. If you need more money wire me. I expect you to drive a hard bargain with our money. I'll give you three hundred cash for expenses on the road. Half of that is part of what you owe me and half of the cowboy's weekly salary will be added until the herd arrives here. Sorry John but I'm not in a charitable mood," Jason added.

"That's all right with me. Losing my plantation and coming here has taught me to be pretty frugal," he assured his lender.

"Good. Then that's settled. You and Amy come over tomorrow night for supper and will discuss the details. OK?" Jason said rising and offering his hand.

Gray Cloud also rose and took Jason's hand. "Thank you for trusting me to be second in charge."

"Trust has nothing to do with it. You have proven your worth a thousand times over. I can think of no other that's more deserving or qualified," Jason replied

John took the offered hand of Gray Cloud and pumped it vigorously. "Neither Jason nor myself could have made a better choice for Segundo," John averred. Jason removed his hat from the peg inside of the door and said to Sarah, "I'll have supper in town tonight and I'll stay there for the night. I'll be back as soon as I can. Would you like to see if Mary will be able to come here to help?"

Sarah paused in her kneading and said, "I think there are enough of us without tearing her away from St. Peter's. Amy, after lunch we can go to your place and help you clean up if you don't mind having my brood along. Laughing Water I'll need your help with the little ones. If Amy will let us spend the night, tomorrow we'll come back here in the morning because I have some canning I have to do. Laughing Water smiled at the two women and nodded.

John went with Jason to the stable so the Rancho Mumia owner could saddle his horse. Spirits soared as the ashes of the Phoenix stirred.

CHAPTER XXXV

AFTERMATH

Two weeks passed and Jason had not received word from Gregory. If he had not heard from his lawyer by next Monday, Jason decided to send another telegram.

During that time, both ranch crews kept busy interring the bodies of the larger beasts destroyed by the fire. Coyotes, magpies, crows, and other carrion eaters feasted in the meantime. The moisture of the thunderstorms and the burnt grassland made many of the cowboys wear their neckerchiefs over their noses to filter the retching smell. John and Jason calculated that at least two more days of this odious work remained before the fresh air would return when they spotted Mary's flatbed headed toward Jason's ranch house. A passenger sat beside her, and a horse tied to the tailgate.

"I'll stay here and help. You go back and see to your guest," John volunteered.

Mary pulled to a stop in front of the house and hopped down. "You and John must have had one hell of a barbecue. Why wasn't I invited?" she quipped.

"We knew you were busy at St. Peter's and we had enough people to deal with the problem," Jason replied.

Sarah came to the door, wiping her hands on an apron. "Well as I live and breathe, Gregory Ellis," she said with astonishment.

"We're glad to see you. What brought you to these parts?" Jason added.

"Trains to Ogden and then the stage to Cascade," Gregory joked.

"Hey. What the hell about me?" Mary added.

"Oh yes, and you too, Mary," Gregory said out of breath. "Remind me to ride my horse back to Cascade."

"Damned Southerners. Go faster than a trot, and they shit their pants," she laughed.

"Mary. Mary," came the cry of two voices from behind their mother.

"Well, somebody around here is glad to see me," Mary said, as she picked each girl up and swung them in a circle. She leaned down and pretended to whisper to them. "If two little girls give me a hand to unhitch the horses and give them a rub down, I'll bet I could find some rock candy in my pocket." This last bit of information produced squeals of delight from the sisters as Mary helped each on the buckboard seat and began to lead her team toward the barn.

"Don't you two just stand there? Come on in. Jason, take Gregory's bag up to the guest room. We'll move Seth to our room and Mary can have his room," Sarah ordered as she stood aside and allowed her husband and their guest to enter.

Jason headed up the staircase as Sarah directed the lawyer toward the table and invited him to sit. "I have just finished three apple pies this morning. I'll put some coffee on, but in the meanwhile I hope you don't mind drinking milk with your pie."

"Not at all," the guest replied.

"Jason do you want some?" she asked her husband who was ascending the staircase.

"No, thanks. I'll just have coffee when it's ready," he responded as he continued his trip upstairs.

"This bad thing here playing is Seth," the teasing mother said as she picked up the baby and gave him a kiss and hug. "Say hello to Gregory," she added, taking the baby's hand in her own and waving at the man sitting at the table. "Now you go on and play and I'll get you ready for your nap in a while." Sarah sat her son down with a corn husk doll.

"Beautiful boy you have there, Sarah. I hardly recognized the girls; they've grown so big," Gregory said.

By this time, Sarah approached the table with what appeared to Gregory a quarter of a pie and a glass of milk. Jason returned and seated himself beside his guest.

"You two go ahead and talk. I have to peel more potatoes for supper. I didn't expect two extra guests. We're so glad to have both of you here. I hope you'll spend a good while with us," Sarah said as she placed more spuds on her work table.

"It'll be just a couple of weeks. I have to get back to Unionville soon and I don't want to over-stay my welcome. Sarah, this pie is delicious. If I didn't know better, I would swear you have Morning Glory hidden upstairs," the solicitor said over a big mouthful of the pastry.

"It should remind you of her. It's her recipe," Sarah laughed as she continued her work.

"What brings you to these parts? As you saw I really need the money you brought," Jason asked.

"Oh. Just a little vacation. When I received your wire, I decided to bring the money in person. I usually see my sister this time of year, but my sister and her husband are in Chicago this month, so I decided to come here. My boy is studying for the bar exam so he couldn't come. He'll be one of the youngest to ever take it. Of course one or two dollars in a certain campaign account didn't hurt. My wife sends her regards but didn't want to make the long trip," the jovial lawyer replied.

"In the past, you have always had others do the bank exchange, and now suddenly you have to do it? Something is just not right, Gregory." Jason observed.

"Jason. You keep talking like that, and you'll make Gregory feel he's not welcome," Sarah censured from the kitchen.

Jason shifted uncomfortably in his chair as Gregory finished the last of the pie and milk and shoved the empty plate, fork, and glass to the center of the table. "Of course he's welcome. It's just that I feel that there is more to this trip than meets the eye, and I hope he will share with me what it is," Jason explained.

Sarah removed the dishes from the table and asked, "Would you like another piece?"

"Definitely, but not right now. If I fill up on the pie, I won't eat supper," he explained. Sarah nodded and returned to her work.

"All right. Let's have it. Why are you here?" Jason pressed.

Gregory let out a sigh and looked directly at his host. "You and Hunter are so much alike. It's hard to keep any secrets hidden from you." Gregory let out another sigh and rubbed his eyes with the palms of his hands. "I have been a lawyer over twenty years. Yes. I admit I have done some pretty shady things I now regret. During my entire career I could defend anything, but I never could understand why one person could murder another person. I always felt if two people just used reason they could solve any problem when it presented itself. Therefore, there was no excuse for murder.

"Within the past two months, I have found myself fantasizing about murder. I began to work out the details on how to do it. I even began to rehearse scenarios for flaws to decide which would be the best method to kill. Your telegram was a wake-up call. I realized I had to leave Unionville immediately, or I might do something I would regret."

“It’s true. My sister and her husband are in Chicago, but I couldn’t wait until they returned to Ohio. It became urgent to leave Unionville now. Your request for funds gave me the perfect excuse, and here I am.”

Jason leaned his arms on the table and noted, “Gregory, I have seen you in some pretty tight spots, and you’ve always kept your calm. I agree that you have done some shady things in the past but, my God, so have we all, and I claim the number one spot on that list. All of that time, the underhanded things you did never included violence. What happened?”

Gregory hissed the response through his teeth. “Bubba.”

Jason considered the problem. “You’ve always known he was a bully and head of the Klan.”

“It’s gotten worse,” Gregory affirmed. “The entire town, black and white, is in fear of their lives from that son-of-a-bitch. Jess Brown stopped him from beating Erasmus Howard to death over at the livery stable because he had left saddle polish on one of the stalls, and when he went to get the sheriff’s horse the sheriff put his sleeve into it.

Jess pulled him off of Erasmus and told him to go his office and calm down. Jess and his wife took Erasmus inside the stable and cleaned him up. That night, Jess’s barn was burnt to the ground by the Klan, and his son got a good beating on the way home from town.”

Gregory added more vehemence to his voice. “Do you remember that dance-hall girl Bubba was sweet on?”

“Yes’“ Jason quietly replied.

“Well, he finally married her. Had a shack built on his old farm place and moved her out there. Her name is Lily Willard. She is a nice girl, no thanks to Bubba. Everyone in town tries to ignore the bruises and black eyes every time she comes to town to do shopping.

About a month ago, she came to the bank and wanted to make a loan. Poor thing. I felt sorry for her, and it was such a small amount. I gave it to her out of my own pocket. The next day one of Bubba's five so called deputies saw her board the stage for Montgomery and told Bubba. The Klan caught up with the stage on the other side of Selma and took her off. No one in town saw her for about three weeks. We feared the worst, but she appeared and did some shopping. She looked as if she had been caught in a herd of stampeding buffalo. When anyone inquired what happened, she would just smile and say that she was all right."

"Oh my God. It's a wonder that he didn't kill her," Jason observed.

"I guess he almost did, by the looks of her. That's when I started to think of ways to kill the bastard," Gregory confessed.

"Jim Sorenson complained to the sheriff about Jess Brown's treatment by the Klan and was found an hour later beaten up in an alleyway beside the sheriff's office.

"Bubba and his five deputies have terrorized the town. He says he sympathizes with the town and the crimes committed by the Klan. He and his cronies have enforced Klan insurance on the businesses there to protect them from a raid by the Klan or the owners being beaten up or their businesses burnt to the ground when their shops close."

"Haven't you tried to get Montgomery involved?" Jason suggested.

Gregory let out a disgusted "Harrumph."The Reconstruction

Government is so corrupt; they don't care about anything unless it has a lot money attached to line their pockets. There is no profit in the doings of a local sheriff and a small town. Our problems must be handled locally. There are still a lot of honest people around but they're helpless to act without proof and people to testify."

Sarah paused in her work and joined the men at the table. "There must be some way to free Unionville from Bubba. What about new elections?"

"The election is over. One of Bubba's deputies controlled the ballot box and counted each blue paper vote as it was placed in the box; a white paper vote would have possibly introduced Klan involvement. How would you have voted? Needless to say he was overwhelmingly re-elected."

"There must be some what to break his strangle hold," Sarah mused.

"There is. Kill the son'-of-a-bitch and his five bastards," Gregory growled.

"No. There has to be another way. Every negative can be molded into something positive if you only take the patience to look for the way," Sarah said.

The front door flew open, and the whirlwind of children entered followed by Mary saying, "No. No more candy until after supper. Which reminds me, what in the hell does a person have to do to get a cup of coffee. Is this house without any food or drink?"

Sarah rose and headed for the kitchen. "The coffee is ready now, and I'll give you a piece of pie to tide you over," Sarah offered.

Alva plucked at Mary's pant's leg. "Seth didn't have any candy. Can he have just a small piece?"

"Sure, honey." Mary reached in her pocket and withdrew a small sliver of the white candy for Alva to give to her brother. "Now take your brother upstairs to play until supper. We big folk want to talk." The children scampered up the stairs.

"How are the ladies at Whispering Willows?" Sarah asked Gregory.

"They're doing just fine. Miss Ann has become interested in charity work and collects a lot of clothes for the less fortunate. Morning Glory and Naomi do a lot of baking and sell it in the merchandise store as well as their restaurant. After buying new supplies, most of the proceeds go to the purchase of food for the needy. Ruth has turned out to be a good housekeeper. The place looks like it did when Mr. Andrew was alive."

"And Lulu?" Jason asked.

Gregory paused a moment to gather his thoughts before replying. "Her good days are becoming fewer and fewer. She constantly wants to fix up Ann for Mr. Harrison's homecoming when she isn't searching for Hunter. When she finally admits the truth, she cries for hours on end. I know it's a terrible thing to say, but she is happiest in her bad days.

"Ruth watches her like a hawk, but she still manages to run away into town looking for Hunter. If someone finds her, they bring her to me, and I take her back, or sometimes even one of the Unionville folk will take her back, usually in tears at being told that Hunter is dead. My God, I feel sorry for that woman."

"No more than I," whispered Jason.

The remainder of the afternoon and evening lightened the mood at Rancho Mumia by telling stories of past events in Ohio, Whispering Willows, and the hilarious tales of Dolly and Mary. About nine o'clock, Sarah went upstairs to make the girls stop rough-housing. By nine-thirty the house became quiet. Gregory had the first restful sleep in many months.

At breakfast the next morning, Jason asked Mary to stop on her way back to Cascade and ask the Garrets to come over the next evening. Today, he wanted to show Gregory some of the ranch and introduce him to Gray Cloud.

"When we get back, I want you to draw up the contract for the loan," Jason informed his lawyer.

"Be glad to," Gregory responded.

"Make sure that you put enough loopholes in it that, if something more happens, John will be able to extend the time limit of the loan," Jason demanded.

"Jason, you're a poor business man, but a good friend," the lawyer remarked. The ranch owner grabbed his hat from the peg beside the door and waved for his guest to follow. Both men mounted their horses as they rode out into the crisp autumn morning.

The next morning Mary informed Gregory that she must return to St. Peter's and prepare the mission for winter. Gregory told Mary to return at the end of next week. "If the next week is anything like this I may not want to return to Alabama."

"I certainly hope you've discarded that terrible idea you had when you arrived here," Jason commented.

Gregory lowered and shook his head. "You have given me courage not to commit a necessary crime. I pray to God all will turn out well when I return." Jason and his entire family stood on the porch waving goodbye to Mary and the departing vehicle. Jason once more was glad he had left Alabama. Perhaps he would have committed the crime Gregory so desperately wanted to do. Suddenly Hunter's voice whispered to him in his mind a phrase his old boss had frequently quoted, "The evil men do lives after them. The good is oft interred with their bones." Jason wondered what, if any, good Bubba had to inter.

CHAPTER XXXVI

GROWLINGS

Gregory enjoyed the first week he spent with Jason. Unionville and its problems seemed a universe away. Jason, along with Hank and the Rancho Mumia crew, taught him the rudiments of droving. Extensive searching in the heavily-treed area abutting the ranch only had yielded less than a third of the original herd from both ranches.

The evening after his arrival, Gregory drew up a contract with enough slack that the addition of three more words would have made it a charitable contribution to John. John and Gray Cloud left with the combined crew from the two ranches the third day of Gregory's visit. Despite the lateness of the season, John assured Jason he would carefully inspect the new herd and would take his time bringing them home, but he wanted to return before winter closed the high mountain passes.

The third day of the second week of Gregory's visit November had arrived and heavy frost covered everything. Jason, Gregory, and skeleton crews had just finished putting the livestock out to pasture when they saw Mary's flatbed approaching. The racing driver waved a white piece of paper as she careened to a perfect halt in front of the ranch house.

"One of these days, Mary, the breaks aren't going to hold, and you're going to wind up in my kitchen," Jason remarked.

"What the hell. It'll save me time trying to get a decent cup of coffee," she said, hopping down from the driver's seat. "Anybody here named Gregory Ellis?" Mary walked forward and waved the letter at the lawyer. "Well, since the damned wall is still up on the house, I guess you're going to have to invite me in."

"Come on in, Mary. Let's see if Sarah has any coffee left," Jason said, wanting to leave his guest alone to peruse his missive.

Once inside, Mary sat at the table while Sarah gave her some of the strong brew. "Don't you ever drink anything but whisky, beer, and coffee? How about water?" the hostess asked.

"With all of the cattle shit and piss around here?" Mary replied innocently.

"I should have known better than ask," Sarah commented as she placed the pot back on the edge of the stove.

The door slowly opened and Gregory entered with his head bowed and holding the letter in his right side. All eyes turned toward him as he walked over and sat in the chair at the end of the table and stared off into space with tears running down his cheeks. Jason went to him and put his hand on Gregory's shoulder. "What is it, Gregory?" Jason asked empathetically. Still keeping his unbroken stare toward the fireplace end of the room, the lawyer handed the letter to his host. Jason nodded his head to Mary to leave the sobbing man alone at the table and join him and his wife in the kitchen. Jason began to read the letter aloud.

Dear Gregory,

There is no easy way to say this, so I'll come right out and tell you. Lulu is dead. The Tuesday after you left, Morning Glory, Naomi, and myself were suppose to take some things over to Maggie Forester. Lulu was with Ruth but she had to go upstairs for some clothing we were going to take with us. We packed all of the things in the surrey and began to look for Lulu. She was nowhere to be found. We checked the stables and found Sergeant missing from his stall. We knew she was off again on one of her escapades. Since she had done this before, we weren't overly concerned. You or somebody in Unionville always looked out for her and brought her back. Since we had errands in Unionville after visiting Maggie Forester, we could easily bring her back ourselves. We spent no more than fifteen minutes at Maggie's because Morning Glory and Naomi had some baking to do that afternoon, and we wanted to get back to Whispering Willows as soon as possible. About a mile from town, we ran into Mr. O'Reilly who had Lulu wrapped up and unconscious in the back of his wagon.

The rest of the story I got from him. It seems she rode into town like the devil was after her. She jumped off of her horse in front of the sheriff's office and began to accuse Bubba of murdering Hunter. She said she had come to him for help with the law and he had lied and betrayed her and had his cronies kill her man. She accused him and his five deputies of hanging Sean and Hunter without a trial.

Quite a crowd had gathered as she kept screaming the accusations. Bubba rushed out of the office still buttoning his shirt. According to Mr. O'Reilly, he grabbed her and threw her to the ground and began to pummel her and call her all sorts of names. At first, everybody watching was too shocked to do anything.

Then, Mr. O'Reilly went over and told him to stop. Just the same, Bubba kept on beating her and calling her names. Mr. O'Reilly said it took him and two other men to pull Bubba off of her and force him back into the sheriff's office. When Mr. O'Reilly returned to the street, Mrs. Ellis and Mrs. Evanston were trying to clean her up as best they could with pieces of their torn petticoats soaked with water from the horse trough. Somebody sent for Doc Haley, but he was over at Louise Thomas's delivering a baby. So, Mr.

O'Reilly put her in the back of his wagon and was bringing her back to Whispering Willows when he ran across us coming into town. Mr. O'Reilly drove back with us and helped carry her up to her room. He said he would keep a lookout for Doc Haley to send him right out, and he returned to town.

We got her undressed and cleaned up but had to change all of the bed linens because her clothing had so much street dirt and blood on it. We took turns in staying with her but she rarely moved. Doc Haley got there about eight and, after examining her, said she was bleeding on the inside, and there wasn't much he could do. About ten o'clock she regained consciousness. Her mind was clear as a bell. The first words she said was that I looked a mess and apologized that she wouldn't be there in the morning to fix me up proper. She thanked Morning Glory, Naomi, and Ruth for all the things they had done for her. She said that she still couldn't understand why Jason did what he did, but she now believed that she was meant to give Sean the ledgers and that it had been her mistake taking them to Bubba. She complained that her life started to go downhill with the end of the war and if the war had never happened, things would have been different for her and Hunter. She talked for about a half-an-hour more about the good times she had before the war. Right in the middle of a sentence she stopped, smiled, whispered "Hunter" and died. I got hold of Reverend Berry and gave her a proper funeral. I had her buried beside Hunter. What surprised me was the number of people who attended the funeral. I never knew that many people cared about her. It seems as if she was Unionville's lost child. Even Lily attended. I know that poor woman paid dearly for that act of kindness.

Bubba has his own version of the murder. Yes, I said murder. I don't care what that filth-of-horse-droppings says. If I wasn't a Christian lady, I would call much him worse than that. He claims that Lulu was disturbing the peace and he came out of his office to ask her to be quiet, and she attacked him. He was sorry she died, but he had to defend his life against her attack. That's like saying the elephant has to defend itself against the flea. He keeps repeating the story in public and, with the help of his deputies, have the people of Unionville publicly agreeing with his version. God forgive me my hatred of that man, but I hope he burns in hell for what he did. There is no need for you to rush back. Everything has been taken care of, and there is nothing you can do. My God, Gregory, I miss her. Every time I brush my hair, I hear her telling me to wear blue for Mr. Harrison's homecoming. I did manage to cut a lock of her hair and put it in the pendant with Andrew's. Now the two people that I loved most, and lost, are always above my heart.

Forgive me, dear friend, for ending this letter so abruptly, but my eyes are beginning to blur so I can hardly see what I am writing. Please give my regards to Jason and his family and let them know the contents of this letter.

Ann

Mary had her arms around a sobbing Sarah. Jason allowed his hand holding the letter drop to his side and stared off into space, but he could not prevent the salty rivulets from cascading down his cheeks. He walked over and sat in the chair next to the stunned lawyer. After tossing the damnable letter on the table, he buried his face in his hands. "I'm going to kill that son-of-a-bitch," he growled.

Sarah broke loose from Mary and ran across the room to her husband. "No, Jason. You've already walked that path. Leave it for Gregory to handle when he returns," she pleaded.

"He's already told us he can do nothing,' he responded. "Somebody has to stop that bastard. What Lulu accused him of is true, and he had to silence her." He paused and looked at the woman standing in the kitchen, "Mary, would you give Gregory and me a ride back to Cascade to catch the coach to Ogden?"

"Sure, if that's what you want," Mary replied, not wanting to interfere with the difference of opinion between husband and wife.

Sarah made another appeal. "Jason, you will be walking the path of the beast again. Don't do it."

"Perhaps. But I owe this not only to Lulu but myself. Maybe it takes a beast to destroy another beast," he rationalized.

"The news has been a sudden shock to you. At least promise me you will think things over before you get to Unionville. I have often told you that even negative things can be turned positive if you just take the time to think it out. At least give me that promise." Jason nodded.

"I hope I'm not forcing you to return early, Gregory," Jason noted.

"Not at all. Lulu was a very wealthy woman, thanks to Hunter and investments I made with the money. I have had her power of attorney and am executor of the will I made her make out. I have to get back as soon as possible and have it probated. We talked it over on one of her good days. She left her money divided between Ruth and Naomi. I felt that Morning Glory had as much money as Lulu did because I have also invested for her. Morning Glory wasn't touching her legacy either so I had Lulu omit her," the solicitor assured Jason.

"That sounded like a good plan. Very well, we'll leave right after breakfast tomorrow." Jason rose. Sarah knew of Jason's need for solitude as she watched him remove his hat from the peg on the wall and walk out of the door.

At breakfast, Jason had another surprise from Sarah. She allowed the children to sleep in after the ruckus they caused on hearing their father would leave for in Alabama in the morning.

The concerned mother didn't want to upset the children further by witnessing their father's departure.

Mary had just hitched the team and Jason had just finished his coffee when he said, "Sarah, I would like for you to take the children to St. Peter's for a couple of weeks. Sister Amadeus can be a big help until I return. John and Amy are going to be busy enough when he returns. I don't want to leave you alone with the children and no one to talk to."

"Just as you order," she replied in a flat voice.

Jason rose and went around to his wife seated at the table and put his arms around her. "Sweetheart, it's not an order. I am asking you to do this, because I really think Sister Amadeus can help out in a time like this." He gave her shoulders a little shake. "I really care about you being alone and thought you would like some comfort. If you don't want to go, then don't. You could invite Laughing Water to stay if you want. She could help you with the children until Gray Cloud returns, and Little Fox can sleep in Seth's room or do both suggestions. Whatever you want. I'm just concerned. You know I don't make demands on you anymore." He gave her a kiss on the top of her head and continued, "I know you think I'm doing something wrong. Perhaps I am, but I have to find that out for myself. So many times in the past, you have been there to signpost the way for me. This is one road I must walk alone."

"Who will come back to me, Jason? My husband or the beast?" she asked with some bitterness.

"I don't have that answer now. I have to do what I must, and you will have that decision to make on my return. Whatever you decide, you have my solemn oath that I shall abide by it without rancor. I gave you my word to think about what I have to do on my trip to Alabama. Somehow I feel this confrontation with the beast will be different. I don't feel the gnawing anger and hatred as in the past. I need those negative feelings to deal with Bubba. I really could make use of them now. I do feel that my beast is dragging me back to Alabama for one last confrontation, and, for what it's worth, I cannot have you by my side. If I can face this trial without you and win, I'll never have to face the beast again. If I lose, you will know on my return, and you only have to ask me to leave, and I shall. I shall deed the ranch and the bank account money over to you. If there is more you want just ask. I'll return to Alabama and face whatever waits for me there. I can only ask that you trust me in this as I have trusted you in the past."

Sarah kept her eyes straight ahead, reached up, and patted her husband's hand resting on her shoulder. She rose and faced him. The glistening tears in her eyes almost made him lose resolve. Through it all she managed a smile. She held his face in her hands and said, "In your eyes I see the beast trying desperately to awaken. Be very careful my love." Sarah released his face. "I'll go get your bag. The children will be getting up soon, and I want to spend some time alone before they come down.

Gregory struggled to put his heavy luggage on the buckboard when Mary muttered, "Damned men. All of their muscle seems to be in their head," picked up the bag and heaved it into the back of the flatbed. She returned inside, relieved Sarah of Jason's luggage and placed it beside Gregory's.

Jason went to the door of the ranch house and hugged his wife goodbye. "I love you, Sarah,"

"I know, my soul mate. I just hope it's enough love to see you through this." With those words, all parties took the first step on a new path.

CHAPTER XXXVII

LIBERATION

Two weeks passed since Jason's arrival at Whispering Willows. At the plantation the atmosphere seethed with anger and not sadness. Jason had formulated a plan to make Bubba accountable for his actions but it would require a little time and patience. Past negative actions by Jason made him an expert in those areas.

With the two men's arrival in Unionville, Gregory promptly began to probate Lulu's will and left the third day for Montgomery. Gregory split the nearly thirty thousand dollars between Ruth and Naomi. Jason had a difficult time convincing the beneficiaries that he had nothing to do with Lulu's decision concerning the will. Only her past loathing of Jason convinced the two women.

Shortly after Gregory and Jason's return, the windfall of hidden gold came into play. On the night of his arrival the former resident of Whispering Willows removed gold from its hidden place in the swamp and took it to Gregory to exchange for Yankee dollars. If it took a great deal of money to get Montgomery involved then Jason had the means. That gold brought only death in its use. Jason hoped what he believed a curse on the gold would provide a respite for the people of Unionville.

On his way to his flatbed to return to the plantation after purchasing Whispering Willow's supplies, a bulky, red-faced figure with baggy eyes stepped off the boardwalk and grabbed the reins of Jason's animals. "What in the hell are you doing back here? I thought I told you to take your black ass out and stay out!" the sheriff fumed.

Jason turned and faced his nemesis. "I had some very important business that I left unattended when I left. As soon as it is complete, I'm going back home," he calmly replied. Jason struggled to keep his voice free of any tone that might provoke the sheriff as he climbed aboard the vehicle.

"How long are you intending to stay?" Bubba pressed.

"After today, it shouldn't take any more than three weeks," Jason answered.

"Well, finish up fast and git the hell back where you belong. We have a nice town here now, and we don't want any smart assed niggers, like you, coming back and causing trouble." Bubba rubbed his chin. "Three weeks, huh? Well, I don't want to see your ugly face in town. Send another nigger from Whispering Willows to do your business. I'm going to make a visit to the plantation in exactly three weeks from today. If your black ass isn't gone by then, I'll make damned sure that it is. Do I make myself clear, boy?"

Jason didn't want any further confrontation, so he nodded to the sheriff and mounted the buckboard's seat. "Sheriff, when I leave, I promise, you will be the first to know." Jason started to flick the reins to depart when a rather pretty woman approached the sheriff and tugged his sleeve. Numerous facial and arm bruises in various stages of healing marred her beauty. "Bubba, may I have some money to buy some material?" she asked in a very low voice.

Bubba turned his attention from Jason to the person who addressed him. "What in the hell are you doing in town? I didn't give you permission to come in," he said in an acerbic tone.

"I finished my chores early and came in to get some cloth to make a tablecloth to surprise you tonight for our anniversary," she smiled.

"We don't need any god-damned tablecloth. The table is alright to eat off of as it is. You and your god-damned stupid, womanish ideas. How in the hell did you get to town? I told you not to touch the horses," he said with rising anger.

"I didn't, Bubba. I walked," she answered in a quivering inflection.

"Well, you can just walk your god-damned ass back home. I don't want you hanging around town. Now git," Bubba finalized.

"Sheriff," Jason called. Bubba had forgotten about Jason's presence. "The road to your farm is on the way. Would you mind if I gave her a lift there?"

"She shouldn't have walked here to begin with, and she should walk back," he growled. Suddenly, a smile came to his face. "No. wait a minute. Let the people see her riding out of town with a god-damned nigger. Maybe then, the people of Unionville will understand what I have to put up with; especially after embarrassing me by going to the funeral of that nigger bitch who attacked me. The people will see how hard it is for an upstanding citizen to be married to a god-damned nigger lover." He grabbed the frightened woman by the arm and escorted her to the passenger side of the vehicle. "Go on. Get up there," he said with a jerk of his head but offered no assistance. Jason slid across the seat of the buckboard and offered his hand to the blushing woman.

After comfortably seating her, Jason gave the reins a flick and headed out of town. The voice of the sheriff rang clearly in back of them. "Now, don't you go stopping in any bushes. I'll take care of you when I get home, nigger lover." Neither passenger looked back. Only when the town disappeared on the horizon did Lily begin to relax. "Thank you for giving me a lift. I hope it doesn't put you too far out," she said.

"Not at all. Tell me Lily, why do you stay with him?" Jason asked.

Lily's lower lip quivered. "I tried to leave him once, and he brought me back. He said that if I ever tried that again, he'd kill me. That is no idle threat," she responded.

The couple rode on in silence for a few moments when Jason asked, "If you had a safe way to leave him, would you?"

He barely spoke the last word when she replied. "Even if I had to do it stark naked in a hurricane," she replied with fervor.

Jason smiled and answered, "I don't think that will be necessary, but, if you're willing to take a chance, I think I have an idea that just might work."

"What? What?" she asked anxiously.

"I have to talk to someone about a few things, and, if they are agreeable, I think I can help. I can't say anymore for now, because I don't want to build your hopes too high if things don't work out," he explained.

"Even the slimmest of hope is good enough for me," she commented almost like a prayer.

"Meet me where your road meets the main road tomorrow at the same time I am going to drop you off. He should be in town, and if everything works as I hope it will, you will be free of him."

Lily covered her mouth with her fingertips. "Oh my God, I hope everything you want works out." She suddenly turned and looked at the man driving the team. "I don't even know your name. Why would you want to do this for me?" she asked in astonishment.

"My name is Jason, and my knowledge of Bubba's brutality goes back a long ways. I have seen him abuse a lot of people, including myself. If there is a way I can stop him from abusing just one person, I'll do it. You, most of all, need my help. The rest of us see him once a week or once a month, but you have to put up with him every single day. If God gives me the means, I'll see that his abuse of you comes to an end tomorrow. Tonight make him an extra special supper. Maybe that will prevent another beating."

Lily reached over and encircled Jason's hands holding the reins with hers. "Thank you for your help. Even if things don't work out, it's still nice to know somebody cares."

Jason gave the battered woman a sad smile and said, "There are more people than you know that care about what happens to you."

During the remainder of the trip, until he discharged her at the entrance road to her shack, neither spoke. Jason remained sitting on the buckboard until he saw the sad figure disappear around a bend in the road. "So help me God, if I have to spend every ounce of gold still buried, I'm going to make sure he'll never touch her again after tomorrow," he swore, rapping the reins hard on the teams haunches.

When Jason returned to Whispering Willows, he immediately sought out Ann and explained to her what had occurred. "God. I feel so sorry for that woman, but what can I do?" she asked with exasperation.

Jason smiled and said, "Plenty." Ann stared at him in disbelief as he explained. "I want to pick her up tomorrow and hide her here until Gregory returns from Montgomery. There may be a document or two she has to sign but after that she can be on her own, and I don't think that Bubba will be bothering her anymore. Will you keep her here for a couple of weeks?"

"Of course," Ann responded with no hesitation or reservation.

"Good. Then effective tomorrow, he'll never hit her again," Jason said triumphantly.

On the following afternoon Jason once more drove the flatbed toward Unionville. As he approached the road to Bubba's farm, he saw Lily glancing up and down the road for other travelers. Jason passed her and turned the rig around and stopped. Two large boxes covered with a tarp rested in the back of the vehicle. Quickly Jason jumped down from the driver's seat and opened the tailgate. "Quick, get between the boxes and under the tarp. In case anyone else is on the road, I don't want them to see you. I hate to make it so uncomfortable for you, but it won't be too long of a drive to Whispering Willows. Miss Ann and the ladies there will make sure you're safe until Mr. Ellis gets back from

Montgomery. After that you won't have anything to worry about."

Jason leapt on the back of the rig and lifted the tarp. Lily quickly clambered aboard between the two boxes, then Jason lowered the cover. Once more he glanced around, but he saw no one on the road. "Just a little longer, Miss Lily, and the beatings have ended," he said as he climbed back into the driver's seat. Luckily, no wayfarers presented themselves on the road back to the plantation, but Jason took no chances until he pulled in front of the mansion. He pretended to examine one of the horse's shoes to make sure that other members of the plantation saw nothing about the new arrival. He lowered the tailgate and whispered, "Miss Lily, quick." The battered woman scrambled out from under the tarp and ran up the verandah's steps and into the house closely followed by Jason.

Ann waited in the hall and escorted the frightened woman to the downstairs spare bedroom.

Jason followed the two women and gently closed the bedroom door behind him. "I see you have some new bruises to go with the old ones," he noted.

Lily rubbed her left cheek and asked, "Are you sure that I won't get you folks in trouble?"

Jason replied, "That should be no problem. You'll be safe here, but I don't want you to leave this house until Gregory Ellis arrives back from Montgomery. This is Miss Ann. She's the owner of the plantation. I know it will feel like a jail but we must keep you hidden." He then turned and addressed Ann. "Miss Lily is about your size, Miss Ann. Dress her in some of your clothes so that anyone passing will think it is you walking around inside. Both of you wear a bonnet, even indoors. That should conceal the difference in hair color. I'll spread word that Miss Ann got a nasty cut on her head from the corner of a table when she tripped over the broom left on the floor by Ruth when she went to get a dust pan and Miss Ann is too embarrassed to allow anyone to see it." Jason then turned and assured Lily. "The ladies will keep you company and take care of your needs until all is safe."

Ann made a small curtsy to her new house guest who burst into tears. Ann rushed to the woman and gathered her into her arms. "There. There." she said as she stroked the crying woman's hair. "It's all over." After allowing enough time for Lily to release her fear, Ann backed away and said, "My, my, but you're a little one just like me." She went to the doorway and called, "Ruth could you come here a minute." Within a moment, another woman appeared in the doorway. "Ruth, this is Lily. She's the house guest we were talking about last night."

"Hello, Miss Lily," Ruth said and gave the woman a hug. "Now Jason, you get on out of here. This lady wants to freshen up and change clothes."

"You're just about my size, and if you will be nice enough to take a few of my things, it will give me a perfect excuse to be extravagant and buy new ones." Ann then addressed Ruth, "I think that old violet one with the pink trim would do just fine for now. I have a similar one I can wear so that anyone looking into the house will think that Lily is me." Unbeknown to Lily the dress in question had a past life span of less than a week. "Oh, and tell Morning Glory to heat some water so the lady can bathe, and have Naomi make up a small tray to tide her over until dinner. Don't let Morning Glory do it or Lily won't be able to eat for a month." She turned back to Lily, "We'll keep the shutters closed in the dining room, library, and the salon so no one will know you are here. Everybody will assume it's me trying to hide my wound." Ann turned and faced Jason. "Are you still here, Jason? Now shoo." Ruth grabbed him by the hand and led him into the hallway. Ann stuck her head out of the bedroom door and added, "Ruth don't forget the undergarments, a pair of black slippers, and two of the same colored bonnets and you may take the rags she's wearing and burn them."

"Yes, ma'am," Ruth replied as Ann shut the bedroom door.

As Ruth went up the stairs, Jason headed out the front door. She turned on the staircase and said, "Jason, you're becoming quite an expert in rescuing women."

He stared at the woman, "At least with Lily, I wasn't the one who caused the need for rescue," he admitted.

Ruth came back down the stairs and confronted the man. "I shall be the first to condemn what you did back in Africa, but did you ever consider that perhaps the gods had that in mind. Mother and I are very happy here. We now have a life we never could have had in Africa, even if my father had lived. Now with the money left to us by Lulu, we never have to worry again. I love Miss Ann and Morning Glory almost as much as mother. Lulu is the second sister I lost. I shall always carry her in my heart. Jason, let go of the past. We all know why you returned. I beg of you, don't do anything to dishonor Lulu or yourself." Ruth gently kissed him on the cheek and went to carry out Ann's instructions.

As he had watched Lulu do many times in the past, Jason watched Ruth ascend the stairs. He went outside and sat on one of the verandah chairs. Ghosts of the past surrounded him. He glanced toward the library entrance. There an angry man sat near the entrance to the library giving a tirade of problems to Hunter for things that seem so unimportant now. Out on the lawn, a brown haired Ann immaculately dressed for a royal ball in a blue gown walked with Andrew's hand around her waist, looking very military in his gray uniform. In the doorway, Lulu anxiously awaited the return of her mistress so she could fuss over some small bit of toiletry. Behind her stood Morning Glory with her famous shoofly pie as a surprise to the returning couple. On his left side with his elbow on the table and smoking a cigar, sat the scheming Sean, watching the couple on the lawn.

Jason bent forward in the chair and buried his face in his hands. "God help me, but I can't turn back now. I must see this path through to the end," he cried out to himself in despair. He rose and walked toward the first willow tree and entered under its comforting umbrella. "Sarah. Sarah." he cried out in anguish. "I need you so now. Help me, my love. I'm lost. Where is the right path I have to walk? A road no longer exists, not even a crossroad. I can see only a thin white cotton thread stretching into blackness. How can it hold the weight I carry? You were always there to give me balance and direction. Help me. I'm lost." He sat with his head resting against the tree trunk, and began to sob.

From somewhere in back of his mind a tender voice called. "My soul mate, I am always with you. Walk the thread and follow my voice. Don't look down, and give me half of that heavy burden you carry. That thin thread is our love. It's stronger than it looks. Step out on it, and come back to me." Jason stood and wiped his eyes on the sleeves of his shirt. "Thank you, my love. I know now what I am doing is right," he whispered. Jason strode out from under the comforting umbrella of the willow into the bright afternoon sun and returned the buckboard to the barn.

CHAPTER XXXVIII

CROSSROAD

Bubba sat alone in his office brooding. Where in the hell did the bitch go? He had checked the stage going east and west with no results. She didn't take any of the horses, and she couldn't have gotten far on foot. Yet, no one had seen her. No one would dare hide her from him. One of his deputies reported that bastard Ellis had left days ago for Montgomery, producing a dead end there. Then, who and where had someone hidden her?

Bubba's anger boiled over as he smashed his coffee cup against the wall. Just wait until he got hold of that whore. She would never leave that farm again even if he had to break both of her god-damned legs. He would lock that bitch up in the house every day he went to work, and if he discovered she had even touched the door knob, he would handcuff her to the bed until he got home. The bitch had made a fool out of him in front of the entire town for the second time, and she would pay. Bubba began pacing the floor; kicking the broken pieces of the cup across the room every time he passed by them. He had his deputies out looking for Lily, and he could do nothing more. He stopped pacing and sat back down at his desk. "I swear to God, that shit head bitch will pay for every single minute she has caused my suffering. Nobody treats me this way," he growled, slamming his fist on the desk.

Without a knock, three strange men, Gregory Ellis, and Jason entered the sheriff's office. Gregory removed his hat, smiled at the sheriff, and said, "Good morning, Bubba. How are you this fine morning?" He stared at the broken pieces of the coffee cup. "Hmmm. I see you've been drinking some really bad cowboy coffee," Gregory chuckled.

Bubba ignored the courteous and sarcastic overture given by the lawyer. "What the hell do you want?" he snapped. "Say what you have to say and get the hell out of here and take that god-damned nigger with you."

"Very well," Gregory responded, "But first let me introduce you to Federal Marshall, Evert Meyers. And these two men are his deputies, Dale Fedor and Edward Goren." At the mention of their names the strange men tipped their hats at the sheriff.

"So what?" he added with contempt. "I'm not in the mood for socializing. Now get the hell out of here. All of you."

Gregory's smile broadened. "I'm afraid we can't do that." He reached into his inner coat pocket and withdrew some documents.

"Here is a divorce decree signed four days ago, granted to a Lily Jenson, nee Willard, from a William Allison Jensen, and signed by Judge Aaron Brooker. As you can see Lily has already signed it. Just sign on the line and you will be free of her forever without paying a single cent. Don't sign and we can all go to Selma and explain to Judge Brooker why not," the lawyer said throwing the document on the desk in front of the sheriff.

"So you were the one who was hiding her," Bubba snorted as he scribbled his name on the document before him. It would certainly be quicker dealing with the situation now than going to Selma and arguing with someone he did not control. Divorce or no divorce she would still pay for her treatment of him as soon as he gathered the Klan.

"Not at all. Gregory responded cordially. Then with a hard voice he added, "You'll never torture that woman again."

"I really don't give a damn. That whore only caused me trouble from the moment I married her. A divorce suits me just fine. Now the people here will recognize I had no choice but to get rid of that nigger loving bitch. Good riddance, I say," Bubba relaxed in his chair and sarcastically smiled back at the lawyer. "Now if you're quite finished, get out, I have work to do," Bubba opened his desk drawer and removed some papers and pretended to peruse them. No one moved. Bubba glanced up and with a backhanded wave said, "There's nothing more to say, and I told you to get out."

Gregory didn't relax his smile. "Our business is not over yet," he said, again reaching into his inner pocket again removing another document and tossing it on the sheriff's desk. "Here is a warrant for your arrest for the murder of Sean O'Casey, Hunter, and Lulu. You will find other charges listed which can be read to you on the way to Selma."

The three lawmen tackled the sheriff and handcuffed his hands behind his back. "You son-of-a-bitch. What do you think you're doing?" Bubba screamed with spittle coming from his mouth.

"Right now? Arresting you. As we speak there are eight more deputies arresting your deputies for abetting in those murders and other crimes. We're transporting you to Dallas County so that you can get a fair trial. I doubt we could find one impartial juror let alone twelve that wouldn't want to see you and your crew swinging from a tree here in Perry County. So, the federal judge has transferred this case to Dallas County," smiled Gregory.

"I'll have your balls for this; you carpetbagger son-of-a-bitch," Bubba screamed as the three lawmen forced him out the door. Gregory and Jason followed him out. People began to gather in the street, wondering why the handcuffed sheriff shouted such obscenities. Gregory clarified the matter by shouting back to the accused felon on a horse surrounded by the three lawmen, "Oh Bubba, I forgot to tell you, O'Reilly will take over your duties here until new elections can be held. Have a nice day," Gregory laughed and waved to the fuming sheriff.

The crowd in front of the sheriff's office began to increase. Gregory considered it time to allay the fears of the people of Unionville. "Folks. Listen to me," he said, waving his hands in the air for attention. "Serious charges of murder and extortion have been brought against your sheriff. He has been taken to the jail in Selma by federal marshals where he is to stand trial day after tomorrow. Is there anyone who would like to stand as a character witness for him?" No one came forward. "Is there anyone who would like to be a witness for the prosecution?" A cacophony of voices accompanied by a sea of black and white hands waved in the air. "Wait a minute. Wait a minute," Gregory shouted over the tumult. "It's not necessary for everyone to make the trip to Selma. Come over to O'Reilly's, and I'll take your depositions. That way you won't have to make the trip."

"And the drinks are on me while you're waiting," Jason added.

With a final shout, the crowd turned and flowed toward the bar. "You were right, Jason. If you can't get justice for free, then buy it. Are you sure you still want to pay for his defense attorney?" the lawyer asked dubiously.

Jason paused to consider the question. "Yes. I want everything to perfectly legal. Have you found one?" Jason asked.

"His name is Don Emerson, and he's a pretty good lawyer. He really didn't want the case, but the court appointed him as well as you giving him a large retainer. He'll do his best for a good defense, but he doesn't have much to work with. I've already given him all of the depositions we have to date, but after today I feel he's going to be overwhelmed. There's no need for you or Lily to come to Selma for another week or two. When I present him with the depositions of today, I'll see he gets an extension to prepare. His problem is that there is nothing on which to base a strong defense with all of these negative depositions. I just hope that he can get Bubba to plead guilty to the more serious crimes and not drag out this farce," Gregory explained.

"Who's prosecuting?" Jason pressed.

"Jim Caffery. He's known to be a tough prosecutor. He has enough testimony that even he says he can attend court, sleep with his feet on the bench, and still get a conviction. He said that even Satan is testifying against Bubba," Gregory responded. "Let's go over to O'Reilly's before the entire town drinks the bar dry." Both men headed for the bar.

As predicted, Don Emerson petitioned for, and received, a two week extension. The Selma courthouse filled to overflowing when the trial began with jury selection which took an additional week. Bubba flew into a rage when Judge Aaron Brooker stepped from the judge's chambers fully robed for jury selection. After the bailiffs restrained the defendant, Judge Brooker looked down from his bench and ruled that he would not tolerate more outbreaks like that or he would have the prisoner tied and gagged. After jury selection Don presented the opening argument that Judge Brooker held the position of a federal judge and this was a civil case.

The judge presented the defense lawyer with the documentation from the Montgomery legislature allowing him to try civil cases since there were few qualified civil judges currently in the state of Alabama.

The next petition wanted the judge to disqualify himself due to bias as he had issued the divorce decree. Judge Brooker stated that he had taken an oath to protect the rights of all citizens and to presume them innocent until proven guilty. The divorce decree had nothing to do with the current charges. He admitted that in Bubba's case it proved difficult, but he intended to uphold the law and remain unbiased and neutral.

The prosecution opened with a list of crimes Bubba allegedly committed and pointed to pile of depositions that formed a white wall on his desk to back up each accusation.

The defense presented a list of hate depositions lacking anything to do with the current accusations and put forth the concept that lawmen became generally hated when they had to enforce the law, and the justly punished struck out for revenge.

The prosecution called Bubba's ex-wife as the first witness. She related a married life with Bubba that would make other trysts appear like a picnic in the park with personal catering service compared to Bubba's Marquis de Sade's treatment of her. The defense tried to discredit her with her past life as a dance-hall girl and prostitute and her married life had nothing to do with the current charges. Lily denied nothing and claimed that during that time before her marriage the nastiest farmhand had treated her like a queen compared to her ex-husband. Her tone of voice and display of bruises made her a very credible witness to the charge of assault and battery listed. Bubba had enjoyed threatening her with the same hangings and beatings given to others while giving others present raid orders as Grand Dragon of the Klan, and she mentioned names of black and white people that had suffered under Bubba's reign of terror. She told of how Bubba and the deputies would meet at Bubba's farm as the Klan and come back boasting how they had just hung some nigger or had beaten up some white citizen of Unionville who refused to conform to Bubba's orders or refused to pay Bubba's Klan tax.

The next prosecution witness caused havoc at the defense table when Caffery announced, "The people call Albert Condon." Bubba jumped up and screamed, "You god-damned, Judas."

Good to his word, Judge Brooker had Bubba tied to his chair and gagged. Even then, Bubba kept mumbling obscenities through the gag and rocking his chair back and forth.

Judge Brooker banged the gavel. "I hope we don't have to go through these scenes when the prosecution calls your other four deputies," he said. Bubba's eyes bulged. His exhibition ceased, and his complexion became that of new fallen snow. Judge Brooker again banged the gavel and said, "An hour recess, and I want to see both attorneys in my chambers, now."

Judge Brooker plopped down on a tall, black leather chair in back of his desk in his chambers and invited the two lawyers to be seated on the chairs in front. "Gentlemen, this is a court of law and not a snake oil medicine show. Mr. Emerson, I expect you to conference with your client when you leave here and demand that he show more respect for this court and his current behavior is not playing very well with the jury."

Don rubbed his forehead and shook his head, "Your honor, I request that I be relieved from this case. I spent the last two weeks challenging depositions that have nothing to do with this case, and I still I have a stack I can't prevent from being entered into evidence. I hired a private detective to search for character witnesses in Unionville and throughout Perry County. There were none he could find. Even those closest to him in the Klan are testifying for the prosecution to save their skins."

"I can assure you his deputies will not get off scott-free. Aside from their admission in abetting the accused, they have individual charges against them for which they will stand trial. I promise to give each of them the impartiality I intend to give Bubba," the judge informed all present.

Emerson gave a deep sigh and said, "All questions I intend to put to witnesses will only damn him more. I have begged him to plead guilty, but he believes he has done mankind a service and should be rewarded and not punished. I can't put him on the stand, or I might as well go up to the witness box and hang him myself."

Judge Brooker sadly shook his head. "Don, you're the best damned defense attorney around, bar none. It's not your fault you have no case, but I know you're doing all you can. That's why Jason hired you, besides the fact that you were court appointed. If there is one redeeming feature in that creature, you'll find it. If it isn't there, it certainly isn't due to your ineptness.

"There are people who take great joy in building and others who take satisfaction only in destruction. Bubba is one of the latter. Those individuals feed on the negative feelings of people and, instead of searching for positive outcomes; they nurture the darker nature of humanity until they drag others down to their level. Their sole solution to anything is destroying everything."

Judge Brooker continued. "Let's do away with all Negroes. What then? The Jews? Fine they're gone. Now who? Catholics?" They're gone, too. Now who? Left-handed people? People who part their hair in the middle? People with blue eyes? There is no end. Even if you gave these people what they wanted, they would desperately search for new victims. Their entire life is eaten up with hatred and destruction. If they had their way of life confirmed, they would have to face the fact of what a nothing they really are. Blaming others' differences which are contrary to their unfounded beliefs gives them proof of their existence and exonerates them from being a nothing. By defending their right to believe that garbage we prove to everybody there is a universe better than they preach. The Bubbas of this world cannot accept that fact. They cannot understand how others can control masses without hatred and bigotry. That essential difference in mass control which they despise so much is called consensual law. Petition to be removed from the case is denied.

Now go back out there and give him the best defense you can. Use whatever means you may. If it is legal, I'll rule in your favor. I meant what I said. I want this to be a fair trial. I insist on giving him every consideration he never gave to others. That will be all, gentlemen, thank you." Both men rose and left the chambers. Judge Brooker sat alone and carefully scrutinized his role in the trial.

The trial dragged out for another three weeks. Some of the citizenry of Unionville insisted on appearing in person to testify. Don Emerson discredited many of the affidavits. Very few witnesses who experienced a Klan raid could attest without a doubt that Bubba participated. The hoods concealed facial features, and most of those attacked by the Klan rarely actually saw Bubba's face. Voice recognition provided no definite proof of participation in a raid due to the cacophony of a Klan raid. Judge Brooker ruled against admitting most of the affidavits concerning the Klan as evidence and Emerson discredited many of the witnesses who did not see Bubba's face during a raid, but the defense lawyer found it more difficult to discredit Bubba's ex-wife, especially when one saw the disappearing bruises, and Bubba's deputies swore he led many of the raids and wore no hood in front of them at times, and they witnessed some of the spousal battery and threats as well as the abuse of the citizens of Unionville.

The deputies spent eight days describing the hangings, the willful destruction of property, and assaults, the deaths of Hunter, Sean, Lulu, and others. Each man's testimony affirmed the previous Unionville deputy's testimony in great detail. The prosecution gave a summation emphasizing the testimony of his ex-wife and the deputies. The defense closed describing Bubba as a not-too-well-liked individual who might have committed certain abuses, but certainly not to the degree described by the citizens of Unionville or by the deputies, who actually performed many of the deeds described. Emerson stated that Bubba's deputies tried to pass their horrendous deeds on to his client in order to save their skins at their forthcoming trials, and one could not accept the word of a dance hall girl and prostitute who probably liked rough sex which explained how the bruises could have occurred.

Brooker followed up with instructions to the jury and sent them to deliberate. Unfortunately for Bubba, the jury had retired for less than two hours and returned with a guilty verdict.

Bubba stood before the judge's bench glowering at the judge. "Do you have anything to say before I pass sentence?" Brooker asked.

"You son-of-a-bitch, you never did like me since the first time I appeared in this kangaroo court and even before that. You granted that bitch a divorce without even consulting me. You and that god-damned nigger over there, and the smart-ass lawyer sitting next to him turned everybody in Unionville against me, even those I trusted most." Bubba went on for the next half-hour ranting about the injustice of the world and the plot to make him personally responsible for all of its woes, and the blame for all of this trouble should rest on the shoulders of the stupid, conniving niggers and the white people of Unionville who refused to obey his interpretation of the law and his attempt at preventing any Klan raid with his Klan tax which would have increased the number of deputies to prevent such raids. Judge Brooker patiently allowed him to rant. Finally, the judge banged the gavel and said, "Bubba you're beginning to repeat yourself. I think you have had your say, and now it is time to pass sentence."

"You have no right to judge me, you bastard," Bubba screamed.

"The state of Alabama says different, and I shall carry out her mandate." Judge Brooker sat up straight. "William Allison

Jensen, having been found guilty of the murder of Sean O'Casey; his hired-man, Hunter; and Ann Harrison's maid, Lulu, by a panel of your peers, it is the decision of this court that you be taken from this court room and hung by the neck until dead. Sentence to be carried out at dawn tomorrow, and may God have mercy on your soul." With a final bang of his gavel, Judge Brooker rose and headed for his chambers.

Two court bailiffs subdued the raging man and headed him toward the railing that separated the spectators from the court proper. Bubba stopped struggling and glared at Jason sitting in the middle of the first row in the balcony. Despite the restraint, he leaned the top half of his body upward and venomously spat out, "I'll see you in hell."

Jason cowed back. Neither the words uttered nor the bulking man threatening him presented any alarm. In full fury before him stood the beast he had so long endured within himself. Jason recognized everything the beast had created in him. That snarl and flashing eyes. Hate. Anger. Murder. Revenge. Need for self-destruction. Jason turned his eyes away. This represented what his life could have become without Sarah. The roaring beast hurled curses at Jason who sat numbly in his seat as the bailiffs led it away.

He sat in the empty court room when Judge Brooker exited from his chambers. The judge looked up, climbed the stairs and sat beside the stunned man. "Well, it's all over. Are you going to watch the execution?" the judge asked.

Jason slowly turned his head and looked directly into Judge Brooker's eyes. "I already have," he whispered. "I get no joy from Bubba's death. I know now that I did what I did for others who could not defend themselves, like Lulu and Lily. Bubba had to be stopped. I only regret that we had to buy justice. I hope one day that won't be necessary."

Judge Brooker put his arm around Jason. "That too is my devout wish and my cross to bear. What you did was right, Jason. The gold you gave me through Gregory did purchase my judgeship that I had tried to obtain in a legal way, but people with more money always jumped ahead on the list of appointments. Gregory's long friendship finally obtained for me a position I have always wanted and had been denied. Despite my following in Reconstruction judges' footsteps in obtaining my post; I swear before God, I gave Bubba as fair a trial as I could, but insurmountable evidence damned him. I really want to be an honest judge. I don't feel that my sentence of Bubba was personal or for financial gain. I based the sentence strictly on the evidence and application of the law. I admit I gained this judgeship by corruption, but I hope to rectify that fact by rendering only fair decisions both now and in the future. Many of my cohorts in Montgomery don't see it that way. If anything, I went overboard to rule things in Bubba's favor because of my personal dislike of the man, but his crimes were just too huge to be ignored. You got him the best defense attorney in Alabama, but even he admitted Bubba had no case. I'm surprised Don did as well as he did."

Jason stood and shook Judge Brooker's hand. The judge warmly returned the handshake. Jason picked up his hat and headed for the balcony's staircase. He paused, took hold of the railing and looked back at the judge. "There is a world of difference between justice and revenge." Judge Brooker smiled and nodded. Jason smiled back, donned his hat and left.

CHAPTER XXXIX

ASSURANCES

Jason cantered his horse back toward Whispering Willows with such calm he believed he rode in a dream. He paused by the area Ann had described as Sean and Hunter's place of execution and clambered down a small hillside by the road to a clearing where remains of a charcoal wooden cross lay on the ground. Yesterday, he would have found it impossible to gaze on this sight. "Why?" he asked the darkened ground, "do you do these things to people who have never harmed you. You hate these people so much because they believe in things different than you or have a skin color different than yours? Why can't we all stand in the sun together? The shadows humanity casts are all the same color." Jason sat on a stump and listened to the small stream coursing its way to the Gulf of Mexico. He stared over at the blackened cross. "If what you're doing is right, why wear hoods? Why do you hide your deeds in the darkness of night? You have your say, yet gag those that differ from speaking and call it just? Is it because the beast is a creature of darkness and detests light?

"Hunter, you did some pretty shady things, but they always had some sort of purpose, not just blind destruction. I remember when you took me to task for making fun of Andrew Harrison's blindness. 'Hate all of the people you want, including me, but have a god-damned good reason for hating them' you said. I really didn't understand what you meant by that at the time. I was no better than," Jason paused and looked around the clearing, "these misguided creatures. They hate without purpose and take the good of humanity and twist it into service to the beast. The cross is a well chosen symbol. The beast takes great pleasure seeing it consumed by fire in the blackness of night.

"I was no better. I hated you for being Masai. One Masai individual had wronged me, and I held the entire nation accountable for his actions. I had my revenge, but other innocents were hurt in the process. The beast could offer me great pleasure in the plotting and execution of my revenge, but the bitter dregs afterward left me looking for reasons to blame others for my actions and seek new victims. Becoming a master of revenge almost destroyed me. Fate threw me a lifeline as my soul sank deeper into chaos. Sarah.

"Hunter, what I can't understand is why you didn't grasp your lifeline, Lulu. Much of what occurred could have been prevented if only you had chosen another path. You were not like other men. Your intelligence far exceeded any one I have ever known, black or white. You had a power to change men for the better. You used it for revenge, like I did, and abused it. You could have been a leader of men and a spokesman for ex-slaves. With your intelligence, you would have found a way for white men to deny you and ex-slaves nothing. It will now take us ages to accomplish what you could have done in one lifetime. Gone. All gone. What a waste.

"Much of what you taught me I shall foster, but I don't have your ability to read men, or absorb and be able to recall every small detail of the past. Nevertheless, thank you for what you did give. I hope you can rest easier now that your killer has been brought to justice. I had thought of waylaying him here and hanging him, but that would not have been justice. That would have been the darkness of the beast, and I would have been no better than your killer. This one time, the beast was dragged out into the light for all to see. It was not a pretty sight. I gave you and Lulu justice and not revenge. Rest in peace, my friends. Rest in peace." Jason rose, returned to his horse, and rode back to the plantation.

On his arrival at Whispering Willows, Jason spent the remainder of the evening in the salon drinking tea and describing the trial to the ladies. He looked hard into the eyes of Ruth and Naomi for condemnation concerning his part in financing Judge Brooker's judgeship which lead to the arrest and trial of Bubba. Only gratitude shone from them.

"What are you going to do now, Miss Lily?" he asked the relieved woman.

Lily stared at the floor and said, "I guess I'll go back to St. Louis. I still have family there, and, despite all I've done, maybe they'll find it in their hearts to forgive me. Naomi has offered to hire me as a waitress, and Miss Ann wants me to stay here until I save enough money to return to St. Louis. When I do go back I'll find something to do. I won't go back to my old way of life. I would like to get married again and maybe have one or two kids."

"Ann reached over and took her hand. "And when you do get married, you must spend your honeymoon here at Whispering Willows. I want to tell that young man all about the wonderful catch he made," she said.

"What about the rest of you ladies?" Jason quizzed.

"Josh Washington has asked me to marry him," Naomi surprised her listeners.

"What?" all replied, stunned by the pleasant news.

"I haven't accepted him yet, but he seems like a nice man. He knows I don't love him, but he says he still wants to make a home for me. Given a little time---well who knows," she chuckled.

"Mama, why didn't you tell me?" her daughter asked.

"Oh, don't go on so, Ruth. I've seen you and Dick Andrews making eyes at each other," Naomi countered.

"Mother, really," Ruth stuttered back, but without a denial.

"Don't forget to let me know the dates of the weddings so Sarah and I can send you two a little something for a wedding gift." He then turned to the hostess. "And you Miss Ann?"

Ann exhaled a long sigh and replied, "Well, I have to spend the next three months fighting with Morning Glory."

"My lord, what for, Miss Ann. The only time we've had words is when you come into my kitchen," the cook defended herself.

"Yes, well that's over for now. I haven't seen my grandchildren since I've returned to Whispering Willows. Gwen has made me a grandmother again. That's four. A lady can't just go traipsing around without a companion," Ann's tone dropped a full octave. "I use to take Lulu." Suddenly the mistress brightened. "And now I have delegated the job to you. Oh dear, from your look I can see the battle has already begun. You have never been outside of Perry County, and we both can be surprised by things we have never seen before," Ann said offhandedly.

"What do you mean 'never seen before' you've been to Charleston hundreds of times," Morning Glory corrected her mistress.

"Yes, but that's not exactly what I had in mind," Ann hinted secretly.

"Miss Ann, what are you plotting?" Morning Glory challenged.

Ann stared at the other members in the parlor for support as she continued. Well, Adam in his import/export business has made a lot of contacts in Europe; even more since he bought out my brother's business. Even as a young girl, I always wanted to see Europe, and now is as good a time as any."

Morning Glory stared at the mistress in awe. "Miss Ann I don't know anything about no kings and queens," the cook commented.

Ann laughed behind a cup of tea. "Morning Glory, I doubt seriously if we'll be traveling in that circle."

Morning Glory made a final plea. "Why don't you take Ruth or Naomi instead?"

"Haven't you been listening? They are close to starting married lives on their own. I can't ask them to leave their husbands for two or three years," Ann explained.

"Two or three years. I can't leave Whispering Willows for that long," Morning Glory affirmed.

"Nonsense. Ruth, Naomi, and Gregory can easily see to the plantation and the restaurant. And it's about time you surrender the recipe for you shoofly pie. Naomi is a very good cook and baker and will keep your secret so that the restaurant and the store don't have to do without until you come back. You're the only one left to go with me," Ann said with delight.

"Hmmm. Well, I'll have to think about it," Morning Glory said cagily.

"I heartily agree. Just make sure you're packed by April first," Ann said.

"Morning Glory, you might as well say yes now. You know Miss Ann always has a means of getting her way," Jason laughed. The cook just smiled and shrugged, knowing the truth of that statement.

"What about you, Jason?" Naomi asked.

"I'm leaving for home in the morning. My business here is through. I'm going to take the friendship of four lovely ladies with me. I just hope Sarah doesn't get jealous," he smirked. "If ever you have need of me, you know where to find me.

"Miss Lily, I know there's a happy life waiting for you out there. Go get it. Naomi and Ruth I hope your marriages are as happy as mine. Morning Glory, you had better stay away from all of those kings and queens. Once they taste your cooking, we'll never get you back." Jason rose from his seat, went to Ann, took her hand, and kissed it. "Besides, you already work for the Queen of the South. Take as good care of her as Lulu would have."

"You can be sure of that," Morning Glory replied and admitted defeat about the forthcoming trip.

Jason patted and then released Ann's hand. "If I'm to get an early start, I had better get some sleep. I wish you all well." With that, Jason returned to his cabin.

When Jason left for Alabama, Sarah and the children had spent two weeks with Sister Amadeus at St. Peter's. The kindness and hospitality the nun showered on them had no equal, but Sarah became restless for the Rancho Mumia and returned. She pleaded for Laughing Water to stay with her until Gray Cloud returned. The first snow had already covered the ground when Sarah and the children resettled back to Rancho Mumia. Sarah busied herself the first few days cleaning two weeks of dust. After that she settled into her daily routine. Jason and his reasons for returning to Alabama haunted her hourly. Two weeks ago, in the middle of the day, she had felt him call her. She couldn't tell if something positive or negative had happened, but she felt in her soul that he had reached out for her. God, she hoped nothing adverse had occurred.

The current month of November blanked Montana with exceptionally large snowstorms. Hank and crew kept a path dug between the bunkhouses and the ranch house in case an emergency occurred. The men had stacked firewood halfway up the wall on either side of the fireplace. One or more of the men checked on Sarah and the children at least six times a day. Mary brought supplies on a regular basis. How she managed those snow-covered roads remained a mystery to Sarah, but somehow she always managed. John and his crew just made it across the pass before it closed due to heavy snow. Laughing Water and Little Fox returned to their cabin but frequented Rancho Mumia. Little Fox and Miriam spent time together making dream catchers and discussing Indian lore or helping the cowboys with the herd. Alva asked her mother to speak with her father about her attending school at St. Peters. Meanwhile she helped her mother in the kitchen and taking care of Seth. Seth had reached the age where he had curiosity for everything around him and both Sarah and Alva had to keep a sharp eye out for him so that he wouldn't hurt himself. Gray Cloud along with Hank made sure the new cattle had no cause to fear wolves or cougars until Jason returned.

Almost three months had passed since Jason had left for Alabama. Sara had sent the children to bed hours earlier and busied herself in the kitchen making bread for tomorrow. Normally, she did this after breakfast, but sleep would not come. She glanced out the window at the small white flakes dotting the black sky. One of the boys would have to do more shoveling in the morning even though it was a light snowfall. Sarah glanced out the window again. There. Coming from the barn. A man. Evidently, one of the hands wanted to keep the path clear now and not have to shovel heavy mounds of snow in the morning. Sarah took down the coffee pot from the overhead shelf. The least she could do is provide warm refreshment for the worker. As the man neared, Sarah put the pot on her work table and ran to the door. It wasn't one of the hands. It was her husband.

Jason paused in the blowing snow and stared at the figure silhouetted in the doorway. At the sight of his wife, he broke into a run and almost slipped on the packed snow. Both wrapped their arms around each other and began a contest to see which one could lovingly pull the other closer.

"Come in before you let out all of the heat," Sarah invited.

Jason knocked all of the excess snow off of his hat and boots and entered. Sarah had gone to the kitchen and picked up the coffee pot again. "You must be frozen. I'll have some coffee ready in no time," she said nervously.

The cold man took the pot from his wife's hand and returned it to the shelf and led her to the warm fire in the living room. After sitting on one of the chairs, he pulled her into his lap. "You're the only warmth I need," he hugged her again. "No, let me correct that. You are the only warmth I have ever needed. You were the missing piece of my life."

Sarah sat up straight on his lap and took his head in both of her hands. She stared long and hard into his eyes and let out a little yelp as she wrapped her arms around his neck and whispered in his ear, "The beast is dead."

CHAPTER XL

FINIS

Jason and John sat on their horses watching their ranch hands wrangle their herds into the summer pasture. Both ranches had nearly completed the spring roundup and branding. The undulating green grass now covered the scorched earth of last fall. Spring brought great promise.

"Oh, I received a letter from Ann. My friend Ruth did get married, but her mother is still being courted. Ann and Morning Glory are in Charleston now. She said that they are going to leave for London on the first of June.

"Ann did have her war with Morning Glory, but not about going. Morning Glory reluctantly would not surrender the recipe for her shoofly pie. Naomi says her shoofly pie is almost as good as Morning Glory's, but how do you measure a handful of flour here, four pinches of salt there, and top it with a steady pouring of black strap molasses for no more than ten seconds. Still, Naomi hasn't received any complaints as yet. Ann had to convince Morning Glory to buy traveling clothes. If she had not insisted, Morning Glory would look like she was ready for anybody's kitchen at all times. Ann finally had to step in and bought Morning Glory a trousseau. She was quite surprised how handsome Morning Glory is when dressed up. She and Gwen's cook had a row concerning cooking which Morning Glory finally won. The food coming from Gwen's kitchen improved in taste. If Morning Glory had not meant so much to her mother Gwen would have made an offer to hire her.

"She heard from Lily who said that her family forgave her for running away, and she's learning to be a secretary. Lily says she's too busy to be bothered with the opposite sex right now. I think it will take a while for her to forget being deserted by one man and physically abused by another."

A horse galloped up to the two men and the rider smiled, "Dad, that cow with the two brands calved again. Boy, that's a tough old heifer. She not only survived the fire, but this is her third calf. You've got to see this one. The bull must have been one that Mr. Garrett brought back. It has a face like its mother, but its body is like its father," Miriam said.

"Miriam, I want you to be careful around the cattle. You're still little enough to get hurt," her father warned.

"Ah, dad, if you had your way, I would wind up by keeping Sister Amadeus company. Hank is letting me brand," she bragged.

"What?" said a concerned father.

"Oh, daddy, I'm just branding, not roping," she turned her horse, headed back to the group of cowboys cutting another calf out of the herd, and shouted back over her shoulder, "yet."

Jason watched as his daughter leapt from her saddle and joined the group of men. "I swear John, that girl is a good reason for men to remain bachelors."

John leaned on the pommel of his saddle and grinned at his neighbor. "Most people work hard to get to heaven, but that girl will storm the pearly gates and shave St. Peter when she goes through." Both men laughed at that scene. "That reminds me, is everything ready for Sunday?" he added.

Jason watched as his daughter removed the smoking brand from the fire and press it against the haunch of a restrained calf.

"Yes. Mary and Hank will be Miriam's godparents, Gray Cloud and Laughing Water for Alva. You and Amy get the big job standing for Seth, Sarah, and myself. Father Felix said not to worry. Everything will go smoothly. This is my second brush with Christianity. I hope that it goes better than the first," Jason observed.

John removed his hat and scratched the back of his head. "Well, at least it will reinforce the morals that you and Sarah have taught the kids.

Jason thought for a moment. "I guess you're right.

"You also told me the story of Rebah and of Konte. There are good and bad in every religion. I guess it rests with the person who does the teaching," John observed.

"Anyway, it's too late now. Mary's coming Friday, and we're all going to spend Saturday in Cascade, then drive out to St. Peter's early Sunday. Gray Cloud, Laughing Water, Hank and Little Fox are going to ride with Mary. Father Felix said he would do the baptisms right after Mass. Why don't you and Amy come along with us? You and I can have one last fling before I become a serious Christian," Jason suggested.

"I'll have to check with Amy first, but I think it can be arranged,' John replied.

"Good. I'll buy the first drink." Jason gave John's back a friendly pat, and both men rode over to the branding area.

Jason, John, Hank and Mary just had sat at a table in the middle of the Silver Spur Saloon when one of the local men approached. "Mary, are you still hiding aces up your sleeve" the stranger asked.

Mary looked up from her drink and replied, "Dave Iverson, you ol' son-of-a-bitch. I don't need any aces up my sleeve to play poker with you. I can beat your ass just holding a hand of blank cards. Wait until I finish my beer and cigar, and I'll prove it.

If your drunkenness doesn't match your stupidity, I'll teach you how to play the real game of poker."

"Oh yeah," he grinned and shot back, "You better hope that your friends here have a lot of money on them because you're going to be borrowing it before the evening's over."

"Go get a new deck of cards from the bartender, and I'll be right over," she said. Dave gave her a two-finger salute and headed for the bar.

"He'd be a good poker player if he didn't scratch his nose every time he has a good hand," Mary told her companions. Mary gulped down her beer and stubbed out her cigar. "Don't worry. I'll be at the christening." Mary stood and went over to the table where Dave eagerly awaited her.

Hank stared after her and asked Jason, "How did that cussing, cigar-smoking, rough-riding woman ever become the best friend of Sister Amadeus?"

Jason chuckled at the question. "Father Felix says the Lord works in mysterious ways," he commented.

"Well, this one was so mysterious, I think God got things a little mixed up," John countered.

Jason nodded and added, "I still wouldn't trade her for the world."

"Me, either. But, boy, she can sure get on your nerves at times," Hank chuckled and took another sip of beer.

John leaned his elbows on the table and looked at the man sitting in the chair next to him. "Jason, I never did thank you for helping me restock." Jason started to say something, but John cut him off. "No. I don't want to hear about 'It was a business deal.' I can read as well as you, and there are enough loopholes in that contract that, if I wanted, I could take nine centuries to pay the loan back, and then only a penny a year. That contract was not written by a business man but a friend. Amy and I just want to say thank you."

"You keep talking nonsense like that, and I'll go over and drink with Mary," Jason insincerely threatened. "Let's change the subject."

"Fine. Have you ever heard from Will or Nat since they left?" John asked.

"Nope. Mary saw one of the cowboys who helped me with my herd. That was about three months ago when she asked about them. Nat had some trouble with the Apaches a while back, but he managed to escape and to get a new name. The Apaches now call him Buffalo Papoose. With all of the names people give him, it's a wonder he can remember his real one," Jason said.

"What about Will?" Hank asked.

"Do you remember that contest with the Flying Double X crew?" Jason asked. Hank nodded. "Well, it seems as if Will has started something new. The Flying Double X men met him the summer after he left here and challenged him again. Some of the local ranches wanted a little of the prize money and put up some of their own. He had a silver belt buckle made out of those he won. Mary's informant said the cowboys fight harder for that buckle than they do for the money. Will is going to make it an annual event that will start right after spring roundup. He's even charging a nickel for those people who just want to watch."

"Well, I'll be. I wonder if anything like that would catch on up here." John asked.

"I don't see why not. Cowboys always take pride in what they do, and like to prove themselves best at doing it. Will has also done a little investment. He's opened a feed and grain store in Albuquerque. It gives him something to do between drives. Farmers with fences are closing off most of the cattle trails. At least the railroads have made cattle transportation easier," Jason observed.

John stretched and finished his beer. "We have a big day tomorrow, so I think I'll head back."

All three men rose to leave but glanced over at the table where Mary sat with a growing pile of chips on the table before her. "Mary, if you keep winning, we're going to make you buy all of the drinks tomorrow night," John said.

"In that case," Mary stood on her chair and yelled. "Hey you jackasses, put down your beer for a minute." Heads at the bar turned to the woman standing on the chair. "Some of you get your god-damned asses over here and get in this game. I need the money." Mary sat back down as four cowboys at the bar took up the challenge.

"She's going to be in a lovely mood tomorrow," Hank commented.

"Isn't she always?" Jason countered. The men laughed and left.

After the morning fog had burned off, the Sunday of the baptismal day blossomed bright. All participants attended Mass and waited for Father Felix to change his sacerdotal garments. The priest exited the church and waved for Jason to speak with him privately.

Sarah watched as Jason looked at the ground, frowned, and shook his head. He left the priest standing in the vestry and approached his wife.

"We seem to have a problem," Jason announced to his wife.

"What's wrong?" she asked.

"Father Felix wants to enter our names in the parish registry, but wants to know our family name," he explained.

"Oh dear, that is a problem. In Africa we were known by one name of a certain tribe. I've totally ignored the fact that family names are important," Sarah said.

"We're going to have to come up with one, and fast. Do you have any suggestions?" Jason asked.

Now it became Sarah's turn to frown and stare at the ground. Suddenly, her brow became smooth as she lifted her head, smiled and stared into her husband's eyes.

He looked at her quizzically and said, "What?"

Sarah never replied but kept staring and smiling. Jason stared a moment more; then suddenly his eyes lit up as he exhaled, "Of course." He returned to the vestry to whisper something in the priest's ear, who responded with a nod.

The ensemble stoically filed into the vestry where a baptismal font stood supported by two marble angels. After identifying the godparents and the pre-ritual of renunciation of Satan, Amy held the Seth's head over the font. Father Felix took the small silver cup and dipped out a portion of the holy water. He stared down at the curious infant and poured a stream of the tepid water over the infant's head saying, "In the name of the Father,"

Seth began to squirm in Amy's arms. What happened? Someone had dumped water on him.

"And the Son," the priest continued as another trickle flowed down both sides of the baby's head.

This could not be tolerated. Seth's eyes focused on his attacker.

"And of the Holy Ghost," the priest finished naming the Trinity, allowing the last flow to come forth from the cup.

Insufferable. Seth emitted a cry of anger that reverberated in the church rafters.

"I baptize thee, Seth Hunter," he concluded.

Somewhere in the golden sunlight of the mission, a cat purred.

THE END

Review Requested:

We'd like to know if you enjoyed the book. Please consider leaving a review on the platform from which you purchased the book.

Milton Keynes UK
Ingram Content Group UK Ltd.
UKHW012208150124
436080UK00006B/770

9 781682 35257